THE THIEVES' LABYRINTH

JAMES McCREET

MACMILLAN

First published 2011 by Macmillan
an imprint of Pan Macmillan, Macmillan Publishers Limited
Pan Macmillan, 20 New Wharf Road, London N1 9RR
Basingstoke and Oxford
Associated companies throughout the world
www.panmacmillan.com

ISBN 978-0-230-74797-5

1 3 5 7 9 8 6 4 2

A CIP catalogue record for this book is available from
the British Library.

Typeset by CPI Typesetting
Printed in the UK by CPI Mackays, Chatham ME5 8TD

THE
THIEVES'
LABYRINTH

Also by James McCreet

The Incendiary's Trail

The Vice Society

It is really wonderful and most interesting to pursue the successive steps of this monster, and to notice the absolute certainty with which the silent hieroglyphics of the case betray to us the whole process and movements of the bloody drama . . .

Postscript to *On Murder Considered as One of the Fine Arts*, Thomas de Quincey, 1853

ONE

—·—·—

Toll-collector Weeton stopped breathing and listened. His finger paused upon a sentence in the book before him. Had he heard the faintest clink of metal on stone?

He looked out through the window of the toll-house, but there was little to see. The broad span of Waterloo-bridge vanished into a swirling nimbus of yellow fog that quite swallowed it after just three lamps: a causeway into nothingness, sepulchral in its silence at that pre-dawn hour.

He exhaled. The sound must have been a chain echoing up from one of the yawning arches beneath. His finger resumed its dry whisper across the page, and he hoped against another suicide on his duty. Fog usually dissuaded the hopeless and unfortunate, for while it was fearful enough to leap into the dark waters, it was surely worse still to plunge blindly into embracing vapour.

The wall clock ticked its hollow wooden seconds as he read. The gaslamps hissed softly. The pages of the book turned.

Then the scream.

Short and sudden, it might have been a gull but for the single outraged note of horror that made it undoubtedly human: a scream of violent death.

Weeton folded the corner of the page with shaking hand and, taking his hat from its hook, stepped from the warmth of the toll-house out onto the bridge.

Cold, moist air settled immediately upon his skin as he inhaled the smoky night. He looked towards the Surrey side, but faced only that impenetrable density of riverine breath. All was silent again.

'Hello there!' he cried. 'Is anyone out there? I am the toll-collector.'

His voice seemed a feeble thing – fragile and insignificant.

'I say! Does anybody need help?'

Fog shifted lazily, suffocating the gaslamps with its sickly hue. Opacity swelled, revealing less, then more.

Then . . . was that a figure? A human form?

He strained to see. There had been legs, a head, perhaps an angular upraised elbow. Then nothing. And the figure had been moving oddly, jerkily – not exactly running, but animated in that manner reminiscent of a dog struck mortally by a cart and attempting an escape on shattered legs.

Coldness had now soaked through the toll-collector's coat. The silence of the empty bridge was replaced by the thudding of blood in his ears.

'I . . . I say! Is there anybody . . . ?'

A figure emerged from the body of the fog: stumbling, staggering, half falling. A man. His face was directed to the heavens, appearing to cry soundlessly with a gaping mouth. Both hands were about his throat.

Weeton stood immobile.

The figure, however, seemed insensible to the toll-collector before him and continued his hectic momentum until, finally, he sagged to his knees and toppled right there at the toll-house door, rolling onto his back with a depleted groan.

Blood jumped from the fleshy wound at his neck. His hands were red with it. His shirt was blotched with it.

'My G—! My G—!' muttered Weeton, kneeling in compacted dung beside the fallen man. 'What happened, sir? Did you see your attacker? Is he still on the bridge? I must ring the bell!'

He rushed inside the toll-house and came out with the hand bell, which he set clanging with a phrenzy born of terror. Would it carry through the bilious miasma of the fog? Would it bring the other toll-collector and constables? Or would it bring the killer himself – out there on the span – leading him to where his unfinished victim lay?

The wounded man twitched and gave a bubbling inarticulate gasp.

'Sir? Do not despair – help will be with us shortly. What is your name? Can you speak? Can you tell me who did this to you?'

The man's eyes, staring madly, turned upon his inquisitor with an unfathomable yearning. A weak rasp came forth: more a gargle from the severed throat than a word.

Weeton leaned closer: 'I . . . I cannot hear you, sir . . . O, where are the constables! Where is our help?'

Again, the victim made his appeal and the toll-collector moved his head lower to hear. The scent of fresh blood dizzied him and he felt hot breath on his ear: sounds that seemed to diminish down and down a tunnel into blackness.

'Sir? Sir! Do not die . . . help will be here shortly . . .'

But the man was dead – chest unmoving, eyes open, the gash in his neck steaming still in the cold night air.

Weeton felt that he was kneeling in blood. He stood on shaky legs to support himself against the toll-house and again urged the bell's clamour, now for his own salvation.

Footsteps echoed strangely from the Surrey side. He raised the bell as a weapon above his head, ready to strike if necessary.

But it was the form of toll-collector Wilkins who was released from the groping folds of the fog and who ran to where his colleague stood.

'Weeton – what is going on?' he panted. 'Is it another suicide? O! What a horrible sight . . . !'

'Did you pass anyone as you came over, Wilkins?'

'I did not see a soul, but I could barely see my own feet. Perhaps in the pedestrian recesses . . .'

'When did this man cross through your barrier?'

'There has been only one in the last hour. It must be he. Yes – it looks like the one, only he wore a top hat before.'

'Are you sure nobody came after this man? I believe there may be a murderer out on the bridge.'

'I am quite sure, Weeton. Nobody came after him, and only one about forty minutes before that.'

'A coster sort, pushing a barrow?'

'Yes, that's right.'

'He passed through my barrier some time past, and I have admitted nobody since.'

'So there is nobody else on the bridge.'

'Perhaps. Where are the cursed constables tonight? We might be victims ourselves.'

'"Murderer", you said? How can it be so if there is no one out there? Do you not recall the man who shot himself some months past? This fellow must have cut his own throat.'

'I heard a scream – a scream of terror. The suicides do not scream that way. They go silently into the river, as you well know.'

'I heard no scream, Weeton.'

'Well, I heard it clearly enough and I will never forget it.'

'If there truly has been a murder, we should inform the Bridge Company. And you should not allow any constables onto the scene. Do you not recall Mr Blackthorne's recent instructions on that matter? He was quite specific.'

'Yes, you are right. Will you go and wake Mr Blackthorne while I see to any constables that arrive?'

'I should not leave my barrier unmanned . . . And if there *is* a murderer about, as you say, I may run into his arms . . .'

'You have already left your barrier . . . and you will be in even deeper water if Mr Blackthorne first hears of this through the newspapers.'

'D— you, Weeton! I will go – but I will tell him you sent me.'

'Just go!'

Wilkins pursed his lips at the dead body on the ground between them, shook his head, and bustled through the Middlesex barrier into a city that was still little more than a dirtily illuminated cloudscape.

It is, of course, the nature of the London fog to descend and liquesce at its own whim. Merely two hours later, Waterloo-bridge presented an entirely different scene. The body of the victim had been removed from its position by the toll-house, and dawn was a flicker in the eastern sky. The full span was again visible across the Thames.

And what a melancholy scene it was in its glistening grey emptiness. The broad avenue was quite immense when seen devoid of pedestrians and traffic, for all passage had now been barred and the thoroughfare closed by the Bridge Company. At each end, a growing chaos of goods wagons, costermongers and river workers let forth a murmur of imprecations at the situation. Meanwhile, Blackfriars and Westminster bridges began to fill with an excess of humanity.

In point of fact, Waterloo-bridge was not completely unpopulated. People at both ends were able to see a diminutive solitary figure at its centre behaving in a most eccentric manner. First he knelt, examining the roadway. Then he walked to the parapet, peering down into the turbid waters. Then he went into some of the recesses beside the pedestrian walkway, vanishing for a few moments as he searched within. In between these studies, he seemed to pause to write in a small book.

Even from a distance of some hundreds of yards, the figure presented a singular appearance. He wore a rather shapeless russet cap that sat in strange juxtaposition to a good suit of rough tweed. Although he moved with the relative agility of one not much beyond forty years, he nevertheless wore an oddly anachronistic salt-and-pepper beard shaped into a point. On his hands were some particularly fine black kidskin gloves that he had not removed, despite his foraging around the dirty masonry.

His name was Eldritch Batchem.

After he had completed his perambulations about the centre of the bridge, he walked back towards the Middlesex toll-house, pausing occasionally along the way to bend and examine some small detail invisible to the massing crowds. Whenever he did so, there was a palpable lull, as if that soiled mote between his leathern fingers were the vital clue that would solve the crime and open the thoroughfare.

Meanwhile, the aforementioned Mr Blackthorne, resplendent in a dark wool surtout and beaver-skin top hat, waited at the Middlesex barrier with his jaw set in consternation. As Bridge Controller for the Waterloo Bridge Company, he considered it *his* bridge, no matter what the burghers of the City might have to say on the matter. He might close it if he liked, and any crime committed thereupon was his to investigate, preferably with all expedience so that no taint of infamy or satirical allusion – 'A penny toll *and* your throat cut!' – could further infect it.

Finally, the investigator arrived at the barrier, where he cast an enigmatic glance over the crowds observing him. He might almost have been searching the dozens of faces for one he knew, but he was interrupted in his scrutiny by the approach of his employer.

'Mr Batchem – I am pleased to meet you,' said Mr Blackthorne, extending a hand. 'I am sorry I could not be here for your arrival earlier, and the toll-keeper told me that I should not approach you during your work.'

'I will not shake hands if you do not mind, Mr Blackthorne.'

The voice was undistinctive, carrying no particular accent or timbre, though the odd pointed beard seemed to lend his words an affable air. His mouth may have smiled, but a lady would have noticed that his eyes did not as he kept his hands by his sides.

'O, I . . . I apologize, Mr Batchem. Do you have evidence there in your hand?'

'Perhaps, perhaps. You were quite right not to approach me, of course. The scene of the crime is critical in its purity and must remain unpolluted for the investigator to do his work. Had you come to me, you might have stepped upon a clue and obliterated that single fragile fibre of truth.'

'A clue, you say? Have you got to the bottom of this case already? I had heard that you have quite a prodigious—'

'The investigator does not blunder into a solution, sir. He

gathers all of the evidence and examines it through a fine lens until the minutest detail is revealed.'

'So you have discovered some clues out on the bridge?'

'There is a quantity of blood. The morning precipitation has diluted it somewhat, but I believe I have identified where the incident took place.'

'The "incident"? You do not call it murder, Mr Batchem?'

'I make no judgement at this juncture. I must talk to the toll-collector who witnessed the dying man and further cogitate upon my findings.'

'But have you found a weapon, or evidence of another person on the bridge? Perhaps you can tell me at least this?'

Eldritch Batchem stroked the point of his beard, either in thought or irritation. 'I found no weapon, but this means nothing. You know my methods, sir. You will receive a full report on my findings later today. Then I trust I will receive my payment.'

'Of course. But perhaps you will tell me whether I may now open the bridge. Have you completed your investigation upon the road and walkways?'

'I have. You may.'

'I thank you, and I look forward to that report.'

Mr Blackthorne made to shake Eldritch Batchem's hand once more, but instead withdrew it with a curt nod and turned his attention to the *mêlée* waiting at the barriers.

Soon, the rattle of carts and the subdued pedestrian chatter of early morning was flowing as normal past the toll-house, observing with morbid attraction the remaining blood of the dead man, itself soon carried on hooves and wheels and soles into the streets of Lambeth or along the Strand until all trace of it was obliterated in the relentless commerce of the city.

In the toll-house, meanwhile, toll-keeper Weeton allowed

his daytime replacement to take position at the barrier and awaited his interview with the investigator. Presently, Eldritch Batchem entered the small space and appeared to scrutinize all that he saw with a comprehensive sweep of the eyes before extracting his notebook and turning his gaze upon Weeton, whose hands had barely stopped shaking since the victim had first emerged from the fog.

'You need not be afraid,' said Eldritch Batchem, his voice sounding somehow distorted in the confines of the toll-house. He had not taken off his russet cap or his gloves. 'I will ask you only a few questions – the same that I have asked the other toll-collector.'

'Very well, sir. But if I shiver, it is on account of the terrible occurrence rather than through fear.'

'Indeed, though I am sure you have seen death before on this structure. You must have seen your share of suicides.'

'I have seen them drop – yes, sir. But there is a piteousness in *their* deaths. They go willing to their ends. This man was not ready to die. I . . . I saw it in his eyes.'

'Let us not speak of such fanciful things. One may see whatever one likes in a man's eyes. If I point out a man to you as a thief, a thief is what you see – no matter what his eyes tell you.'

Weeton looked into the eyes of his interlocutor and saw only unblinking attention. 'I cannot agree. I saw—'

'Yes, let us discuss what you saw, and what you heard. An investigator must know every small detail in order to solve a case. You have said to others that you heard a metallic clink shortly before the scream – is that correct?'

'That is so.'

'Have you heard such clinking sounds before during your duty?'

'The fog is a trickster, sir. One might hear a cough from

across the bridge as if it were by one's side – or one might fail to hear a fellow shouting. I thought it came from the bridge, but it may have come from the river: mooring chains, perhaps, beneath the arches.'

'Inconclusive.' Eldritch Batchem noted the comment in his book and underlined it. 'What of the victim's utterances after he fell?'

'No words, sir. Just noises: breathing, groaning, cries of pain. I could barely hear anything at all, even in the silence at that hour.'

'Was there anything in his hands as he fell?'

'Nothing, sir. They were bloodied. I believe he lost his hat on the bridge, for Wilkins said he admitted a fellow wearing a hat.'

'Indeed? Are you sure it was he: the same fellow admitted by Wilkins?'

'I . . . I thought there was no other man on the bridge.'

'I have not said so.' Eldritch Batchem smiled and again stroked the end of his beard as if catching his interrogatee in a falsehood.

'I believe he was the same. There could be no other.'

'Very well.' A further line entered the notebook. 'May I see your hands? Both sides. Thank you.'

'They are still shaking from the shock of it, sir. Why do you ask?'

'To see if there is blood on them, or on your shirt cuffs.'

'I am not sure what you—'

'No matter. Did you look in the gentleman's pockets once he had expired?'

'Certainly not! What are you suggesting?'

'Nothing at all. I am asking a simple question for which I require an answer.'

'I did not, and the Bridge Company can speak for my good character if anyone maintains anything to the contrary. Am I a suspect in your investigation, Mr Batchem?'

'In any investigation, one does not limit oneself to whom one suspects. The evidence is the silent witness and it alone is to be understood. You were the last to see the man alive, is that right?'

'I and the murderer.'

'You will not speak of murder to anyone once you leave this place. It is not for you to decide. I am the one in possession of all information – not you. Now, look at this earring I found in a recess. Do you recognize it?'

'How would I? I do not examine the ears of every person who passes through my barrier each day. As long as the toll is correct—'

'Please answer simply "yes" or "no".'

'No. People leave things on the bridge every day. I have a cupboard full of them here. Sometimes they come back asking after their lost articles – mostly they do not.'

'I see. I trust you have been directed by Mr Blackthorne not to speak to any police constables?'

'Yes, sir.'

'Good. The police are poor investigators and I would not like them to muddy the waters. I go now to examine the body. Thereafter, the verdict will become public knowledge. Good day to you.'

And with that, Eldritch Batchem stood, made a curious bow, and walked without further pause into the passing crowds, his russet cap visible for just a few moments before he vanished into the crowd.

Toll-collector Weeton now felt the fatigue of the night's experiences settle heavily on him. He picked up his book, took his hat, bade goodbye to the daytime toll-collector and set off south along the bridge to his home in Lambeth.

At mid-span, though, he had occasion to pause in interest. It was hereabouts that Eldritch Batchem had been making his earlier investigation. No visible trace of the incident now remained among the dung and dirt trodden by the traffic, but he leaned on the cold stone balustrade to linger where the man had died.

Daylight had arrived but weakly and light-grey cloud was striated with blue over the city. At this hour, the great chimneys of Southwark were still largely idle and the black pall of a million household flues had not yet obscured the vista. St Paul's towered above all in sculptural eminence, and countless black spires raked a distant band of pellucid horizon soon to be lost in smoke. Over to the east, the slender Monument caught a flicker of nascent sun and briefly flashed its gilded crest. Here was the greatest city on earth, seemingly empty from this vantage, but seething with life.

And death. As if remembering something, Weeton took his book – a rather torrid tale – from a pocket and turned to the page he had folded on hearing the scream. He put his finger on the very sentence interrupted by that incident and traced it again:

Horror hides in darkness, and every heart resides in endless Night.

People passed – strangers all – walking with their own concerns along that patch of fatal roadway. Few knew of the crime at that time. In following days, however, that single death would become just one element in a far more terrible series of events.

TWO

There were some who might have asked why Inspector Albert Newsome of the Metropolitan Police's Detective Force had not been the investigator walking about Waterloo-bridge that morning. Had he known of the incident, he would have been asking the same.

In fact, the inspector was sitting in a Thames Police galley beneath London-bridge at the very moment the toll-collector was making his way home. Perhaps it was the early hour, or the chill down on the water, or the stiff blue uniform he was unaccustomed to wearing, but the inspector's expression that morning was one of stubborn lugubriousness.

Even without the scowl, his face beneath the badged cap was one that seemed perpetually irritated. His twisted red hair and bushy eyebrows gave him a somewhat windy appearance, and his wiry frame was the spring set to trap any criminal foolish enough to underestimate him. Unpopular he may have been, but other policemen spoke of him as rat-catchers are wont to speak of a champion terrier: if not with fondness, then with a certain respect for his fortitude.

The two constables sitting facing him in the galley held their oars across their laps and were pleased to look out among the shipping rather than at their recently appointed superior.

'There, sir – can you see?' said one of the constables. 'There is a wherry towing another, both with passengers. Shall we row upon them?'

'I believe the security of the nation will be unharmed if we overlook that particular crime,' replied Mr Newsome.

The constable knew well enough not to respond, and tried to avoid the expression of his fellow sitting behind him. The galley remained tethered to the chains under the arch, gurgles and wave-slaps echoing strangely about them as the stream sucked past the mossy stonework.

'Sir?' offered the second constable. 'Two ferries going there through the fourth arch at the same time, sir? Should we row?'

'No, constable. We will not row. There has been no accident. No lives have been lost in that infringement of the shipping regulations.'

The wake of the ferries reached them and rocked the boat so that the oars rattled thickly in the oarlocks.

'I say, Inspector,' began the first constable who had spoken, 'did you hear of the incident at Waterloo-bridge earlier this morning? A fellow of that division told me of it as I came on duty.'

'What incident? Another suicide?'

'Possibly . . . but there has been talk of murder. A man had his throat cut in the fog before dawn. I heard that Eldritch Batchem was appointed by the Bridge Company. They say he is the greatest detec—'

'I will thank you not to use the word "detective" in the same breath as "Batchem". The man is a nuisance and unworthy of the name,' said Mr Newsome.

'Yes, sir.'

'A murder, did you say?'

'Yes, sir. I heard that no weapon was found on the victim, but also that nobody else was on the bridge at the time.'

'Curious, but it rather sounds like a suicide to me. The d—— river absolutely reeks today, does it not?'

'No more than usual, sir,' answered the second constable.

'It is quite putrescent. Rotten eggs, mud, tar . . . and excrement.'

'As I say, sir: the usual.'

The inspector reflected yet again on how many aspects of the river he despised. The black-brown water was the least of them: that frigid stew of hospital refuse, slaughterhouse effluvia, street dung, city sewage, manufactory poisons and the saturated souls of innumerable suicides. Its very surface was variously a swirling solution of mud, a rainbow-hued slick from the gas works' outflow, or an animal-corpse bath.

This magnificent Port of London, so called, was to him but a conglomeration of irritants almost beyond tolerance. From the bridge down to Horseferry Pier, it was nothing but a dense glut of ships too diverse to enumerate, a passage barely three hundred feet wide winding between their pressing hulls. Not merely 'boats' – as his constables had been quick to inform him – but colliers, schooners, punts, barges, smacks, skiffs, cutters, lighters, hoys, barks, merchantmen, wherries, and sloops.

No doubt there *was* one hundred million pounds of cargo in the warehouses of that district. No doubt it *was* the richest and largest free port upon the earth. But the marine districts of Wapping, Shadwell, Limehouse, Poplar, Blackwall and Rotherhithe were nevertheless sinks of such notorious vice and infamy that no amount of precious ambergris or attar of roses could mask their stench. Ratcliff-highway alone kept the undertakers of the east busy, whether from natural or unnatural deaths.

One learned, of course, after time and whether one wanted to or not, to read the river: the slim difference at one hundred yards between a Dutch eel boat and a Hastings smack; the ochre sail of a distant barge compared to the start-ling salt-starched white of the returning whaler; the loaded boats low in the water and the unloaded waiting for their ballast; the leaning yards and looped canvas of the ship long in port, or the oakum scent of the vessel heading outwards newly supplied with rope. In that sense, and to an ex-beat policeman, it held at least some similarity with the streets. It was a vast, singular street to belittle all others – the oldest, the busiest and the most dangerous in London.

For their part, the constables of the Thames Police did not dare ask why this eminent detective had so recently and inexplicably adopted the uniform once more to come among their number – particularly as he did so with such obvious reluctance. True, they gossiped as constables will about an alleged scandal, about a criminal's death in custody or an al-tercation between Inspector Newsome and the Metropolitan Police Commissioner Sir Richard Mayne – but none could agree on the truth.

In fact, if we were to follow the inspector's history back a number of months, we would have found him in Sir Rich-ard's office at Scotland Yard, facing once again the stern glare of the commissioner's intelligent eyes over the top of that broad desk.

'So, Inspector – what punishment are you to face?'

'Sir Richard – I feel I must deny all knowledge of this ledger that you say you found in my office.'

'I do not *say* I found it. I found it. And I will have no more of that insolent tone. I would be quite justified in ejecting you from the force in ignominy for what you have done.'

'Sir – if, for the sake of discussion, I *had* compiled a secret catalogue of the vices of London's eminent people . . .'

'Dispense with your conditional clause, Inspector. Your grammar cannot exculpate you.'

'Justice was the sole spur to my action, sir. I sought neither personal advantage nor salacious entertainment.'

'That may be, but you have disgraced the Force with your actions. It is not just the ledger, but also your handling of this recent case. You have let others get the better of you. If your behaviour were known outside this office, you would now be on the street: a common citizen. As it is, you are a senior policeman with an illustrious – if tarnished – record dating back to our very beginnings.'

'Thank you, sir.'

'Nevertheless, you must not escape punishment. As of this moment, you are no longer a member of the Detective Force—'

'Sir! I must protes—'

'I say you are not a detective! Tomorrow you take up a position with the same rank in the Thames Police. You will supervise two constables in a galley in the Upper Pool and you will work with your new colleagues to limit petty smuggling and river infractions wherever you may see them.'

'I believe I would rather be a citizen.'

'Enough of your petulance. It is that sort of attitude to authority that has brought you to this. I expected gratefulness for your unimpaired rank, but I see I am entirely correct in my course of action. Do you have anything further to add?'

'No . . . Yes, I do. Under what circumstances could I earn again my position in the Detective Force?'

'Finally, a question worthy of your character. I will say only this: your position remains open. When you have demonstrated to me once more that you are the man to fill it – when you show me the virtues of a righteous and true investigator – then you will return. And only then. I believe there will be ample opportunities on the river. Now – make yourself known at the Wapping Police Office tomorrow at six o'clock. They are expecting you.'

'Righteous and true . . .' mumbled Mr Newsome with a scowl, his eyes unfocused upon the water.

'Sorry, sir?' said the first constable. 'Were you speaking to us?'

'Nothing. It was nothing. Are you watching the river?'

'Yes, sir. But I have seen only the things that do not interest you.'

'That is enough impertinence, Constable. Do you not read *the Times*?'

'I occasionally look at the sporting intelligence, sir . . .'

'Well, if you were a little more literate you might have looked at the correspondence. In recent days, there have been a number of letters concerning improprieties in just this stretch of the river: alleged corruption among the Custom House officials. That is the kind of thing we should be looking for.'

'Yes, sir. Alas, I have seen noth— *Wait!* Do you see over there by the collier being unloaded?'

'Where?' Mr Newsome stood in the galley for a better view. 'Which one? Point it out. There are dozens of the infernal things.'

'There . . . just short of Tooley-stairs,' said the constable, directing his finger into a thicket of hulls. 'Something in the water. I saw something rise above the surface . . .'

Mr Newsome stared where directed but saw only sooty timbers lapped by the greasy swell. 'What was it? What did you see, Constable?'

'I would not like to say for sure, but it might have been a body. I cannot see it now. Perhaps I was mistaken . . . some piece of debris . . . a wool bag.'

The three of them scanned the water for any sign.

And then there it was: a dark hump rising from the depths. It might have been a garment buoyed with air or a half-floating bale . . . were it not for the pale skin and the hair.

'Row, boys!' shouted Mr Newsome. 'Put your backs into it and row!'

The tether was unhooked, the oars splashed and they were off with a jerk, the inspector standing now with a kind of practised harpooner ease and his eyes fixed unblinkingly on the body.

The bobbing thing was now clearly visible at the surface. Others had seen it also and a clamour arose upon the collier, where coal-blackened lumpers leaned overboard to point. A boathook was handed from man to man to extract the object, but Inspector Newsome shouted to them:

'No! Do not hook it! You may damage evidence!'

The galley pulled rapidly alongside the collier with a bump. The first constable tossed a rope up to the coal-lumpers and the two vessels nestled against each other.

Close to, the corpse wallowed face down in water stained black by coal dust. It wore a dark pea coat, and the white flesh of the forehead was revealed briefly as it bobbed amid the waves.

'Hand me that hook now,' called Mr Newsome to the lumpers above.

The boathook was passed down into his outstretched palm and he manoeuvred its end carefully under the arm of the body, straining to turn it over in the water. A face appeared, revealing dead eyes and a flap of bloodless skin hanging loose from the left cheekbone.

'Take the arms, boys,' he said. 'Careful now, he is d——heavy.'

Together, and with the shouted accompaniment of the lumpers, they struggled to heave him into the galley, which pitched alarmingly under their exertions. Finally, and with much muttering from the constables, the legs flopped over the gunwale, dragging about two feet of rattling iron chain after them.

'Well – what do you make of that?' said the inspector, examining the chain about the ankles. 'It looks like our swimmer was not meant to surface.'

The dead man lay sprawled in the bottom of the galley, his saturated clothes creating a pool of dirty water about him. If there was any wound, the blood had long since passed into the river.

'What do you think, sir?' asked the first constable, squeezing water from his own jacket cuffs.

'I think I would like to get this man back to the station at Wapping and see what he can tell us about why someone would wrap his legs in chain.'

'Do you think it is murder, sir?'

'Closer investigation will tell us more, Constable. But I most definitely hope so. To your oars!'

THREE

Among the manifold thieves in London, perhaps none is more notorious than the pickpocket. The cracksman may take greater risks as he ascends buildings, and the embezzler may make more money for his troubles, but it is the pickpocket whose name lives in infamy among visiters to the city. In France, in Germany, in Holland and, indeed, across the world, they speak of his skills in tones of half-admiring outrage.

For there is nothing to the pickpocket so ignoble as mere *theft*. The 'lift', as he terms it, is both a science and an art, learned through many years of apprenticeship during which he who reaches maturity without being transported earns the respect of his fellows and may call himself a master. As such, he has his own closely guarded techniques to prey upon the gullible and innocent.

Observe him, for example, on Oxford-street, where he is accustomed to working with an accomplice. They loiter together before jewellers' windows, smoking cigars and casting surreptitious glances inside to see in which pockets the customers deposit their purchases. The cigars, of course, are no coincidence. When the ill-fated customer eventually exits, it is into a great puff of finest Havanah, which causes him or her to blink and blindly accept the sincerest apologies from the courteous smoker who has so thoughtlessly breathed upon them. No matter that the other rapscallion has extracted the necklace in the velvet box from their jacket pocket and made off down a side alley without so much as being seen by his victim.

Or see the pickpocket lounging in the restaurants of the finest hotels with just a porcelain cup of tea and that day's *Times* before him. He could very well be one of the guests himself with his fine linen and new boots, but he is watching the others with far greater attention than he gives to his newspaper. He notes, for instance, how the elderly gent with the top hat pays for his drink and slips his pocketbook into a right trouser pocket. Or he notes how the Belgian tourist constantly pats his breast pocket to see if his daily allowance has been lifted by the unscrupulous men of whom he has been warned. These two will soon be visiting the Tower, or Parliament, or St Paul's, and the observant tea-drinker will be there close by them in the pressing throngs.

Indeed, there is only one man that strikes fear into the heart of the master pickpocket: the person who knows his techniques and who watches him as closely as he watches his victims – the detective.

Were one to visit the Sol's Arms public house on Wych-street, or the Brown Bear opposite Bow-street Magistrate's Court, one might hear these light-fingered fellows discussing the figure of the detective. And one might be surprised to hear the commingled dislike and respect they reserve for their sole predator.

In fact, let us eavesdrop on just such a conversation in one of the smoky rooms of the Sol's Arms on the evening of the day that had begun with the Waterloo-bridge incident.

'Did you hear about Jacobs?' says a thief with a clay pipe in the corner of his mouth. 'He was pinched at Ascot last week with a pocket full of watches. He's got transportation – seven years.'

'I heard,' replies a Haymarket loiterer. 'A sorry business, that. Who got him? Was it Sergeant Jenkins?'

'No – Jenkins is working on a murder at Chelsea.'

'Was it Newsome then? I heard the inspector was after Jacobs for ages.'

'No, not Newsome, the ———. He seems to have vanished of late.'

'And good riddance. He is the worst of them.'

'Someone said he is working on the smugglers at Wapping,' observed a corpulent omnibus pickpocket.

'Is that right? I must tell the boys down there to watch out,' says a Custom House-wharf thief.

'A year ago, gents, I would have said for certain that it was Sergeant Williamson who got Jacobs,' opines the pipe-smoker with a knowing glance around his colleagues.

Silence follows the utterance of that particular name. The gathered criminals nod to themselves or exchange looks, each reflecting on their experiences of Sergeant George Williamson.

'Aye, he was the best of them,' says the Custom House-wharf thief.

'And the worst,' says the omnibus thief. 'The man had eyes in his back, I swear.'

'Well, he may no longer be a detective, but he is still our foe,' says the pipe-smoker, smirking at his privileged information.

'What? I heard he is now working at the Mendicity Society,' says Haymarket. 'We're no fakement writers to worry about his interest.'

'Your information is old, and you would be advantaged to know what I know: Williamson has been engaged by the manager of the Queen's Theatre on this very street. If I remain contentedly by the fire with my pipe tonight, it is because he is on duty at this moment, keeping his hawkish eye out for our kin . . .'

At this intelligence, half a dozen people left the bar with some rapidity, bound, no doubt, for the theatre further down Wych-street so that they might sound the alarm among any fellows planning to work the crowds: *Beware! Williamson is on duty!*

There was one, however, who showed no such concern. He sat alone at a corner table, spurning contact with the others. One might have said he was Italian from his sallow skin, the gold ring in his ear and his long, oiled hair, but he did not speak to reveal his origins. Rather, he finished his brandy with a jerk of the wrist and turned out of the house, guided towards the theatre by the sound of the crowds and the false dawn of gas flares flickering about the house *façades*.

The Queen's was a-buzz with one audience leaving and another queuing for access. Smiling faces were reddened with garrulous mirth and gin, all the revellers bedecked in their finery and seemingly unconcerned about the possible thieves in their midst. Was this not, after all, a well-lit place in a populous and broadly reputable part of the city?

On any other night, a significant proportion of the crowd might well have been the class of pickpockets we met at the Sol's Arms – but not this night. Those who had not already been warned would soon have fled the area if they had seen that sober, straight-backed figure standing on the theatre steps.

Even in his top hat, George Williamson was not a physically imposing figure. He was of a rather meagre build, slightly bow-legged from his years on the beat, and his face scarred by a childhood attack of the smallpox. It was his eyes that one noticed, for they seemed effortlessly to see everyone and everything at once. Wherever people pressed together; wherever there was a rapid movement; wherever a person appeared to look around suspiciously, Mr Williamson's gaze was there: examining, watching for signs and techniques catalogued mentally during his former years with the Metropolitan Police.

Beside him stood a much bigger man, easily six feet tall and with enormous shoulders. *His* face bespoke no great intelligence, but he seemed a doughty sort: trustworthy and not conspicuously violent of temperament, despite his evident strength. His name was John Cullen and he, too, had once been a policeman.

'Did you hear about the Waterloo-bridge murder this morning, sir?' asked Mr Cullen, not taking his eyes from the shifting crowds before them.

'I heard that no conclusive evidence was found,' said Mr Williamson, without turning. 'Keep your attention on the street.'

'Yes, sir. Did you also hear that Eldritch Batchem was called to investigate?'

'So I hear. Have you been observing the fellow with the pearl buttons there – he standing by the railings?'

'Pearl buttons? I . . .'

'He is not queuing and has not exited the theatre. Watch him carefully.'

'I will . . . I am. Did you hear about that other case of Batchem's, where he found the infant's body on Blackfriars-bridge?

Cut in eight pieces it was. He traced markings on the towel wrapped around the body to a place in Whitechapel that—'

'Concentrate, Mr Cullen. We are working.'

'Yes, sir. I am watching them all.'

Mr Williamson continued to scan the street. The crowds were thinning now as the theatre filled and the previous audience trickled out into the night – but something had caught his attention.

It was no pickpocket he identified, but a girl. Though merely nineteen, she walked like a princess with her head held high and with her pale face quite luminous in the gaslight. Men paused to stare; women cast icy glances of disapproval. The girl was clearly a magdalene, albeit one confident in her superior beauty.

And as she strolled past the theatre with her advertisement of possessible glamour, she cast a smiling, dark-eyed glance at Mr Williamson – a glance he felt like sudden embers in his blood as memories flooded his mind. It was Charlotte: the girl he had attempted to interview recently on another case.

He blinked. He flushed. He looked down at his boots as if to avoid the dangers of her smile.

And she was gone as quickly as she had come, seemingly absorbed back into the bustle. Had she really looked at him . . . or had he been just one of the hopeless males caught in her sweeping gaze? One thing was unfortunately clear: he had taken his eyes from the crowd for too long – long enough for a lift to occur.

With a rapid refocusing, he applied his attention urgently to the scene he had witnessed just seconds previously, attempting to recall an exact *tableau* of the street before his distraction. He pictured who had stood where, the relative proximity of each to the others, the trajectories of their movement.

'There . . . by the street lamp,' he said, almost to himself.

'Sir?'

'There has been a theft by the street lamp,' said Mr Williamson, still urgently scanning the people. 'A lady with a black bonnet tied down with a white ribbon. She carried an umbrella with a horn handle. Do you see her now?'

'A theft, sir? I saw the lady you describe, but I saw no lift. I believe I was looking in that very direction.'

'I saw nothing also, but it has occurred – you may be sure of that. I have no idea what was taken, but the perpetrator was likely a southerner who was loitering thereabouts. An Italian perhaps. He wore a gold earring and I believe his hair was worn long and tied back. No hat.'

'I thought you did not see anything.'

'I did not see the lift, but I had noticed that man a few seconds before I was . . . before I looked elsewhere. I cannot see him now. He must have moved the moment I looked away from him.'

'Are you sure, sir?'

'Yes. Do you see him, or the lady I referred to?'

'I believe the lady has gone inside the theatre. As for the other, I admit I did not notice him at all. What do we do now? We have not a victim, a crime or a criminal.'

At that moment, a scream came from the lobby and the very lady they had been speaking of ran towards them with an expression of great agitation.

'O! O! Are you Mr Williamson?' she asked, her hands all a-flutter and her face flushed red. 'The manager has told me to talk to you. My bracelet! It is stolen!'

'Describe it to me, madam,' said Mr Williamson.

'Well . . . I . . . it was a silver bracelet about half an inch wide. I had it when I stepped down from the cab because I recall hitting it against the door and checking to see if it was damaged . . .'

'Was it jewelled or otherwise decorated?'

'No. In truth, it was rather a plain thing, but given to me by my brother. Did you or your lofty companion here not see who took it from me? You have been standing here.'

'Hmm. I believe I know who took it from you. Do you recall seeing an Italian-looking gentleman walking near you?'

'Not at all.'

'No matter – it was he.'

'Well, where is he now? And where is my bracelet?'

'Madam – I believe I will be able to put my hands on that bracelet within the next hour. You may go into the theatre and enjoy the show – I will be here with the bracelet when you return.'

'And I, sir?' said Mr Cullen. 'Should I accompany you?'

'No – the next audience has almost entirely entered. We have two hours until they emerge. In the meantime, you will keep a look out for that gentleman with the gold earring, though I fear he will not return here.'

'Where will you go, sir . . . in case the manager asks why you have left your post?'

'Tell him I have gone to reclaim his customer's stolen item.'

And with this, Mr Williamson tipped his hat to the lady and set off west along the street with a determined gait.

'How does he know where to look?' said the lady to Mr Cullen.

'Madam – I really could not say.'

When Mr Williamson entered the Sol's Arms a few minutes later, it was as if a freezing wind had just blown through the place. Glasses paused midway to lips and the murmur of conversation died to a silence punctuated only by the creak of chairs.

'Good evening, gentlemen. I am happy to see all of you here rather than outside the Queen's Theatre tonight.'

The pipe-smoking man gave a short laugh and raised his glass: 'George Williamson – I trust that this is not a business call. You no longer have the authority to arrest any of us, in case you had forgotten.'

'Peter Cunningham,' nodded Mr Williamson in response. 'I may no longer be a policeman, but I know where to find a constable and point out a criminal to him when I see one. Are you still picking pockets at the rail termini?'

The man addressed as Cunningham smiled stiffly. 'I am sure I do not know what you mean. You must be thinking of another man.'

'Perhaps that is the case. Much as I would like to spend time talking, my "business", as Cunningham puts it, concerns one of your brethren. And I believe he is not one whom you would seek to protect. I am speaking of a man with long, dark hair and a gold earring – an Italian, perhaps . . . and I see from the glances among you that he was sitting in the corner earlier this evening.'

'He is not one of us, Williamson,' said Haymarket. 'Came here tonight and didn't speak to a soul. First time we've seen him, as well. That's not polite on another man's ground.'

'Hmm. As I suspected. Did anyone hear him speak? Or did anyone speak *to* him?'

'I did,' offered the barman. 'He said just one word: "Brandy". Not even a "please" or "thank you".'

'Yes, I believe you London thieves are quite particular

about your social decorum. What of that single word – did you hear a foreign accent?'

'Indeed, but I could not say for certain what it was.'

'Did anyone else converse with this man?'

Nobody had.

'One more question and then I will leave you in peace. It is rather a hypothetical enquiry. If any of you gentlemen happened to see me on duty on the theatre stairs, would you lift a worthless silver bangle from a lady before my very eyes?'

This provoked a few barks of laughter and some expletive-laden comments to the effect that only someone with a penchant for time in gaol would attempt such a thing for so meagre a prize.

'Hmm,' said Mr Williamson with a nod. 'As I suspected. I bid you good night. Let us hope we do not meet again in a professional capacity.'

Out on Wych-street, he turned east without hesitation and walked within minutes towards the cab stand on the corner of Holywell-street. A cabman was sitting upon his perch with a blanket over his legs and a cigar in his mouth.

'Good evening to you,' said Mr Williamson. 'Have you seen an Italian-looking gentleman walk this way? He had long, dark hair. It would have been about fifteen minutes ago.'

The cabman looked into the brim of his hat and cocked his head on one side in a show of earnest cogitation. His cigar tip glowed dimly.

'Ah, I see,' said Mr Williamson, reaching into a pocket. 'Here is a shilling for your trouble in remembering so far back.' He flicked the coin up into a grubby palm.

'As you say, sir: long dark hair,' said the cabman, recollection illuminating his face. 'But he looked like no gentleman

I ever saw. Never trust a man who don't wear a hat – that's what I say. He went down towards Milford-lane there, looking behind him as he went. Glared at me something shocking, he did, just on account of me watching him. What's it come to if a gent can't watch another—?'

'Thank you for your time.'

Mr Williamson strode towards the entrance of Milford-lane, but paused there beneath a lamp. Something was awry. This road led directly down to the river, with alleys connecting it only to Water-lane and Essex-street. Anyone taking such a route would be seeking either the waterside, where there was no pier . . . or a means to turn unnecessarily back on themselves. As a young constable in uniform, he would not have hesitated in venturing down towards the shore in pursuit of a thief. But as an older man, a simple private citizen with some recently acquired scars and more experience than he might choose, he allowed himself some caution.

Unfortunately, he had made the lady at the Queen's Theatre a promise. And there *was* something undeniably odd about the occurrence on Wych-street that would not let him rest. He clenched his jaw and began to walk down the street.

As he proceeded further, the noise of carriages around St Clement Danes faded behind him. The smell of the river came faintly over cobbles and, after another dozen yards, it seemed his own footsteps were the only sound. He might have been that constable again: alone on the city streets, his every sense alert and the truncheon his only protection from murder. Such instincts, once learned, did not leave one.

Approaching the alley to Water-lane, Mr Williamson stopped. He had heard nothing. There was no other person to be seen. And yet . . . he had the most compelling sense somebody was standing near, observing him. It was the same curious sensation, he realized now, that he had felt on the steps of the theatre.

The alley before him was not lit by gas, but vanished into darkness between the houses. A shiver of apprehension went through him. He was no longer young.

'That was an impressive lift you made at the Queen's tonight,' he said quietly, as if speaking to somebody by his side. 'But you will not lure me into those shadows if that is your aim.'

There was no response from the alley – no sign at all that anyone was there.

'I bid you good night – I hope we meet again.' Mr Williamson backed away from the alley entrance and retraced his steps back along Milford-lane towards the traffic, checking periodically behind him. Nobody followed.

As he came to the end of the street, he passed a house where a family was dining. The large ground-floor window cast its bright gaslight out into the darkness and he stopped for a moment to watch the cook serving steaming potatoes from a tureen to the seated people. Muffled conversation and the weaker notes of a piano in another room drifted out to him.

Then, quite unexpectedly, a maid appeared at the window and saw the strange man in the top hat staring into the house. With a chiding look of disapproval, she spread her arms wide and jerked the curtains firmly closed.

And Mr Williamson made his way back to the theatre alone.

FOUR

Those who knew Sir Richard Mayne, Commissioner of the Metropolitan Police, knew that he was a man of scrupulous fairness, piercing intelligence and impeccable morality. However, when his office door at 4 Whitehall-place slammed with colossal force on that morning following the Waterloo-bridge death, they might also have reflected upon his fierce protectiveness of the Force's good name.

Waiting in the office that day was Mr Blackthorne, the Waterloo Bridge Controller. A not unimportant man himself, he was nevertheless somewhat cowed by the fearful bang of the door and the uneasy silence that followed as Sir Richard took his seat behind the great oaken desk.

Minutes seemed to pass without the commissioner acknowledging his visiter. Instead, and seemingly deep in thought, he slowly folded a letter he had been holding as he entered – a letter that had evidently caused him a degree of consternation. In the flat grey light from the window, he looked rather drawn and pale. Then, with a deep sigh, he finally looked up and into the expectant eyes of the bridge controller.

'Mr Blackthorne – I must begin by thanking you for accepting my invitation to converse,' he said.

'It is my honour, Sir Richard. We at the Bridge Company are most keen to aid the police in any way we are able.'

'Except, it seems, in the pursuit of crime.'

'I . . . beg your pardon?'

'You know very well what I mean, Mr Blackthorne. I refer to the death on your bridge yesterday morning.'

'The suicide, you mean? If that was a crime, it was one against divine law, not human. I see, or intend, no insult to your men . . .'

'In the first instance, it has not been proved to me or to the Metropolitan Police beyond reasonable doubt that this *was* a suicide—'

'Sir Richard – you may have read in today's newspa—'

'And in the *second* instance, perhaps you might explain to me why my constables were prevented from entering the bridge to satisfy themselves whether this was a suicide or otherwise?'

'Sir Richard – I need hardly remind you that the bridge is private property . . .'

'And I need hardly remind you, Mr Blackthorne, that crime has no ownership. If a murder occurs in a private house or in a palace, it is the province of the law – of my men – to seek out its perpetrators. You had no right to prevent their access.'

'With all respect, I absolutely have that right. As bridge controller, I may close the thoroughfare any time I wish, whether for repairs or for an investigation.'

'A crime was committed on that bridge, Mr Blackthorne. Where is the body? Where is the inquest? Where is the word of the law? You are preventing the hand of justice.'

'Forgive me, Sir Richard; perhaps I have not made myself clear. The death yesterday morning was a suicide. There was nothing to investigate: no crime committed but against the self and no law broken but the religious.'

'You say there was nothing to investigate, but you called in your own investigator: this ludicrous mountebank Eldritch Batchem. Why would the Bridge Company go to such lengths for a mere suicide?'

'Sir Richard – as you may know, Waterloo-bridge has been termed "the noblest bridge in the world" by Canova. It is the pride of the city: a glorious feat of engineering. Much as I am aggrieved to admit, it has also of late earned a reputation for . . . for the unfortunates who wish to leap from its parapets. We at the Bridge Company absolutely *resist* that reputation. I have made clear to my toll-collectors that any suspicious death upon the bridge is to be reported to me directly. I do not wish to add murder to the infamy already heaped upon the structure, and I intend to address any such ambiguity personally.'

'So you are implying that you would have a murder more fortuitously termed a suicide by an amateur "detective" to protect the name of your structure?'

'Certainly not! And I would have you know that Mr Batchem is a highly respected practitioner of the investigative arts.'

'Respected by whom? Not by I or any of my detectives, who have spent years perfecting their vocation under the aegis of the law. This Mr Batchem approaches police work as an idle hobbyhorse.'

'I am sorry that you feel this way. I meant no slight to you, Sir Richard, or to any of your detectives. The truth is that your Detective Force is known to be . . . somewhat slow in its investigations and I wished only to expedite—'

'*Slow?*'

'That is to say . . . the . . . er lengthy process . . . I mean, the machinations of the . . .'

'I believe you wish to express that the Detective Force is a thorough and professional body of the finest investigators ever to walk these London streets. They take as long as necessary to find the true solution. And they do not take out advertisements in *the Times*'s classified pages selling their wares like some common Bermondsey hawker of coals.'

'Forgive me, Sir Richard. I see I have insulted you.'

'I and the entire Metropolitan Police.'

'Well, I can only state that the Bridge Company has already made generous concessions to the Force, whose constables may pass without toll along the bridge as many times as they wish each day.'

'Is this a threat, Mr Blackthorne?'

'It is not. It is not. I have no wish to earn your antipathy further. May I offer the apologies of the Bridge Company on this matter, which I feel is actually a great misunderstanding. I will take your concerns back to the company and you may be sure that the board will communicate formally with you shortly . . . if that would be a satisfactory resolution to this unfortunate situation.'

'I will wait for that communication, Mr Blackthorne – and for a change in policy. In the meantime, I have *this* to deal with.' Sir Richard held up the letter he had folded earlier.

'Then I will show myself to the door, Commissioner. You are a busy man and I do not wish to inconvenience you further.'

Mr Blackthorne closed the door behind him with a soundlessness to rival the thunderclap of the commissioner's earlier ingress.

Now brooding alone at his desk, Sir Richard rubbed his eyes and looked at the folded letter. He slipped it inside his waistcoat pocket and rang for his clerk, who appeared at one of the internal doors to the office.

'Yes, sir?'

'Arrange for the steam launch to collect me at Whitehall-stairs in five minutes.'

'You will not take the carriage, sir? It is ready to leave.'

'No. The launch will be quicker. I am going to the Custom House. Send a fast galley ahead to instruct the inspector general I am on my way.'

And with his stern expression unchanged, the commissioner of police took his coat and hat and went out to the stand by the riverside, glancing east along the brown waters to the pale arches of Waterloo-bridge, half concealed even at that short distance by the steam and smoke of the city. On the police launch, he would unfold and read again the letter he had received that morning, versions of which had already appeared in a number of morning editions:

Dear Commissioner Sir Richard Mayne

May I first introduce myself? You might already have heard tell of my recent efforts about the city, but I am Mr Eldritch Batchem: he who was engaged by the Waterloo Bridge Company to investigate the late death upon the span. No doubt you will be astounded to learn that I have already found the solution to that little mystery, whose investigative process I propose to delineate for you here, that you may derive some pleasure or enlightenment from my methods.

I admit that the evidence upon the bridge itself initially offered little aid to the skilled investigator, for the dampness of the fog upon the stone surfaces had obliterated my opportunities to read any footprints. I did, however, find a quantity of blood in the middle of the roadway approximately above the fifth arch from the Surrey side. This had been diluted but not dissipated by the atmospheric moisture, and I adjudged it to be the point of injury. No weapon could be found on the bridge.

A careful examination of the area around the blood stain turned up a lady's silver earring in the eastern pedestrian recess nearest to where the body lay, and a handkerchief approximately ten yards south of the body, both of which I dismissed as the kind of things lost on the span each day.

As you may have heard, the victim managed to stagger to the Middlesex toll-house, where he expired. Although the dying man was unable to convey anything coherent to the toll-collector in his dying breaths, his corpse itself would provide me with the solution to the mystery. Thus I had it removed to a place where I could examine it away from the attention of the many newspapermen seeking my intelligence on the matter.

Well, I made a thorough search of the victim's clothes, which yielded the initials W.B. on sundry garments. In the left coat pocket, I was pleased enough to find a playbill for my own forthcoming address at the Queen's Theatre on Wych-street. In the right pocket, I found a bundle of blank Custom House unloading warrants signed by Principal Officer Gregory. Other pockets revealed little of note: a pocketbook, a number of coins amounting to 4s 6d, and a small Sheffield penknife with pearl scales.

Perhaps your first thought, Commissioner, is that the penknife was used to inflict the fatal wound. You would be wrong in such an assumption, however: there was no blood on the knife, and, in any case, what man would cut his own throat and then carefully fold away the blade before putting the weapon in his pocket?

No doubt you are also thinking that the unloading warrants suggest the victim was an employee of the Custom House. Though the body itself bore no such uniform, insignia or paraphernalia of a waterside worker, I nevertheless examined the body and clothing closely and was perspicacious enough to find a small stone in the left shoe – a stone, mind you, of the exact colour and dimensions of the gravel upon the Custom House terrace. This was my corroboration of what the warrants suggested.

As you might expect, my next action was to request that Principal Officer Gregory of the Custom House come to where I was examining the body and look at the dead man's face in order to identify it. It was thus with great melancholy that Mr Gregory said he knew the victim as one William Barton, a tidewaiter of the Custom House. The blank unloading warrants, said Mr Gregory, had been stolen some days before, and the victim had been one of the suspects in that crime. (Note also the corroboration with the initials W.B.)

Commissioner – I will torture you no longer with the solution: William Barton was the victim of nothing more than suicide brought about by his own guilt and fear of impending discovery.

'What is the evidence?' you may cry.

Well, there was not another soul on the bridge at the time of the incident. Each person who passed through the Surrey or Middlesex toll-houses was accounted for at the other end – at least in the hour or so preceding the death, when the fog descended. The last was a costermonger with his barrow. Where there is no other suspect, there can be no suspicion of murder.

Ah, but you will say the toll-keepers themselves could be suspects. They were, after all, the only two people on the bridge apart from the victim. Naturally, I took such a consideration into account and examined both of the gentlemen for traces of blood. There was none, and also no opportunity for them to clean their hands prior to my arrival. Nor, indeed, was there any obvious motive: nothing was stolen and there was no benefit for the toll-collectors in such a course of action.

'What of the weapon that bisected his throat?' you may ask – a question worthy of your position. Let us put ourselves in the position of the victim (as any good detective must do). Here is a man who is suspected of a serious crime; he is in danger of losing his employment and being shamed before all of his fellows. He stands to lose his good name, and possibly also any bond he may have put up in trust as an employee of the Custom House. Would not any man quail before such a fate? No – he simply takes his razor and walks out to the loneliest place in London: Waterloo-bridge in a fog. There, he makes a single slash at his own neck, using the fatal momentum of his arm to fling the offending tool over the parapet.

'Mere fancy!' you mutter. 'Supposition!' you conclude. Not at all – the toll-keeper of the Middlesex side heard metal striking against stone. Since no other metal article could be found on the bridge, we may assume it was the lethal article itself: the razor.

I trust that you will pass this letter on to your men in the Detective Force (if they do not read it in today's issues) that they may benefit from my methods.

Most respectfully yours,
Eldritch Batchem Esq.

Sir Richard held the letter with whitened knuckles. Much as he would have liked to rip it into shreds and cast it into the river, there was much in it that deserved more attention. In the meantime, the steam launch was finally approaching his destination: Custom House quay.

As usual, the river about that point was frenetically a-bustle. Steamships from Hamburg, Rotterdam, Antwerp and Havre seemed to suckle like piglets at the embankment, spilling chattering passengers and luggage down gangplanks onto the gravel and into the arms of Customs officers waiting to check for significant importations of china, books, instruments, millinery and sundry other goods masquerading as personal effects. Fishing boats jostled for space among the larger vessels and, indeed, the Pool hereabouts was so dense with dark-bodied ships that there seemed to be almost no visible water at all.

The bell of the police launch cleared a space in the traffic and finally Sir Richard was able to get ashore to crunch rapidly over the gravel for his appointment with the inspector general, who, it must be said, was no more enthusiastic about his impending meeting than Mr Blackthorne had been.

'I thank you for seeing me at such short notice,' said Sir Richard, shaking hands and taking the proffered chair in the large office overlooking the quay. The din of the embankment echoed up to where they sat.

'I admit I was given very little advance warning,' said the Inspector General of Customs, Mr Jackson. He was a nautical sort, his long greying beard giving him the air of a captain, and his dark-blue jacket with brass buttons suggesting a ship's bridge rather than an office desk.

'I trust you have seen this morning's editions, Mr Jackson?'

'Indeed.'

'What do you know of this tidewaiter William Barton and his pocket full of unloading warrants?'

'Forgive me if I lecture you, Sir Richard, but we speak of a small piece of a much larger process. Such warrants are issued by this building (from the Long Room directly below us, in fact) so that any ship which has rightfully declared its cargo manifest may be docked at its point of destination and unloaded, the cargo being warehoused under bond until duties are paid for its release. The unloading warrants found on the body of Barton should not leave this building until ship details and cargo manifests have been logged in our ledgers by the relevant clerk.'

'Then how does one explain such a quantity of blank warrants in the possession of a tidewaiter, all of them apparently signed by Principal Officer Gregory?'

'He signs large quantities of these things at one moment and stores them, as do other principal officers. I suppose it would not be beyond credulity for someone to discern where they are stored and to steal some.'

'You seem unconcerned by this gross case of fraudulence, Mr Jackson.'

'I am concerned, but I am unsurprised, Commissioner. A tidewaiter is not a highly paid employee; his job, after all, is simply to sit about on incoming or outgoing ships and wait for the correct documentation to arrive that he might observe legitimate unloading or loading. As a moderately paid man, he finds himself thus in sole charge of many thousands of pounds' worth of valuable cargo. Might he not occasionally turn a blind eye to some minor illegality?'

'"Minor" you say? Am I not correct in thinking that a fraudulently completed unloading warrant allows the ship to unload its entire cargo anywhere it likes, without the Custom House knowing of it? I do not call that "minor".'

'We hope that our employees are men of integrity and discretion, Sir Richard. Indeed, our landing-waiters (who register arriving ships) require two references and a five-hundred-pound bond. Alas, the tidewaiters often work unsupervised and are prone to staying with us for a short time. At the busiest periods, we have difficulty employing enough of them.'

'I must repeat, therefore: how does a mere tidewaiter manage to procure these warrants? Surely he would need help from others? Others more senior than himself . . .'

'I think I see the direction your questioning is taking, Sir Richard. I suppose you are referring to the recent correspondence in *the Times* concerning alleged corruption among officers of the Custom House.'

'Well, what of it?'

'Of course, the correspondent was anonymous . . .' said Mr Jackson.

'But evidently also someone with an intimate knowledge of the Customs processes along this river.'

'That may be. But to accuse my landing-waiters *en masse* of being corrupt, and to accuse this institution of masking corruption at a higher level is frankly rather fantastical. There will always be dishonest men, and we attempt to find them. There is nothing more to it than that, Sir Richard.'

'Merchants have been complaining for some time that there is no record of their cargo and, therefore, that they are unable to pay their duties. Fruit has gone rotten under bond while landing-waiters' logbooks are "missing".'

'Our processes are not perfect. Logbooks are sometimes handed between landing-waiters as they move from wharf to wharf. There is a huge amount of documentation . . .

but may I be bold enough to ask what concern this is of the Metropolitan Police Commissioner? I am happy to welcome you, but admittedly rather nonplussed as to why you take a personal interest in this.'

'A man was killed yesterday morning on Waterloo-bridge: one of your men who was apparently engaged in some questionable business. The Thames Police are also under my jurisdiction and I will not be made a fool of if smuggling is flourishing beneath my very nose. I trust you are my ally in this earnest wish for legality.'

'Of course, Sir Richard. But I believe the death of William Barton was suicide, was it not?'

'That has not been the verdict of the Metropolitan Police, no matter how many newspapers it may appear in. Was this Barton under investigation as claimed in the articles?'

'Naturally, I spoke with Principal Officer Gregory when I heard he had been called to identify the body. He told me that Barton was a recent appointment and that there had been some reports of . . . of irregularity in his work.'

'Irregularity?'

'The man had seemingly vanished during his duty a number of times. On being questioned, he said he had been stricken with a persistent cough and forced to take a drink of tea to calm himself. Not particularly creative as an excuse, I grant you. We were in the process of checking his claims when he died.'

'This was no reason for him to kill himself, surely.'

'Rather not – though he would have faced transportation had we known of those warrants. Assuredly, he could have simply not arrived for work today and we would have been glad of his absence. That would have been the simplest path.'

'That is what I suspected.'

'Is there something more to this incident than has been made public, Sir Richard?'

'I cannot be certain, but you can help me to discover the truth, Mr Jackson. I wish to task a number of my clerks with going through your records for further irregularities over previous months—'

'That is rather an imposition. We are very busy here and—'

'All you need to do is provide a room for my men and supply them with records of arrivals, loading and outgoings for the past six months. You need not concern yourself with any vessel currently or henceforth in your ledgers, thereby inconveniencing you not an iota. I believe that this data, once scrutinized, will reveal any patterns of discrepancy that will benefit both you and I in the battle against smuggling. Nobody else need know of the results. Are you afraid of what we might unearth?'

'Not at all. But I feel this response is quite out of proportion to a simple suicide. May I ask you if I am being told everything? I am not insensible to the fact that your Inspector Newsome has recently been assigned to the Thames Police. He is a detective, is he not?'

'He was a detective and may be again. At present, he is simply aiding the Thames Police in their work.'

'Nothing more than that? I do not like to feel that I am being observed.'

'Mr Jackson – it is the work of the Thames Police, among other duties, to be vigilant for any depredations upon the water. It matters not who commits them or where. You tell me that there is no corruption among your ranks and I am obliged to accept your word. Should events prove otherwise, we will speak once again.'

'We certainly shall.'

'Very well. I thank you for your time and I presume you will be most welcoming to my clerks when they arrive tomorrow morning.'

Thus did Sir Richard retire from the office of the inspector general and return to the quay, where the launch was waiting for him. Indeed, he was so preoccupied with his thoughts that he barely noticed the gentleman who brushed roughly against him while disembarking from a steam ferry. Had Sir Richard noticed, he would surely have recognized the man as one whom he had not only previously imprisoned, but whom he had also once engaged on a very unusual case.

The two would be meeting again soon enough, but it may prove interesting nevertheless to take a few steps backwards before revealing the identity of that particular ferry passenger.

FIVE

As Sir Richard had travelled beneath the arches of Blackfriars-bridge that morning, he would have passed the stately row of merchant's houses on the north shore: testaments to the diligence (and rapacity) of those traders in timber, coal, sperma-ceti and spices who had made London the destination of the world's fleets. From the river, these edifices appeared even taller and grander, their *façades* diminished not a jot by the many leaning masts and the rows of ochre-sailed barges set-tled on the mud before them.

One of these residences, between Puddle Dock and the bridge stairs, was a particular curiosity. A thin, two-storey building, it seemed to have been shouldered into place by the taller ones each side. Indeed, one might not have said from the river whether it was an independent structure or an extension of its neighbours. From Earl-street at the rear, it was quite invisible and offered no apparent door to the thoroughfare.

As for the inhabitants of that singular home, there was much debate among other residents of the row. Some main-tained that the owner was one Harold Smith, an importer of linen. Others knew the gentleman in question as William

Smart, a minor ship-owner holding cargo somewhere in the east of the city. All remarked on the somewhat terrifying aspect of the gentleman's manservant: a lofty Negro with a damaged left eye that presented but a milky film to the world. Neither resident brought trouble to the area, however, and so the merchants thereabouts did not – as merchants generally do not – enquire too closely into the other man's business.

That morning, then, as Sir Richard had passed under the bridge, the master of the narrow riverside house had been reclining in a sturdy leather chair with his back to the window. He was holding an old edition of *the Times* on his knee and scanning the personal advertisements with his light-grey eyes. One might have said, from his well-made clothes and the good taste of the room, that he was a gentleman. But the crooked nose and lightly scarred knuckles suggested a more eventful past than most of our gentlemen are accustomed to. His real name was Noah Dyson.

'Listen to this, Ben,' he said, reading to the large Negro sitting in a similarly accommodating chair by the fire. '"The writer of the anonymous note to Mr Swales makes an erroneous assumption as to the identity of the person referred to." If that is not a blackmail case, I do not know what is. Or how about this one: "If Mr Parrack, formerly butler to the late Lord Young will make his address known to G.D. at 14 Rathbone-place, he may hear something to his advantage." What do you make of that, Ben? A legacy? Or more blackmail?'

Benjamin gave a great *basso* laugh and put down his book. He was indeed a unique specimen, the opaque eye and his large size – all of it hard muscle – lending him a fearsome air. A horrifying scar of twisted skin about his throat suggested a too-near acquaintance with the gallows at some point in his past, while further scarring at his temples and

48

nose hinted at some time in the prize ring. He did not respond in speech to Noah's question, but instead described a number of curious shapes in the air with his hands, swooping, squeezing and punctuating with his fingers until he had completed his thought in that language.

'No, I am not *bored*, Ben. These entries are quite fascinating. Each one is a story in itself; one must only pull at its strands to uncover the larger truth. Do you not occasionally look at the faces on the streets and wonder at their secrets, their cares, their guilt – their crimes? Do you not see in these pages those secrets laid bare?'

Benjamin, now reading again, smiled and used a single hand to indicate 'no' without looking up from his page.

'Well, listen to this one: "If M.R. will write immediately, M.S. will go to see her". That is evidently a story of romance. He is pursuing her against the will of her parents, but they have been maintaining an illicit correspondence all the same. It seems her parents have been getting the upper hand and this is his desperate attempt to renew that correspondence. That is *my* interpretation.'

Benjamin, still focused upon the book, simply shook his head. He had not the slightest interest.

'And this is an interesting one: "ποταμιάνοι: αυγή στο τηγάνι" – some manner of vulgar Greek by the looks of it. One does not often see foreign tongues in the personal advertisements. I wonder what it—'

Benjamin slapped the covers of his book together and remarked (one might assume from the pointed nature of his gesticulations) that he had had enough of his friend's incessant talk and was taking his book to a place where he might read in peace.

'Suit yourself, Ben. I will see you at supper,' said Noah.

Alone now, he applied himself once more to the paper and saw on the next page that Benjamin, despite his professed lack of interest, had circled one of the advertisements in dark pencil for Noah's interest: *Five guineas reward – lost on Tuesday this week between Custom House quay and the Tower, a gold and diamond brooch in the shape of a swan. Bring the article to Mivart's Hotel and ask for Miss Roberts to claim the reward.*

He smiled. Many mistook Benjamin for his manservant, but no man could wish for a truer and more loyal friend. They had fought back-to-back on more than one foreign shore, sailors' knives in hand and their clothes hanging in bloody strips from their bodies. They had known such privation that a shared forecastle bunk was their only comfort, and yet they had also enjoyed wealth beyond many men's imaginations. That, however, is another story entirely.

Noah tore the circled message carefully from the paper and folded it into his trouser pocket. He then stood and turned to look out at the river, where a fully loaded steam ferry was leaving a churning wake for a coal barge to traverse on its way up to Westminster. The manufactory chimneys of Southwark were pouring their incessant smoke into a grey sky. Idly, he looked at the mantel clock and seemed to weigh how best to spend his afternoon.

He looked again at the advertisement Benjamin had circled, and, as if making a sudden decision, he quickly extracted a dagger from a drawer and slipped it into a leather sheath beneath his jacket. His top hat and dark overcoat were next, and then he was descending carpeted stairs to emerge into a narrow alley that brought him onto the private wharf facing the river. In just a few minutes, he was standing with a dozen others at the Blackfriars ferry pier.

As they waited thus, the gathered passengers heard the unmistakable chant of a street hawker coming down the stairs from the bridge:

'*Eldritch Batchem! Eldritch Batchem!* The greatest detective of modern London and investigator by royal appointment!' cried a man in a garish rust-coloured suit as he walked among them. 'Hear him speak on "The Mind of the Murderer" at the Queen's Theatre . . . !'

A playbill was thrust into Noah's hand by the cryer. He scanned the first few lines:

THE MIND OF THE MURDERER REVEALED

Esteemed private investigator by Royal Appointment
Eldritch Batchem addresses the people of London on
the science of detection and on the special case of
the murderer . . .

He crumpled the paper and threw it into the river, where it was almost instantly sucked into the boiling water beneath the arriving ferry's circular paddles. The swell splashed up against the pier, a billow of acrid smoke washed over faces, and the hatch-boy on board yelled 'Stop 'er! Stop 'er!' down to the hidden engineer.

The gangplank was lowered into place and, after a sudden cataract of passengers off and on, the hatch-boy was relaying the skipper's hand signals from the bridge to the engine: 'Half-a-turn-astern! And another . . . easy now! Easy now! Full speed ahead now!'

Noah climbed the stairs to take a seat on the upper deck that he might better observe the passengers, who presented a common enough selection: here a group of enthusiastic visiters from the provinces in their outdated fashions, pointing vigorously at the shoreline as if every warehouse were a palace and every spire the dome of St Paul's. Here a minor clerk heading for St Katharine's, *his* mind occupied with how many wagons would be available to transport his hogsheads of beer. And here, sitting before Noah, was a governess with her young charge: a boy whose clothes said he was from a wealthy family, but whose unkempt hair and muddy knees said he was still just a boy at heart. His inquisitive eyes seemed to be fixed on Noah's wrists, which, where they emerged from the coat cuffs, revealed the kind of scarring that comes only from incarceration in irons.

Seeing the boy's glances, Noah winked and reached beneath his waistcoat to extract the dagger, which he used affectedly to scrape a clot of mud from his boot heel, enjoying the wide-eyed stare it elicited.

The game soon ended, however, when the intended object of Noah's trip walked by with a scent of perfume to counteract the river's stink. Her linen and lace were suggestive, and the flash of ankle as she strode made that suggestion fact: she was a street girl using the ferry to advertise herself to the many professional men upon the Thames. Noah stood and walked towards where she stood at the rail, the line of her outthrust hip exhibited to best effect in the black dress.

'Good morning to you, miss,' he said.

'I don't talk to policemen, sir. Call me superstitious, but I just don't.' Her smile said that she might, nevertheless, make an exception for Noah.

'What makes you think I am a policeman?'

'I can just tell.'

'Well, I assure you I am not – and if I were, I would be legally bound to tell you. Is that not correct?'

'I . . . I suppose so.'

'Miss – I believe you can aid me greatly. I see that you have rather an attractive brooch there at your breast . . .'

'Why, and I thought you were a gentleman! A fine one you are, looking at my—'

'Please, let us dispense with such banter. I can see immediately that it is not a genuine diamond, no matter what your benefactor may have told you. Even so, I will buy it from you.'

'It is not for sale, at least not to one so rude as yourself.'

'It is worth perhaps two shillings, but here is a sovereign.'

'I . . . well . . . all right.'

'But before you remove your brooch so readily, let me explain my terms. I will give you your sovereign but you will keep the brooch. For the money, you will disembark at the Custom House and simply make your way to the Tower. If I do not meet you there after ten minutes to collect the brooch, you may keep both the brooch and the sovereign.'

'I say, what is this all about, sir? I am no criminal.'

'It is simply as I say. All you need to do is walk to the Tower with my money in your pocket. Do you agree?'

The ferry passed under an arch of London-bridge, casting a shadow over them. For a moment they might have been in a watery cave rather than at the centre of the world.

'I will do it,' said the magdalene, finally seeing no disadvantage in the deal.

'Good girl. Go now so that you are among the first across the gangplank. I will observe you and will follow.'

The engines altered their tone. The paddles slowed their thrashing of the water. From up on deck, the broad Custom House quay looked like chaos: all hawkers, clerks, merchants, idlers, visiters to the Tower and, of course, the lines of continental passengers with their luggage.

Noah looked carefully over the crowds. As a child of the

streets, he saw the city unlike other Londoners. Those raised in the comfort of a home lived their lives among a limited network of roads, seldom venturing beyond the known shops, offices and residences of friends. To one who called the whole city his home, every metropolitan space had a life and character of its own. At a glance, and often from their pace or gait alone, he might pick out the stranger, the worker, the beggar and the thief. He saw not mere streets, but catalogues of characters.

And there was one who attracted Noah's attention after just a few moments. The man was waiting, but evidently not for a vessel, for he showed no urgency or interest in moving closer to the embarkation points. His left arm appeared to hang limply in a soiled sling around his neck, yet he showed no awareness of caution for his damaged limb as the people pressed all around him.

The gangplank was lowered and the ferry passengers surged across it. Noah watched the man with the sling, who had positioned himself in a place where the people would flow past him. As they did so, each one was scrutinized with a rapid up-and-down glance . . . until the street girl walked by, looking over her shoulder to see if Noah was watching her. At that moment, the 'injured' man stepped in front of her, causing her to almost trip. A swift mutual apology was effected, and then both went on their ways.

Noah smiled and stepped quickly to join the remaining disembarking passengers, all the while keeping his target – the 'one-armed' gentleman – in sight. He would never again see the girl, who had earned her sovereign but lost her brooch.

Once on the quay, Noah assumed the role of a passenger waiting for the Havre ferry, all the while watching with growing amusement as the 'one-armed' man bumped into numerous other people too distracted to notice that they were missing their pocketbooks, bracelets, tiepins, handkerchiefs or brooches. Finally, after about half an hour, good sense dictated that it was time the thief left his workplace lest somebody find their property missing and remember being jostled by him.

Noah followed, himself accidentally colliding with a fellow he recognized instantly as none other than Commissioner of Police Sir Richard Mayne. The eminent gentleman was mercifully too preoccupied to pause, however, and Noah managed to keep his quarry in view while reflecting ironically on how the city threw people together.

Moving north, he was not at all surprised to be led around the Tower, up Rosemary-lane and then into that warren of alleys north of East Smithfield, where sundry low receivers of stolen goods are to be found. With many a backward glance (but little observation) the 'one-armed' man turned repeatedly left and right through a maze of filthy passages before finally entering a dilapidated marine store whose unsellable wares spilled out into the narrow passage before it.

A few moments later, he was joined by Noah in a shop that was tiny and made to seem smaller still by the improbable multitude of rubbish piled on its shelves and floor. The tin cups, rusted tools, oiled capes, sacks of mouldy ship's biscuit and coils of well-worn rope together gave off a powerfully musty scent. Behind the counter, the proprietor was talking to the thief but paused mid-sentence to look dubiously at his new 'customer'.

'Sure yer got the right shop, mate?' he said.

'I believe so,' said Noah. 'I am looking for . . . excuse me a moment . . .' He took the newspaper clipping from his pocket and unfolded it. 'Yes – I am looking for a "gold and diamond brooch in the shape of a swan".'

'Ha! You must have problems with yer peepers, mate. I can do yer a length of rope or a tin bucket, but I don't sell no jewel'ry. Yer want old Levi down the alley – he'll do for yer.'

'No – I am sure this is the place. I have just followed this poor fellow here, having spent part of my morning watching him steal from passengers at Custom House quay. I trust that you are his customary receiver and that – as thieves are wont to do – he has reserved that particular plot as his own. Therefore, this is the most likely place for me to find my brooch.'

'I don't think I like your tone,' said the 'one-armed' man, squaring up to Noah. 'Call me a thief to my face, will you?'

Noah smiled and casually extracted his dagger, which, without a moment's hesitation, he thrust downwards into the arm within the dirty sling. It stuck there, upright, and quivered slightly at the handle.

The 'one-armed' man showed not the slightest reaction of pain, but the proprietor let forth a throaty laugh and slapped the counter in his mirth.

'Balsa wood, I presume. Or is it pine?' said Noah, tugging the dagger free of the false arm.

'Ha ha! He's got yer there!' said the proprietor to the man with the sling, who – seemingly nonplussed by the boldness of the gentleman with the dagger – was now sheepishly releasing his concealed arm from a hidden vent in the side of his jacket. He looked Noah up and down. 'You are no policeman. What are you?'

'I have come for the brooch. Not the one you took today from the street girl – you can keep that. I want the one shaped like a swan.'

'What makes yer think it's here, if it ever was,' said the proprietor, his smile fading rapidly.

'Because a small receiver such as yourself does not sell his spoils piecemeal to the larger receivers – you store up your treasures until you have a quantity to tempt them. Because it was taken only a few days ago. Because if you do not give it to me now, you will both be very sorry.'

'You are only one and we are two,' said the proprietor with mathematical assuredness.

Noah merely grinned. 'Gentlemen – let us be civil. It would not inconvenience me at all to use my dagger on you. But in truth I am not remotely interested in your thievery. I have no intention of harming your free-enterprise endeavours – nor do I intend to inform the local constables what goes on here. All I want is that swan. Then I will bid you good day and never return to bother you again.'

The two criminals looked at each other and then at this gentleman who so affably threatened them with violence.

'What is it worth to you?' asked the proprietor.

Noah sighed and shook his head. His right arm flashed out in a blur and the edge of his hand struck the throat of the 'one-armed' man, who fell loudly to the dusty wooden floor. He writhed there, groaning, with his hands about his neck.

'That is the end of my patience,' said Noah to the proprietor. 'The swan, if you please, or I will similarly disable you, search this place and take it.'

The shopkeeper peered over the counter at his fellow on the floor. Then he opened a drawer to his right, rummaged briefly among its contents and placed the swan on the counter with a defiant glare.

'That would have fetched me a pretty price,' he said with a clenched jaw.

Noah examined the brooch and saw that the stones were real, as well they might be for a lady resident of Mivart's Hotel. 'Well, now you may go home to supper with a throat that works. Good day to you, gentlemen.'

And to expedite the conclusion of Noah Dyson's day, he did indeed make his way to that hotel, where he handed the brooch to an effusively grateful Miss Roberts and received the five guinea reward. If it looked like chivalry to her, it had been merely an afternoon's entertainment for him: a diversion from the tedium of which he had grown so tired.

Indeed, he did not even keep the money. Within minutes of collecting it, he had dropped the coins into the basket of a pale and sickly girl selling watercresses on an Oxford-street corner. It was, after all, an insignificant sum to him, but one that, to her, would be the certain difference between life and death.

Such *ennui* was soon to end, however, for his next call was south across Waterloo-bridge towards Lambeth, where the door he knocked upon was opened by a gentleman of our recent acquaintance: one George Williamson.

SIX

'What can you tell me about this body I found yesterday, doctor?'

Inspector Newsome looked at the naked form on the examination table in the surgery of the Thames Police station house at Wapping. It was a man of about thirty years, moderately built, with little bodily hair and with a number of obvious wounds about the torso and limbs. Now washed clean of the river's filth, the pale body appeared less horrifying than when found, though it had been opened and sewn closed again in the meantime.

'I can tell you, Mr Newsome, that this is no place for me to be doing work of such a variety,' said the surgeon, an earnest gentleman more accustomed to reviving half-drowned would-be suicides or dockworkers. 'This is neither a dissection room nor a morgue.'

'Your help is most gratefully received, doctor. I need to know everything: the provenance of every wound, and the cause of death.'

'Is this not a matter for an inquest? I really do not see the need for me to have examined the body here in the station.'

'No doubt there will be an inquest, doctor, but justice

occasionally does not appreciate waiting – particularly if there is a murderer on the loose.'

'Do you suspect as much?'

'I suspect only what I have cause to – which is why we are in this room.'

'Well, he did not drown – I can tell you that. There was no water in his lungs. The chain about his ankles may have been to weigh him down in the water, but he was already dead when thrown in.'

'Not enough chain, evidently. What of the cut on his left cheek there?'

'Difficult to say. It seems to have been caused by a significant impact rather than by a sharp instrument. The skin has been torn from the bone in an irregular shape: a rip rather than a cut.'

'Have you any idea as to the cause of that impact?'

'It could be anything really. If he has been in the river some time, it might be the hull of a boat, a ferry platform, something on the riverbed . . .'

'Or the weapon that killed him?'

'I think not. The cheekbone is not broken so the force was not colossal.'

'And this ragged area about his left shoulder? That does not look like a blow.'

'I will come to that in just a moment. If you are seeking the cause of death, however, I rather suspect it was the blow to the back of his head here.' The doctor indicated a shaved area of discoloured scalp. 'The scull is quite shattered beneath the skin.'

'I see. What of those minor abrasions about the wound? He has them also on his elbows and knees.'

'My guess would be that they are the result of the body

churning along the gravel of the riverbed for some time, abrading through his clothes in those bony places. I pulled a good many fragments out of the wounds.'

'How long do you think he was in the water?'

'Based on the numerous suicides I see, I would guess no more than two or three days. The cold water has preserved the body if anything.'

'Is there any way to tell whether that blow to his head occurred before or after he went into the water?'

'I am afraid not, Inspector Newsome – only that he did not inhale river water.'

'Well, the chain tells us he probably did not slip and fall, hitting his head as he toppled into the river. Somebody wanted him not to be found.'

'It seems the most likely conclusion. I did, however, find something exceptionally curious in that wound on the shoulder. It is rather inconsistent with the other injuries.'

'Yes?'

The surgeon went over to a stone basin and returned with a small metal bowl, which he held out for examination.

'What do you make of that, Mr Newsome?'

'My G—! Did you find that in the body?'

'In the shoulder, as I say. I had to dig it out of the flesh.'

'Is it really what it appears to be?'

'Indeed – it is an exceptionally large mammalian tooth. An incisor, most probably, though I could not say from what animal.'

'A very big one, it would seem.'

'Certainly. And not one indigenous to the river or its environs either. It is like no fish tooth I have ever seen.'

'Could this have happened prior to the body going into the water?'

'That is even more curious. There was some sand inside the wound beneath the tooth. It may have worked its way in there, of course, but it suggests the tooth went into the body *after* the body had been submerged and washed about the river. I might even venture that the body was washed up on a bank during low tide and attacked there as carrion.'

'This is most interesting, doctor. What manner of beast could do that?'

'I cannot say. Certainly none that seems native to the city. Of course, there are stories among the mudlarks of "beasts", but they are simple people and prone to idiocy.'

'Is that right – the mudlarks? I may look into it further. In the meantime, I wonder if you can tell me anything of the man's profession?'

'From his naked body alone? I am a doctor, not a necromancer. I would expect his clothes to tell more about that story. Have you not examined them?'

'I have, but a man may wear any clothes he likes – or be dressed in them by another. You raise your eyebrows, doctor, but such things are part of my experience. Let us look at his hands, for example: no calluses upon the palms and no oakum or tar beneath the nails. That tells us he was not a common seaman. Likewise, there are no fresh cuts or abrasions on the fingers, which reinforces the assumption he was no mere river labourer. As for the feet, they are also relatively free of calluses or misshapen toes, meaning . . .'

'He wore good boots.'

'Precisely. He was wearing them when found, but the body tells us they were his own.'

'What else did his garments tell you, Inspector?'

'The pea coat is indicative of a mariner, it is true – as are the canvas trousers. As with the boots, they were of a reasonably good quality, so I presume our man was a ship's mate. We also found a folding marline spike in his pocket with the initials "M.H." branded into its handle.'

'So we can safely assume the man was a sailor.'

'It would seem so. He had a pocketbook with some money in it – alas, nothing more that would identify him. The chain about his ankles was standard medium-gauge iron that might be found anywhere along the Thames. It must have been attached in a hurry, or else there was initially more, for as we know, it was insufficient to act as an anchor.'

'Well, I am sure this is all most intriguing, Mr Newsome, but I have finished my examination and I have other duties. Shall I arrange to have the body interred as usual?'

'Yes, thank you, doctor. But before you do so, I would like Constable Jones to make me a detailed pencil likeness of the victim's face. You may leave it on my desk when it is done . . . and I will take that tooth with me.'

'I was hoping to keep it as a curiosity . . .'

'It is a clue in an investigation. I must take it from you.'

'Very well, Inspector – if you must. Where does your investigation go now?'

'Back to the accursed river again. I need to discern, if possible, where that body might first have entered the water.'

'I wish you luck. The tides are a mystery that few understand. In fact, you might want to speak to a retired pilot many of the constables consult on such riverine matters. He goes by the name of John Tarr, though he is sometimes termed "the Thames sage".'

'*Tarr*? I fear you are mocking me now, doctor.'

'I am quite serious. He claims it as his family name. He can be found at Pickle Herring-street, apparently. Everyone knows him there, although I hear he is somewhat eccentric.'

'Perhaps I will seek him out. In the meantime I thank you again for accommodating me regarding the examination of "M.H." here.'

In a city born of its river, can there be any place more representative of that heritage than Pickle Herring-street on the Surrey shore? Its stairs, wharf and warehousing were as familiar to those ocean-rovers of glorious Elizabeth as they are to Victoria's merchants, and the bustle about those alleys has not ceased for centuries of trade.

Coal dust crackles underfoot, barrels roll down planks from wagons, cries echo from cavernous storage spaces, and the tackle of innumerable cranes rattles and creaks at loading platforms. High above the thoroughfare, criss-crossing wooden walkways convey clerks from office to office so that one might fancy being upon the deck of an enormous brig rather than a street. And everywhere, the smell of cargoes: oranges of Spain, the pungent fish basket, the musty wine cask, tobacco's sweet scent, and the odd enticement of tar. It is said that dogs go mad here.

At the shore-side stairs, waves slap at moss-mottled stone and rinse the steps with solutions of sand. And as the river went about its timeless business that afternoon, a police galley crossed between colliers and smacks from the Tower to steer among the tethered wherries of the watermen.

One might be assured that those particular gentlemen of the river were, as ever, reluctant to meet any Thames policeman, whatever rank he might hold. For as a teacher has to apply the birch now and again to his charges, so the uniformed men of the river are obliged daily to figuratively lash the waterman for his fractious nature.

'Ho! Come to investigate my stolen wherry, have you?' shouted one.

'Nah – they've come about the young feller had his brains splashed all over by that dray Tuesday last,' offered another.

'Hush your blather!' said a third. 'They'll be here about that body we pulled out two months gone. Better late than never!'

These jibes raised a collective laugh from the other water-men, which the constables in the galley bore with their usual professional fortitude as they stowed the oars and tied up to a chain. Their inspector, however, seemed less placatory.

'Make way, mongrels!' said Mr Newsome as he stepped from the galley up the stairs and into the group of ruffians. 'You think yourself wits, but your humour may have earned you trouble. Constables – while I am about my business, I want you to check that all of these wherries are numbered and logged to the last letter of the regulations. Any that are not will be towed away and destroyed on my return.'

A mutter of discontent rippled through the watermen and the constables in the galley smiled to each other, momentar-ily pleased to be working with their unorthodox superior.

Thus it was that Mr Newsome made his way past the fishing-net frames and smack baskets to the main artery of Pickle Herring-street itself, which, on that afternoon, seemed less like a public highway and more like an eruption of cargo from the overloaded vaults around it. Wire-bound bales stamped with merchants' marks were piled as high as a man on both sides, and barrels tumbled chaotically in wait for the cranes. Everywhere, men toiled with weight and wheel to process the trade of the world.

'Excuse me,' said Mr Newsome, addressing a foreman supervising the hoisting of tobacco bales into a third-storey aperture, 'I am seeking a certain John Tarr of this street. He is an ex-pilot, I believe.'

'Aye – ten yards on,' replied the man, waving an arm but not taking his eyes from the swaying package. 'Turn right at Walden's Wool. You'll find him down Tripe-alley.'

Mr Newsome walked as directed among the wagons (mindful of the waterman's allusion to the pedestrian who had recently fallen under their wheels) and saw the sign of the wool warehouse. Turning right as directed, he could see the river and the manifold masts of the Pool at the conclusion of Tripe-alley, but there was otherwise no sign of habitation – just the blank brick edifices of warehouse ends. He muttered a blasphemy and started to pick his way through a muddy tangle of worn rope, rotten timber and cat-chewed rat corpses.

'John Tarr! Are you down here? John Tarr, I say!'

At the alley's end, the *silhouette* of a figure appeared: squat, stolid and wearing a formless corduroy cap upon its head. A long, thin cigar protruded from the mouth.

'John Tarr?' said Mr Newsome, seeing the face properly now. The man had the leathery look of a South Sea mariner, his face etched with lines like a whaler's hull after a three-year voyage. A lifetime of pulling on oars and ropes had given his arms and shoulders some natural bulk, though he seemed to be doing nothing in this place other than watching the vessels upon the water. A rough-hewn bench by the muddy bank appeared to have been situated for the very purpose, and the ex-pilot beckoned his visiter to come closer.

'Aye, I am Tarr.' The voice matched the face: a brine-seasoned, weather-hewn instrument that exhaled a cloud of smoke from the twig-like cigar.

'What are you doing down here, Mr Tarr, if I may ask. I see no houses.'

'I might ask the same of you, Inspector.'

'You know me?'

'I saw the galley row over from the Tower and I saw you in it. Two constables and their inspector is standard for a galley. You held no oar. Won't you take a seat and watch the river with me?'

'Thank you – I will. Your sight is certainly acute. I am Inspector Newsome of the Detec—, of the Thames Police, and I am told that you are the man to speak to concerning the tides of the river and . . . and other related matters.'

'I was a Trinity House pilot. I was a waterman. I have been a ferry skipper. I know the river as well as any man, and I know it as little as any man.'

'Well, you are better placed than I am to answer my question. If a body washes up among the colliers of the Pool on the Surrey side about fifty yards east of London-bridge, where might it have entered the water? Is there any means of calculating it?'

'Ho! Do you know women, Inspector?'

'Women? What has that to do with the question?'

'A woman is a force of nature, Inspector. One might learn no science to predict her actions. She is like fire or the sea – a mystery to men, and a great danger. The river is like a woman – only less predictable, more lethal.'

Mr Tarr took the cigar from his mouth and pointed to his interlocutor with it as if adding a glowing full stop to the proclamation.

'I see,' said Mr Newsome. 'Perhaps, in my ignorance, I have mistaken the daily change of tides to be a somewhat predictable pattern—'

'"Predictable", you say? Perhaps before Old London-bridge was demolished – but no longer. Did you know that the flood tide has greater velocity on the Surrey side of Blackfriars when the Middlesex side simultaneously has flat water? Shoals appear and disappear at their own whim. When the north-easterlies blow uninterrupted, the channel chokes on water and breaks its banks. And yet dead water will appear mid-flow, stirring flotsam as the tides flow round. The bed of the river is to blame, of course. It is dredged, it is shifted, it is moulded by accretions of human filth from the sewers. Who knows what it is doing there beneath the cloaking water or what secrets it holds? Predictable? No. No. It is *haunted*.'

'Haunted?' Mr Newsome maintained his mask of earnest enquiry with difficulty.

'How many lives are lost to it every year? Fifty? One hundred? There are forty jumpers annually from Waterloo-bridge alone. Multiply that by centuries and ask yourself: where do those damned souls go? Not to heaven, certainly – not with the taint of their sin upon them. No – they remain there in the depths, in the cold blackness. It is *their* sorrow that animates the tides. They call to others, and keep them at their pleasure before releasing their flesh back to the world.'

'I recall reading a more scientific explanation, but no matter. Perhaps an example will prove more helpful. Last month, a woman's body was pulled out of the river at Blackwall. She had leapt from London-bridge four weeks previously – but where had she been since then? At the bottom of the river? Moving out to sea and back again in a ceaseless cycle? Is there something in the tides or the patterns of the river that make Blackwall a more appropriate place to find bodies fallen in at the bridge? Then again, some bodies falling from Waterloo-bridge have been reliably found at Cuckold's Point. Some bodies are never found at all. There *must* be some knowledge not known to almanacks but known to men such as you.'

'Some places are darker than others, Inspector. They harbour more souls and seek more to share their hopelessness. Waterloo is doubtlessly one such place. They are the spots where your bodies linger, unseen, until delivered up once again to the sun.'

'Well, I see I have wasted my time coming to you for information, Mr Tarr.' Mr Newsome made to stand.

'The river becomes darker, Inspector. Time was when every vessel moved by the power of wind or arm alone. Time was when every vessel was natural wood. Now all is steam and iron and copper. We have lost our feeling for the river and have made it just another thoroughfare to suit our ends. And yet it continues to claim souls, does it not? What would we see if the waters were to recede and reveal the history in its mud? The ribs of Roman galleys? The ribs of men sacrificed to religion, commerce and despair? Predictable? Ho! Predict your own end, Inspector!'

Mr Newsome stared sidelong at the ex-pilot to discern if he was mocking, or merely mad. The latter seemed the likelier assumption, so he began walking towards Tripe-alley.

'I will bid you good day, Mr Tarr. I leave you to the comfort of your insanity.'

'Beware the beasts of the river!'

The inspector stopped and felt for the tooth in his pocket.

'"Beasts?" I thought you spoke only of souls?'

John Tarr touched the side of his sun-seasoned nose and winked.

'Look at this.' Mr Newsome returned to the bench and held the tooth between thumb and forefinger so that Tarr could see it clearly. 'What manner of river animal has a tooth like this?'

'Inspector – there are things down there in the blackness that no man has ever seen. O, we sometimes see their shadows or the flick of a tail. We sometimes see the body of a cat vanish in a splash with an unseen snap of jaws; we sometimes see shapes in the low-tide mud made by no human foot; we sometimes hear noises at night made by no human throat. Your tooth tells me nothing I do not already know.'

'I see. Well, once again, your "expertise" appears to be quite incoherent. Thank you for your time.'

John Tarr made a mock salute and turned his attention back to the river, his cigar still smouldering at the corner of his mouth.

Mr Newsome shook his head and returned to the clamour of Pickle Herring-street, more assured than ever that the river made mad those who worked upon it. As he passed the wool warehouse, a terrible faecal-vegetal reek assailed his nostrils and he was forced to rapidly pull out a handkerchief to cover his nose. He looked around for the origin of the smell and his eyes met those of a very odd little man standing on the opposite side of the street.

The fellow might have been a boy of fifteen from a distance, such were his dimensions, but in fact he must have been twenty-five years old. His face seemed utterly devoid of expression – almost, indeed, as if his features had been painted onto a wooden effigy of a man: two round brown eyes, a spatter of freckles, an unremarkable nose and a mouth-shaped mouth. The dark hair was matted with filth, and it was evidently he who was so noisome. Passers-by exclaimed in disgust as they walked by, allowing him significant space. He returned Mr Newsome's look of disgust without interest or recognition.

The inspector was hurrying to be elsewhere, however, and did not stop to give the encounter further thought.

SEVEN

It might be said that one has not truly experienced London until one has visited the theatre. Admittedly, there is much to be said of a stroll along Oxford-street or a cup of coffee on Fleet-street, but for an authentic view of city life, one attends a theatre such as the Queen's. And on that evening two days after the Waterloo-bridge incident, Wych-street was veritably a-swarm with people flocking to hear Eldritch Batchem speak.

It had been uncharitably noted by some that it was no mere coincidence that a playbill for this show had been found in the pocket of the unfortunate tidewaiter William Barton . . . or at least that Mr Batchem had reported thus. Wags in certain other quarters had joked that the investigator himself had slain the man just to popularize the evening. Such are the comments of cynics, but the fact could not be denied: the thrill of the dead man advertising the fame of his own death's investigator was a story too delicious to resist.

Accordingly, the auditorium was filling rapidly, each part relative to the price of its seat. In the gallery sat London's common men and women: a heaving and raucous mass of unalloyed humanity that exuded a sour reek of bodies, smoke and gin. Some scratched at dirty collars; some feasted on handfuls of meat pie bought especially for the occasion; some peeled off boots to ease their work-worn feet. All chattered and laughed with the crass manner of the streets. Perhaps nine in every ten women were there in a purely 'professional' capacity.

The stalls were perhaps a little more refined. Here, decorum competed with affectation to demonstrate that two shillings more per seat made one a 'theatre-goer' rather than a groundling animated only by vulgar entertainment. Were one to scan the rows in this part of the theatre, one would have noticed among the throng a single Negro face: Benjamin. Beside him was Noah Dyson, and beside *him* was Mr George Williamson (relieved of pickpocket duty tonight on account of attending the show). John Cullen was once again by his mentor's left hand, seemingly gleeful at this, his first visit to a 'real' theatre rather than the sordid penny gaff.

A number of people would have been intrigued to see this peculiar quartet together, and Commissioner Sir Richard Mayne was one of them. Sitting alone in his private box, he had at first believed himself to be mistaken when he saw George Williamson sitting in the distant stalls before him. Using his opera glasses, however, he was able to verify that it was indeed the illustrious detective who had once worked within the ranks of the Detective Force. And there, either side of him, was an ex-constable and a known felon.

Inspector Albert Newsome was yet another who, seeing the Negro face, had noticed the four sitting together and wondered at the import of such a grouping. In his experience, it was a fellowship that promised only inconvenience. Fortunately, none of them seemed to have noticed him sitting a few rows to the rear and to their right.

By now, the theatre was quite filled to capacity and the vast banked horseshoe of seating writhed with figures and murmurs. Smoke drifted thickly through the light of the large gas chandelier hanging from the gaudy gilt ceiling.

'Is that Sir Richard in the box?' said Mr Cullen to his neighbour.

'It is,' replied Mr Williamson. 'And he has seen us.'

'Do not turn, but Inspector Newsome is also sitting three rows behind us to the right,' said Noah. 'I saw him in the lobby as we entered. He pretended to be tying his bootlace.'

'There are many policemen here tonight,' said Mr Williamson. 'Whether to mock or revere Mr Batchem, I could not say.'

'Which do you favour, George?'

'First I will listen to the man – then I will make my judgement.'

'Of course. Tell me – why do you study the gallery so intently, George? Are you expecting to see somebody in particular there?'

'Hmm. It is idle habit – nothing more.' Mr Williamson extracted his watch somewhat irritably. 'Where is Mr Batchem? It is time for the performance to begin . . .'

At that moment, the deep-red curtains on the stage twitched and a thrill went through the audience. A cheer went up from the gallery. The theatre manger emerged from between the folds and made a bow.

'Ladies and gentlemen – welcome! Welcome! Tonight we are privileged indeed to have the pleasure of an audience with a man who has lately captured our interest in the public sphere, in the newspapers, in the annals of crime and—'

'*Get on with it!*' yelled a voice from the gallery, followed by much spirituous mirth.

'I . . . well, without further preamble, I give you Mr Eldritch Batchem: investigator *extraordinaire*!'

Applause of an enthusiastic (if not yet fully convinced) manner went up, and the curtains were drawn back to reveal that same figure glimpsed previously on Waterloo-bridge. He seemed a smaller man on the immensity of the bare stage, dressed in his customary tweed suit and odd russet cap. Indeed, there was a suggestion, almost, of vulnerability about him that hushed the crowd to an improbable silence.

Cowed he may have been, but the way he strolled to centre stage showed little trepidation. There, he stroked his pointed salt-and-pepper beard with a gloved hand, eyes cast downward at the boards, and nodded to himself as if lost in thought. One might have heard the very rustle of his clothing as expectation rose.

('Quite the showman, is he not?' whispered Noah to Mr Williamson.

'Hmm,' replied the latter.)

Finally, Eldritch Batchem looked up, giving the impression that he had stumbled quite by chance upon an audience gathered in his honour. He cast a meaningful look around and smiled, though his eyes were black glass. When he spoke, it was with a calm, clear voice that carried to the furthest recesses of the auditorium.

'Who among you, I wonder, is a murderer?'

A flutter of scandalous pleasure passed through the gallery.

'I say again: who among you is a murderer? No doubt you abhor the thought! No doubt you reject outright the very idea that you – a Christian, a son, a daughter – could be capable of such a soul-staining act. But that would be your mistake! Why? Because we are *all* murderers.'

He paused to let his voice and his challenge dissipate among the multitudinous faces before him. There was doubt in the stalls, cynicism in the boxes and a horripilating desire to disbelieve in the gallery.

'Who is the murderer?' said Eldritch Batchem, pacing head down now in a soliloquizing manner and stroking at his beard. 'Is he (or she) not the one with the wild light of insanity in his eyes? Has he not wet, fleshy lips and dirty hair? Does he not sweat, as we are proverbially led to believe? O, we have all seen the death masks of these killers, and we fancy that we can see their murderous intentions – even in death! – merely in the cast of their features. We see images of men in the newspapers and, because they are called "murderer", we *see* a murderer . . . but I ask you: could not that face just as easily be the face of a poet shaped in plaster for posterity?'

('I regret to admit that he makes a salient point,' whispered Noah.

'Hmm. Let us see how his oration develops,' returned Mr Williamson.)

'There are those who may say the murderer *is* a poet: an artist of the criminal world because he breaks both human law and the divine. I disagree, ladies and gentlemen. I disagree most wholeheartedly. The murderer is a man (or a woman) like any one of us because he is *weak*. Not omnipotent, not super-human, not an aberration of morality. No, he is all *too* human. It is his humanity that makes him murder – not because he is strong, but because he has failed to fully become a civilized man.'

Here, Eldritch Batchem paused again, staring up at the ceiling and caught in the reveries of his address. He might almost have been quite alone upon the stage and seemingly engaged in a dialogue with his own soul. The gallery perceived his immersion and were even more spellbound. Was the man an actor to capture them so? Or did he truly have a deeper knowledge of the murderer's mind? The silence pleaded to be filled with more, and he timed the hiatus precisely before resuming:

'But do not take *my* words as authority, ladies and gentlemen. I am a simple investigator. Consider, rather, some words more fitting to our venue here and let us hear what the Bard has put into the mouths of *his* murderers. Says the first:

> *I am one . . .*
> *So weary with disasters, tugg'd with fortune*
> *That I would set my life on any chance*
> *To mend or be rid on't*

'Says the second:

> *I am one . . .*
> *Whom the vile blows and buffets of the world*
> *Hath so incens'd, that I am reckless what*
> *I do, to spite the world*

'What do we make of this pair of murderers? Our first is a desperate man who cares not for his own life, who is tired and punished by fate. Are there not debtors in our prisons who might speak so? Our second is perhaps more how we perceive the murderer of our city: a crazed and maddened figure who acts with violent impetuosity. Even in this, however, he seeks – like a child – to anger a temperate parent. *These* are your murderers: weak fellows! And are we all not weak on occasion? Do we not all stumble briefly on the path of righteousness?'

A cough punctuated the quiet – a cough from a private box to Eldritch Batchem's left. He looked up and beheld the commissioner of police holding a handkerchief at his mouth.

'Sir Richard Mayne? Is that you, sir? I am honoured.'

A colossal susurration of comment rolled through the audience and three thousand pairs of eyes went to the box, where the red-faced gentleman sat with an expression carved in vermilion granite. Fingers pointed and a ribald laughter tinkled in the gallery.

'Perhaps our august guest in the private box there is privately saying to himself: "That is all very well, Mr Batchem, but those murderers are drawn from the fancy of a great writer rather than from our real city streets." Too true, sir. Too true. So I will proceed to some murderers of recent note as a means of illustration.

'Who does not know the name of Daniel Good: this man who severed the arms and legs of his female victim, disembowelling her and burning the entrails in his fireplace? Three thousand policemen could not find *this* gentleman as he drank at Hampstead or sat in plain view to have his hair cut at a barber's! Perhaps you will say that *he* is the kind of murderer you are thinking of?'

('If Sir Richard becomes any redder, I fear he will suffer apoplexy,' whispered Noah.

Benjamin covered his snorting laugh with a handkerchief.)

'I say "no",' continued Eldritch Batchem. 'Daniel Good was a weak man. His appetite for the female form was uncontrolled. He had spent time in Millbank penitentiary for killing a horse *by tearing out its tongue*, if you please! He was a suspected incendiary and a petty thief whose secret was discovered when he tried to make off with some stolen breeches. Why, the man was an utter failure as a member of our species.

It is said he was also vain, combing his hair from each side to cover his naked pate. Who would fear such a man? A weak and mortal man.'

'What about Greenacre?' came a shout from the gallery.

'Ah yes – James Greenacre. No doubt you shout his name because he was reputed to be a thinking man, an intelligent man . . . and another dismemberer. It was he, of course, who carried his female victim's head in a canvas bag across London – by omnibus, no less! – to dispose of it in Stepney lock. A calculating, inhuman man you might say. On the contrary, he was a fantasist and liar, an atheist who slept in a strait-waistcoat while at Newgate lest he take his own life . . . though, of course, he protested his innocence to the last.

'*These* are your murderers: the weakest, most venal, most hopeless, most selfish and godless of men. Any one of us here could be these men but for the love of a parent, but for the teachings of the Church, but for the paternal hand of the law. The way of weakness leads to death and damnation, but the way of moral strength leads to salvation for all.'

Eldritch Batchem paused, his finger raised as if to punctuate the thought and his glistening eyes focused somewhere among the gilt heavens of the theatre's ceiling. Silence reigned. Then, slowly, he seemed to return from that sublimity to cast a smile across the thousands of faces before him.

'Ladies and gentlemen, this concludes the first part of our evening', he said. 'I thank you for your ears.'

And with this, he bowed deeply, adding a theatrical curlicue of the arm.

The auditorium at first yielded but a patter of applause, as if people had not quite registered the conclusion of the address. Then the gallery stirred itself into action and the patter built into a more thunderous response, fuelled further by no small contribution from the stalls.

'What is your impression?' said Noah over the noise.

'He has said nothing we do not already know,' said Mr Williamson. 'But it pleases the common man to think investigation is an art rather than a science.'

'Is it not both?' said Noah.

'Hmm. I leave the consideration of art to artists. I note that Mr Newsome is not applauding.'

Noah turned in his seat to peer at the sour expression upon the inspector's face. 'Ha! Was he not one of the men working on the Daniel Good case?'

'I believe so. He was never keen to speak of it.'

'Look – the theatre manager has taken to the stage once again,' said Mr Cullen, pointing.

And the manager had indeed ventured onto the boards once again in order to shake Eldritch Batchem's hand. When that gesture was met with blank refusal, however, a laugh went up from the cheaper seats. Red-faced, the manager attempted instead to attain silence so that he could speak.

'Ladies and gentlemen! Ladies and gentlemen, please! After the interval, Mr Batchem will speak further on the life and philosophy of the investigator, and perhaps entertain us with stories of some of his cases. At the present time, though, he has consented to take questions from the audience. Will anybody be the first? Who will offer a question for Mr Batchem?'

The theatre rapidly took on the absolute quietude of the classroom when the master asks for a reader. Feet shuffled. There were a number of coughs. Then came a (no doubt) gin-fuelled query from the gallery:

'Mr Batchem – you says bad things 'bout murderers. Aren't you afeared of being murdred yoursel?'

79

Laughter animated the crowd, but dissipated when it became clear the speaker was quite prepared to answer.

'Sir – murderers often prey on the weak because they are weak themselves,' said Eldritch Batchem. 'Their women, their children, their inferiors. What have I to fear from a man like Greenacre? He has no interest in one such as me.'

'He might kill yer for yer money!' returned the original inquisitor, again provoking mirth.

'Ah – but then we are describing a different category of criminal altogether: not the *classic* murderer of the criminal annals, but a man who can only kill as if by accident! A bully or common thief for whom slaughter is but an occupational hazard.'

'It sounds like you almost revere the murderer, sir.' (This from an earnest gentleman in the stalls.)

'"Revere", you say?' pondered Eldritch Batchem with another barbate stroke. 'Not at all – but I take an interest in the classification and study of these malefactors. It is a fascinating subject, even if the subjects themselves are aberrations of our civilized condition. By knowing the evil of the human heart, one may better fight the criminal.'

A preparatory cough came from that private box to the left of the stage. And a new hush came over the gathered throng.

'Mr Batchem,' said Sir Richard Mayne with a clear, unwavering voice, 'you speak of fighting criminals and of investigation – but what of remuneration? You take considerable monies for your work. Why not work for the Metropolitan Police if eradicating crime is your aim?'

'Do you not also receive a wage for your work, Sir Richard? Do your constables and inspectors not receive a wage? I am no different in that respect.'

'Except that you choose to investigate only robberies, blackmail cases and embarrassing private concerns,' said Sir Richard. 'For all your talk of murderers, you leave those cases to the brave men of the police because there is no money in them for you.'

'I fear you are wrong, sir. Only two days ago, I was called to investigate a very nasty incident on Waterloo-bridge – which I am sure most of our audience has read about.'

A murmur among the three thousand seated there said that yes they had indeed read of it.

'"Suicide" you called it,' said Sir Richard. 'I cannot contradict because I was forbidden access to the facts of the crime. No doubt many of the people here tonight also read of your shameless self promotion in mentioning a playbill for your show found in the dead man's pocket. A highly fortuitous occurrence, would you not say?'

'I certainly would *not* say that, Sir Richard!'

Sensing that the tenor of the dialogue was making the audience restless, the theatre manager stepped forward. 'Thank you, Sir Richard, for your contribution, but perhaps we will let another ask their question . . .'

Sir Richard smouldered and leaned back in his seat with folded arms. Eldritch Batchem appeared to smirk into his beard.

'Who else will speak?' encouraged the theatre manager.

'I. I have a question,' came an assertive voice from the stalls: Inspector Newsome.

'Mr Batchem says that three thousand policemen could not find Daniel Good. But Mr Batchem did not find him either. In fact, Good was found in Tonbridge, Kent, by an ex-constable of Metropolitan V Division who recognized him.'

'Inspector Newsome is it?' said Eldritch Batchem, peering exaggeratedly into the crowd. 'I see you are not wearing your uniform tonight. I congratulate you on your memory, but perhaps you are forgetting more recent events. Were you not the detective in charge of the Lucius Boyle case – that evil murderer and incendiary also known as "Red Jaw"?'

At the name of this particular criminal, a great mutter went up among the audience. Lucius Boyle had been a murderer to make Good and Greenacre look almost angelic.

'As I recall,' continued Eldritch Batchem, 'you chased *that* criminal all over the city and could not catch him even as he committed a murder among a crowd of thousands at Newgate! Nor could you apprehend him as he sailed slowly away in a hot-air balloon. Or was that the fault of Detective Sergeant – rather, *former*-Detective Sergeant – George Williamson? I see he has also attended this evening to learn about the art of investigation.'

Mr Williamson flushed with embarrassment as the massed audience turned to look in his direction, but did not rise to the bait. At his side, Mr Cullen felt a stab of anger at the humiliation and threw out his own question:

'You mock respected detectives, Mr Batchem – men who face danger every day. Perhaps you can tell us, with all your wisdom, what makes a great detective?'

'A fine question from the burly fellow there,' said Eldritch Batchem. 'I will answer such things more fully after the interval, of course, but let me summarize now. A great detective does not guess – he knows. A great detective has intuition and knowledge in equal measure. A great detective understands his fellow man and reads him as one might read a book. And, finally, a great detective has a keen intelligence – keener, in the end, than his quarry the criminal.'

Eldritch Batchem nodded to himself, evidently pleased with the apophthegmatical nature of his answer. Mr Cullen struggled for a *riposte* and could find none.

'Well – that is all we have time for in this first part of the eve—' began the manager. But there was to be one more question . . .

'Wait! I have something to ask.'

The speaker was a gentleman in a private box to the right side of the stage. His voice carried great authority, and his appearance suggested considerable wealth. He did not wait for the manager's permission to continue:

'I have heard much tonight about the nature of crime and criminals, and I believe I have a challenge for some of those present, if detectives they truly are.'

'Let us hear your challenge,' called Sir Richard from the other side of the stage. 'Whatever it is, I am sure the Metropolitan Police's Detective Force is more than adequate to your purposes.'

'Yes, share your question that a *true* investigator might solve it,' added Eldritch Batchem, looking at the boxes either side of him in turn.

The auditorium was once again as silent as a midnight altar.

'Very well,' said the wealthy-looking gentleman. My name is Josiah Timbs. I am a merchant and ship-owner of this city who recently suffered a substantial loss. I know not who is responsible, or any of the circumstances, but here, tonight, I offer the sum of one thousand pounds to him who will solve this crime and return my property to me.'

'*I* will do it!' shouted the drunken man who had asked the first question that evening. Laughter briefly filled the place.

'That is a generous sum, Mr Timbs,' said Eldritch

Batchem, once more stroking his beard. 'What manner of a loss would account for a reward so significant?'

'Mr Batchem, Sir Richard . . . you other investigators present . . .' began the ship-owner, 'I hardly know how to say it, so incredible is it to me that this crime has occurred in the modern city of London. Gentlemen – my ship, the brigantine *Aurora*, has been stolen.'

A hubbub immediately animated the crowd and the theatre manager did his best to restore calm.

'Excuse me, Mr Timbs,' said Eldritch Batchem, when he could make himself heard. 'Did you say your *ship*? An entire vessel?'

'Quite so. The *Aurora* is my four-masted brig. It has vanished utterly from the Port of London with half of its seamen aboard and with a full cargo. It might not be a murder, but it is certainly an outrage. What do you make of *that*, you detectives? What will you do about *that*?'

A pandemonium of speculation and wonder now quite seized the audience. Eldritch Batchem looked up to see Sir Richard staring glacially down at him and the former seemed to smile with those dark glass eyes.

EIGHT

If Eldritch Batchem had been a minor public figure before that performance, he was a greater one thereafter – not least because a number of newspapermen had been in the audience to hear his comments about the Metropolitan Police and the challenge from Mr Josiah Timbs. The following day's papers seemed to mention little else.

A recurrent theme in all of them was the provenance of the strange investigator himself, who, barely six months previously, might never have existed. The first recorded instance of his investigative work, of course, had been that scandalous case of the infant cut in pieces and left in a package on Blackfriars-bridge. Then there had been the lesser-known case of the banker's clerk who absconded with cash left in his care. It had been around that time that people started to speak his name more widely.

It need hardly be said that any mystery about his identity vanished when he was said to have investigated that notorious case of theft from the Green Drawing Room (anteroom to the very throne room itself) at Buckingham Palace. Whether it was the Queen herself who requested his involvement, or whether he was engaged by an attendant to Her Majesty remains somewhat ambiguous, but the man had ostentatiously used his 'By Royal Appointment' appellation since that occasion.

One thing was certain: the Green Drawing Room case made the title of 'detective' suddenly fashionable in London. For the first time, one began to see examples in the personal advertisements of *the Times* for investigators with 'Private Enquiry Addresses' who would, for a fee, trace one's missing jewellery, recover one's absconded husband, or observe one's wife unbeknown to her. Nothing, it seemed, was quite as exciting as the life of the detective. Indeed, for a month or so, one might have seen a notice on the first page of *the Times* for:

MR DENT'S ADVANCED
COLLEGE OF DETECTION

Those gentlemen wishing to learn the science of investigation may attend this course, designed and ratified by erstwhile genuine detectives of the Bow Street Magistrates Court. For instruction in the finer points of clue-finding, reading the criminal face, 'Swell Mob' cant and deductive philosophy, apply to Mr Aloysius Dent, 14 Oxenden-street. Gratis map of 'Murderous London' with lesson one, and a 'Certificate of Detection' on completion.

Yet the man who seemed to have stirred the interest remained an enigma. Nobody knew him. Nobody could remember hearing the name previously. He attended no club and had been to university with not a single person who could recall him. It was rumoured that he lived not in a house or apartment, but alone at Mivart's Hotel. In fact, had he not spoken English with such unaccented fluency, one might have suspected him of being a foreigner.

At least, this was the common interpretation of events. There is, in truth, always someone who knows the bigger story – always one man who is able to burrow beneath popular perception and the obfuscations of rumour to strike at the facts with unerring accuracy. And, inevitably, there was one who knew.

It was I.

To some, I am a penny-a-liner: a self-supporting newspaperman who measures the size of his next meal in column inches. To others – notably those old men of Paternoster-row and Haymarket – I am an occasional producer of popular broadsheets, arcane encyclopaedia entries, sundry poetry (or, rather, doggerel) for all occasions, and dramas that play too often to an unappreciative audience of one. Speaking for myself, I am a novelist well accustomed to the rigour of the nib, the ceaseless scraping upon paper and the oil-lamp blindness of extended lucubration.

Perhaps the reader has read a copy of my book on an earlier illustrious case of George Williamson (the copyright of which I was obliged to sign away to avoid another penal spell). Or perchance my more recent volume on another case of that investigator has found favour . . . before the copyright of that one also was taken from me on account of my non-payment of printing fees. Alas, I had been somewhat less prolific following those works on account of my being imprisoned at Horsemonger-street gaol in Lambeth.

It was not, as some malicious wags may have implied, for plagiarism that I found myself incarcerated thus. Nor was it for the penning of false begging letters, fraudulent inquest reports or defamatory satire – some of which accusations might have been previously levelled at me. No – I was resident in the debtors' wing of that gaol thanks largely to the personal impoverishment occasioned by my latter *opus* and the incomplete repayment of printing costs thereof. Such are the results of publishing at one's own risk.

So it was that, while another great case had begun to play out on the streets of the city, I was confined between dusk and seven each morning to a room with four iron bedsteads (alas, no pillows or sheets), a cruelly chilling stone-flagged floor, a reeking privy emptied but once a day, and three other dolorous gentlemen similarly abused by Fortune.

Nevertheless, one should not think that I was isolated from events. As befits a fellow of infinite resource, I had rather set about establishing that mildewed cell as the centre of a web to trap every fruit fly of gossip, every moth of rumour and every fat buzzer of news floating above those London streets. Each newspaper left behind by a visiter was a *reservoir* of information for me to absorb. And, of course, I was not idle in my writing, producing regular scandal sheets for the presses that I might better peck away at my debt (like a sparrow at the dome of St Paul's).

In short, even in my confinement, I scented the story and used the flavour of it to build a feast in my mind to sustain me where the oatmeal gruel and pulpy vegetable stews of Horsemonger-lane could not. It was also within those imprisoning walls that I happened to learn more of Mr Eldritch Batchem . . . or at least of a possible previous incarnation.

On the day after that notable theatrical address, I was reading *the Times* for possible further news of the Waterloo-bridge case or of the body dragged recently from the river. Unaccustomed as I was to receiving visiters of my own, I instead used the broad pages of that esteemed organ to hide myself as I eavesdropped on the conversations of those who came daily to see my cell-fellows.

Burley was one such inmate: a tailor by trade, but a failure by inclination, he was a faded and worn wisp of a man who had spent much of the previous decade in one or other of the city's debtors' gaols. Grey of skin, hair and suit, he did some occasional stitching work during the days with the futile aim of mitigating his debt – but his chief value to me was in his brother-in-law Charles: a loquacious sort who would visit each day but Sunday to tattle and chatter like a maid of all work.

'I declare, I had a capital evening yesterday,' twittered this Charles the day after that eventful show.

'O yes?' said Burley, with gibbet enthusiasm for another tale of unknowable pleasure.

'Yes indeed! I went to the Queen's Theatre to hear that fellow Eldritch Batchem – you know: the investigator chap.'

'O yes?'

'He spoke about murderers: Greenacre, Good, Lucius Boyle . . . all the best ones. And there was a terrific episode before the interval when some merchant chappy said his brig had been stolen entire. And Sir Richard Mayne – the police commissioner himself – was there in a box, and he said he would investigate, and—'

'O yes?'

'. . . and, well, I had the strangest impression I had seen this Batchem before.'

(At this point, I fear there was a crepitant convulsion of my newspaper as I reached for a pencil to scribble details over the police notices.)

'O yes?'

'Indeed. He has a strange sort of pointed beard, this Batchem. That, combined with a rather peculiar russet cap he wears, does rather tend to hide his face but for the eyes.

However, it was something in the cast of his eyes, combined perhaps with the inflection of his voice, that struck me.'

'O yes?'

'Do you remember when you were in Whitecross-street gaol, just after you lost your premises?'

'O. Yes.' Burley now rather had the look of the medieval martyr hewn in lichened limestone.

'Well, I would swear before any judge that this Batchem was at Whitecross-street at the same time you were. He was not called by the same name then. Nor did he have a beard or wear a red cap. No – he was called something quite different: "Crawford" or "Cowley" or "Crowell" or some such. But he did seem to wear leather gloves, as I recall. But I tell you: the voice and the eyes were highly suggestive.'

'O yes?'

'Indeed. The voice . . . you know? It seems rather odd, does it not, that two years past, he seems to be a debtor with a different name and now he is an illustrious investigator addressing thousands at the theatre? Somebody should investigate *that*, don't you think?'

'I suppose so, Charles. In truth, I cannot recall the man you refer to.' (A rare conversational gambit from the threadbare tailor.)

'What? Well, I have a distinct recollection of him. Most curious. Ah, did I also tell you about the young lady I have been calling upon?'

'O yes?'

By this point, however, my keen journalistic mind was working phrenziedly at the potential story I had just overheard. Were there even a shred of truth in it, it was the sort of thing that might earn me a juicy commission to cover my debts and free me from that place.

Accordingly, I left old Burley to the garrulous tortures of his brother and walked out towards the yard, cogitating upon how I might extend my reach beyond the walls to learn more. Then I remembered with a flash of excitement: had not a turnkey of my acquaintance at Horsemonger-lane previously held a position at Whitecross-street? I immediately sought him out.

As usual, he could be found in the warder's lodge with a mug of tea and a newspaper. He was an affable sort, and what I learned from him, though exiguous enough, was intriguing. There had indeed been a 'Crawford' or 'Cowley' or 'Crowell' at Whitecross-street, and my turnkey recalled the fellow in question with some clarity on account of his being allowed the rare privilege of a private room. The debtor's stay there had been brief, but what had struck the warder more than anything was the general eccentricity of the gentleman combined with a mania for privacy.

So fastidious was he (said the turnkey) that his every limited possession was stored with almost geometric precision: his razor and other bathroom articles laid out perpendicularly parallel to the eighth of an inch; his clothing brushed and folded with the greatest care; his few books kept always in strict alphabetical order (by author), and his newspapers catalogued by date. And, while many freshly incarcerated insolvents will initially spurn the company of other debtors through humiliation or low spirits, this fellow never settled into his ward.

There was one more thing that marked the fellow out. Though private in nature and not in the least troublesome for most of the time, he had been known to fly into most terrible rages. On one such occasion, it had been something so trivial as a warder knocking over a pile of sorted newspapers – an act that moved 'Crawford' or 'Cowley' to such a fury that he had to have his hands prised from the throat of the poor turnkey.

Could this unusual man have been the same who called himself Eldritch Batchem? There was no beard, no russet cap, no apparent aspirations to lauded investigation. Certainly, I was in no position to judge further . . . at least not as long as I remained unable to resolve my debts. That time would come soon enough, and I would return gloriously to the cab stands, public houses and itinerant street lads who are the true authorities on the city's happenings.

In the meantime, and as I garnered more shreds of information from other sources, Eldritch Batchem himself had spent little time luxuriating in the triumph of his evening at the Queen's. Assuredly, he stepped with perhaps a little more pomp than heretofore, and stroked his beard with a more practised air, but he had seen his chance to eclipse the Metropolitan Police and there was no time to be lost while the Detective Force gathered its wits.

Thus, on the very afternoon I was quizzing the turnkey at Horsemonger-lane, our be-capped investigator had taken the first logical step in chasing the vanished brig *Aurora* and was down among the carpenters, canvas cutters, rope weavers, biscuit-bakers, blacksmiths and instrument-makers of deepest Wapping. He was looking for crimps.

As any sailor (or river-district constable) knows, there are generally three kinds of people awaiting a ship as it finally tosses its ropes ashore: the multifarious shore-side workers, the ruddy-cheeked whore, and the crimp. It is the latter, of course, who offers most. The finest beds, the cheapest beer, the most wholesome nutriments, and the most convenient lodgings for rapid shipping – all such lies roll off his tongue like poetry. Never mind paying now, he says to the tars rolling down the gangs onto solid land – they can pay him in full after they have collected their payment from the shipping office. They can pay him in full after he has kept them drunk for three weeks, inflated their bill, paid their women and gone quite through their wages before they even receive them, heading back out to the horizon with a throbbing head and no recollection of land.

Accordingly, Eldritch Batchem was working his way along the dozens of taverns on Wapping-street asking if any of these crimps had welcomed the crew of a ship called the *Aurora* recently, and whether any of them might be resident. He had already visited the Ship and Pilot, the Golden Anchor, the Ship and Whale, and the Marline Spike before meeting any fortune.

The obstreperous sot who owned the Marline Spike had offered the investigator little but invective, yet there happened to be two sailors on the cobbles outside who had heard the exchange.

'Ho, sir! You there wi' the child's red cap on,' hailed the taller one of the pair, evidently a number of days into his prodigious intake of liquor.

'Are you referring to me, sir?' said Batchem, turning.

'Aye, mate. Was yer 'quiring 'bout th' *Aurora*? The brig out o' Calais?'

'Indeed. Do you know of it?'

'Know o' it? I was a —— seaman on it two . . . three . . . some days hence!'

'Is that so? You may be of considerable importance to an investigation I am conducting.' The investigator took out his notebook and pencil. 'I had heard that half the hands were lost with the vessel.'

'Well . . . my 'ands is both accounted for. Are yer wi' the newspapers?'

'I am an investigator. Tell me, sailor – where did the *Aurora* dock? She did not land where expected?'

'Aye, that's right enough. Should o' roped up at St Kath's, but the tidewaiter said there were no place and we 'ad to wait. After a bit, first mate said we could go ashore by lighter on account o' our thirst for beer and whores!'

'I see. Do you recall the name or the appearance of the tidewaiter who came on board? This is really rather important.'

'Youngish chap I s'pose . . . I didn't pay him much 'eed. He spoke to the first mate, not to me.'

'Did the mates accompany you on the lighter?'

'The mates stay aboard for offloading, don't they?'

'Of course. How many of you eventually came ashore by lighter?'

'O, seven or so. And the master. I don't recall p'cisely.' The sailor turned to his fellow, who was leaning against the wall of the public house with heavy limbs and an expression of spiritous idiocy. 'How many o' us came ashore on the lighter, Pikey?'

He addressed as Pikey moved his eyes towards the origin of the question and merely gaped in wonder at the function of speech.

'Well, it was 'bout seven,' said the taller sailor. 'And the master.'

'What of the ship herself? What happened to her thereafter? Have you met any of your fellows hereabouts who stayed aboard?'

'I 'ave no idea, mate. And I 'ave no care. Never saw the ship again after I came ashore. I got money to drink! What is all o' this 'bout?'

'It is an investigation I am conducting. You may have heard of me – my name is Eld—'

'An 'vestigation? You police, then? If I'd known you were police I wouldn't of spoke to yer!'

'I am not a policeman. I am something quite different. My name is Eldri—'

'——— copper! I don't talk to no coppers!'

Eldritch Batchem recognized that the interview was at an end. He made his little bow and continued on his way along the high street in search of any more sailors from that unfortunate vessel.

And as he strolled, his nose was assailed by a quite hideous stench of effluent that caused him to resort to use of his handkerchief. He looked about the street, perhaps expecting to see an open sewer, but there was no evidence to be seen. At the same time, as he hastened his step to escape the stench, he had the curious notion – that queer tickling at the base of the neck – that he was being watched.

Others in the thoroughfare seemed to show no particular sign of interest in him, so he glanced at the upper-storey windows, at shadowy doorways and at a passing omnibus for signs of his observer. But no curtains twitched, no figures lurked and no sign of *surveillance* presented itself. He hurried on.

NINE

'Inspector Newsome – you are no longer under my direct command. Did I not make it absolutely clear? Furthermore, you are neglecting your duty on the river by being here.'

Sir Richard Mayne occupied his customary position behind the oak desk at Scotland Yard. Standing before him, Mr Newsome was dressed in the uniform of the Thames Police and was indeed absent from his official duties. His constables waited impatiently for him in the galley at Whitehall-stairs.

'Sir – if I may speak frankly . . .'

'You generally do, Inspector. That is a significant proportion of your failing as a senior officer.'

'Eldritch Batchem, sir – he cannot be permitted to escape his recent slurs upon the name of the Detective Force—'

'And he will not be permitted to do so. The case will be solved and we will prove conclusively that justice is best served by an official body.'

'Sir – if I were to be reinstated in the Detec—'

'No. I already have Inspector Watson of the Detective Force working on this case. Any assistance *you* can offer will be through your duties on the river . . . wait, do not attempt to interrupt me! Your duty with the Thames Police allows you access to the wharfs and docks and warehouses of the entire Port of London. If the *Aurora* is to be found, she is likely to be found there.'

'So I am to remain in uniform . . .'

'That was our agreement: until you prove yourself. Now – since you are here, perhaps you can tell me something about the body you apparently pulled out of the river four days past.'

'It was nothing. Just another suicide washed up by the colliers. We have no identity as yet.'

'Really? I heard that there was a length of chain about the legs. An odd sort of suicide, was it not?'

'One might think so if one had not worked on the river, sir. It seems they shoot themselves, poison themselves or weight themselves and *then* leap into the waters. I surmise that they want to be absolutely sure of reaching oblivion.'

'And what of the hurried *post mortem* you allegedly arranged at Wapping station? That was not standard procedure.'

'I am thorough in my work, sir . . . but, may I ask how you came to hear of the examination? I rather feel I am being spied upon.'

'Not at all. The superintendent at Wapping merely mentioned it to me and questioned whether you understood that you are no longer a detective. Do you?'

'I wanted to be sure that it was indeed a suicide. As you say, the chains were suspicious. But the surgeon's report was quite conclusive: drowning with some injuries sustained after death.'

'I see. That is what I assumed, but perhaps in future you could spend more time on the water with your constables . . .'

'Yes, sir . . .'

'Is there something else you would like to tell me, Inspector?'

'Sir Richard – I am confused. You clearly had no intention of entertaining my request to work on the *Aurora* case, and yet you agreed to receive me this morning. Was it to ask me about the suicide? I feel there is something more afoot.'

Another man might have smiled, but the police commissioner was content to nod an acknowledgement of his interlocutor's perceptiveness.

'Good. That is the Inspector Newsome I know. I will explain further in just a moment, but I am just waiting . . .'

Sir Richard took out his pocket watch and flicked open the case. There was a knock at the door and the clerk appeared. 'The gentleman for whom you are waiting has arrived, Commissioner.'

'Very good. Show him in.'

The figure of George Williamson entered the room carrying his hat in both hands before him and looking ill at ease. Sir Richard stood to receive him.

'What is this!' erupted Mr Newsome.

'Silence, Inspector,' said Sir Richard. '*You* have been given admittance despite my better judgement – might not we extend that invitation further?'

'This man is no longer a member of the police, Sir Richard. I must protest in the strongest terms.'

'I asked for your silence, Inspector. Mr Williamson is my guest in a purely informal capacity.'

Sir Richard came out from behind his desk to shake Mr Williamson's hand.

'George – I thank you for responding to my letter. It has

been a long time and I have been remiss in passing on my regards since you left the Force.'

'Hmm. I imagine Mr Newsome here has been informing you of my activities over the last year or so,' said Mr Williamson.

'What is that supposed to mean?' said Mr Newsome.

'Gentlemen!' Sir Richard held up placatory hands. 'This animosity between you is something I neither understand nor condone. Collaboration is the more effective strategy.'

'The man collaborates with criminals,' said Mr Newsome.

'And I see that *you* are back in uniform,' offered Mr Williamson.

'That is enough,' said Sir Richard with finality. 'Let us go and sit by the fire. I have something to share with both of you.'

The three moved to the leather wing-back chairs by the hearth. Sir Richard stoked the coals as the two ex-detectives took opposing seats: one scowling, the other still looking highly dubious about the whole affair. Neither seemed to notice the neat pile of papers or the pen and ink-stand on the fireside table between them.

'George – I understand that you recently discovered the truth about your wife's death,' said Sir Richard, taking his seat. 'I am happy that you were finally able to solve that most private of crimes.'

'Hmm,' said Mr Williamson.

'Do not question him too closely on how he went about his investigation,' said Mr Newsome.

Sir Richard fixed him with a gimlet eye: 'Inspector – your current uniformed attire should be proof enough that your investigative methods are not beyond reproach, so let us dispense with such accusations. It is actually rather fortuitous for me to have the two of you in one room today. You are both fine, but flawed, detectives – by temperament if not by employment – and I believe that justice is in earnest need of your like.'

'Hmm. I have found justice to be a strange mistress,' said Mr Williamson. 'Things are done in her name that would shame some criminals.'

'You are quite correct, George,' said Sir Richard, 'and that is why the investigation of this case must be an exemplar of righteous, honourable detective work: an investigation that will stand the scrutiny of any judge, whether legal or moral.'

'Forgive me for saying so, sir,' said Mr Newsome, 'but you speak as if the three of us had already made a covenant over this *Aurora* case.'

'You are eager, as always, to reach the conclusion, Inspector. Well, let me reveal my thoughts. You gentlemen have solved some of the greatest mysteries to face the Metropolitan Police, whether working together or at odds with each other. And yet you have both demonstrated qualities unbecoming of a detective. I will not dwell on these – rather I will say that the Detective Force is a better body with such as you within it.'

'But you have told me—' began Mr Newsome.

'I have told you that you are to remain with the Thames Police, and that is the fact. What I have perhaps not made clear is that my offer also extends to Mr Williamson.'

'What!' ejaculated Mr Newsome.

'I know of no such offer,' said Mr Williamson.

'The offer is this, gentlemen.' And Sir Richard extracted two sheets from the bottom of the pile of papers on the table that stood between them. He handed one sheet to each man.

Contract of Compliance

I, ..., accept the challenge of
Metropolitan Police Commissioner Sir Richard Mayne
to pursue the whereabouts of the missing brig *Aurora*
and all circumstances relating to her disappearance
(including any touching upon Customs and Excise
regulations). I also accept and understand that the first
to solve this mystery (to the complete satisfaction
of the Police Commissioner) will be reinstated at their
former rank within the Detective Force and begin duty
once again with a clean record.

This contract is applicable only on the conditions
that the above signatory agrees to, and abides by, the
promises to:

- Break no law, whether knowingly or unknowingly, in
  pursuit of the case.
- Fraternize, associate or otherwise collude with no
  known or suspected criminals in pursuit of the case
  (other than questioning them where strictly
  necessary).
- Behave at all times in a manner that brings honour
  and respect to the name of a police detective.
- Cease from any unfair or underhand practices aimed
  at inconveniencing or otherwise disrupting the efforts
  of his competitor in this challenge.
- Do nothing that will physically harm or defame
  Mr Eldritch Batchem as he pursues the same case
  (though he might not offer the same courtesy).

Signed:.............................
Witnessed:.............................(Sir Richard Mayne)

Mr Newsome was first to finish reading, having frowned with particular consternation over the itemized points. Nevertheless, he did not hesitate in reaching for the pen on the table and signing his name to the contract.

Mr Williamson took longer over his read. Finally, he addressed Sir Richard:

'I believe this contract makes a number of assumptions about my previous behaviour.'

'George – you are fundamentally a good man and an honest man. I make no reference to things I may have heard previously, but I saw you at the Queen's Theatre two nights ago in the company of a man who has been in gaol and who, but for events I would rather not dwell upon, should have been transported. This contract is to prevent that kind of taint from attaching itself to the police. Are you prepared to sign it?'

'I am no longer a policeman.'

'You are right, George,' said Mr Newsome. 'You are not a policeman. Why not enjoy your other work in peace, without the threat of daily danger.'

'The choice is yours,' said Sir Richard to Mr Williamson. 'Though I cannot comprehend how a man of your talents could be content toiling in an office of the Mendicity Society in pursuit of mere begging-letter writers, or standing on theatre steps looking out for common thieves. Yours is an ability to be tested against greater crimes, and with the entire apparatus of the Metropolitan Police supporting your efforts.'

'Hmm. I am content enough in my way.'

'Might you not consider this a sport then?' offered Sir Richard. 'A test of your wits against those of that buffoon Eldritch Batchem? I can promise you no wage – you would investigate entirely in your own capacity and with your own resources, whereas Inspector Newsome here has the uniform of the Thames Police to aid him. The odds are not in your favour, and it is likely the Detective Force will solve the crime before you or the inspector can. If you wish, sign the contract and then throw the job back in my face when you are the triumphant challenger. '

'He will not win!' scoffed Mr Newsome, almost to himself.

'One thing further, George,' said Sir Richard. 'If you will not sign, I cannot reveal any further particulars about this case, which the merchant Timbs has since relayed to me. You will go on your way with my blessing and I will communicate the details to Inspector Newsome alone, who will have less competition in his quest.'

Mr Williamson looked at the inspector, who was grinning malevolently in response. Here was a gentleman who, just a few months before, had left a man to die so he could instead pursue his own glory. Here was a man for whom treachery was a tool of 'justice' and ambition. Here, more to the point, was a man who had engineered Mr Williamson's expulsion from the Detective Force on the spurious grounds of his being injured and unfit for duty.

He signed.

Mr Newsome scowled.

'Very well,' said Sir Richard. 'Let us begin.' He reached for the pile of paper on the table. 'As I say, I spoke at length with Mr Timbs this morning and learned all I could from him about the circumstances of his missing ship, a four-masted brig out of Calais. Unfortunately, he told me that he has already given precisely the same information to Eldritch Batchem. Perhaps it would be most expeditious at the outset if you both simply asked me questions to discern what you need to know. Who will begin?'

'Do we know exactly when the vessel vanished and from where?' said Mr Williamson, taking out his notebook.

'We know from Custom House records that the ship arrived at Gravesend six days ago,' said Sir Richard. 'Mr Timbs, however, did not go to St Katharine Dock to view his cargo until the morning of Eldritch Batchem's performance. It was then that he discovered no sign of it, or of the *Aurora* herself.'

'What was the cargo?' said Mr Newsome.

'Almost entirely French silk: shawls, handkerchiefs, gloves and a large number of bolts in different colours. I have the exact quantities and colours if you need them. Also, there were some few packages containing scammony, *radix rhataniae* and quassia – sundry ingredients of the apothecary, I understand.'

'Hmm. They are all products with an exceptionally high duty,' said Mr Williamson. 'Smuggling is the obvious motive, although it would be exceptionally bold to take an entire cargo. But one thing above all confuses me: the ship sailed from France with silk of that country, yet I believe those other items originate in the Orient.'

'You are correct, George,' said Sir Richard. 'Although the ship had sailed from France, it had first been in the Orient. It seems to have been one of those vessels that collects and delivers its cargo according to whichever ports are on its route: cedar wood here, tortoiseshell there *et cetera*. This was the final leg of the voyage.'

'Have any crewmen come ashore?' said Mr Newsome.

'The master of the ship came ashore with some seven sailors aboard a lighter, owing to the designated landing place being temporarily unavailable. This master, who lives near the docks, has been thoroughly questioned and his answers are gathered here. I am afraid he has nothing useful to report – the ship lay at anchor in plain sight before St Katharine Dock when he left it. He cannot recall a single suspicious circumstance. Oddly, none of the seven sailors has yet applied to the shipping office to collect his money from the voyage. My constables are seeking them as we speak.'

'They will be utterly intoxicated by now,' said Mr Newsome. 'In a few days, they will go to the office accompanied by their crimps and hand over all of their earnings.'

'I am assuming the vessel was legitimately registered,' said Mr Williamson.

Sir Richard consulted his papers once more. 'Indeed. A landing-waiter logged the ship's correct name and cargo manifest, both of which were later recorded in the Long Room at the Custom House. A notice also appeared in *the Times* the following day to that effect. A tidewaiter was then put on board to oversee the cargo until a berth could be secured at St Katharine's. However, when an unloading warrant was eventually supplied by the Custom House, the ship, its crew and its cargo had vanished.'

'And the tidewaiter? Did he also vanish?' said Mr Williamson.

'He, too.'

'There must be a record of his name,' said Mr Newsome.

'I have it here,' said Sir Richard. 'His details appeared on the docket supplied by the landing-waiter to the Custom House. His name was William Barton.'

'Wait . . .' Mr Williamson felt a tremor of recognition. 'Was Barton not the man who committed suicide on Waterloo-bridge four mornings ago?'

'The very same. Perhaps you see now, gentlemen, why I give so much attention to this case. The gauntlets thrown down by Eldritch Batchem or Josiah Timbs are the least of it.

How does a tidewaiter from a stolen ship find himself dead upon an empty bridge?'

'What do we know of this Barton?' said Mr Newsome.

'The man was quite a recent employee and was not well known to other tidewaiters. He was also under investigation for sundry irregularities. Clearly, we must all question the unofficial verdict of suicide in the light of what we now know. As for that particular avenue of investigation, I fear it has gone cold. The body has been buried and the bridge itself has since had many thousands of feet over it. We have Eldritch Batchem and the Bridge Company to thank for that travesty of justice.'

'I do not wish to ask a foolish question,' said Mr Williamson, 'but may we understand that the *Aurora* has not docked anywhere at all?'

'*Officially* – at least, under that name – she has not. It is the paradox of the river that at any moment there are scores of vessels loading and unloading in plain sight. Each one should be under the control of a Customs man, but does anybody ask if the papers are in order? It is likely that the cargo was unloaded somewhere before the very eyes of those paid to prevent such depredation.'

'Did I not read that this suicide Barton was found with numerous blank unloading warrants?' said Mr Newsome. 'If he had them with him while aboard the *Aurora*, he might have signed the name of any ship and any wharf to them and offloaded anywhere he liked.'

'That is precisely right,' said Sir Richard with a tight jaw. 'A ship is in that sense like a man: change his name, change his clothes, change his customary place and he becomes invisible though he stands beside you in the crowd. I rather suspect that the *Aurora* sits somewhere on the river as we speak.'

'I may be wrong, but I believe a *four*-masted brig is a relative oddity,' said Mr Newsome, surprising even himself with the knowledge. 'They are built for speed and to carry a smaller crew. There cannot be too many of them in port.'

'I will bow to your greater experience on that matter,' said Sir Richard. 'I hope you are correct. So, gentlemen – what can we surmise from the facts as they stand?'

The two detectives appraised each other, evidently unwilling to be the first to speak.

'O, come now,' said Sir Richard. 'I am certain that two men of your ability have already reached the same conclusions. Let me hear your thoughts, if only to clarify them in my own mind. Mr Williamson, I am certain you have observations on the matter . . .'

'Hmm. My first is that unloading a brig is likely to take approximately eight or ten hours and to involve a good number of lumpers. Were it not for the fact that there must be ten thousand such men at work in the Port of London, questioning might have begun with them. Even then, it would be a huge task for the police.'

'Quite so. Although, as the inspector has said, a four-masted brig is perhaps more memorable than other ships of that size. It may be remembered.'

'The receivers around the river may know something,' said Mr Newsome. 'The huge amount of silk must find its way into the nefarious marketplace one way or another.'

'I think not,' said Mr Williamson. 'Most of those fellows deal in smaller quantities. Unless that cargo is broken up and distributed piecemeal, I suspect we are largely unaware of those who form the superior category of receiver – they who handle such high-risk consignments. Perhaps the silk merchants themselves may be approached . . .'

'And give up the source of their illicit, duty-free sources?' scoffed Mr Newsome. 'Unlikely.'

'Hmm. I rather suspect this is not the first occasion such a notable theft has occurred,' said Mr Williamson. 'The majority of large-scale depredations are likely settled between the merchants and insurers. Sir Richard – may I assume you are already working with the Custom House on this question?'

'You are correct, George,' said Sir Richard. 'I have men in the Custom House as we speak searching the records for ir-regularities. Moreover, there is one further piece of evidence that I have so far withheld from you. Mr Timbs gave it to me during our interview.'

Sir Richard took a piece of folded paper from his sheaf and unfolded it to reveal a small handwritten note, which he held up by the corner so the two other gentlemen could examine it. As he turned it, they saw that the text in fact appeared on the back of one of the ubiquitous playbills for Eldritch Batchem's recent show.

'Mr Timbs received this note on the same day he dis-covered that his ship had been stolen. It was delivered to his home address – no doubt to demonstrate that the writer knew where he lived. It is, as you see, handwritten, but the hand is not especially distinctive.'

He laid it on the table for Mr Williamson and Mr Newsome to read.

Timbs

*We have your brig Aurora. Do not look for it. Do not
go to the police. Take your insurance and be content.
If you do not heed this warning, you will be sorry.*

Mr Williamson picked up the playbill and sniffed. He examined the folds. 'It smells of the river: mud and sewage. The folds are grubby, suggesting a writer or deliverer with dirty hands. Was there an envelope?'

'No. It arrived just as it is, folded with the theatrical information outwards and then stuck between door and jamb. Mr Timbs heard a knock at the door, answered it, and assumed it to be a piece of advertising.'

'Has Eldritch Batchem seen it?' said Mr Newsome.

'Indeed he has, though we do not know his thoughts on the matter. Mr Timbs shared it with him on the night of the performance. What do you make of it, George? You have some experience with letters.'

'As you say, the hand is indicative of nothing but an education. It does not even offer the courtesy of a "Mr", but uses only the surname. It is a warning plain and simple. I would say that the "we" is significant – a group rather than an individual. It might be an idle choice of word, but, of course, no mere individual could be behind a crime of this size.'

'Do you not wonder that the writer has thought to specify the name and type of the vessel?' said Mr Newsome. 'Only one is missing; surely no more detail is necessary?'

'Not at all,' said Mr Williamson. 'The merchant likely has more than one ship. Naming it reinforces that the note is authentic . . . and a seafaring man likes to differentiate his vessels, hence the "brig". Let us remember that there is such a thing as *over*-examining one's evidence, Inspector.'

Mr Newsome coloured. 'In that case, *ex-Sergeant* Williamson, perhaps you might tell us why the note appears on a theatrical flyer for Eldritch Batchem. Surely *that* is highly suggestive, especially when we recall that the suicide William Barton had such a paper in his pocket also.'

'Suggestive, yes – but conclusive of nothing. A coincidence is often just a coincidence. There are hundreds of the flyers about the streets at the moment. It would be a matter of the greatest ease for our letter writer to take one from a hawker or simply pick one up on an omnibus.'

'I take a different view of coincidence, myself.'

'So what would you have us believe, Inspector?' said Mr Williamson. 'That somebody is attempting to implicate Eldritch Batchem in these crimes? It is rather an obvious attempt if so, and rendered futile by the evident pleasure that the man himself seems to have taken from mentioning the flyer found in William Barton's pocket. That in itself seems entirely dubious. I gather nobody else examined the body of Barton but Mr Batchem, who evidently saw the opportunity for some self-promotion.'

'Very good, gentlemen! Very good,' said Sir Richard. 'I am heartened to see two minds such as yours wrestling with the evidence, even if you are at odds. I feel sure that this is a case we can solve before Eldritch Batchem does.'

'Sir – may I enquire: what, if anything, the Metropolitan Police knows of Eldritch Batchem?' said Mr Williamson. 'I have read about him in the newspapers, of course, but there must be more information.'

'The man is a nonentity!' said Mr Newsome. 'He is a buffoon in a ridiculous hat, albeit with a degree of wit that appeals to the common man. He is a showman – not a detective.'

'I admit that I have very little to offer you,' said Sir Richard. 'My first thought was that he was one of the old Runners. You know that many of them have continued to work privately since they were subsumed by the Metropolitan Police. However, I am assured by my contacts that

Eldritch Batchem is unknown to them. In truth, the man seems to have appeared from nowhere. His methods are oblique and his clients, understandably, do not speak. It is possible, indeed, that we will learn more merely by investigating this case alongside him.'

'Hmm,' said Mr Williamson, closing his notebook and putting it away in his waistcoat pocket.

'I wish you both good luck in your respective endeavours,' said Sir Richard, now standing. 'There is much to be gained, and much to lose. Investigate according to the terms of the document you have signed and we may soon be together once more. Until then, I have no plans to meet again until the case is solved.'

And so the two gentlemen went out into the streets with little more than a wordless glance as their leave-taking. For all their pliant discussion at Sir Richard's behest, we might be certain that each had withheld more than he had said. Now the *real* investigations would begin.

TEN

Inspector Newsome made his way hastily back to the galley waiting for him at Whitehall-stairs. A light rain had begun to fall during his audience with Sir Richard and the drops were stippling the brown surface of the river. So intent was he in his thoughts, however, that he did not pause to curse the water beading upon his hat and coat, carrying with it the smuts of numberless chimneys and the oily scent of the gasworks.

The fact was that he knew something greatly to his advantage in the *Aurora* case. Unknown to Eldritch Batchem, to the police commissioner and to Josiah Timbs, the inspector had spent the earlier part of that morning seeking out the master of the missing vessel. It had been a matter of the greatest facility for him – wearing his persuasive uniform – to talk to a number of clerks and sundry ship-owners at the Custom House until he learned that the *Aurora*'s master lived just north of Upper Thames-street. Thereafter, it had been no trouble at all to leave his constables once again lingering afloat in his absence as he called upon a rare survivor from that fateful vessel.

It was, naturally, the purest ambition that had motivated

the journey. Inspector Newsome had decided personally to solve the *Aurora* case even before Sir Richard's contractual arrangement, and his keen detective's mind had made the paralogical leap native to all great investigators: what if the man he had pulled from the river was connected to the case at hand? Did not his clothes bespeak a mariner of a mate's rank? Was not the body fresh enough to have been in the water those few days since the ship went missing? And was not the chain about his ankles highly suggestive of felonious activity? It was a pattern of supposition too tempting to ignore.

The master of the *Aurora* had opened the door within moments of Mr Newsome rapping on it. 'Yes, officer?'

'Sir – were you the master of the missing vessel *Aurora*?'

'I am. Who are you? Did Timbs send you? Have you news of the ship?'

'Thames Police, sir. I know that you have been questioned on the matter of the—'

'Quite comprehensively. I saw nothing out of the ordinary. The procedure was as always when we dock in London, but for the delay in reaching our berth and the business with the lighter. I believe I have nothing more to say on the matter.'

'There is just one more thing, if you please . . .'

Mr Newsome reached inside his coat and gently removed a piece of paper folded into quarters. He opened it to its full extent and showed the pencil sketch of the not-drowned man to the master. 'Do you know this face, sir?'

'Why, yes – that is the very image of Hampton, the first mate. Is he . . . dead?'

'I am not permitted to say, sir. I was merely asked to come to your address and ask you about the drawing – for the purposes of recognition only. I suspect that we have men looking for him.'

'It looks like a mortician's illustration made after death. What is that mark on his cheek there?'

'I am afraid I have no further knowledge. Thank you for your time, sir.'

Mr Newsome folded away the sketch, tipped his hat and began to make his way back to his waiting constables.

'Wait! What is your name? Where did you obtain that picture?' called the master.

But the inspector was hurrying back to his galley at Dowgate-stairs on his way to that meeting with Sir Richard at Scotland Yard. No doubt news of this impromptu visit would soon find its way back to the commissioner, but not before he had exploited any advantage to be had and destroyed the sketch.

Accordingly, his first instruction to the constables on stepping back into the galley after his meeting at Scotland Yard was to row east to the large stretch of exposed mud near Blackfriars-bridge.

'Inspector Newsome, sir?' said the first constable as the oars rattled thickly in the rowlocks. 'We were talking while you went on your . . . errand . . .'

'Congratulations, Constable.'

'I mean to say . . . we have been asked by the superintendent at Wapping why our galley has not been seen more often in the Pool, where we are supposed to be on duty . . .'

'And what did you answer?'

'That we have been obliged, on occasion, to pursue suspected smugglers or to give chase to a ferry.'

'Very good, Constable. Initiative is a fine skill for a policeman to have.'

'But is it not rather a . . . a lie?'

'A lie is a complicated thing, Constable. Sometimes it is truer than the truth, and often more preferable. You can rest assured that whatever duties you pursue in my galley are in the strictest interests of justice. You may not perceive this immediately, but your job is to row and to observe. It falls to *me* to think one step ahead of the criminals on this pestilential channel.'

'Yes, sir . . . but . . .'

'But you would rather be watching for wherries towing each other, or an overloaded ferry, or a lumper dropping a bottle of beer into his pocket, or any number of other such catastrophic injuries to the morality of our nation – is that right? I wonder what you would do if you came upon a man being slaughtered in an alley by a crazed sailor wielding a knife. No doubt you would enquire whether the knife had been legitimately purchased.'

'I . . .'

'Constable – what would you say if I told you that the names of you and your fellow here may one day be used with reverence by your colleagues when they speak of the crime you helped me to solve? What today seems like a mild diversion from your ascribed duty will subsequently be called a great investigation by the historians of the Metropolitan Police.'

'Well . . .'

'Good. I am glad we have discussed the matter. Backstrokes now, gentlemen! Bring us alongside the mud here where these wretched beings toil in the mire.'

The 'wretched beings' alluded to were the unfortunate mudlarks of the Thames. 'Mud', however, was perhaps too charitable a description of the matter of the bank on which the two-dozen-or-so filth-caked souls strode thigh-deep. Freshly uncovered by the receding tide, it was a glistening brown surface of semi-gelatinous slime on which departing waves had revealed a timeless detritus of fractured clay pipes, shards of patterned porcelain, sodden coals, frayed rope and the ballooning bodies of cats or dogs washed eternally up and down the stream. The abominable stench of it – soil from the great flowing bowel of the city itself – was nauseating.

'You there!' called Mr Newsome to a rain-sodden skinny boy nearest the galley.

The youth thus addressed was a pitiable sight indeed. Thin to the point of near starvation, he stood mid-shin in the loathsome stuff and wore tattered clothes so caked in multifarious generations of wet mud, damp mud, drying mud, and desiccated mud that he half appeared to be born of it as opposed to visiting it tidally. He looked up with an expression of bestial awareness, his hands dripping.

'Yes – you there,' said Mr Newsome. 'Come closer, boy. I wish to speak with you.'

The youth blinked, and, unspeaking still, picked up his mud-laden basket and approached the galley with glutinously sucking steps. He wore no shoes, but the matter of the bank left dark stockings of glistening opprobrium upon his pale legs.

'Good. Have you been a mudlark long?' said Mr Newsome.

'Aye, since I wus so 'igh,' replied the boy, holding his hand at the height of a five-year-old child (allowing, perhaps, for partially submerged legs).

'Excellent. Do you frequent only this bank?'

'No, sir. I goes all 'bout the river, right down to Cuck'old's-point. There's good pickin' down yonder: I found nails an' good copper down Cuck'old's. Found a gent's watch once, too.'

'Do you ever see strange footprints on the mud? Perhaps at an early tide? I do not mean footprints made by men or women, but by . . . by something else.'

The other mudlarks, bent double in their silent searches, had been moving gradually closer to listen. Now they paused, palm-deep, wrist-deep, elbow-deep, as if debating whether to return to the primeval clay whence they came.

The boy turned to look behind him at an older woman whose dress was but a mass of dirt-stiffened folds about her.

'What? What is it, boy?' said Mr Newsome. 'Does that woman know the answer to my question?'

'Mary says she 'as seen the monster's feet in the mud. She's deaf, and she is . . .' The boy glanced behind him once more and tapped his temple with a horrifying digit.

'Call her over. Call this Mary,' said Mr Newsome.

'*Mary!* Mary – come an' talk to the buzzer,' shouted the boy.

The crone raised her head, collected her basket and trudged towards them with ovine obedience. She paused beside the youth, her face quite devoid of anything that might be termed a thought or feeling. Close to, a number of wiry silver hairs could be seen bristling at her chin.

'Tell 'im 'bout the monster!' prompted the youth with continued volume.

Something flickered in her rheumy eyes and she nodded, chewing at long deserted gums. 'They's a monster all right. I seen its prints – bigger than a man's 'and!'

'Where? Where have you seen this?' said Mr Newsome, loud enough to be heard.

'O, down Wapping and Lime'ouse . . . Middlesex side.'

'What do they look like, these prints?'

'A monster! It 'as fingers, three or four of 'em – only

bigger than a man's 'and. And deep, too – it's a big brute. Come from the sewers, it does.'

'The hag is a lunatic,' murmured one of the constables.

'The prints go to the sewers, do they? Have you seen the beast itself?' said Mr Newsome, seeing that the fleeting light of sapience was soon to ebb from that creased walnut face. He pulled the yellowed tooth from his coat pocket and held it up for the woman to focus on. 'Does it have teeth like this?'

She peered at the incisor, but her awareness had faded and it seemed she had already forgotten both the question and the context. 'Did yer find it by the river?' she said.

'Never mind that, woman. Have you seen this animal?'

'The monster? I have seen its prints down Wapping and Lime'ouse . . . Middlesex side.'

The mud-caked youth shrugged as if to say that he had warned the inspector.

'Very well.' Mr Newsome put the tooth back in his pocket. 'I will not delay you people longer. Please – go back to your foraging.'

The oars banged against the gunwale once again and the galley pushed off from the bank, moving out mid-stream to continue east and leave that band of unfortunates to their sodden labour. There, in that ancient ooze, they trod the very stuff of London's history between their toes: composted Elizabethan suicides, rusted nuggets of long rotted ships, martyrs' ashes, corroded Roman currency, bones of Atrebatean battles, and the poet's humble turd.

'Is that really a tooth from the river, Inspector?' asked the first constable as they passed under the shadow of London-bridge.

'Perhaps. I aim to discover precisely that,' said Mr Newsome.

'Does it touch upon a crime you are investigating?'

'That is no concern of yours, Constable. We are heading for Hermitage-stairs.'

'May I enquire why, sir?'

'No. Take care of the ferry's wake there . . .'

The galley was rocked by the heaving wake from a west-bound steamer, causing their oars to slap the surface. Moored ships crowded thickly about them now. The sky was criss-crossed with masts and the air thick with the scent of coal. Here were the entrances to St Katharine's and the London Dock, those great and venerable basins towards which men and vessels from across the world made their way.

But not Mr Newsome. When he stepped onto the slippery stairs just beyond Hermitage Dock (leaving, once again, his constables to the chaffing of the watermen), it was to visit that curious street weaving north between the immense ware-houses of the docks on each side: Nightingale-lane.

Heavy wagons and drays formed almost the entire traffic here, their sturdy wheels crunching ceaselessly as they loaded and unloaded the commerce of the globe. During the day, its blank, canyon walls gave it the sense of a street out of the common pattern – a channel that was neither here nor there, seemingly not ending or originating anywhere of note. At night, however, one did not venture this way, where the lofty blank-faced walls made shadows darker still and where the noise of the unending carts might mask a gargling cry.

There was, nevertheless, one notable address at which Mr Newsome might find an answer to his persistent question concerning the tooth. He heard the place long before he saw it, and smelled it even before that.

Jehosaphat's Extraordinary Bestiary was only one of a number of such wild-beast emporia about the docks, but it was certainly the most celebrated for its variety of stock and the esteem in which it was held by those private collectors for whom a barely credible oddity of nature was the most fashionable thing one could wish . . . at least until it died for want of its native sustenance, to be replaced by something more outlandish still. It had been Jehosaphat's that had first brought an elephant to London, and the first also to exhibit a rhinoceros. Those glorious days had passed, but it remained the only place one might purchase a jaguar or hyena – or where sun-browned mariners may bring their feathered, scaled, hairy or otherwise-furnished captives for a healthy sum of rum money.

The bell on the door rang as Mr Newsome entered, but he did not hear it over the ornithological cacophony that greeted him. Cages were everywhere: on shelves, on hooks, on twine hanging from the ceiling and upon the floor itself. And in each was a bewildering diversity of parrots, parakeets, cockatoos and macaws letting forth their respective screeches, creaks, croaks, rattles, screams and whistles. Within that general maddening din, the inspector thought he could additionally hear some shrill but indistinct *words*, which these birds were alleged to utter. Beside the counter, a cord-tethered pelican pattered its feet and looked down its long beak at the visiter as if in mutual disapproval.

'Yes, sir?' said a human voice.

Mr Newsome looked towards the counter but saw nobody.

'Here, sir,' came the voice again from an open doorway leading to a room deeper within the shop.

The inspector removed his hat and ventured towards the door to look inside, where a man wearing thick spectacles, a worn black suit and a battered hat with bird ordure upon it sat hunched over a cluttered desk of papers.

'How did you know I had entered the shop?' asked Mr Newsome, noting the ubiquitous grey splatter and replacing his hat with alacrity. There was no clear view of the street door from this anteroom.

'Why, I heard the bell, sir. And Gerald told me,' said the man, turning from his business at the desk to face the new customer.

Mr Newsome looked around to see if he had missed the gentleman named 'Gerald'. Instead, a rusty shriek assailed his left ear:

'——— copper! ——— copper!'

'You must forgive Gerald,' said the bespectacled man, in fact the eponymous Jehosaphat himself. 'It amuses the sailors to teach crude words to the birds on their voyages and Gerald has a vocabulary that will earn him no respectable home. I admit, I do wonder how he recognizes the uniform. Still, we do not mind working together, do we, Gerald?'

'——— ———!' said Gerald.

'Well, that is quite enough profanity for one day,' said Jehosaphat, shaking his head. He placed a blanket over the cage to the sound of squawked blasphemies. 'Now, sir – you do not strike me as a bird man. What is your pleasure . . . or are you here on police business?'

'Indeed I am. I have come into the possession of an animal tooth and I was hoping you might be able to identify the animal from it.'

'Of course I will look if you have it with you now, but I fear there are so many animals that . . . O, that is a very large incisor! Most definitely from a carnivore. May I look closer?'

Jehosaphat took the tooth and shifted papers aside on his desk to find a magnifying glass.

'Yes, yes – a large carnivore. A crocodile, perhaps, or one of the large felines . . . or the largest of the lizards.'

'Might it be a swimming animal?'

'I cannot speak for the piscine varieties, alas. The earth and the air are the natural habitations of my animals, though I will say that looks like no fish tooth to me. Theirs are more aculeate. Even the fearsome shark has a more triangular weapon, and . . . hmm, this is also no cachalot ivory.'

'Could it be from some beast native to these shores?'

'O no! No, no . . . even our island's largest dogs cannot boast a weapon such as this. In fact . . . will you accompany me to the yard? Perhaps I can show you something similar.'

The two gentlemen exited through another door into an enclosed courtyard of multiple iron-barred cages, which reeked unlike anything Mr Newsome had yet encountered on the streets or on the river. It was a pungent, feral smell that seemed to mingle urine, droppings and matted hair. Without quite knowing why, the inspector paused and felt an uncharacteristic shiver of fear.

'You need not worry,' said Jehosaphat. 'All are safely locked away, see?' He indicated a sleek black cat that glared back at them with imperious disdain.

'A jaguar,' said Jehosaphat. 'He has the kind of tooth you showed me, albeit somewhat smaller. Perhaps his neighbour . . .'

They looked in the next cage, where an enormous tiger lay on straw staring at the sky. Its gaze flickered at the arrival of the visitors but remained otherwise fixed.

'These beasts seem not at all dangerous,' said Mr Newsome.

'Ah, they bide their time, sir. While caged, they soon learn that it is futile to rage and roar against their fate. So they merely wait. There is food and water; I light a brazier on cold nights to warm the courtyards. But if I were to unlock the cage of this tiger, he would rip out your throat in an instant and feast upon your still living body.'

'Has such a thing ever happened here?'

'We had a boy once – a foolish boy – who put his arm in the cage. He lost a hand.'

'Have you ever had an animal escape?'

'O no, sir. The courtyard is quite closed and the cages sturdily constructed. The occasional bird manages to flee the shop, but they often return when they see the city they find themselves in. I perceive that you have a particular reason for asking . . .'

'If not from your emporium, is it possible that such a beast as this tiger could find itself free in the city?'

'Possible? Why, certainly. Do you recall the incident a few years ago at the menagerie on Exeter-change? Their elephant went insane and escaped into the street, where men shot at it for hours with muskets. Then there was that outrage a couple of years past when a jaguar like this fellow here was being offloaded at a wharf and its wooden cage was fractured in the fall from the crane. It ran off into the streets and took a child in its jaws as it went. Such accidents do occur.'

'What happened to that jaguar?'

'O, I do not recall. It may have been killed shortly afterwards amid the traffic. Such animals become quite crazed when faced with the noise and the bustle of the city.'

'I see. Might such an animal survive on the streets, or by the river, if it managed to avoid the traffic?'

'What curious questions you ask!' said Jehosaphat, exhibiting a look of concern now, despite his jocularity. 'The large felines require a quantity of meat to live. If they could get that from the markets, or hunt it, then I suppose they might survive . . . but would not all of London be aware of a beast stalking horses upon the street?'

'True. But a man could keep and feed such an animal if he so wished. Certainly, you do so.'

'It is possible . . . but I admit I am more and more perplexed. Is the tooth you showed me from an animal you suspect to be free in the city? That would be a very dangerous thing indeed.'

'You need not concern yourself over that, Mr Jehosaphat. I found the tooth and it intrigued me. Nothing more than that. I thank you for your kind attention and for showing me these animals . . .'

'I am happy to be of help, sir. But take care – if you should encounter such a beast, do not attempt to approach it. Rather, stay very still and show no signs of fear or aggression.'

'Thank you, but I have no intention of putting myself in danger. Good day to you.'

And so Mr Newsome left Jehosaphat's Extraordinary Bestiary to return to his constables, musing as he did so that the more he learned about the mysterious incisor, the less sense it seemed to make. Could it be that it had been purposely left in the corpse as a wilful misdirection?

He was passing the corner with Burr-street and turning the questions over in his mind when he became aware of the same hideous smell he had encountered on Pickle Herring-street. Pausing at the coincidence, he looked up and saw precisely the same odd little man he had glimpsed at Pickle Herring: the freckled face, the painted emotionless eyes and the hair stiff with dirt. On closer examination, the clothes also seemed quite saturated with either mud or dirty water.

For his part, the little man simply stared back.

'You there!' said Mr Newsome crossing the road to reach the malodorous fellow. 'I want to speak to you.'

But the challenge was enough to stir the man from his immobile stance and dead-eyed gaze. He turned quickly on his heel and began immediately to run down Nightingale-lane towards the river.

'Halt! You there! Stop! Police!'

Mr Newsome gave chase, mindful of the fact that they were fortuitously running towards his galley and the two waiting constables. He kept up his cries accordingly.

'Thief! Stop! You there! Stop that man! Constables! Constables!'

The little man emerged at the end of the street, followed rapidly by the clamorous Mr Newsome. By now, the two constables were standing in the galley to locate the source of the alarm. On seeing their inspector running, they quickly understood the situation and bolted up the stairs to block the little man's flight.

Mr Newsome kept up his momentum and ran straight at the back of his quarry, who had momentarily paused in panic to look for means of escape. Thus all three policemen were able to converge upon the man with a clatter of footfalls.

There was no struggle. Evidently accepting his situation, the reeking fellow wordlessly dropped his arms and allowed the cuffs to be placed around his wrists. Apart from his panting, there was no emotion to be read in his face.

'Who are you? Why do you follow me?' said Mr Newsome, himself quite unused to the exertion.

No reply.

'What is your name? Are you working for Eldritch

Batchem? Speak, man, or you will face the full wrath of the law!'

No reply.

'I see. Then it is the cells at Wapping for you until we can loosen that tongue.'

Together (and with some obvious reluctance on the part of the constables to touch such a vile-smelling specimen of humanity), the three policemen manoeuvred the man into the galley and cast off for the short row to Wapping station.

But the prisoner was never to arrive.

Within moments of the galley moving out into the channel between shipping, the little man simply stood and leaped head first over the gunwale into the stream, his hands still cuffed behind him. The galley rocked madly and threatened to capsize.

'My G—! He has killed himself!' said Mr Newsome, gripping the sides of the boat and staring at the disturbed water where the man had plunged in.

He did not resurface.

ELEVEN

It is oftentimes remarked among the older policemen that, once a man has habitually trodden a beat, that route is burned not only upon his memory but upon his very way of thinking. The rhythm of his boots, the heightened sense of awareness, the feel of the cradling masonry about him: all conspire to make his peregrinations thereafter one lifelong beat, whether or not he wears a uniform and steps out in the name of justice. Those who have been accustomed to a nocturnal duty note the phenomenon even more acutely.

Mr Williamson was of the latter class. No longer a constable, he nevertheless took a curious comfort from a stroll about the city. There was no wife to await his return, no familial bustle to draw him back – just a cold hearth and a bed which, of late, had become more a source of distress than of repose. So he walked – often for hours at a time.

He clearly had much to think about on that day of the meeting with Sir Richard and Inspector Newsome at Scotland Yard. Other men might have cast a lugubrious glance at the rain and decided that the warmth of a coffee house was a more preferable place to gather their thoughts, but Mr Williamson seemed in no way inconvenienced. Rather, he simply turned up his coat collar, pulled on his gloves and set his course northwards towards the traffic of Trafalgar-square.

There is, after all, beauty to be found in the sodden metropolis. Just as snow and bright sun will create altogether distinctive scenes, so a spring rain will reveal the city's wonders. Spires quiver in puddles, horses snort steam, gas illuminates long avenues of silver, and already soot-stained stone is made darker still with leaking streaks. Not all poetry need be hopeful.

Who could say what thoughts animated the mind of Mr Williamson as he walked these streets? He appeared not to see the people around him, and showed no interest in the shop windows or in the corner vendors. He was unaffected by the scents of baked potato, of roasted pork, and of coffee-imbued tobacco clouds emanating from the convivial rooms along the way. Indeed, it was not until he approached Hay-market, almost at dusk, that he seemed to lift his head and finally observe the crowds.

The theatres were not yet open for business, but their sundry parasites were. As he walked, he observed the insouciant pickpockets, the watchful beggars, the small hawkers of flowers and fruit . . . and the street girls.

No doubt they all saw him and knew him for the policeman he had once been. Uniform mattered not – everything could be discerned in the eyes. These were people who, for one reason or another, were used to not being seen, or seen only by a certain few. Thus was it that, as Mr Williamson took up his viewing position in front of the Haymarket Theatre, a telegraphic communication passed among those various miscreants: watch out for there is an investigator in our midst.

''Ello, lovey!'

Mr Williamson looked to his side and saw a moderately attractive girl smiling at him. 'I am not interested,' he answered, returning his gaze to the street.

'O, sir! I seen 'ow you been lookin' at us girls these past ten minutes and I knows that you are *indeed* interested!'

'You are mistaken. Move along now.'

'Are you lookin' for a particklar girl? P'raps I know 'er if you tell me 'ow she looks. I don't mind losin' the custom to 'elp a gentleman find what 'e's lookin' for.'

'I told you I am not interested. Go about your business; I will not hinder you.'

'As you please! But don't say I didn't try to 'elp you find your girl.'

The magdalene gave Mr Williamson her professional smile once more and nudged him with a *coquettish* hip before walking on. He blushed at the contact and felt a sudden rush of humiliation. Walking was the thing – it was time to move on.

He headed northwards along Windmill-street to Brewer-street, then west. Had someone been following him from a discreet distance, they might have reported he was walking without a destination, walking merely to be moving and thinking. He might, indeed, have said the same himself if questioned on the matter.

It was quite by chance, therefore – nothing more than an accident of the deeper mind and the suggestive but inchoate pattern of the streets themselves – that he found himself in Golden-square, standing before a grandiose-looking house whose curtained ground-floor windows revealed but a slash of gaslight within.

Mr Williamson paused for some time before the house.

Had someone been following him, no doubt they would have pondered why he lingered thus, looking at that one particular ground-floor window. At one point, it seemed he was about to approach the door and knock, but it was the merest shadow of intent. Certainly, there was some agitation of indecision in his demeanour as he twice made to walk away before returning.

Was he expecting to see someone in particular? Was he expecting to be seen? Was he, perhaps, imagining what manner of activity was taking place behind those heavy damask curtains and suffering some unknowable emotion at the images that played in his mind?

It was indeed a curious display, and most assuredly one that he would not want anybody who knew his name to witness – let alone *two* such persons.

Morning, of course, brings absolution. Once the dandies have been carried away; once the street girls have returned over the bridges and the gutters have been cleared; once the victims of the darkness have been recovered and given last rites, then the city is reborn to fall again.

On that particular morning, the modest house of Mr Williamson – usually so silent – was a-bustle with the clatter of crockery as John Cullen prepared tea at the stove. A greater number of chairs had been procured in the living room and Noah Dyson was sitting beside the fire with Benjamin and Mr Williamson, the latter having just summarized his meeting with Sir Richard (albeit omitting, for now, the fine print of its conditions).

'What will you do, George?' asked Noah. 'I was not aware you had any great desire to return to the Detective Force.'

'I myself am not certain of that desire,' said Mr Williamson, looking into the flames.

'Does it not seem curious to you that he would invite you to Scotland Yard and make such an offer?'

'Perhaps, but you saw the challenge thrown down by Eldritch Batchem at the theatre. Sir Richard is determined to solve this case. If I am to investigate, it is to be purely in my own name so that no taint can affect the commissioner or the Metropolitan Police.'

'Still – to pit you against Inspector Newsome like that is rather an odd strategy by the famously predictable Sir Richard . . . or perhaps he knows you well enough to know that this would be impetus enough to tempt you.'

'Very likely you are correct, Noah.'

'Well, you know that I myself have no great affection for the inspector, and I must say I am inclined to aid you in your challenge. I admit it seems an intriguing mystery . . . and, as Ben keeps reminding me, I *have* been somewhat restless of late.'

'It is a challenge to all of us – that's what it is!' said Mr Cullen, shakily carrying the teacups and pot on a tray to the table by the fire. 'Perhaps I am speaking only for myself when I say that I miss the excitement of our previous collaborations.'

'It is easy for you to be excited, Mr Cullen,' said Mr Williamson. '*You* did not experience physical assault or the threat of imminent death as we others did in those cases to which you refer. None of us walks willingly into danger.'

Benjamin clicked his fingers for attention. He had been paying characteristically close attention to the discussion and spoke now in his artful arabesques of palms and fingers so that Noah, observing intently, might translate the thoughts into the vulgar tongue.

'Ben says that the case of the missing brig points to a

number of larger questions: the likelihood of a very significant smuggling enterprise . . . at least one example of murder . . . and the greatest mystery in all of this – the person and purpose of one Eldritch Batchem. For any one of these reasons, he says, the case is worth investigating . . . but in combination they make for a truly interesting challenge. Of course, he *would* say that.'

Ben smiled at this last observation and good-naturedly made a single gesture with his hand and the crook of the opposing forearm that seemed sufficiently explicit to require no translation.

'Hmm. Ben makes some valid observations,' said Mr Williamson. 'May I ask, though, which murder he is referring to?'

Ben slashed a hand across his scarred neck.

Mr Williamson nodded. 'Yes – the tidewaiter William Barton on Waterloo-bridge. His death – or at least the instrument of it – is evidently an important part of this puzzle. I assume we are all agreed that it was clearly not suicide?'

'I have read Eldritch Batchem's account of his "investigation", as I am sure we all have,' said Noah. 'Any intelligent man would question some of his suppositions.'

'But what of the fact that there was nobody else on the bridge at the time of the death?' said Mr Cullen, sensing the onset of one of those investigative jousts he had been privileged to witness previously within this curious group.

'Absence – or *perceived* absence?' said Mr Williamson. 'It is said that everyone passing across the bridge was accounted for at the other end for an hour before the incident. Is it not entirely possible that someone could have loitered within one of the pedestrian recesses *before* that time, emerging some hours later to attack the victim only once the fog had settled?'

'Perhaps,' said Noah. 'But where did this person escape to

once the fog lifted and Batchem arrived? The bridge was indeed empty then. Not to mention that the (extraordinarily patient) killer would have had to know in advance that his victim would cross the bridge at a certain time. Is it possible he even had some intuition of the impending fog to mask his actions?'

Benjamin made his customary cough and added his own digitolocutionary comment. Noah nodded.

'Ben says the killer could have quite easily escaped over the bridge parapet in the thickness of the fog. That could explain the absence of the weapon.'

'Hmm. That would have been a quite hazardous and rather skilful escape,' said Mr Williamson. 'Waterloo-bridge may not be the highest, but it is high enough to attract numerous suicides.'

'It stands thirty-five feet at high water, I believe,' offered Mr Cullen, seeing his chance. 'London-bridge is forty-two.'

'Very good, Mr Cullen,' said Mr Williamson. 'There was also, of course, the mention of a sound in the fog: metal striking stone. Perhaps that was something to do with the killer's escape rather than the sound of a weapon?'

'Batchem did not venture to question anyone at the foot of the bridge,' said Noah. 'Had he not been so convinced of his own cleverness, he might have learned something more by doing so.'

'If I may ask a question,' said Mr Cullen, 'why would anyone kill this fellow Barton in the first place? If he was aiding smugglers, surely he was of use to them?'

'You are correct, of course,' said Noah. 'We have no idea why he would be killed – especially in this manner – but the very fact of his being killed is what we hope to discern, moving from that point of discovery to the next and the next. George – I know that you could apply some genuine detective vigour to the investigation of that murder. Will you visit the bridge?'

'There is unlikely to be any physical clue now that so many thousands have traversed,' said Mr Williamson, 'but I could indeed speak to the toll-collector and to anyone below the bridge.'

Mr Cullen's teacup rattled upon its saucer. 'Does this mean, then, that we will pursue the case? Are we to compete with Eldritch Batchem and win back Mr Williamson's rightful place in the Detective Force?'

Ben looked to Noah and nodded.

Noah looked to Mr Williamson and shrugged.

'Hmm,' said the latter. 'Let us agree only that we will make preliminary enquiries to see what manner of case this is. Nothing more. There is certainly no need, Mr Cullen, to begin ornamenting any of our endeavours with talk of grandiose challenges or of my returning to the Detective Force (which, I might add, has many able men and may solve the mystery before we attempt to do so). Simplicity is the key – we must ask only what is at the root of the disappearance of the *Aurora*.'

'As Ben has implied, the cargo of French silk is too obvious a fact to ignore,' said Noah. 'The duties are currently so high that it is almost impossible for an honest merchant to make money from imported silk – which is no doubt why much of what passes for legitimate business in our city shops is actually based in smuggling. I am sure I could walk into any cloth warehouse in the city and find you silk never logged by the Custom House.'

'Well, in that case, perhaps you and Ben can locate the cargo of the *Aurora* and investigate its origins,' said Mr Williamson. 'That is the most likely avenue to a solution.'

'What of Eldritch Batchem?' said Mr Cullen. 'Should we be aware of *his* actions?'

'I think his investigation of the Waterloo-bridge incident tells us all we need to know about his quality as a detective,' said Mr Williamson. 'We need not concern ourselves with him.'

'I mean, rather, that he may himself be implicated,' said Mr Cullen. 'What if his conclusions on the Waterloo death hide a more personal involvement? It was certainly a very great coincidence that a playbill was found in the victim's pocket . . .'

'I suspect that there never was a playbill in Barton's pocket,' said Noah. 'That will have been a self-aggrandizing flourish of Batchem's prior to his show – a harmless, albeit cynical, ploy.'

'That may be,' said Mr Williamson, 'but what makes you think, Mr Cullen, that the man is involved in any way other than his job for the Bridge Company? The man might be a fool, but it is quite another thing to be a party to murder. It seems to me that his only motive is the urge for public acclaim.'

'I . . . I do not know,' said Mr Cullen. 'He is a strange man. Watching him at the theatre the other night, I had the distinct feeling that I was seeing an actor in a role rather than a man . . . O, I cannot explain it!'

Benjamin clicked his fingers with some urgency and responded to Mr Cullen's words, looking to Noah for a voice.

'Ben says he had the same feeling . . . he thinks that we should not disregard Batchem as a factor in any efforts to solve the case . . . that it is a shrewd man who appears to make sense even as he lies . . . and that Ben, too, would not be at all surprised if we discover some deeper involvement.'

'Hmm. Hmm. What do *you* make of the fellow, Noah? You are a good judge of men.'

'I admit I agree with you, George. The man is vain, histrionic and has perhaps half the mind he thinks he has. Nevertheless, he made some salient and interesting points in his address. I might not agree with all of them, but I acknowledge their cohesion if nothing else. There is decidedly more to the man than what he presents. I assume I am not the only one to have pondered the oddity of his dress?'

'You are referring to the russet cap,' said Mr Williamson. 'I admit I have seen nothing like it; he must have them made for him. Of course, I have asked myself why. It is true that one may often know a man by his hat – a silk or beaver top hat, a broad-brimmer, a tricorn, a corduroy cap – and make assumptions about his station or vocation. But what does one say about a hat with no precedent? Its wearer becomes unique: a madman or a genius. Is this, perhaps, Mr Batchem's own reasoning on the matter?'

'You make a keen observation,' said Noah. 'His rather garish tweed suit, also, craves attention, as does the affectation of the gloves worn indoors. We have certainly seen enough of the man to acknowledge his theatricality. Indeed, Mr Cullen has accurately noted his role-playing air. I submit that the pointed beard is also part of that role. Do you recall how he toyed with it during the show to lend himself a thoughtful manner? In fact . . . between the cap and the beard, there is little of his face revealed. I would not be at all surprised—'

'– if it were all actually a disguise,' finished Mr Williamson.

Noah smiled and nodded. The four of them pondered upon that possibility as the fire crackled in the grate.

'Who *is* Eldritch Batchem?' said Mr Cullen. 'Somebody, somewhere, must know the man, even if he now wears a disguise. Somebody must recognize his voice, his dress, his mannerisms.'

'You are quite wrong,' said Mr Williamson. 'How many now inhabit this city? Two million? One might live within two miles of a person and never see him, or one might see him every day and not notice him. A man alters his dress, grows a beard, changes his name, wears a russet cap . . . and he becomes another man entirely. Why, you may well have worked alongside Mr Batchem as a constable in the very same division, Mr Cullen.'

'I knew every man in my division and could name them all . . .'

'I merely make an example, Mr Cullen.'

'Well, we should remain aware of the man,' said Noah. 'At the very least, it may be interesting to see where he is looking as he investigates this case.'

'What can *I* do?' said Mr Cullen. 'Mr Williamson is to investigate the bridge. Noah and Ben will investigate the receivers. There must be something for me . . .'

'Which additional aspect of the case do *you* think should be pursued, Mr Cullen?' said Mr Williamson.

'Well, we know that some of the *Aurora*'s seamen came ashore . . . and it seems likely that they have spoken to others . . . or that there are lumpers who have unloaded her. I could infiltrate the docks and ask questions among the men there. If they are anything like constables, they will have all the gossip.'

'Very well, then that is your task,' said Mr Williamson. 'Only, take care – the gossip that is of benefit to you can also turn against you.'

'I will leave this very moment!' said Mr Cullen, finishing his tea at a gulp and striding to fetch his coat.

Ben also stood, communicating to Noah that he would accompany Mr Cullen as far as the City and make preliminary observations concerning the receivers.

Thus, with the bang of the street door, the two sat in silence: one maintaining his gaze into the fire and the other watching the reflection of the flames thereupon. Noah waited for Mr Williamson to speak. The moments became minutes.

'What is the matter, George?' said Noah, finally. 'I do not believe the innocuous Mr Cullen has affected your mood so with his enthusiasm.'

'No. It is not he.'

'Then what is preoccupying you? I know that I am liable to become listless when I have nothing to occupy myself, but you seem to have become quite melancholy since your meeting with Sir Richard.'

'Noah – I have never enquired too closely into your life, for it is not my business to do so. We have shared a number of experiences, but I . . . I do not even know where you live. I do not know what you do to sustain yourself. I do not know how much – if at all – the accusations Sir Richard and Inspector Newsome once made about you are true . . .'

'George – why do you ask these things now? I cannot see how they affect our acquaintance. You are no longer a policeman to care about such things, and my past is precisely that.'

'Call it curiosity if you will. What manner of investigator would I be if I did not enquire how a fellow of mine comes to be independently wealthy even after he is forced by the police to give up a house to protect his anonymity?'

'That was some time ago . . .'

'I know of few men who could give up a house and not be financially broken by it. I have heard rumours – no matter from where; they are everywhere – that you are a dealer in opium. Is this true?'

'I will admit to being an importer and refiner of that commodity. It is not against the law and I make a good living from it. If I do not advertise the fact, it is merely because my clients appreciate discretion. The recreational use of opium, as you know, is not always associated with the greatest morality or restraint.'

'Hmm. Hmm.'

'And I live by the river, between Blackfriars and Southwark bridges if that further satisfies your curiosity . . . but – forgive me – I do wonder at your sudden interest after all we have seen and done. Has Sir Richard been asking questions? Is your association with me something to blacken your name?'

'I may no longer be a policeman, Noah, but justice and truth remain important principles in my work, whatever that work may be.'

'I understand, George. It is common enough for an intelligent man – when he looks into himself – to find doubt and conflict. We are all engaged in internecine battles between our higher honour and our base urges.'

'What are you referring to? I asked only about your—'

'There is no need to be ashamed. Your Christian morals asphyxiate you, George. Appeal instead to your detective's rationality.'

'Noah . . . I feel we are speaking of different matters. I have said nothing to you about any anxiety of mine.'

'You were at Golden-square last night.'

Mr Williamson shuddered as if he had been struck. He reddened. Then his face became more ominously pale.

'Have you been following me? This is outrageous! I . . . I . . .'

'George – listen. The occurrence was quite innocent—'

'Innocent? It is nothing short of a betrayal!'

'Yes, you were followed – but not by my intention. If you will listen to me, I can explain.'

'Hmm. Hmm. Explain, yes – then you may leave.'

'Benjamin was out at Haymarket last evening (he has an inexplicable love of the theatre) and saw you standing out-side on the street. He was about to approach you when he saw another fellow observing you: a man of Italian appear-ance wearing long hair and an earring.'

Mr Williamson came abruptly out of his reproving glare. 'Italian, you say? And watching *me*?'

'Quite so. Ben immediately perceived that you might be in danger, if only of having your pocket picked (the man looked very like a thief) and so he began to observe your observer. The man kept you in his sight for the whole time you waited, then followed you thereafter to Golden-square, leaving you only when you returned home. *That* is how I know. Ben feared for your life and would have sprung forth in your defence at the merest hint of danger.'

'I was completely unaware . . .'

'Precisely, George. You were preoccupied with other things. There was no reason to suspect you were being followed, but you were and did not notice. In itself, that is a strange thing.'

'What . . . where did this Italian-looking fellow go after I returned home?'

'Ben followed him back to Oxford-street – a suitably busy location, no doubt – where the man evidently perceived he was being shadowed and simply vanished. Perhaps he knew even before that point and chose to lead Ben there. Whatever the case, it was quite an impressive performance. What do you make of that?'

'I . . . I believe I have seen that man before: five nights ago outside the Queen's Theatre. He made a quite skilful lift while I was distracted by . . . by someone in the crowd.'

'Distracted? *You?* What would distract you while you are at work? What is it, of late, that provokes you into such cogitations?'

'I do not know. There is some . . . some plan afoot but I cannot explain it.'

'May I ask what drew you particularly to Haymarket and Golden-square?'

'I often take a walk in the evenings. I am surprised Ben has not seen me before if he frequents those streets.'

'The girl Charlotte . . . the one you questioned for that recent case . . . does she not live at Golden-square? And is her pitch not Haymarket?'

'A man might walk anywhere he likes. There are magdalenes on every street.'

'There is no need for anger, George. Your personal affairs are no business of mine.'

'Quite. And I do not consort with prostitutes if that is what you are implying!'

'Even if you did, there is no sin or shame in it. A man has desires. It is nature's way.'

'I have no such desires.'

'Very well, very well – we need never speak of it again. Of more immediate concern is this Italian fellow and the nature of his grander design. Who is he and why does he follow you?'

'I have no idea. Could it be the hand of Eldritch Batchem at work?'

'If it is, George, I am at a loss to explain his purpose. I am certain of this much, however: we will likely be seeing more of such strategies.'

TWELVE

———•·•———

Noah could not have been more correct in his assertion. The following day's edition of that scurrilous rag *the London Monitor* (home to scandal, misinformation, gossip, and frequent litigation) was to set new standards for what might be expected in the much-pursued case of the missing brig. Only a *verbatim* excerpt of the offending article will suffice:

THE STANDARD OF
THE MODERN DETECTIVE?

Since the astounding revelation at the Queen's Theatre, Wych-street, four days ago, some of London's 'finest' investigators have been falling over each other to surpass the esteemed Eldritch Batchem in the race to solve the mystery of the vanished vessel *Aurora*. But who are these gentlemen, and what are their pedigrees as 'detectives'?

Let us first take G.W. This gentleman was once a policeman – a genuine 'detective' no less! – who participated in the investigation of the celebrated Red Jaw murders. He was on the very gallows platform itself when Lucius Boyle performed that notorious murder amid the pressing crowds, but could only stand by impotently as the felon strolled away! Is there any truth in the rumours that this ex-sergeant once collaborated in aiding a prisoner to escape from Giltspur-street prison? We could not possibly say! Could it be the case that this is also a man who has consorted with common prostitutes in the so-called 'investigation' of recent crimes? Modesty (and his honour the magistrate) forbids us from stating the facts more clearly! And what of his acquaintance with criminals? More of that in a moment . . .

Then we have A.N., an active policeman – albeit one who has plummeted like Icarus from his former status as a senior 'detective' to find himself once again in uniform. Why has this happened? We could only speculate! Might it be his reputation for uncouth manners? Or perhaps it is his readiness with a truncheon? We cannot confirm (or deny!) the recent shameful reports of his bursting into the Continental Club like a maniac, only to be taken away by constables of his own paymaster, the Metropolitan Police. Is it true that, even now, he neglects his duty upon the river to pursue personal matters? As to suggestions that he has frequented houses of ill repute 'in the course of duty', this organ will say nothing . . . !

Next we have the enigmatic figure who we shall simply call N.D. – if that was ever his real name. We admit we know very little about this fellow, except that he is said not only to be a convicted criminal but also an escaped transportee! What is his profession? Why does he pursue such cases? What was his relationship to the murderer Boyle? Is it true that he owns a manufactory at Limehouse, whose produce would raise more than a few eyebrows? We cannot answer these questions, and this perturbs us! He is, after all, the man said to be working alongside the once-upstanding G.W.

And who is the dusky Negro who is often seen with

both N.D. and G.W.? Nobody who has seen his horrifying countenance will forget it in a hurry, towering Cyclops that he is! While others of his ilk beg in the gutter, hoist rope at the docks or dance and jig upon the common stage, *he* strolls elegantly about town in the finery of a gentleman! From where does he draw his income if he is but a manservant?

Finally, there is the failed constable J.C., who has gone over to the side of those he once sought to put in gaol! No uniform for this burly fellow any longer – he prefers it when the street girls cannot see him coming!

Is this, then, the standard of the modern detective? Transgressors, failures, criminals (or their cohorts), and mockers of justice? Let us see us who reigns triumphant in this investigation . . .

It need hardly be mentioned, of course, that *the London Monitor* has never been blessed with the impartiality of our finer press. If a man pays rather more for an advertisement than strictly required, he might not be entirely surprised to have his own articles accepted with only the lightest editorial touch.

I would like to state that I have never written for such a base publication . . . though that would be a lie. A writer produces words as a manufactory produces bricks – he cannot be responsible for what is done with the buildings once the blocks are made. Indeed (to further labour the device), it would be my words that would eventually dismantle the walls around me, reducing my debt, brick by brick, until I could walk through the language-built aperture to freedom.

To that very end, I had been spending my days at the small card table in my cell, producing articles on investigation and other matters related to the *Aurora* case, and then quizzing the printers' boys for further news when they came with the proofs for correction. These canny scamps can seldom read for themselves, but they spend most of their lives in the compositors' room or by the editor's side and know too well that, for a crust or a coin, they can be bribed for the very latest intelligence even before the presses begin to whir.

Thus it was that my continued incarceration inconvenienced me hardly at all in the accumulation of the news on the streets, though my loss of bread to the printers' boys was threatening to render me dead through emaciation before I could write myself liberated. That minor hardship, along with the incessant cold that palsied my slender fingers and drove needles into my wrists, was tolerable for the time being.

In truth, I was busier than I had ever been. The fashion for all things investigatory, combined with Josiah Timbs's challenge at the Queen's Theatre, had generated numerous opportunities with the common press. And as one who had some prior knowledge of the Detective Force myself, I was a natural enough choice to provide a voice on Messrs Newsome, Williamson and Mayne.

Nor had I been dormant on the matter of Eldritch Batchem, who, it seemed, was highly selective in his availability to the gentlemen of Fleet-street. Following his acceptance of the challenge by Mr Timbs, he had not spoken to anyone but the merchant himself. Was he a genius of self-mythology, or had he something to hide? My journalistic nose rather suggested the latter.

I had been unable to extract more information from the turnkey who had worked at Whitecross-street (a dull fellow with a duller memory), but he assured me there was a fellow of his on another corridor of Horsemonger-street who had also worked at Whitecross at the same time and who might have more to say about the inmate called 'Crawford' or 'Cowley' or 'Crowell'. And since there was not the least likelihood of my trusting an interview to anyone but myself, I had no choice but to engineer a temporary transfer to that corridor – the one with the solitary cells – in order to effect that conversation.

It was, fortunately, a matter of the greatest ease. The law may inform us that only dissenters and those of the Popish persuasion may be excused from Sunday service in gaol, but the warden and chaplain were of a different view: all debtors were to attend chapel or face three days in a solitary cell on half rations. Accustomed as I was to perfunctorily mumbling Old Testament platitudes for the sake of my gruel, it was but a matter of letting forth an inventive (and generally rather artful) blasphemous tirade the next Sunday in order to find myself immediately escorted to the solitary cell.

On taking up my new residence – quite by chance in the lunatic cell with coir matting and canvas on its walls – I was soon able to locate the turnkey in question, who proved to be somewhat more cogent than his colleague. He did indeed recall the fellow who may have been an earlier incarnation of Eldritch Batchem, and, better still, the dubious debtor had been a resident on his very wing. Yes, I was told, the inmate had been highly methodical; yes, he had also been rather secretive and irritable if disturbed in his rituals. But there was more . . .

It seems that this Crawford ('I feel sure it was Crawford . . . or Crowley') was possessed by disturbing dreams that would cause him to speak or even shout in his sleep. It had been the nightly bane of neighbouring debtors, who quite disliked the man anyway for his haughty demeanour, and was altogether disturbing to the guards, who eventually took the unorthodox step of removing him to a private room.

As to the nature of these nocturnal exclamations, they were largely incoherent, as oneiric monologues are wont to be. Nevertheless, there was a tone and inference that was clear enough to the guards who pressed ears to the cold iron door so they might perhaps afford a glimpse into the tortured soul of the curious fellow under their charge. For all of his diurnal order and control, the sleeping man was a vortex of despair.

Assuredly, I pushed the turnkey for more detail regarding the words, the names and the terms used in those midnight cries, but he recalled only the broadest tenor: discomfort, unease and great sorrow. I persisted. Was there not *something* that remained in his memory of those nights – some teasel-like expression or otherwise distinctive nomenclature he had not heard before or since? Was there not one salient phrase he could repeat to me that would capture the spirit of this Crawford's pillow-smothered, sheet-twisting agonies of sleep?

'Liveridge.'

That was all. Was it a name? Was it a place? Was it an imperfectly heard and misremembered conglomerate word: a mere accretion of inchoate phonemes? Was it 'Live Ridge' or 'Liver Edge'? Regrettably, it was all my turnkey could offer in terms of detail on those somnolocutionary outbursts.

I had worked with such meagre tools before, and would again. Somehow, later, it would all coalesce. And if I could sustain myself long enough in that wretched penitentiary to pay off my debt, I would be the man to deliver the story into print for a sum fully deserving of its exclusivity.

As for the whereabouts of my subject Eldritch Batchem, he was undiminished in his search, and could that day be found in the place where the *Aurora* should have arrived if such ill fate had not befallen it: St Katharine Dock.

With its towering, all-encircling warehouses and retractable bridges, its clanging cast-iron paving, its many hundreds of vessels and many thousands of workers, its clatter of commerce and the relentless rumble of the treadmill cranes, St Katharine's might almost be a city unto itself. Seek the sky here and one instead sees multiplicitous spars, yards, crosstrees, masts, wrapped sails, limp pennants, loose rigging and the endless jib-festooned brickwork behind which is stored the produce of the globe. One smells molten tar, musty oakum, salt-soaked timber and the feral reek of sailors – all carried upon the river's earthy perfume.

Along these characterful wharfs did Eldritch Batchem stroll, conspicuous in his appearance even among the carnivalesque maritime spectacle of tattooed torsos, turbans, sashes, and skins of every hue. Here, the oddities of the world commingled, and yet the investigator was no less strange in their company.

Perhaps it was his assumption that the brig had in fact docked here regardless of what the documentation maintained. It would have been a simple enough matter to land under a different name – commodiously effected via those fraudulent landing warrants – and to unload without the merchant being any the wiser. Had Mr Timbs or his agents made their way to the warehouse to collect his cargo, they would simply have been told that no such stock and no such ship existed. Meanwhile, the vessel itself would by then have long sailed away to be used again, or scuttled mid-Channel on some moonless night.

Or perhaps the russet-capped fellow was pursuing a different line altogether. Ships here load and unload continuously to the song of rope on pulley, and as they do so their bottoms are filled or emptied of the ballast that keeps them stable upon the oceans. Since no ship receives ballast without the knowledge of *somebody*, Mr Batchem may have decided upon this as his next avenue of enquiry.

He had most likely already enquired at Trinity House (that monopoly of ballast upon the river) and learned that no outgoing ship named *Aurora* had requested gravel. That much was to be expected, though the thorough investigator always reassures himself of the obvious before delineating it so. The next logical step was to speak to the truckmen and ballast-heavers themselves – those grimy, gritty labourers in their collar-covering hats who toil with the shovel at a thousand portholes across the Port of London.

And here was such a pair at St Katharine's, going about their work with a determined silence marred only by the rhythmical *slench* of the shovel's edge into gravel and the occasional spatter of ballast against the wooden hull. Eldritch Batchem watched with admiration how the burly heavers cast their loads up from the barge with unerring accuracy, and with hardly an upward glance, through a narrow aperture into the lower holds of the ship, where another would be raking it level in near-total darkness.

Finally, a muffled voice came from inside the vessel and the heavers stopped their labour to wipe grit from their sweating brows and reach for bottles of beer beneath a canvas sheet. By and by, one of the pair saw that they were being observed from the quay and nudged the other, whose face was skyward with the last of the bottle draining into his throat.

'Gentlemen,' said Eldritch Batchem, meeting their gaze, 'I admire your skill. Every man must have a skill, must he not? I myself am a detective.'

The two ballast-heavers looked up at the curiously dressed man and then at each other. If they had understood his words, they made no sign of wanting to reply.

'I mean to say that your work with the shovel is most accurate. Do you work only here in the dock, or also among the wharfs of the river?'

Again, the two gentlemen looked blankly back at their interrogator.

'I wonder if you gentlemen understand plain English? Or perhaps you have a foreman I may speak to rather than my disturbing your rest period any further . . . ?'

One of the men gestured towards the hull with a bottle-clasping hand.

'Your master is inside there? May I cross into the vessel and seek him out?'

The answering shrug may have been an affirmative, or an expression of the purest indifference.

Eldritch Batchem bustled away from the ballast-heavers and towards the deck of the ship, whose hollow-sounding boards had evidently just been swabbed clean. There seemed to be not another soul on board.

'Hello! I say – is anyone below decks?' he called.

No answer.

He descended a rough wooden stairway into the murk and was assailed with the reek of dank wood, caulking and the cellar mustiness denoting the now empty ship's most recent cargo of wine barrels. There was still no one to be seen, so he ventured still deeper, stepping carefully around the coils of rope and neat piles of bolstering timber that must have held everything in place on some storm-lashed crossing.

'Ho! Hello! I am looking for the ballast man. Your two heavers advised me I may descend . . .'

Darker and deeper he went, until he might have been descending into the depths of the sea itself, where sunlight penetrates only dimly and where shadows may be abysses or leviathans. Down there in the vessel's bowels, below the water level itself, one might indeed have been within the belly of a great fossilized beast, its ropy viscera and broad mossy ribs glistening with a perpetual mouldy sheen. The smell of the river now seemed stronger: the aroma of the gravel. By and by, a flickering light emerged from the depths: the lamp of the ballast-raker.

'Hello there! I am Eldritch Batchem – you may have heard of . . . O! You surprised me!'

A rough-hewn and filthy face, made ghoulishly dysmorphic in the shadows of the lamp, had appeared in the frame of a still lower hatchway. It did not seem well disposed to any visitor, but this did not stop Eldritch Batchem venturing down the final steps into the gravel.

'What in the name of C—— are you doing below decks?' said the ballast-raker. 'Are you a ——— fool? There is no civilians permitted on board. Be gone!'

'Sir – if I may ask a simple question regarding any recent loading of ballast for a four-masted—'

'Are you ——— deaf? I said be gone! This no place for a tourist. Go – or I will make you!'

'There is no need for rudeness, sir. A crime has been committed and I am invest—'

The ballast-raker took two rapid crunching steps and

grasped the front of Eldritch Batchem's tweed jacket with a tremendous grip, drawing his face to within inches of his imminent victim's.

'I said *be gone!*'

'This is intolerable! I am an investigator . . .' said Mr Batchem, struggling for balance on the gravel while trying to prise the iron fist from his clothing. It looked rather like he was going to suffer an injury if he did not immediately heed the advice given.

Then something changed – something in the eyes of Eldritch Batchem.

What had previously been fear became something fearful. A dread calm came over him and he ceased his grappling with the other fellow for a moment . . . a moment that caused the assailant to himself pause, relax his grip, and seek the face of his 'victim', now set in an unsettling expression of dead-eyed rage.

With a strength giving lie to his proportions, Eldritch Batchem pushed with all his might and sent the ballast-raker careering into the ribs of the hull, where his head collided solidly with the timbers. He fell to his knees there, stunned, and put a hand to his profusely bleeding scull. In this other hand, he held one of his attacker's gloves, pulled off during the violent encounter.

'Perhaps that will teach you the cost of insolence!' said Eldritch Batchem, restoring his clothing and demeanour to normality.

But the injured man, his head ringing and the blood trickling through his fingers, could not take his eyes from the bare ungloved hand brushing at the tweed jacket. At first, it was confusion that made him stare. Then, the more he looked, the queasier he began to feel.

Eldritch Batchem perceived the focus of the stare and swiftly put his hand in a jacket pocket. With a dark muttering, he then made to ascend the stairs back to the light, but turned before passing through the hatchway, his eyes again assuming that dark glare.

'Tell a soul what you have seen, sir, and you will certainly regret it. That is a promise.'

THIRTEEN

It was about a year ago that a man crossing Waterloo-bridge took it into his head to hoist a loose kerbstone over the parapet into the river. Instead, it landed upon the scull of a young man standing on a ballast machine below, killing him outright. The same year, another man boasted to his fellows that he could walk the bridge's length atop the parapet. He fell and drowned. Once again, in that same year, a heavily decomposed body was found under the second arch from the Surrey side. Nobody ever discerned the identity of that unfortunate. And we need not expand further upon the death of Samuel Scott on that selfsame span: accidentally hanged before a crowd of thousands in his own show of fearlessness.

In short, it might be said to be the most notorious among all the city's great crossings. Ask any waterman plying his trade below its graceful ellipses and he will tell you: there are upwards of forty suicides annually from its lofty edge – and that does not account for the deaths upon it through accidents, the winter exposure of indigents or abandonment of infants. Is there a stretch of thoroughfare in any city in the world so blackened with ill fame as Waterloo-bridge?

Of course, it is not only death that finds associations

along that granite span. It is also the bridge of lasciviousness, infamous for its assignations in the recesses after dark, and for the torrent of common prostitutes who swarm north from Waterloo-road to the lights of Middlesex between seven and nine each evening, only to return at nine the next morning, crapulous and in disarray. It is a place where both innocence and lives are lost – a fine example of our city in miniature should one be required.

Yet during the day, it is as chaotic with traffic as any of the larger bridges. Not as busy as London-bridge, to be sure, but certainly noisy enough that Mr Williamson felt the urge to occasionally hold his hands over his ears as he ventured along the pedestrian walkway to the place where the newspapers (and Eldritch Batchem) had indicated the fatal incident had taken place.

If he looked deep in thought that morning, it was not the case of the *Aurora* that was uppermost in his mind. Indeed, he might not himself have been able to say which of the conflicting emotions in his head was the strongest. Was it the naked humiliation of being slandered in that article of *the London Monitor*? Was it the slur upon his proud record as a policeman and as a detective? Was it the accusation – whether true or not – that he had aided the escape of a felon?

Or was it the shameful and defamatory reference to his associations with prostitutes – with *that* prostitute? With Charlotte.

It was worrying enough that Eldritch Batchem – for it was surely he behind the article – knew so much about his competitors on the case. Evidently he had had them all followed or otherwise investigated in some depth. Was that the task of the curious Italian . . . ?

Mr Williamson paused suddenly, causing a number of

people to stumble, muttering, behind him on the bridge. What if it had been no coincidence that he had been distracted that night outside the Queen's Theatre? He had assumed that the incident had been purely accidental – it was, after all, her pitch. But what if the Italian and Eldritch Batchem had somehow inveigled Charlotte into serving their purpose, knowing that she would certainly catch her victim's eye – and that he would react as he did?

'Stand aside, won't yer, mate?' shouted a man brushing swiftly past Mr Williamson (who was still quite stationary in the centre of the pedestrian walkway).

He moved absently out of the flow to the stone balustrade overlooking the river and laid a hand on its cold surface. One fact in particular did not make sense to him: the episode outside the theatre had happened two days *before* any mention of the missing brig had been made. Could Eldritch Batchem really have been observing him for so long? And, if so, for what earthly reason? The questions multiplied until they questioned themselves . . .

This would not do. Mr Williamson called upon years of experience and attempted to clear his thoughts of all confusion. There was a case to be solved, and the solution to it would likely bring all other mysteries to a conclusion. Today, the death of Mr William Barton was the thing. He began to walk once again.

It seemed frankly ridiculous to assume that he would find any physical evidence there among the rolling wheels, clopping hooves and persistent footfalls of thousands, but a detective will always check before he is sure. And as he looked at the roadway of compacted dung cut into ragged ruts by carriage wheels, he knew that all trace of William Barton was forever vanished.

Behind him, a pedestrian recess stood empty – the one in which Eldritch Batchem had claimed to find an earring – and he stepped into it to be away from the pedestrians. Could it be that someone had lurked in this very space for hours, seeing the fog descend and waiting, waiting for the expected footfall of the tidewaiter? Certainly, it did not seem to be the sort of thing a lady wearing earrings would do.

He examined the walls of the recess and, as expected, found nothing indicative there. Indeed, from this vantage, the view along the bridge itself was limited: one would have had to peer out continuously to see someone coming . . . and the fog would, in any event, have made such caution quite un-necessary. Similarly, the high walls of the recess (a deterrent to suicides) made visibility of the river or city to the east dif-ficult. Anyone waiting to see or hear a signal that the victim was approaching would, in fact, have been inconvenienced by being in the recess (even if there had not been a fog).

Mr Williamson's keen brain examined the problem from all points of view. If the theory of the recess-lurker was doubtful, perhaps Benjamin's suggestion of the killer escap-ing over the side was the correct solution.

He stepped out on to the walkway once more and turned his attention instead to the stone balustrade on each side. He first moved northwards, examining each inch of the masonry for any sign, not knowing at all what he was looking for, but knowing he would recognize it when he saw it. After ten yards or so of nothing unusual, he retraced his steps and conducted the same meticulous search southwards. He did not look for long.

Three yards beyond the recess, he came upon a small peculiarity in the stone: a jagged indented hole taken out of the granite. He pressed a finger into it and noted that the lack of grime suggested it was relatively recent. On one knee now, he examined the walkway beneath the hole and confirmed what he expected to be the case: there were a few tiny chips remaining where they had fallen. No doubt the larger piece had long since been kicked away by pedestrians. In the fog and the damp, Eldritch Batchem clearly hadn't noticed it at all – or simply not given it any further thought.

Mr Williamson smiled ruefully to himself. He had been wrong because he had not considered the most unrealistic of all possible solutions.

A hole of this kind did not suggest escape at all, but arrival. Granite is an exceptionally hard stone and would not have been so scarred by having an iron slipped over it. Scratched, possibly, but not chipped. No – a grappling iron must have been tossed up from the river itself and landed at this spot with a chisel-like impact – an impact loud enough to be heard by the toll-collector in the silence of the night. Eldritch Batchem's assumption that the noise had been the razor hitting the parapet when thrown by the dying man now seemed even more ludicrous.

Mr Williamson placed both hands on the parapet and peered over to check the stonework there. What he saw caused him to smile again. There were a number of greasy scuff marks where it seemed someone had braced their shoes against the stonework to climb the final stretch before the parapet. And was that also the merest suggestion of where a tarred rope had abraded against the lip of the edge, leaving a murky line? Such marks would have been difficult to see in the pale dawn, and even more invisible with the bridge stained by rain or fog. But in the clear daylight, the marks could not be denied.

Nevertheless, it was a feat to be disbelieved by any

rational man. What manner of being would be able to toss an iron and rope thirty-five feet upwards in a dense fog and hit the balustrade? What manner of human monkey would be able to scale a rope swinging half under the great gaping arch and, furthermore, to descend, probably onto a boat moored mid-stream? The iron would then have had to be disengaged from the balustrade with an immense whip of the rope. The whole would have required a colossal feat of strength, balance and nerve – and also of determination. Why not simply cudgel the fellow as he walked along a darker street?

More and more, the murder of William Barton seemed to be a significant one. Mr Williamson took out his notebook and added what he had seen, estimating measurements and peering over the side once more to be sure of his bearings. In a moment, he would go below the bridge to do what Eldritch Batchem had not, but for now there was the toll-collector Mr Weeton to be questioned.

Having enquired at the Bridge Company offices, Mr Williamson had learned that Mr Weeton was still working the night shift, although he had put in a request to move to days. That duty was to conclude in a matter of minutes, so Mr Williamson hurried towards the Middlesex side, weaving between pedestrians that he might not miss his opportunity.

He was just in time, catching the toll-collector as he was about to leave the toll-house.

'O, I have already spoken to the fellow in the red hat,' said Mr Weeton, 'and to a gentleman from the police. I have told all I know.'

'I would be most grateful if you could spare just a few moments more to answer my questions also,' said Mr Williamson, still panting slightly from his progress across the bridge.

'Are you a newspaperman? I have been instructed by Mr Blackthorne not to speak with any—'

'My name is George Williamson. I—'

'Wait – I have heard that name . . . Are you the same fellow who worked on the Lucius Boyle case. The detective? I have read all about it.'

'I am he. I will not take more than ten minutes of your time . . .'

'O, all right – but only because you are a detective. I am a furious enthusiast of such work and read everything I can on the subject. But let us step back inside the toll-house. Timpkins will not mind, and it is a little quieter inside.'

The aforementioned Timpkins was the toll-collector just beginning his duty, and he was busy enough at the toll-gate to offer just the merest nod as the two men went inside the house to take seats by a small cast-iron stove that smelled of coal smoke. Once settled, Mr Williamson removed his hat and turned to a fresh page in his notebook.

'As I say, sir, I told everything to that Mr Batchem,' said Mr Weeton. 'I am not sure how I can help you.'

'With respect, you may have answered his questions, but you did not necessarily tell him everything you know. The questions can be as important as the answers. Let us begin with the sound you heard – it was metal on stone, is that right?'

'Indeed. I am told it was the razor hitting the parapet.'

'Is that what it sounded like to you? Would you have heard such a minor sound from some hundreds of yards away?'

'The fog plays tricks with sound, sir. It was late . . . I was afraid . . . Mr Batchem has said—'

'Hmm. If I were to take a razor and strike it against the

stone now, would it sound the same? Or was the sound more like something being dropped – something heavy like a chisel or pry bar?'

'Why . . . yes, I suppose that was more like it . . . but no such item was found. And the man's throat was cut, not his head beaten in . . .'

'Let us deal only with the evidence, not yet what it might mean. Did you hear anything else? Footsteps, shouts . . . ?'

'Nothing more . . . not until the man came out of the fog and fell at my feet.'

'Ah, yes. It seems he said nothing to you about his experience.'

'Just noises, sir. Moans . . . gargling . . . the sounds of death. No words.'

'What manner of noises?' Mr Williamson poised ready to write.

'Sorry, sir . . . what do you mean? They were the groans of a dying man.'

'A man never makes a mere noise. He makes a sound: *Ooo*, or *Aaah*, or *Urrr*. Think carefully – what manner of *sound* did the dying man make?'

'O, I see! You are thinking he was perhaps trying to make a *word* with his ruined throat. Very clever.'

'Hmm.'

'It was a sort of *Orrr*. Then it was more like . . . well, it was more like a prolonged *fffff*. I suppose that was his dying breath.'

'Perhaps. Did you notice anything strange about the man's appearance?'

'He had lost his hat out on the bridge, I suppose. And he was covered in blood.'

'Was his clothing in any disarray? More so than would be

expected from his hectic path to this toll-house? Were all of his buttons fastened? Were his garments torn at all?'

'No . . . I cannot recall anything like that . . .'

'Hmm. You are being most helpful, Mr Weeton.'

'Really? Mr Batchem seemed quite unimpressed with my account. He even asked me if I had gone through the dead man's pockets. Can you imagine?'

'Did he indeed?' Mr Williamson added the note into his book and underlined it. 'There is one more question. Eldritch Batchem claims to have found a number of items upon the bridge, notably an earring in a recess. Is such a thing common in your experience?'

'Quite so. I told Mr Batchem as much. This cupboard here is full of such things.'

'May I see?'

'Of course. We have some most interesting oddities.'

Mr Weeton took a ring of keys from a hook on the wall and unlocked the cupboard door. He looked inside, choosing among the items there, and began to select some for Mr Williamson's interest, placing them on a tabletop for viewing. Each had a small paper tag appended with string, describing when and approximately where on the bridge it had been found. Coins were in tiny envelopes marked with the same information.

'It is mostly keys, jewellery and coins, sir. Anything smaller than a sovereign we give to the orphan home, but we also get some surprises. What do you think?'

Mr Williamson stood and looked at the things on the table. There was one very fine diamond ring that must have been worth many hundreds of pounds; a piece of dark wood carved into an obscene tableau of Leda and the swan; a lethal-looking dagger with an ornamental handle in the Turkish style; a pistol with a stubby wooden grip; a moisture-curled book: *Dr Stuart's Anatomy of the Heart* . . .

'Does anybody return to claim such items?' said Mr Williamson. 'The ring alone is not something one would lose without searching the entire city.'

'Sir, I am not an educated man, but I see my share of humanity upon this span and I have learned that people are strange. I imagine that each of these items has a story all of its own – a story dark enough to warrant its loss (or at least its remaining lost) being of benefit to somebody. Do you, a detective, not wonder at such stories yourself?'

'Hmm. Stories are often lies in my experience. What is this item here?'

Mr Weeton took the object between thumb and forefinger and held it up for a clearer view. 'Ah, it is perhaps our oddest piece in the collection, sir. I am surprised you have not read about it before. Look closely and you will see what it is.'

Mr Williamson moved in to scrutinize the curled brown specimen. It might have been a piece of wood or a twist of animal gristle, but the ridged and opaquely yellow flake at its end told a different tale. 'Am I looking at a human finger?' he said.

'Indeed, sir. That's exactly what it is. See the nail there . . . the joint, and the nub of bone at the end?'

'And it was found here on the bridge?'

'All items are found items, sir. The date on the tag says it was logged a year ago. I am told that, when found, it was quite fresh and pink with life, but time has withered it into this rather sorry object. It caused a stir at the time. The Bridge Company even took out an advertisement in *the Times* . . . in fact, I believe there is a copy of it in the cupboard.'

Mr Weeteon went again to the cupboard and withdrew a

curled and faded scrap of newspaper, which he handed to Mr Williamson:

FOUND on WATERLOO-BRIDGE on Wednesday: a human (middle?) finger of indeterminate gender, measuring almost four inches from joint to tip and in a state of relatively good preservation. Return of the digit on application to the offices of the Waterloo Bridge Company (proof of loss required) . . .

'A curious item to be sure,' said Mr Weeton. 'Nobody came forward – or rather, none of the pranksters who did so were missing a finger. I often wonder, though: was it severed on the bridge? Was it dropped by a passing gull? Was it carried in a pocket? It is a delicious mystery, is it not?'

'Quite. I thank you for your time, Mr Weeton. You have been most helpful.'

'A pleasure, sir.'

Mr Williamson returned his notebook to its pocket, put on his hat, nodded a goodbye and stepped out once again into the flow of people, leaving his interrogatee with the odd impression that he had said far more than he himself knew.

Below the bridge seemed almost as busy as the span itself. Churned and furrowed by ceaseless ferries, the river slapped at muddy brickwork, sucked at timber pilings and gurgled among the dozens of natural recesses. Steam whooshed from boilers and the choking black smoke of funnels washed back and forth through the huge arches to sting the eyes of waiting passengers.

Mr Williamson looked among the crowds and saw what he was looking for: a waterman smoking a long-stemmed clay pipe at his station by the stairs. The fellow seemed an unusual specimen of his kind in that he was not haranguing passengers in a semi-threatening tone to take a trip in his wherry. Rather, he simply observed the bustle about him with a good-natured smile.

'Good day to you', said Mr Williamson to the waterman. 'I would like to ask you a few questions if you have a moment.'

The waterman, pipe still in his teeth, looked his addresser up and down. 'You are a policeman?'

'Of a sort. Were you at your station on the night of the suicide six nights ago?'

'You are fortunate, sir. I would normally not be here at that early hour, but I was returning from an evening of leisure early that morning and stepped down here to inspect the water.'

'To "inspect the water"? I am afraid I do not . . .'

'You may have heard of me, sir, for I have a certain renown along this shore. No other man has pulled as many suicides from the river as I. Twenty to this day. I find that I have an odd aptitude for seeing them where others see only a log or other flotsam. So, I came down just to have a look.'

'It was very foggy that morning was it not?'

'It was indeed. So much so that I saw nothing and made my way home. I suppose it was about the time of the death according to the accounts in the newspapers, but as you say . . . the fog was as thick as I've seen it.'

'Tell me – in your experience on the river, would it be possible for a man to stand on a boat below the arches there and throw up an iron to the parapet? Then could that man climb up, later returning the same way?'

'Ha ha! What you describe is quite fantastical!'

'But is it possible? I accept that such a feat would be difficult.'

The waterman chewed his pipe and rubbed his chin. 'Well, it certainly would be difficult. There is the tides, the darkness, the fog. I dare say there are seamen who can climb a knotted rope to that height, but throwing it is a different matter . . .'

'Hmm. You are a fellow of the river. Were you to perform the task yourself, what materials would you need?'

'A puzzle, eh? Let me see . . . well, I suppose I would use a dredger's boat: they are very stable vessels. And while I was at it, I might get myself a dredger also – those lads who haul the gravel by hand have arms of iron. If not one of those, then a whaler's harpooner; there are sometimes a handful of those about the docks. Then I would need two men to row and one to climb. Yes – that might do it: four men and the vessel.'

Mr Williamson added the information to his notebook. 'You are quite sure you saw or heard nothing on that morning?'

'Sir – it was foggy, dark, and I was drunk.'

'Very well. I thank you.'

Mr Williamson was about to ascend the stairs to the bridge when something caught his eye. Two men wearing unusual coats and hats with wide soft brims were engaged in an odd activity further along the shore. Using long hoes, they were attempting to gather some object from the river's surface.

'Toshers,' said the waterman, perceiving Mr Williamson's interest. 'Sewer-hunters – they are waiting for low tide and will enter the sewer mouths hereabouts in search of their treasure.'

Mr Williamson walked past the ferry platform to where the two men had now managed to hook their object ashore. He was about to ask them if they had seen or heard anything that night when he saw what the object was.

A long, rectangular board with scrollwork at its corners, it was badly charred all over. Still, as the 'toshers' turned it over to confirm that it was indeed the nameplate of a large vessel, some vestigial letters could be partially discerned – a blackened and fire-eroded conglomeration of vowels to momentarily pause Mr Williamson's heart:

Au - - - a

FOURTEEN

Noah Dyson had received the article in *the London Monitor* with no less consternation than had Mr Williamson. If nothing else, it meant that Benjamin's visibility about the city had been significantly increased now that people were looking out for a tall 'Cyclopean' Negro dressed in fine clothes.

Unlike Mr Williamson, however, Noah felt no humiliation. Rather, two questions plagued him: how did Eldritch Batchem come to know the things he knew? And how best could one respond to this man who used such underhand tactics to unsettle his competitors? It was an unworthy play of the sort that even Inspector Newsome would not have countenanced.

Nevertheless, an opponent reveals more than they wish when they overplay their hand, and the nature of the inadvertent intelligence contained in that article was of use to Noah. It alluded, for example, to the escape from Giltspur-street gaol that had occurred some months previously when Noah had been aiding Mr Williamson on a case. Necessarily, that event – which had ostensibly led to the latter's dismissal from the Detective Force – was known only to a very few: the warders of the gaol and some senior policemen. True, constables are notoriously indiscreet gossips, but it seemed unlikely that Sir Richard's men would have discussed it abroad, or that the gaolers would have been permitted to speak freely on the matter. Could it be that with all of his lofty 'private investigation' among wealthy lawyers and bankers, Eldritch Batchem had somehow sniffed out the rumour?

Then there was the fact of Noah's initials – perhaps the most concerning matter of all. His own neighbours did not know his real name, and his business contacts knew him only by a variety of monikers. Even among the police, only a handful had any reason to know his true identity, though that selection did, admittedly, include Inspector Newsome, who cared little for the anonymity of his one-time nemesis. Indeed, the only positive element in that otherwise worrying exposure of truth was that no mention had been made of Benjamin's name. One would assume that to know one name was to know the other, but the omission may have been pure oversight. The overall assumption seemed unavoidable: Noah – and most probably his co-investigators – was being closely followed.

A skilled pursuer might, for example, easily have stood within earshot and heard Noah's name being used by another. That they had not yet heard Ben's was of the purest coincidence. Such an explanation would also account for the connection with the cargo at Limehouse: somebody had simply followed Noah there, and thence to any number of clubs or private residences that purchased the high-quality refined opium for their own medicinal or sybaritic requirements.

If this in turn were the case, two attendant questions presented themselves. One: Noah had not visited his warehouse for some weeks past on account of waiting for a fresh shipment to arrive – in fact, since before the case of the *Aurora* was known to any of them. And two: *nobody* followed Noah Dyson without him knowing about it. A child of the city streets and of the crowd, a needfully suspicious man, and a man of constant readiness for danger, he was intuitively cautious and observant. It would take a true master, a veritable artist of pursuit, to shadow one such as Noah.

The Italian?

Had the man not invisibly followed the usually very perceptive Mr Williamson without being seen? Had he not also been audacious enough to make a lift in plain sight of the detective? Here was a man with skills not to be underestimated. Eldritch Batchem, for all of his other faults, was to be congratulated on finding and employing such a fellow. But who might he be?

Noah himself usually had the benefit of much privileged intelligence. Through the gentlemen's clubs, through politicians, and through his more dubious activities about the city, he knew much of what happened beneath the veneer of news headlines and common knowledge. He had a 'criminal's map' of the city in his mind that no cartographer would dare print (the vantage points of pickpockets, the hunting grounds of prostitutes, the rooftop routes of cracksmen) and he had a mental index of most notable beggars, hoaxers, robbers, dissimulators and receivers – but this Italian was truly an unknown specimen.

Perhaps another man, knowing what Noah Dyson knew, would have been apprehensive at venturing out onto the streets that day. Rather, it filled him with an almost childlike enthusiasm. Here, in the Italian, was a worthy adversary. Here was an opportunity to play out on the streets a more serious (and possibly more deadly) version of those innocent games he had once engaged in with his fellows when they had raced in rags about the legs of horses, not caring about the next meal until hunger told them to steal it. Here, in short, was a genuine challenge: a trial of wit, nerve and skill.

Accordingly, when he left his house by the river early that morning, it was in full preparation. The man exiting the door that day was recognizably Noah Dyson. Anyone observing the address would expect no less. In fact, the only notable difference was the black walking cane he carried on this occasion, it being his habit never to carry one.

If he took Earl-street and then Water-lane northwards rather than the more direct Bridge-street, it was no doubt to avoid the crowds (and the opportunity for an observer to hide in them). He certainly evinced no awareness that he suspected such an observer as he strolled towards Ludgate-circus, the iron ferrule of his cane tapping at the road almost as if to direct the attention of anyone watching. But then a curious thing occurred as he stepped into the bustle of that larger thoroughfare.

In a flash, he retracted the cane by means of an ingenious system of articulated hinge points, folding it into a foot length. Almost simultaneously, he shrugged off his black overcoat and rapidly turned it inside out, putting it back on as a bottle-green one. Anyone emerging into the busy street along the same route Noah had taken would have looked in vain for the fellow they had been tracking. The metronomic black cane was quite vanished and there were too many black coats to count.

As for the gentleman in the green coat and a folded cane up his sleeve, he was already aboard an omnibus heading east. Or rather, he was inside the 'bus among a half-dozen other passengers, of whom only the merest shape could be seen from outside (owing to the windows being misted by their collective breath). Though undoubtedly slower than walking among those central streets, it was nevertheless a fine conveyance for the man who would not be observed too carefully.

It was also, reflected Noah, a suitable place to gather one's thoughts, for despite the constant jerking stops and starts and the cries of the liveried 'cad' to prospective passengers, conversation is rare upon the plush cushions within. No matter that ten or twelve people sit there – each is as wilfully oblivious to his neighbour as if he were quite alone, staring fixedly at his shoes, his newspaper or the blurry outline of the buildings through misty glass. On the omnibus, only the French and the Americans speak (the former, volubly, to each other, and the latter, at volume, to everyone else).

On any other day, Noah would have engaged in his habitual pleasure of surreptitiously observing the other passengers to discern their stories, for, in their yearning anonymity, they invariably revealed more about themselves than they realized. The fellow with the canvas bag sitting opposite, for example: see how he nervously holds the bag close to his thigh as if its contents are of great value . . . or something to elicit great guilt and horror. Or the young lady who, on boarding, casts an apprehensive glance at the other passengers before sitting in straight-backed, staring discomfort until her stop. No doubt she is going to an appointment that no one should know about. But no – today, such people barely intruded on Noah's thoughts.

Foremost upon his mind was his opium store at Limehouse. The accusatory tone of the article in *the London Monitor* would certainly be enough to cause problems for him if officers of the Custom House read the piece and decided to cross-reference their records with any stock found there. And it need hardly be said that Noah had not been as assiduous as he might concerning the payment of duties on his raw opium. He had already lost a house to the machinations of a criminal; it would be too much to sacrifice his business to another.

Thus, as the passengers boarded and alighted, and the lofty buildings of the centre gave way to the warehouses and trade traffic of more riverine *locales*, Noah became more apprehensive at what he might find at his destination. An opium refinery is not especially hard to find if one knows the smell of its steaming chimneys and expects to see a preponderance of Oriental faces about the area. Nor, as the 'bus rattled on, was he ignorant of the possibility that the whole thing was an elaborate trap – that the Custom House men would be lying in wait for their merchant to arrive.

In the event, the worst of his fears was confirmed. Having approached on foot for the last half mile, cutting through muddy alleys and loitering in doorways to confound any persistent pursuer, he emerged at a street corner facing the warehouse to witness another desecration of his privacy.

The massed Chinese workforce was standing moodily outside in their white 'pyjamas' and the large wooden loading doors had been thrown open to the street. Customs men (denoted by their brass arm badges) seemed to swarm about the place, directing the burly lumpers in their employ to confiscate all that could not be accounted for – which was everything. The chimneys gave forth but the merest vapour, having evidently been smothered by the torrent of authority.

Noah's fists clenched in white-knuckled fury. The game had just changed irrevocably. What had seemed a test of investigative wit was now a matter of cold retribution. Eldritch Batchem would pay for this – not only by losing the challenge, but also by losing everything else he had to lose. Those were the rules he had established when he had the article inserted into the pages of *the London Monitor*.

Still lurking on the corner there, Noah became aware that his foreman, Hong Li, had seen him. The aged China-man, who rarely communicated anything as revelatory as a facial expression, remained as teak-faced as usual and made no sign he had seen Noah. Rather, he made the most subtle shake of the head and his eyes sought out his employer with a clear enough message: go now . . . flee while you can and we will meet again in this or another life.

Noah nodded and withdrew. He had urgent work to do.

As Noah had demonstrated those few days previously with his pursuit of the missing swan brooch, the city's receivers of stolen goods are clear enough in their categorization. The riverside ruffian – who most likely also runs a shop, a crimp-house or some other maritime business – will take whatever flotsam and pocket-smuggled contraband that dockworkers bring him, but can sell it to a greater practitioner of the trade only if he saves up his finer specimens and sells them on *en masse*.

These more professional receivers, in turn, will specialize in their trade, be it jewellery, spirits, fabrics or tobacco. They may even maintain a small storehouse or floating repository of goods that buyers can visit as they do a shop, for let us not imagine that smuggled goods are in any way rare. It is said that those materials attracting the greatest duties (silk, essences, furs and the like) account for as much as forty per cent of the goods sold *legitimately* in our respectable gas-lit emporia.

As is ever the case, though, the grandest criminals are the ones who operate in plain view and maintain all the hall-marks of esteemed respectability. While Customs investigators chase after the minor operator in a muddy alley somewhere off the Ratcliff-highway, the glittering store on Oxford-street or Regent-street sells vast quantities of goods that have come into the city without the sacrificial blessing of a duty warrant.

It was with this knowledge that Noah re-entered the city centre – still taking the greatest care to check his wake for anyone of an Italianate cast – and made his way to that grand shop on Ludgate-hill, which is known to all ladies of the metropolis as quite the premier vendor of silks, muslin and linen in all of London.

He was not at all surprised to find the place a-bustle with females of the finer sort gleefully cooing over the cool touch of the latest import from Paris or Brussels. Nor was the proprietress surprised or disappointed to see a man waiting patiently at the counter. He was, if she were fortunate, one of those who maintain a mistress and who will do whatever necessary to fulfil *her* pleasure that he might continue to enjoy his own. Her professional smile flashed accordingly into life.

'Good day to you, sir. I perceive that you are seeking the finest cloths for a special lady . . .'

'I am indeed inclined to buy some silk products,' said Noah, adopting a loftily pompous tone. 'Gloves and shawls.'

'Very good, sir. I have a wonderful selection for you to choose from . . .'

'I should say that I am minded to buy rather a large quantity.' Noah took a piece of paper from his pocket and pretended to read from it: 'Forty-three pairs of long ivory-coloured gloves, an equal number of short silk gloves in black, and one hundred silk scarves in at least three colours. I have sizes for the gloves. All must be of the very finest quality, which I have been assured you can supply.'

'Why . . . that is rather a large order. I am not sure . . .'

'I represent the Swiss National Opera, ma'am, and I am charged with procuring costumes for the entire cast of a production that will entertain the crowned heads of a number of nations. If you cannot supply me with what I need, I must go elsewhere – Paris directly if need be, though I admit I am somewhat pressed for time . . .'

'I . . . did not say we could not manage an order of such a size, sir. It is just that—'

'And I should add that I expect to receive a substantial discount for buying such quantities.'

The proprietress maintained her smile only with the greatest commercial rigour. Her eyes showed that calculations of an entirely different sort were taking place in her brain. This customer seemed genuine enough; his story had a certain air of plausibility; his clothing appeared well made; his arrogance was of the sort to be expected from one with power and money. Her decision was made. She beckoned Noah towards a door behind the counter.

'Let us adjourn to the back room, sir, where I think we can come to an agreement that will satisfy all parties.'

Noah stepped past the counter and through a door into a large storeroom in which the bulk of the shop's stock was arrayed on serried shelves lining every wall. Shipping crates marked in French (and further appended with sizes in chalk) were stacked in the centre of the space, with aisles between them so that the assistants might have quick access lest a customer suffer the indignity of delay.

'Well, it seems you have plenty of stock here,' said Noah. 'I will take this.'

'Sir – if you wish to benefit from a . . . a more competitive price, I would ask you to wait a day or so. We are expecting shortly to take an order for a very large quantity of silk items and I will make certain your needs are met.'

'But I can see many gloves here! Did I not express myself clearly upon the urgency of my need?'

'Yes, indeed, sir. But as I say, the goods we are expecting are of the very finest quality and . . . they come to us by way of . . . from a more beneficial source regarding cost . . . which naturally we pass on to our most special customers . . . men such as yourself, sir, who will not be satisfied by anything other than the very, very best French silk newly imported into the city.'

'The best, you say?'

'O yes, sir! Nothing like it! France must weep to lose such finery from its shores.'

'I see. Well, that is the quality I am seeking. When can I have it?'

'A man will come here in a day or so – it is always around this time of the month – and he will take our order. The merchandise is then delivered the very next day.'

'A man? What man? I hope there is nothing underhand here . . .'

'Certainly not, sir! He is . . . he is,' she wrinkled her nose as if in distaste, 'he is the agent of our supplier. I cannot be more specific about his arrival as he is somewhat . . . eccentric. But if you return here on Saturday I am sure we will have your order packed and ready to take away. If you are able to pay us a percentage of the price as a deposit . . .'

'Yes, yes . . . I suppose that will be all right. Saturday, you say? Well, that is rather late, but if the price compensates me for the wait . . .'

'O it will, sir. You will not find a better price in London.'

'Good, good. Then I thank you for your service.'

And so Noah was obliged to pay rather more than he would have wished by way of a deposit for goods he would never see, let alone buy. He had, however, got the information he needed and could now act upon it.

Doffing his hat to the ladies at the counter, he turned to exit the shop . . . and walked directly into a man entering at some velocity. Their eyes met. They knew each other.

'*You!*' said Inspector Newsome.

'Inspector Newsome – that is a particularly fine uniform you are wearing.'

'I should . . . I should . . . What are you doing here?'

'A little shopping. I needed some new gloves.'

'It is pure coincidence, I assume, that the missing brig *Aurora* was loaded with silk of the exact variety sold by this shop?'

'Precisely that: a coincidence. I was indeed at Eldritch Batchem's performance – as you know – but why would I be interested in locating that vessel? I have no need of the money—'

'That may change. Have you been to Limehouse recently?'

'Ah, you are referring to the article in *the Monitor*. I was most amused to read about *your* recent experience at the Continental Club, though I admit I already knew of it. Your visits to "houses of ill repute" were perhaps more of a revelation . . .'

'The author of that libel will pay, you can be certain. Are you working with George Williamson?'

'What on earth do you mean by that? I am here for gloves, as I said.'

'You cannot work with him. It is not permitted.'

'"Permitted"? Are you my keeper now?'

'I could arrest you, Mr Dyson. You are known as an escaped transportee.'

'I thought we had resolved that discussion some time ago.'

The inspector glared into Noah's pale-grey eyes and remembered the night some months past when he had retired to bed to find a dagger and a warning under his very pillow.

'Why are *you* here, Inspector? Is it also a matter of purchasing gloves?'

'It is police business and none of your concern.'

'Well, I will leave you to your business. The proprietress is most helpful.'

'If I discover that you are working with George on this case . . .'

'You will be quite helpless to do anything about it. What are you afraid of, Inspector? That you are not the investigator you believe yourself to be?'

The two men remained standing, almost chest to chest, at the door of the shop. Customers inside nervously avoided glancing at the scene, while the girls at the counter looked to each other at a loss what to do.

The situation might well have turned to violence, but at that very moment there came a boyish shout from the street outside. At first indistinct, it soon came closer: a newsboy heralding the headlines of the afternoon editions.

'*Horrible discovery at London Dock! Bodies found in vault!*'

Noah and the inspector stared at each other once again.

Then they were both suddenly out of the shop as swiftly as their legs would carry them.

FIFTEEN

The day had started much as any other at the magnificent London Dock, whose tireless labour sang to the tune of chains, hammers, boots and the coarse oaths of lumpers as they attended to the many acres of tobacco, wine and spirit warehouses. In packets, crates, bottles, bundles, bindles and chests, the produce of the entire world was there hoisted, wheeled and pushed into its duly allotted place: the hides, horn, spices, coffee, tea, rum, brandy, cork and precious perfumed essences to supply the capital of commerce with its daily desires.

In the spirit vaults, the air was dense with the cold-stone mustiness of the barrels. Great diaphanous webs of black mould swayed from the ceiling, while rats could be heard skittering invisibly among oaken ribs. At one end of that vinous nave, a team of warehousemen were re-weighing a consignment of French brandy by the dim light of Davy lamps before loading it into the iron callipers to be lifted to the wharf for shipping. Any sign of inconsistency with the original unloading warrant and there would be questions from the Custom House men.

'Wait!' called one of the men as the large Limousin

hogshead dangled ominously on the measure before him. 'This one is below weight.'

'By how much?' said another.

'By enough. Put it to one side and let us weigh the remainder.'

The suspect barrel was rolled to the wall, but the next and the next and the next – five in all – also proved to be underweight. Tense glances were exchanged – the manifest declared that the entire consignment had entered the vault at the correct weight. Somebody was going to have to face the head warehouseman.

'Let us consider this closely,' said one of the men as they all stood with folded arms around the five suspicious barrels. 'Is there any sign of a leak?'

They each took a barrel and examined its staves, hoops, head and stopper. Then they went among the frames to look for evidence of puddles. Nothing – no signs of spills.

One of the men rapped on a barrel with his hammer. 'Ho! Do you hear that?'

Each sounded their barrel, tapping the correct specimens for comparison.

'There is something in these barrels that is not only brandy,' spoke one for all.

'Let us be sure. A barrelful of fluid rolls straight,' said another.

Space was cleared and they laid one of the five hogsheads on its side. A hefty kick sent it crunching across the floor, wobbling on its axis as it went: proof enough of what they suspected.

'There is something solid inside these barrels,' said one.

'Who puts a solid thing in a barrel? Spirits and wine, yes. Grain or syrup, perhaps . . .'

'Whatever is in these five, it is not only brandy. And it is not on the manifest.'

'We must open one. Who will fetch Frederick?'

The head warehouseman, Mr Frederick, arrived with grave demeanour and checked all documentation. The merchant in question was sent for and informed that five of his barrels were underweight. He agreed that they should be opened in order that an investigation might be started. A cooper was called.

And so it was that Mr Frederick and the five warehousemen stood by, casting sidelong glances at each other as the cooper set about the head loop and quarter loop with his hammer and chisel. As he worked, brandy began to bleed from between the loosening staves. Was it just the fevered imagination of the observers, or was it perhaps a redder hue than normal?

'You might want to stand back,' said the cooper as he prepared to remove the barrel head.

The staves parted like the segments of a large wooden orange and brandy flowed freely through them, washing towards the observers and filling the vault with its heady aroma. Then the cooper fully extracted the circular head and peered inside, squinting against the powerful alcohol vapour and the dim light of the lamps.

'What is it?' asked Mr Frederick.

'I cannot be certain,' said the cooper. 'Bring a lamp, won't you.'

All gathered round with their Davy lamps to look into the dark round eye of the cask.

'My G—!' whispered Mr Frederick as the thing became clear in the light. 'Fetch a policeman. Quickly! Go!'

There was certainly some surprise when Sir Richard Mayne himself appeared at the docks with a number of constables from division A. Noah Dyson and Inspector Newsome were next to join the already gathering crowds, followed shortly afterwards by Mr Williamson, who had heard the news from a ferry full of excitable passengers heading west up the river and rushed to the scene.

By that time, all five of the barrels had been opened and tipped on their sides so that their grisly contents could be dragged out into the lamplight for inspection. It was indeed a sight to challenge the strongest of constitutions.

Five male corpses, each fully dressed in seamen's clothing, lay arrayed upon the warehouse floor. Though entirely whole in terms of limbs, their exposed flesh had been rendered spectrally white and wrinkled into premature old age by the potent effect of the strong spirit in which they had been pickled. Rather than humans, they appeared instead to be effigies moulded coarsely in ridged pork fat: lips swollen and twisted, eyes dead and milky, fingernails warped like damp wood shavings. Mercifully, the only smell was that of the sweet brandy itself.

For his part, Mr Frederick was maintaining a polite defiance under the interrogative assault of the policemen.

'Sir Richard – the unloading warrant specifies a hundred barrels of fine French brandy. They were unloaded and weighed a month ago and have been here since. I see no way that these bodies could have found their way into the barrels in the meantime. I assure you that these vaults are exceptionally secure.'

'It would seem not,' said Sir Richard, trying not to look upon the five forms before him. 'Is it possible that a cooper could have gained access at night and opened the barrels to put the bodies within?'

'It is very unlikely, sir. We have watchmen of course, and the vaults are locked at night. Even if a cooper were to gain access and do as you say, the loss of spirit would have been evident on the floor the next morning.'

'Unless he and his accomplices – whose existence is beyond question in this endeavour – collected and took away the excess spirit to hide their crime,' said Inspector Newsome, pushing his way to the front of the crowd and nodding a greeting to Sir Richard (who did not seem especially surprised to see him there).

'But . . . why?' Mr Frederick turned to his other warehousemen for support, of which there was none. 'Why would somebody go to so much trouble to put these unfortunate men in barrels? It makes no sense whatsoever.'

'And that is precisely why it is so suspicious,' said Sir Richard. He turned to the constables by his side: 'Men – these bodies are to be removed to a police surgery and examined minutely under the supervision of the Detective Force. There may be no obvious cause of death other than immersion in brandy, but I want to know precisely what killed each of them. I also want every stitch of their clothing to be examined to discover any clues to their identities.'

A familiar voice came from the crowd: Mr Williamson.

'Hmm. Might I also suggest that the ship-owner Josiah Timbs, or his master, casts an eye over these spoiled faces. Identification may thus be expedited.'

'A capital suggestion, Mr Williamson,' said Richard with the merest flash of personal acknowledgement. 'We will do just that.'

Inspector Newsome scowled. 'If these men do indeed prove to be the missing mariners of the brig *Aurora* – which I am sure we are all thinking – my suggestion is to check once again whether (and if) their wages have been collected. That way a timeline of their deaths might be reconstructed.'

'Another fine point,' conceded Sir Richard. 'It will be done.'

The name of the *Aurora* had sent a thrill of recognition

through those gathered in the vault, and now a greater murmur animated the space. Could it be true? Were these the lost souls of that bewitched vessel, washed up here on a tide of spiritous liquor? The story would be in a hundred public houses by dusk.

'Very well!' said Sir Richard, sensing that the congregation threatened to expand still further, 'let us have everyone out of the vault but myself and the constables here. This is now a scene of investigation . . . Mr Newsome, Mr Williamson – I refer to you also. This is now a matter for the Detective Force, who will no doubt soon arrive to take up the case. You must both leave.'

The crowd began reluctantly to exit the vault, looking back that they might drink in one final glance at the bodies. Among them, Noah also did his best to commit the entire scene to memory.

But even as the people left, a clamour erupted elsewhere in the dock and cries could be heard coming closer to the spirit vault. Those departing made way for a young man approaching with an expression of the greatest agitation.

'Police! Police! There is another one – another body at the Pipe!'

'What? What is this?' Sir Richard held up a hand to the onrushing youth. 'Becalm yourself, boy. Breathe, and tell us what this is about.'

'Come quick, sir. They have found a dead man in the Pipe!'

'The Pipe . . . ? I . . .'

'The Queen's Pipe, sir . . . what we call the furnace . . . won't you come quick?'

'Very well. Constables – you stay here and see that these bodies are not disturbed; I will go to secure the other scene. Lead the way, boy . . .'

And as Sir Richard (with the sundry other interested

investigators) was pursued by an ever-growing retinue up-wards and outwards towards the colossal chimney towering over London Dock, perhaps a brief illustrative interlude upon the subject of the 'Pipe' will permit them time to arrive there.

The simple fact is this: any commodity warehoused in the dock may be released only on full payment of the duties owed according to the rates of the time. Should these monies not be paid, the cargo is destroyed. Whereas the other docks see fit to bury what cannot be used, London Dock takes a more complete approach and sends it all up the 'Queen's Pipe' – so called because Her Majesty's duties have not been paid. No matter whether it is Havanah cigars, New Zealand mutton, French silk gloves, pocket watches of Germany or African ivory, all is fed to the fire. (Only tea, which has been known to set the chimney ablaze, is exempted and reserved for interment.)

As for the ashes scraped from the great conical chamber of that fiery beast, they are sold by the tonne and variously prized by a number of eager buyers. The blacksmith prizes its sifted iron nuggets as the finest and hardest metal available; the soap manufactory reckons tobacco ash to be the *ne plus ultra* of its kind; the farmer is pleased to scatter the destruc-tion of nations upon his fields; and the treasure-seeker makes sly reference to the droplets of pure silver and gold to be garnered from the grey masses. In such ways is annihilation turned to profit.

The visiter approaches, as did Sir Richard and the pursu-ing throng, through the tobacco warehouse towards a door with the royal crest and 'V.R.' marked upon it. Beyond that, one enters a space of quite furious heat, where the iron mouth of the furnace is fed and where sacks of doomed pro-duce lie all around.

The heat was not the only sensation. A distinct smell of

cooked flesh also filled the room – something indefinable whose nearest animal comparison was perhaps pork. Its origin was not difficult to detect.

Two human legs, detached at the knee joint, lay below the open iron shutter of the furnace. Each one wore a shoe, stockings and the charred remains of trousers that had partially bunched about the ankles. The rest of the body, evidently, had gone inside the furnace and now revealed itself as a charred and twisted form whose thigh bones protruded in their pinkly roasted state from the frame.

All present made the obvious deduction: the legs had cooked until so tender that the lower legs had literally dropped from the knees. A sound of vomiting came from the back of the crowd around the door.

'My G—!' said Sir Richard.

'I found 'im just like that,' said the furnace-master, standing by the huge brickwork cone. 'Came in this mornin' and there 'e was.'

'So this incident occurred overnight,' said Inspector Newsome, again at the forefront of the bustle attending the scene. 'During what hours is the furnace unmanned, and who has access to it during those hours?'

'The fire burns twenty-four hours, sir, but I needn't be 'ere for all that time,' said the furnace-master. 'I loads it up and lets it work. Durin' the night, I let it burn itself low, then starts again next day. This must of 'appened durin' that time, though quite 'ow, I 'ave no idea. I locks the door when I'm not 'ere lest someone pilfers the goods to be destroyed.'

'The door has not been forced,' said Mr Williamson from the back of the accumulated group. 'Are there duplicate keys?'

'Of course, sir,' said the furnace-master. 'The watchmen

'ave 'em, and the tobacco warehouse foreman also . . . in case the chimney starts afire.'

'Good. I require a list of all who have keys,' said Sir Richard. He indicated the legs on the floor: 'Do we know who this gentleman might be? Is he perhaps an employee of the docks? Is anybody thought to be missing?'

'It is nobody known to me,' said the furnace-master. 'As far as I can tell.'

Noah – who had thus far been maintaining an inconspicuous profile in Sir Richard's presence – whispered something to Mr Williamson, who looked at the disembodied legs and nodded his agreement.

'Hmm. Hmm. I believe I may know the identity of our unfortunate victim.'

The crowd hushed accordingly.

'You have our attention, Mr Williamson,' said Sir Richard. 'Proceed.'

'I have seen those shoes before. The chase-work on the buckles is quite distinctive, and the heel is worn slightly more on the left shoe. I noticed these points when I last saw them four days ago. At that time, they were on the feet of Mr Josiah Timbs, owner of the missing brig *Aurora*.'

This intelligence again set the audience a-buzz. The bodies in the barrels . . . the body in the furnace . . . the missing vessel. It had the makings of a delicious scandal.

'Right – I want everybody out of this room,' said Sir Richard with a determined gesture. 'Everyone back into the tobacco warehouse. This also is a crime scene. Mr Williamson and Mr Newsome – you may remain momentarily . . .'

The eager observers (Noah included) were pushed back from the furnace chamber and the door closed so that Sir Richard remained closeted with the two other gentlemen (and the semi-clothed legs mocking them from below the

'Queen's Pipe'). The men looked at each other in silence for a moment, perhaps not knowing where to begin.

'This is . . . this is quite ridiculous,' said Sir Richard. 'What on earth is happening? The bodies in the barrels and now . . . *this*. Gentlemen – I want it to end as quickly as possible. Your thoughts please – and let us not worry about revealing anything to "competitors". The reputation of the Metropolitan Police may be at stake.'

'If this *is* Timbs,' said Mr Newsome, 'I rather suspect his killers were more serious about their warning than he was. They might have killed him anywhere, and in secret. *This* is a declaration of intent: they are not to be underestimated or ignored.'

'I fear you are correct, Inspector,' said Sir Richard. 'To bring the body here and leave it thus is an outrageous act. But who are *they* and who are they communicating with? Surely they do not expect the police to cease the investigation through any such coarse terror as this?'

'Hmm. I believe the murders discovered here today are for the benefit of the police only tangentially,' said Mr Williamson. 'The bodies may have been left anywhere in London for us to find. Why the London Dock, and why in such a manner? The men in the barrels make for a particularly gruesome exhibition – one that will be told by sailors and river folk for years to come. As such, it is a fine illustration of what can happen to those who do not collaborate. Was the murder of William Barton on Waterloo-bridge a similar case, I wonder: a highly conspicuous murder where an invisible drowning would have done just as well?'

'Murder?' said Mr Newsome. 'There is no evidence that Barton—'

'On the contrary – there is more than sufficient evidence he was murdered, and very likely by somebody he knew.'

'Whom do you suspect?' said Sir Richard.

'I cannot be certain, but my findings thus far, combined with today's discoveries, can suggest nothing more than some connection with river trade and smuggling. Beyond that, I cannot offer anything more coherent.'

'Sir – if I may take custody of the bodies and examine them . . .' began Inspector Newsome.

'You may not. This is a matter for the Detective Force, as you know. They will discern whether the bodies in the barrels are the remaining crew of the *Aurora* and, if so, how they found their way into the spirit vault. Likewise, they will investigate the identity of these disembodied legs. I trust that you gentlemen will find avenues of your own to pursue.'

Mr Williamson and Mr Newsome exchanged glances.

'In the meantime,' continued Sir Richard with a stern expression, 'may I enquire about that article in *the London Monitor*? You can imagine what embarrassment it has caused me. I will not tolerate disrespect of that sort to stand, and you may be sure redress is being sought via the appropriate legal channels. Who is the writer? What have you found?'

'Eldritch Batchem,' said Mr Newsome. 'It can only be he.'

'Are you certain of that, Inspector?' said Sir Richard.

'I cannot prove it, but he seems to be its greatest beneficiary, and he is the only investigator in the piece not to be pilloried. If he did not place it, he knew of it and paid to have his name kept out.'

'Very well. Your reputation was not enhanced by it, and you know what calibre of men I want in my Detective Force. As for you, Mr Williamson, I trust that the accusations about you are out of date.'

'In fact, Noah Dyson was here today in the crowd,' said Mr Newsome with a smirk. 'I believe he whispered something to Mr Williamson.'

'I saw him, Inspector,' said Sir Richard, 'so there is no reason for you to play the over-eager pupil. In fact, I am inclined against my better judgement to consider it an unfortunate coincidence that will not be permitted to occur again.'

Mr Williamson caught the unblinking gaze of the police commissioner and returned it with an assurance sorely infected by doubt.

'Every man deserves the benefit of a second chance,' said Sir Richard. 'Even you, Inspector.'

'Sir,' began Mr Newsome, 'if I am not to investigate the scenes of these crimes, how am I to pursue the investigation with any rigour?'

'By using your ingenuity, Inspector – as any detective does on a difficult case. You will also stay within the remit of your duties with the Thames Police. Now – I must ask both of you to leave. The constables will secure this room and the men of the Detective Force will take over.'

Sir Richard opened the door and allowed the gentlemen to exit, whereupon Mr Newsome veered immediately into the tobacco warehouse and Mr Williamson made his way outside and towards the dock gates.

'George! George! Wait a moment,' came a voice from among the cargo. It was Noah, running to meet him.

Mr Williamson did not slow his pace. 'I am sorry, Noah. There is something urgent I must do. I cannot stop.'

'George – has it not occurred to you how strange it is that we were all here today? All *except* Eldritch Batchem? Where was *he*? Why did he not deign to visit this most important occurrence in the case of the *Aurora*? George – will you not stop for a moment? What is so pressing? We have much to discuss.'

'I am sorry, Noah . . . I must . . .'

And Mr Williamson strode on without looking back, leaving Noah standing both perplexed and concerned in his wake.

SIXTEEN

If Inspector Newsome seemed in a hurry as he bustled about the tobacco warehouse, it was perhaps because he saw an advantage to be exploited. The men of the Detective Force had not yet arrived to scatter accusation and to fatigue everyone with their questions, so there was a brief opportunity for untainted interrogation.

It had taken mere moments to learn from sundry labourers that both the tobacco warehouse and the spirit vault were securely locked during the hours of darkness (the furnace-master being the only one with access to the former). Indeed, the sole employees permitted to enter the stores at night were the five watchmen, whose job it was to ensure that no fire – not even a pipe or cigar – could spark into life amid so many millions of pounds worth of precious stock.

Accordingly, the fellow responsible for guarding the tobacco warehouse soon received a visit from Mr Newsome in the watchmen's private sleeping quarters. A healthy fire was burning in the kitchen grate and a broad dining table was as tidy as one might imagine in a residence inhabited by five unmarried men.

'I am grievously tired, sir,' said the gentleman in question, one Herbert Ball. 'I am accustomed to sleeping once my duty is finished, but the dock master told me the police would be along.'

'And here I am,' said Mr Newsome. 'I presume you are going to tell me you saw nothing at all last night.'

'That is right. There was nothing of which to be suspicious.'

'Describe your rounds to me – in detail if you please.'

'Well, I have my supper here in the watchmen's residence, then I take my lamp and I take a stroll about the wharfs to look for smoke – the sailors are terrible ones with their pipes . . .'

'Sailors reside on board their vessels, is that right?'

'Only some of them, sir – usually the older ones. The younger men stay in the city. None is allowed to smoke inside the dock.'

'Fine. Proceed.'

'After my general rounds, I enter the tobacco warehouse and walk about each floor looking for any flame or sign of crime, and I have never seen anything in all my time here, sir. Thereafter, I come back to the residence for a cup of tea and then start all over again around fifteen minutes later. The other men each patrol a different warehouse: spirits, wines and the rest.'

'I see. So there are five of you continuously walking about the dock at night.'

'That is right, sir. It is most secure.'

'And I suppose it never occurs that you five watchmen time your rounds so that you might meet back here together for your tea, leaving the entire dock momentarily open for dubious activity? I observe five cups together there at the table . . . and also a deck of playing cards dealt out into five hands . . .'

'I . . . the rounds are coordinated . . . there are always—'

'Mr Ball – I am not interested in the rules; only the reality interests me. You are not facing any prosecution. Simply confirm if my assumption is correct.'

Mr Ball nodded glumly, his eyes upon the floor.

'There seems to be no sign of damage to the door of the Queen's Pipe. How might that be explained?'

'I cannot explain it, sir. The furnace-master has a key; the watchmen all have keys; the warehouse foreman has one – but none would admit a stranger in the night. We would surely lose our position for doing so.'

'I fear *somebody* will find himself thus inconvenienced. In summary, it seems you are telling me that the tobacco warehouse and the furnace were left unobserved for a period perhaps between thirty minutes and one hour, depending on the duration of your route around the dock. Is that correct?'

'Well . . . it is quite common . . .'

'Is that correct?'

'Yes, sir . . . or rather . . . in fact, there may be one *other* man who saw something.'

'Who? Somebody else who patrols the dock? Another watchman?'

'Not exactly, sir. He is . . . well, he is not officially tasked with doing a round, but I suppose he is the one man who might be anywhere in the dock during the night hours. He is allowed access to every area, above and below ground.'

'Who is this man? I need to speak to him.'

Mr Ball's face underwent a curious transition from amusement to doubt and then distaste.

'Well?' said Mr Newsome. 'I do not have time to wait upon your answer. Who is he and where do I find him?'

'He is called Baudrons: the cat master. You might find

him in the low building between the south-west corner of the main dock and the basin.'

'The *cat master?*'

'I will not attempt to describe him, sir. Better that you go and see for yourself.'

'I will do that. Thank you for your time, Mr Ball. And may I suggest taking more responsibility over your work in future.'

'Yes, sir. What about the other watchmen? Will you not question them also?'

'Other policemen will be along shortly to conduct that task. I suggest you make some coffee in preparation for their visit. In the meantime, I bid you good day . . .'

And as Mr Newsome ventured through the dock to locate the man known only as Baudrons, his questions to dock workers about the fellow were met with either utter ignorance of a 'cat master' or a smirking oddness that made the inspector increasingly curious. Directed finally to a rather dilapidated wooden building with grimy windows, he rapped on a weather-worn door using a knocker in the likeness of a cat's face.

'Mr Baudrons?' he called. 'It is the Thames Police. I have some few questions for you. May I enter?'

No sound came from within.

Mr Newsome turned the handle and pushed the door. It was not locked, so he entered.

An unspeakable smell assailed his nostrils the moment he stepped inside: a sharp compost of ammonia, stale fish and some unidentifiable feral scent that evoked damp hair or the smell of the gallery at a low theatre. There was no light except from the filth-encrusted windows and he was forced to shuffle tentatively down a corridor with one hand against the wall.

'Mr Baudrons? I found the door was unlocked . . . I am Inspector Newsome of the Thames Police. Are you here?'

Still no response from inside the building.

The smell became stronger, catching at his throat and causing his eyes to water as he ventured nearer to a dark room at the corridor's end. He tried to breathe more through his mouth and, as his eyes became more accustomed to the dimness, he saw that dozens of cats were silently pacing the floor around him.

A curious sound seemed to emanate from a room ahead:

'Heeeere.'

Mr Newsome made his way through the prowling cats and came to a room that was in almost total darkness. Only the flames from the grate gave out a flickering illumination that showed perhaps ten more cats lying before it in various states of languorous prostration. The smell here was at its most powerful, inflected with the boiled-meat odour of whatever was simmering in a tin pot above the fire.

'Heeeere.'

Mr Newsome looked for the source of the sound but the room seemed not to be inhabited by any sentient being. Instead, there were more cats: cats peering back at him from shelves; cats populating a sagging old sofa; cats wheedling about his ankles; cats seemingly spilling from every surface. Tails twitched into question marks and whiskers quivered as small noses investigated their investigator. From somewhere in the building came the warbling cry of a rutting female.

'Heeeere: on the ssofa.'

Mr Newsome stared where bidden and saw a human arm rise from a writhing multiplicitous pelt of dormant felines. Lying at full length, the man was all but covered with the animals, his heavily bearded face emerging from the fur as an incongruously human element. In the shadows, it was not clear whether the sable mass atop his head was his hair or yet another slumbering cat.

'I am seeking Mr Baudrons. I presume you are he.'

'They call me sso. Won't you ssit?' The arm indicated a straight-backed wooden chair by the sofa.

Mr Newsome pulled the chair closer to the reclining form, wondering what manner of deformity or affliction caused the fellow to hiss so. In the half-light, the man's features were limited to hair and eyes. As he sat, a cat jumped up onto his legs with a warble and he brushed it off with an irritable backhanded swipe.

'Sshow ssome resspect for my ssoldierz, won't you?'

'I am not fond of cats, sir. Nor dogs, if pressed on the matter. I like animals only inasmuch as they feed me.'

'If you would sspeak with me, you will resspect Jeremiah'z mood.'

Baudrons appeared to nod assent to the cat named Jeremiah, which then ventured another leap onto the visiter's lap and began to paw at his trousers preparatory to settling for a nap. Mr Newsome pursed his lips and resisted the urge to swiftly open his legs. Meanwhile, another be-whiskered specimen viewed him suspiciously from the nearby table edge.

'Mr Baudrons – there was an incident last night at the Queen's Pipe and I have been informed that you are often on patrol about the dock at night. Exactly what is the nature of your role as "cat master"?'

'Ratz!'

At this word, a palpable shiver of awareness went through the room, ears twitching and drooping eyes flickering open for an instant lest the common enemy skitter audaciously across the boards.

'You are a rat-catcher? Well, I suppose every dock must have one, but—'

'Not I – my troopz! I feed them; I care for them; I train them to combat their foe: the R-A-T. They are the workerz; I merely esscort them about the vaultz and sstoreroomz that I might collect the long-tailed cadaverz my ssoldierz leave behind. Admittedly, I do alsso catch live onez for the fightss.'

'I see. And in your nocturnal duty last night, did you see or hear anything unusual at the tobacco warehouse? I am sure you have heard about the discovery there.'

'A terrible buzinesss. It waz Jethro alerted me to the horror.'

'Jethro? Who is Jethro?'

'He ssitz to your left – on the table there.'

Mr Newsome turned to look at the cat named Jethro: a battle-scarred ginger tom with a leonine head, gnawed ears, one empty eye socket and a single yellow fang protruding from a mouth set in baleful disapproval. Policeman and tom exchanged a stare of mutual distrust.

'Old Jethro is my finesst ratter. He will take on the big-gunz – almosst az big az himsself ssometimez. Quite fearlesss iz Jethro. He called to me at the Pipe: called me to ssee.'

'He . . . *called* you?'

'O yess – all of the ssoldierz will call me when they make a kill or find ssomething of note. Izn't that right, Jethro?'

Jethro gave a dry creak of a meow to his master, evidently in the affirmative.

'In thiss casse, it waz the body – or rather the legz. I believe Jethro had a little lick at the sstumpz – he likess his meat well done.'

'So – let me understand this: you found the body during the night but reported it to nobody? You allowed your cats to desecrate the remains and returned here leaving the outrage to be found by others?'

'Rodentz are my buzinesss, ssir – not dead bodiez.'

'I see. Did you – or perhaps Jethro – hear or see anything thereabouts that made you suspicious? A strange sound? A strange smell?'

'Well, now you mention it, ssir, the catz were ssomewhat odd lasst night: more tentative than uzual. They sstayed closser to me than is their habit. Perhaps it waz the ssmell.'

'The smell of the burning body?'

'No, ssir – the ssmell of the ssewerz. It waz quite powerful lasst night.'

'Really? Is it common that you can smell the sewers here within the dock?'

'Not common, no. Ssometimez in the fog . . . ssometimez if the wind iz from the easst. On my honour, I have never ssmelled it az bad az lasst night.'

'Are you sure it was the sewers? Might not it have been, for example, a man who had the smell of drains about him?'

'That iz posssible, but my catz fear no man and they were unuzually sskittish.'

'Is it conceivable that there was a man, or men, inside the warehouse at the same time as you and your cats?'

'Doubtful, ssir. What man do you know who iz sstealthier than a cat?'

Mr Newsome pondered what he was hearing and looked once again around the malodorous room that seemed to undulate with silent fur. Fiery eyes blinked back at him and countless nostrils explored his scent. A quick glance to his left showed him that Jethro was evidently still unimpressed.

'Mr Baudrons – you are clearly something of an authority

on cats. Do you know anything about the larger variety: tigers, jaguars and the like?'

'One cat iz much like another. Ssome are larger. Were Jethro az big az a lion, I dare ssay he would be a veritable monsster.'

'No doubt. Some say that there may be such animals loose in the city – escapees from menageries or the docks. What do you make of that?'

'It would not ssurprize me a jot, ssir. There are ssigns. I have lost catz to the ssewerz. They go in there out of curiossity, az catz will do, and never return – or return injured. If you don't believe me, witnesss Judith. Judith? Where are you, girl?'

A throaty trill came from near the fire and a creature roused itself from the hearth to approach the cat-ridden sofa. If its gait was curiously lop-sided, closer inspection showed its rear right leg and tail to be entirely absent.

'Sshe went down the ssewerz along Wapping and came out like that. I thought sshe would die, but the dock ssurgeon ssaved her. I have retired her now.'

'Am I right in thinking that no rat could take a leg like that?'

'No rat that I ever knew of, ssir.'

'Do you know that certain mudlarks believe there to be a monster that emerges from the sewers?'

'I may have heard az much.'

'Mr Baudrons – I would like to show you something.' Mr Newsome took the tooth out of his breast pocket and held it up in the firelight that the cat master might see it.

Jethro smelled it first, however, and let forth a terrifying hiss, his back arching and his hair standing up in a quite alarming manner. The flames shone in his single eye and Mr Newsome made to move away for his own safety.

'Calm down, Jethro!' said Baudrons, pulling himself into a sitting position.

Cats tumbled from him amid much protestation and his fuller form became more visible: a man no more than five feet tall and with a dark beard that extended to his breast. A number of his teeth also seemed to be missing. He reached out a grubby hand to take the tooth from Mr Newsome.

'Interessting. It doz indeed sseem to be a feline tooth. Big one, too.'

'Could an animal of that size survive alone in the city? Mr Baudrons? In the sewers perhaps?'

'There are ratz a-plenty in the ssewerz . . . the occazional tosher, perhaps . . . sslopz from the sslaughterhouzez – aye, there iz no doubt ssusstenance enough. Sstill, I would be ssurprized if ssuch a beasst could lasst without a man to take care of it.'

'Intriguing.' Mr Newsome put the tooth back in his pocket. 'There is one final thing. We have not discussed the bodies in the spirit vaults. I believe that men may have entered it unofficially at some time in the last fortnight. Have you seen or heard, or smelled, anything untoward in your duties during that period?'

'In truth, I have not. I am but one man and fifty catz; I cannot be everywhere, even if my ssoldierz can be. In fact, I rather ssusspect that my job and yourz have more than a few ssimlaritiez in that resspect.'

'Really.'

'Why, yes: we sseek a foe by sstealth. We look for cluez to his exisstenz and venture into his lairz that we may know hiz wayz. We musst almosst become like him, don't you think?'

'If you say so.'

'I do, ssir. Indeed, I ssee that you purssue an enemy: a

clever foe who, like the R-A-T, is a masster of his art. He lurkz; he watchez; he sstrikess when the hour of ssilence is upon the world – in darknesss.'

'And how would you, with your particular wisdom, recommend that I catch this foe?'

'In the same way I do, ssir: with a higher intelligence, by lying in wait where your enemy will be, by luring him, by making him confident. A big rat will kill a cat, but the cat who knowz hiz foe always triumphz. Look at Jethro there: a proud ssoldier!'

Tomcat and detective again shared a glance of mutual distrust.

'I see. Well, I thank you, Mr Baudrons. That has been most edifying.'

Preparatory to standing, Mr Newsome opened his legs swiftly and watched with barely disguised satisfaction as the dozing Jeremiah started awake and dropped to the floor.

'You are unkind, ssir,' said the cat master with a disapproving tone.

The inspector was about to offer a riposte when a spray of reeking urine spattered against his left shoulder. He turned to see Jethro strolling slowly away with a one-eyed parting glare, his final comment delivered.

Outside in the stark daylight, Mr Newsome breathed the relatively pure air of the dock and dabbed disgustedly at his coat with a handkerchief. He could not remember having visited such an unpleasant place as part of an investigation (though he would very shortly change his opinion on that point).

The case of the *Aurora* – initially something of a minor curiosity – was becoming odder with every step. By this stage, he would normally expect a pattern to be emerging:

the merest glimpse of a trail to be followed, but a glimpse all the same. Here, the detective was presented only with a clutch of disjointed pieces. Indeed, it was almost as if clues were being left wilfully to confuse an investigator.

There was the tooth, of course, which might or might not have bearing on the body of the first mate dragged from the river. Certainly nothing else about the corpse offered any further aid as to the circumstances of his death. Had he died at the same time as his fellows who later found themselves sealed up in barrels?

And what of those bodies in barrels? There seemed little doubt that they would be revealed as the missing mariners of the *Aurora* – those who had remained after the tidewaiter was taken on board. But why the risk, the ingenuity and the sheer horror of entombing them thus when their discovery was certain? If such conspicuous shock was the aim, it had most likely succeeded – but to what end and with what audience in mind? Was it a warning? Was it a perverse expression of malice? Or was it a threat made real?

On the latter point, at least the death of Josiah Timbs (whose shoes were indeed quite suggestive of identity) might be linked to the letter he had been sent. What had it said? *Take your insurance and be content. If you do not heed this warning, you will be sorry.* It had clearly been no idle threat, but again: why the public horror, the stealthy illegality of entering the dock at night, the outrageous *theatricality* of it all?

Eldritch Batchem – the man's name could not be kept separate from the events. His very absence from the dock that day was perhaps the most suspicious fact of all – this man who seemed to live upon the stage and the page of popular interest. If ever there was a case to truly set the man's name down in investigative lore, this would be the one.

Then there was the most curious, and perhaps the most significant puzzle of all: the noisome little man who had leapt from the police galley two days previously. Why had he been watching Mr Newsome, and on whose behalf? Why had he chosen the cold and filthy embrace of the Thames rather than a gaol cell? And how did one explain the sewer smell described by Baudrons if indeed the little man had drowned (as he surely must have with the irons about his wrists).

As for Mr Williamson, he was obviously pursuing the case with vigour – and contrary to the document he had signed in Sir Richard's office if Noah's constant presence was to be correctly understood. Evidently they had already investigated the Waterloo-bridge incident and the receivers of illicit silk merchandise. What was next? In his previous role, Mr Newsome would have had them followed, but now he was handcuffed by the loathsome uniform of the Thames Police.

And, again, he cursed his inability to follow first hand the investigation at the tobacco warehouse and the spirit vault. His erstwhile colleagues at the Detective Force were good men, but they lacked his tenacity, his fire, his latitude in interpreting the letter of the law.

Amid such a chaos of clues, there seemed to be only one common strand, one clear course of action. And it lay in the sewers.

SEVENTEEN

The extent of the public hunger in those following days for details of the London Dock murders can hardly be conceived. In the lesser journals and street scandal sheets, hastily sketched images of the spirit-blanched barrel corpses and the half-baked legs of Josiah Timbs (who had indeed been proved to be the corpse) had people crowding around the street patterers to pay their penny for a twin tale of terror. Even in the better newspapers, each detail was sought and discussed with a degree of attention more often reserved for the coronation or death of a monarch. None, it seemed, could resist the delicious horror and the commercial significance of the deaths, which together contributed the ingredients of a perfect story.

Indeed, as an iron rod upon a church spire attracts the bolt from the aether and channels it to the earth with crackling fury, so the *Aurora* case became the new focus of the current investigative mania. Everybody, it seemed, in every club and on every omnibus, had thoughts upon the matter and discussed them at length. Constables, meanwhile – more often figures of derision or distrust – quite revelled in their new attractiveness to a population positively galvanized to know more.

It was, in short, a situation highly fortuitous for a man of my talents. I could barely produce enough articles, opinions and quasi-fictitious eye-witness accounts from my cell at Horsemonger-lane, and each day saw an almost constant parade of printers' boys to and from my small table. All the while, news came to me from these canny lads and from the visiters of other debtors, who were quite giddy with the novelty of the latest great murders.

'Have you heard?' said young Charles, that garrulous demi-relative to our worn tailor Burley. 'Have you heard about the shocking murders at London Dock?'

'O yes,' said Burley, himself seeing only the benefits of a fatal immersion in brandy.

And as I wrote nearer to my release from debt, the *dramatis personae* of the notable case itself were engaged in various activities across our great city . . .

John Cullen was grievously tired. For the last few mornings, and according to his own suggestion at Mr Williamson's house, he had been attending the crush of hopeless humanity that gathered before the London Dock at seven-thirty each day that they might be permitted to work themselves into exhaustion for the price of a few more days' reprieve from hunger.

As a big man, he was able to push his way to the front of the crowd at the gates and had been fortunate enough to be chosen each day by the calling foreman (who, in truth, required many more men due to the persistent north-easterlies). At least, Mr Cullen was 'fortunate' if that word described the opportunity to blister one's feet in the crane wheel, risk one's fingers in the winches or strain one's back moving cargo upon the wheeled trucks. He had so far ventured his hand at all such endeavours, and liked none.

He had, however, been offered the chance to associate with all manner of lumpers, balers, hoisters, packers, whippers, shovellers, warehousemen, lockers and general seamen in his activities about the dock. And his initial stilted attempts to glean information had become, with regular practice, the occasional artful expletive and some acquired riverine idiom, a relatively effective interrogation technique. The tough working men of the docks may have been frugal with their words, but a phrase here or a hint there was enough for the investigator to catch a scent.

On that particular day, he could be found inside the sixteen-foot treadwheel with five others, working the ropes that powered the cranes that hoisted the bales from holds and swung them into the warehouses. The noise of footfalls and the grinding axle was constant, but the men liked to talk as they completed their halting thirty miles a day.

''Ow long yer been dockin', mate?' said Mr Cullen (in his improvised argot) to the fellow walking to his left.

'O, for a couple of years. I am a watchmaker by vocation, but . . .'

'Aye – I knows 'ow it is. Times is 'ard. Yer 'ave to do what yer can to bring in the pennies.'

'That's certainly the case, Mr . . . ?'

'Call me John, mate. Look 'ere – I've heard talk that there's ways to make a bit extra. Some of the old 'ands say there's extra unloadin' to be done, "unofficial" like. Yer 'eard about that?'

'Well, I . . .'

'We're all mates here, ain't we? If there's a shillin' to be made on the sly, I'm not particular about who's payin'.'

'I have not done it myself . . . but I have heard other men say that some vessels are unloaded further after leaving the dock. They take some lumpers with them. That is what I have heard . . .'

'Aye, *that's* the work I'm after. Enough of this ——— walkin' in circles, says I!'

The six men trudged on, boots resounding, all of them gripping the rough rope supports for balance. Around the dock, other treadwheels ground away at their own labour for hour upon hour. Then finally came the shout to halt for a break. Mugs of beer were passed hurriedly through the struts so the walkers could refresh themselves before turning to walk in the other direction.

'You should talk to Rigby, the foreman of the eastern wharfs,' muttered the man to Mr Cullen's left, wiping the drink from his lips with the back of a hand. 'He sometimes has extra work.'

'Is that right, mate?' replied Mr Cullen in a similarly con-spiratorial undertone. 'I'll see about it when I get out of this ——— wheel. My thanks to yer.'

Benjamin's expression as he sipped his coffee was one of intermingled disgust and incredulity. Before the large plate-glass window of that Ludgate-hill coffee house, an itinerant 'Negro band' was going about its performance with the absurd gusto of their kind. Replete with coarsely blackened faces, exaggerated woolly wigs and tattered straw hats, the five-man *troupe* jigged spasmodically and sang travesties of American slave songs to the unfaithful tune of a lone guitar – all quite oblivious to the genuine specimen of ebony humanity observing from the window behind them.

He was dressed, as ever, in the manner befitting a gentle-man about town: a fine dark suit, well-made boots, and his silk top hat worn at a quirky angle. Indeed, he seemed even more resplendent than usual, perhaps as a sign of defiance against the attempts of that article in *the London Monitor* to cow him. One-eyed he may have been; half-strangled he may have appeared; tongueless and silent though he was, a mere journalistic slur was not enough to keep him at home.

And as Benjamin watched the mock Negros bring shame to their true race, one of them – perhaps sensing the gaze of ageless accusation upon them – turned and saw his dark audience. His song dried in his mouth. His feet ceased their idiot jig. He elbowed his neighbour to turn. The others also stumbled to a pause. Then all five stood transfixed: preposterous of garb, risible in endeavour, and diminished in dignity.

One ventured to raise a smile and a wave of 'brotherhood', but abandoned the gesture in the face of its piercing monocular response. In a moment, they were gone.

Benjamin returned his gaze to the silk emporium directly opposite: the reason for his continued tenancy at the coffeehouse window. Noah had earlier recounted the details of his encounter at the shop and made clear the task: keep a lively eye for anything suspicious, anything out of the ordinary. At some point in the day, an agent of the smugglers was likely to arrive (provided Inspector Newsome had not since returned to reveal the truth about that spurious representative of the Swiss National Opera). As to the possible appearance of that agent, there was but a single tenuous clue: the woman in the shop had referred to him as 'somewhat eccentric' and had wrinkled her nose on thinking of him. It was barely suggestive, but perhaps it would be enough.

Benjamin ordered another coffee and leafed through his newspapers once again for any articles he may have missed. The customers entering the silk emporium during the morning had been entirely conventional: well-presented ladies with their mothers, gentlemen of a certain age purchasing for women not their wives, sundry tradesmen . . . but nobody who appeared to be associated with smuggled silk – nobody who appeared conspicuously cautious, watchful or sly. By noon, he had begun to think it a quite futile task.

Then, as the clock struck one and the endless coffee had finally become gall in his mouth, there was a man in the street who looked like he might very well wrinkle a nose or two. A short fellow, with a boy's face, no hat, and clothes that seemed never to have been washed was looking artlessly about him as he approached the shop and loitered at the entrance to the rancid alley alongside it. Here was no *connoisseur* of fine silk. The odd little chap gave a final appraisal of the street and then disappeared quickly into the alley.

Benjamin readied himself.

And within minutes, the pestilent man re-emerged into the flow of pedestrians to set off eastwards, appearing not to notice the tall Negro walking some dozen yards behind him.

Noah Dyson was also out among the crowds, reflecting that, despite the maddening clatter of the carts, the pungent dung, the unending bustle of the faceless multitudes and the discordant hawker's chorus, he was more at home here – a nameless, street-swallowed stranger – than he had been anywhere in the world. Here was his childhood playground, his school, his stage, his home.

At the same time, however, the city was as much foe as friend. Eyes were everywhere and a man might be observed from a thousand places as he walked. Accordingly, Noah was again attired in his ingenious reversible coat and carried a discreet palm-sized mirror so that, by means of innocuous gestures, he could glance behind him any time he felt an observing presence.

Among the numerous other things to ponder as he strolled – Mr Williamson's increasing oddness among them – foremost in Noah's mind was Eldritch Batchem. The man's temporary absence from the investigation, and particularly from the London Dock two days previously was highly suspicious. Could it be that the death of the ship-owner Josiah Timbs and the concomitant loss of reward had diminished the investigator's enthusiasm? Whatever the man's activities, the repercussions from his article in *the London Monitor* could not be forgiven. Something decisive had to be done about the meddling amateur – at the very least by discovering more about him.

Noah had so far discovered that his quarry had refined tastes. Eldritch Batchem customarily ate at the Albion on Aldersgate; he drank porter at the Cock in Fleet-street, and he took his coffee and cigars at the Divan on the Strand (where he was known as a keen chess player, though an obstreperous loser). It had been at the latter address that a corruptible secretary had informed Noah of the weekly delivery of fine Havanahs to a certain 'E.B.' resident at Mivart's Hotel on Brook-street.

Of the many hotels in London, this was perhaps the most fitting abode for 'E.B.'. Temporary home to deposed princes, disgraced lords, ladies travelling incognito and diplomats engaged in political duplicity, Mivart's was quite accustomed to the discretion born of secrecy. Here, a man was whoever his calling card proclaimed him to be, and more convincingly so if it featured a crest. But where money buys silence, it might also buy favours when one knows the right porter, cook or chambermaid.

Thus, not ten minutes later, Noah was dropping a sovereign into the palm of a lad dressed in the hotel's livery. The grinning fellow reciprocated with a wink and a key drawn ceremoniously from his brocaded breast pocket.

'Number twenty-four, sir. I must have the key back in one hour sharp or the manager'll have my guts. The room's to be cleaned at twelve sharp.'

'One hour will be quite enough,' said Noah. 'Are you quite sure he will not return?'

'He's only just left, sir. Won't be back before supper. Never is – feller of habit is Mr B. For an extra shilling, I'll send a girl up to warn you if he does, though.'

Noah could not help but smile at the acquisitive skill of the lad, remembering his own days as a wit-driven scamp on the city's street corners. He handed over the coin and made his way upstairs along silent corridors to the *sanctum sanctorum* of door twenty-four.

At first glance, the interior appeared already to have been cleaned – or, at least, to have been unoccupied for some time. The bed was made, the curtains were tied back, all drawers and cabinet doors were closed. There was no sign of the man's clothing. Only a faint smell of cigars suggested any trace of an inhabitant.

Noah went first to the large mahogany wardrobe and opened its twin doors to reveal contents that surprised even him. Six identical tweed suits hung on the hooks within, accompanied by six identical soft russet caps arranged with seeming eighth-of-an-inch precision on the central shelves. None of the pockets held anything more than lint or the tiniest flakes of tobacco. In the drawers, six sets of black gentlemen's undergarments and six folded shirts were similarly laid out with geometric exactitude. As Noah bent closer in wonderment, he saw where faint pencil lines had been etched in the baseboard to direct the specific lie of each stocking.

Caught now between amusement and growing unease, he next addressed the bedside cabinets. Here also, there was no obvious sign of use – no used water glass, no cigar ash, no hair strands or marks. But positioned quite centrally inside one drawer, Noah discovered a slim, leather-bound ledger that retained its aromatic new-hide scent.

He sat on the bed and opened the book on his thigh, seeing immediately that it was a *collage* work of newspaper clippings (each pasted meticulously in date order) pertaining to Eldritch Batchem's life as an investigator. Assorted head-lines told their own story:

DISMEMBERED INFANT DISCOVERED
ON BLACKFRIARS BRIDGE

PRIVATE DETECTIVE CLAIMS:
'I KNOW THE SOLUTION'

GENTLEMAN DETECTIVE SOLVES
BLACKFRIARS CASE

DOVER – FUGITIVE CHILD & CO CLERK
CAPTURED

THEFT FROM BUCKINGHAM PALACE
MR BATCHEM INVESTIGATES
THE GREEN DRAWING ROOM

WATERLOO-BRIDGE DEATH WAS
SUICIDE SAYS BRIDGE COMPANY

Noah checked the dates: six months from start to finish. Before that grisly case on Blackfriars-bridge, Eldritch Batchem might not have existed at all. Here, between the boards of this ledger and within the few pieces of furniture of this anonymous hotel room were the materials for a character in a story rather than for a living, breathing man. Had there been other stories: other hotels, other suits, other ledgers, other names and other lives for this curious fellow?

Already certain he would find more mere stage properties, he nevertheless made a cursory examination of the bathroom and found scissors to trim the beard, a razor to define its edges, a hairbrush to *finesse* the russet cap's perch, a pair of tweezers for . . . for what? To control each individual hair? No other scents or treatments or personalizing items presented themselves.

Returning to the bedroom, Noah sat on the edge of the bed and looked around for some further hint of the inner man, for the soul of Eldritch Batchem – but there was only absence. The roar of the metropolis sounded at the window-panes. The sky beyond was a swirling grey *palette* of smoke.

What had Noah hoped to find? Had not his experience taught him that there were few easy solutions, and still fewer happy ones? Certainly, there were those who might, with some legitimacy, observe *his* life in similar terms. The false names, the disguises, the long absences, the past that did not bear too great a scrutiny – such are the characteristics of those suckled at the cold and sooty breast of mother London.

Mr Cullen walked with weary legs towards the eastern wharfs of London Dock. It was now four o'clock and the exodus of working men was flowing towards the gates, their faces drawn, their limbs heavy, their stomachs empty, and their clothes be-smirched with sugar, flour, tobacco, pitch and sweat.

As anticipated, the foreman he sought was not difficult to locate. His sleeves were rolled to the elbow and his formid-able forearms were a veritable canvas for the tattooist's art. As he lifted and pulled, those tendon-rigged muscles ani-mated sinuous serpents, uncoiling ropes, storm-lashed seas and ladies in states of unembarrassed *déshabillé*.

'Mr Rigby, sir?' ventured Mr Cullen.

''Pends who wants him, don't it?' Mr Rigby did not look up from the roped bale occupying him.

'I'm a day casual, sir. I was told I might ask you about earnin' an extra shillin'.'

'Told by 'oo?'

'Some feller in the treadwheel . . . don't know 'is name . . . don't mind about no names. It's only extra shillin's I'm after. Was I directed to the wrong man, sir?'

'What do you expect to be doin' for your shillin'?'

'Anythin' you like, sir. I'm strong. I'm good with the tackle an' the trucks.'

'Know your way 'bout the river, do you? Know your brig from your bark?'

'I'm no seaman. I lift and I carry; I ask no more than for that.'

'You certainly look like a sturdy one . . .'

'I have lifted whole barrels alone, sir.'

''Ave yer? Well, there might be an unloadin' job at Wappin'. Wait about the gates a while as the men go 'ome. I'll send a man for you before dark if we needs an extra lumper.'

'Aye, sir.'

Mr Cullen exited the docks as bidden and availed himself

of some steaming pea soup from the vendors there. He might have enjoyed the repast better, however, if the air about the gates had not been polluted so by a remarkably malodorous little man who insisted on loitering thereabouts . . .

Benjamin followed the dishevelled little fellow only a few yards to the east before he turned south towards Water-lane. Even at a distance, the odour of the man was highly offensive – a compost of drains, river water and something more unspeakable still that seemed to emanate in all directions and cause people in the street to react with disgust. The fellow himself appeared neither to notice nor care, walking doggedly onwards to Earl-street.

Observing from a careful distance, Benjamin found himself becoming increasingly alert. Though there was no obvious pursuer, he had the oddest sense of being observed. And surely the direction also could be no coincidence: inevitably towards his and Noah's own abode. Was it imagination, or did the reeking man actually cast a glance sideways as he passed the door of the very house?

He continued on, however, down to the stairs below Blackfriars-bridge where he was fortunate enough (or was it planned thus?) to board a ferry about to depart for Greenwich. Benjamin followed, glad of the crowds, and took a seat towards the rear where he could watch all comings and goings. If the little man knew of his dusky shadow, he showed no concern, electing instead to stand at the rail radiating his odious stench.

Still, there persisted in Benjamin the curious sense of being watched. With his startling appearance, he was quite accustomed to the stares of children and the occasional gasp from ladies, but this was different: a sustained invisible gaze that seemed to have begun almost as soon as he had exited the coffee house on Ludgate-hill.

He scrutinized the passengers in vain for an observer, but nothing seemed odd or misplaced – nothing, that is, but the absence of oddness where its presence was felt. Dusk was approaching, and with it a sense of foreboding that told him to end the pursuit. The route past his home had been strange enough, but allied with this feeling of ambiguous malice there seemed sufficient reason to disembark at the very next stop.

Only Noah's sense of urgency prevented Benjamin from doing so. Cautious by nature, he nevertheless recognized that his intuition of danger added credibility to what had been only assumption. Whatever the little man's connection to the silk emporium, it seemed certain to lead somewhere secret, somewhere illicit – somewhere, indeed, where the trusty Negro was being inexorably lured despite his better judgement.

On leaving Mivart's Hotel, Noah's continuing search was little more than guesswork. If Eldritch Batchem was still seeking the *Aurora*, the most natural place to look remained the river and its environs. That was where any surviving seamen or smugglers might reside, where the bodies of those related to the case had been found and where all the mysteries seemed to vanish into the churning black waters.

Fortunately, Eldritch Batchem's unnervingly unchanging wardrobe suggested a particular disinclination to assimilate himself into new environments. If he *was* there among the yards and alleys of Ratcliff-highway, he should be easy enough to locate.

Noah had taken pains not to make the same error. On passing into the eastern regions of the city, he had stopped at the first marine store he came across and purchased an old oilskin coat to replace his customary reversible surtout. Combined with one of those wide-brimmed hats favoured by the criminal classes for its ability to hide the face, the resulting *ensemble* had transformed him into one who would not attract a second glance among the denizens of the docks.

Indeed, it was no doubt the very aborigineity of his outfit that permitted him the remarkable good fortune he experienced within minutes of beginning his search. He was asking among the cabmen, vendors and common trollops of the street for sightings of the russet cap when he caught a glimpse of something that set his higher instincts buzzing.

There on the corner of Betts-street was a man whose entire demeanour showed him to be engaged in a surreptitious pursuit. He loitered without waiting, looked without seeing into shop windows, and moved with a feline grace that showed him ready to pause, turn and vanish at a moment's notice. It was a masterly performance, made all the more fascinating by the detail of the man's hat, which, though it mostly concealed the long dark hair beneath, did not hide a gold earring.

The Italian?

Noah instinctively felt for his dagger in its leather sheath. The Italian had not noticed him, but was rather occupied with some other target out of Noah's line of vision.

Walking along the opposite side of the street with his gaze focused intently upon the reflections in the windows, Noah affected an aimless saunter to mask his steel-spring alertness. Within seconds he would be able to peer around the corner and observe whoever or whatever was being watched so intently by the Italian.

If Noah had seen Inspector Newsome going about his

investigations under that Mediterranean gaze, it would have been no great surprise. Had the target been Mr Williamson, at least a precedent had been set for that mode of *surveillance*. Whatever the identity of the pursued, it would surely provide some advantageous perspective on the Gordian knot of the *Aurora*'s disappearance.

In fact, the object of the Italian's gaze was a gentleman standing on the street corner and engaging a cabstand waterman in conversation. He was clearly not a difficult man to follow on account of his russet cap and garish tweed suit.

And suddenly there were even more questions.

EIGHTEEN

Mr Williamson looked up from his notes for the countless time and stared, unseeing, out of the window. It was not the chattering clatter of the coffee house that distracted him so. Nor was it the incessant hooves and wheels and busman's cries of broad Pall Mall stretching before him.

People outside walked by in unending procession, oblivious to their observer's gaze. It was a veritable catalogue of evening-time London: earnest men with appointments, laughing ladies with none, shuffling tomb-bound beggars, the sprightly costermonger with his barrow . . . and, of course, the street girls – the street girls with their silk and lace, their flashing ankles, their dark eyes seeking the merest flicker of appreciation from a male gaze.

He clenched his jaw and returned his eyes by force of will to the notebook. There, in his neat, small writing was all he knew (and did not know):

William Barton – Custom House tidewaiter murdered on Waterloo-bridge with blank unloading warrants in his possession (most likely for smuggling). The registered tidewaiter of the Aurora. Why killed, and why in such an outrageous manner?

Barton's murderers – Most likely skilled seamen to climb and navigate so in a fog. A harpooner also? In whose employ? Who might know them? Did Barton?

Barton's last utterance – Could his 'Orrr' be a strangulated attempt at 'Aurora'? What of 'ffff'? A name? A place? A time?

The Aurora – What of the charred name plaque? Is the entire ship thus consumed, or merely its identity? How did the board find its way to that part of the Thames, and from where?

Josiah Timbs – Owner of the vanished brig: murdered in the furnace of London Dock seemingly following a threat from the purloiners of his vessel. Again, why so conspicuous? Why this location above others? Did the murderer(s) leave any clue?

The seamen in barrels – Presumably those who remained aboard the fateful ship. How did their bodies get into barrels and into the spirit vault? Again, why such a curious – almost theatrical – act of discovery? Planned to coincide with the discovery of Timbs? Who were the coopers responsible? Mr Cullen to ask about the docks for any intelligence . . .

Eldritch Batchem – Who is he? What is his true role in all of this? Is he watching? Was his piece in the Monitor motivated by something other than competition? Why did he not attend the discoveries at the dock? Where is he now and what is he investigating?

The Italian – spy of Eldritch Batchem? His interest in me? How long has he been following? What does he know?

The missing cargo – Fine French silk. Benjamin and Noah to investigate receivers . . .

Mr Williamson again looked up, this time catching his own reflection in the plate glass. He avoided its eyes.

Noah Dyson – this man who had once risked his life in pursuit of the truth behind the death of Mr Williamson's wife, Katherine; this man who had sacrificed his own private anonymity to investigate where Mr Williamson could not; this man who was said to be an escaped transportee and thief . . . this man who now stood arbiter between his friend's return to the authority and respect of the Detective Force or a life chasing pickpockets and begging-letter fraudsters.

A large clock in the coffee house began to chime above the human noise. Mr Williamson took out his pocket watch to verify it. He closed his notebook and returned it to his coat. There was an appointment to keep – one to which he went with conflicting hope and desolation.

'Please take a seat, George. I appreciate your coming to see me.'

Sir Richard Mayne had been sitting contemplatively by the fire in his office at Scotland Yard but stood now to shake his visiter's hand.

'Take a seat, George. May I ask the clerk to bring you tea?'

'No thank you, Sir Richard,' said Mr Williamson, resting his top hat on the table between them. 'I assume that whatever it is you have to tell me will also be communicated to Inspector Newsome – if it has not been already.'

'That is correct, George. I do not deal in favourites. An expedient solution to this mystery is all I seek. Recent experience suggests that it is simply more peaceable to discuss matters separately with the two of you.'

'Hmm. Have you any further intelligence on the murders at London Dock?'

'The Detective Force has made a thorough investigation, but I am afraid there is little to show. As we thought, the body is indeed that of Josiah Timbs. The furnace was almost certainly accessed with a duplicate key during the absence of the furnace-master. It being night, there were few available witnesses, and the watchmen follow a rather imperfect system that seems to place a regular cup of tea above their attention to duty. In short, nobody saw anything and there were no probative discoveries made in or near the furnace.'

'That is perhaps the greatest clue in these deaths,' said Mr Williamson, taking out his notebook to append his existing thoughts. 'Whether or not there was wider collusion in their commission, the villains evidently knew enough about the nocturnal workings of the docks to plan their activities carefully. The more I see of this case, the more I am convinced it stretches far beyond what is visible.'

'You are more correct than you realize, but we will come to that in a moment. The bodies in the barrels were indeed the missing crew of the *Aurora*. No attempt had been made to empty their pockets or otherwise disguise their identities and the master of the vessel was able to identify all of them by a combination of clothing labels and direct recognition. Poor man – he was quite nauseous in the surgery where we examined his erstwhile crew.'

'Hmm. What was the cause of death?'

'All were struck fatally on the back of the head with a blunt instrument – a hammer perhaps. It seems they may have been made drunk first, however, as each had a quantity of brandy in their stomachs. It was not in their lungs, so we deduce they were embarrelled *post mortem.*'

'Have all of the mariners now been accounted for?'

'All but one. Investigations among the marine districts have turned up a handful of the crew who claim that seven seamen and the master left the vessel by lighter prior to its disappearance. Remaining on board were the three mates and three older sailors. I am told the older men like to remain on board.'

'So – we are to account for six bodies. There were only five barrels.'

'Indeed. The first mate is the only one unaccounted for, but it seems the inspector may have something to say about that.'

'Mr Newsome? Why is that?'

'The ship's master has since told me that an unnamed officer of the Thames Police came to his door on that day you both signed the contract and showed him a pencil likeness of the first mate before fleeing without explanation. I rather suspect that the hasty policeman was our Inspector Newsome and that the body he pulled out of the river prior to Mr Timbs's challenge was the first mate.'

'I presume he has not mentioned that avenue of investigation to you?'

'I am sure it is merely an oversight.' Sir Richard's expression was rather one of faith than certainty.

'Hmm. What of the manner of interment? How did the bodies get into the barrels and the barrels into the spirit vault?'

'It is another tale of general ignorance. What seems clear, however, is that five of the original consignment were replaced with the fatal casks some time between the *Aurora*'s disappearance and the discovery of the bodies. The new barrels were identical in size but evidently fashioned from a different kind of oak. A cooper noticed the detail once the barrels were examined in daylight.'

'Were there any other differences in the barrels? These could be highly informative.'

'Let me see . . . there were some minor . . .' Sir Richard looked through a sheaf of papers beside him. 'Yes – the five new barrels showed evidence of both muscovado sugar and tobacco about their girths. It seems they were rolled from, or through, other warehouses at some point. Of course, we have no idea if this was before or after the bodies were put inside – or whether it was at the London Dock itself. Our investigators looked into the sugar warehouses there, but there was no evidence to suggest anything untoward had occurred. Even if it had, why roll the barrels through the tobacco warehouse for no reason? It is nowhere near the spirit vault.'

'Hmm.'

'George – I am sure you have given some further thought as to why these murders were carried out in such a shocking manner and arranged so conspicuously. Have you reached any conclusions?'

'You have said it yourself, Sir Richard: nobody saw anything. Nobody knows anything. I can only imagine that the very audaciousness of the crimes was intended as a warning to all that assisting the police, or resisting the criminals, was inadvisable.'

'Whom do you mean by "all"? And what might they be offering resistance against?'

'That is where my knowledge ends, Sir Richard. It seems clear that the disappearance of an entire vessel must touch upon many other points: the Custom House, riverworkers, dockworkers, warehousemen, merchants . . . Some may be paid to stay quiet; others have nothing to lose but their pride. But it takes only one weak link in the chain of corruption to destroy the whole endeavour. Was that link a greedy William Barton? Was it a heedless Josiah Timbs? Was it a crew that would not be bribed to look away? We will likely never know – all are dead. Examples have been set. More information is needed if we are to progress.'

'Have you any such information to supply, George?'

'I have been pursuing my own investigation. I would tell you what I have discovered, but I fear you would be bound to reveal whatever I know to Mr Newsome, would you not?'

'I must be fair in all things. At the same time, I can tell him only what I have been told. It is more important to me that the case is solved rather than that all parties have equal information.'

'Very well, Sir Richard. In that case, perhaps you can tell me more. You alluded earlier to the broad reach of this case – have you further intelligence on that matter?'

'Indeed. On the day after the Waterloo-bridge incident, I exchanged words with Inspector General Jackson of the Custom House and I established a number of my clerks there to examine recent records for signs of irregularity. That report arrived before me this morning and its findings are . . . well, they offer more complication than clarification.'

'Sir Richard – before you continue, did your men experience any difficulties or obstructions in their duties?'

'Yes, I follow your line of thought. The men of the Custom House were as helpful as they could be, but each of my clerks received anonymous threats similar to the one sent to Josiah Timbs. One of them was attacked after dark and injured about the head . . . though naturally no concrete connection with the *Aurora* case can be made.'

'I trust that you have ensured their safety? Recent events have shown the need for caution.'

'Yes. The men are currently removed from the city.'

'Hmm. Does your report reveal anything more about the missing brig itself?'

'Very little. There is no record of ballast being issued to a ship of that name, suggesting either that it was not unloaded at all and left the Port of London as it was, or that it was unloaded and departed under a different name.'

'The most likely explanation,' said Mr Williamson.

'Quite.'

'But if that were the case, there would surely be a discrepancy of an "extra" ship leaving port – one that had not entered. Does the Custom House record such aberrations?'

'Not as a matter of course; they are simply too busy to do so. However, a careful tabulation and cross-referencing of inward- and outward-bound ships reveals irregularities where they exist. It is laborious work, which is perhaps why nobody sought to disguise or amend the ledgers.'

'How widespread is the phenomenon?'

'As an illustration, the ledgers show that there are currently three ships in port which, however, do not occupy their allotted berths. That is, they appear to have arrived some weeks ago, but cannot be located and have not left under their original names. For all intents, they exist only as documentation. The vessels may never have physically entered London at all.'

'What is the listed cargo of these ships?'

'As one might expect: cargo with high duties. I have men seeking the merchants, owners and mariners of these vessels, but . . . you know what the process involves, and how reluctant people are to speak.'

'Hmm. Has no merchant reported his vessel missing as Mr Timbs did?'

'There was apparently an instance similar to the disappearance of the *Aurora* some six months ago. Heated questions were asked in the Long Room at the Custom House, but the owner suddenly took his insurance and sought no further information. He has declined to be interviewed by the police.'

'I imagine we know why. What of departing ships? Presumably some leave the port without appearing to have entered?'

'Oddly enough, we located no such instances. It means nothing, of course. Only a ship loaded with dutiable cargo is registered outgoing. We could check about the ballast with Trinity House, but . . .'

'Yes . . . a laborious process. The *Aurora* is the case at hand.'

Mr Williamson looked through his pages of notes, hoping to see a single thread of sense emerging. 'It seems safe to assume that all of these irregularities are connected – that we are observing the visible elements of a much larger *in*visible organization.'

'I concur, though there is nothing more to suggest it than the necessity of some higher supervisory or authoritative element. As you say, it is an enterprise that touches on so many other functions. There must be a single head to which the tentacles lead. Who could that be? What manner of criminal could so orchestrate the endeavour?'

'Sir Richard – I am almost afraid to consider it. This is a man, or a group of men, who thinks nothing of committing murder – someone with allies across every aspect of our marine commerce. The Port of London is a city within the city: numberless warehouses, ships, men, cargoes, Customs officials, merchants . . . it is task beyond even the Metropolitan Police to see everything and know everyone.'

'That is precisely the reasoning of the criminals behind the *Aurora*'s disappearance, Mr Williamson. It will not do. The Detective Force exists to demonstrate that higher intelligence, diligence and honour will always vanquish criminality.'

'But I am no longer a member of the Detective Force.'

'Indeed you are not, George – but you were once its most stalwart investigator. Do you not reflect upon those years with satisfaction and pride? Do you not long to return to your rightful place at the heart of justice?'

'You have read the piece in *the London Monitor*. Is that truly the calibre of man you seek? All that was written was . . . is true.'

'Do not think, George, that I am ignorant of the world here in my Whitehall offices. Inspector Newsome has already made such an assumption to his detriment. I am quite aware of that unfortunate business at Giltspur-street gaol. Why do you think I accepted your precipitous "resignation" without question? It was the honourable thing to do . . . and I am not so *naïve* that I do not appreciate how much Mr Newsome benefited from it. But every man has the capacity for repentance, George. Every man may be cleansed of his sins and reclaim his faith . . . if only he can find it within himself to do so – to eradicate evil and follow instead the path of righteousness. I hope I have given you the opportunity to follow that path . . .'

'Sir . . . you have certainly done as much.'

'Very well. I trust you will do what is right. Let us speak no more of such things. There is one final matter I hoped to ask about: you said at the London Dock that you had evidence concerning the Waterloo-bridge incident. Are you able to share it with me without compromising your own private investigation? I ask merely because it would be of the greatest benefit to me to refute Eldritch Batchem's original "solution" publicly and to approach the Bridge Company with the true series of events.'

'It is quite simple, although admittedly somewhat incredible. The murderer ascended the bridge from the river using a grappling iron and a rope. Once upon the span, he murdered William Barton and descended the same way he had come.'

'You are quite certain of this?'

'As certain as I can be. I use evidence where Mr Batchem uses supposition.'

'Good. Your word is sufficient; leave the finer details with my clerk and I will see that this news is reported. But tell me, George – do you think Eldritch Batchem capable of artifice over his version of the crime: the suicide interpretation? Could it be that he knew of the murder all along and chose not to reveal it? Could it be that he is involved in a larger deception?'

'Hmm. Everything I have seen of the man shows him to be little more than a theatrical performer. The worst he can be suspected of is inserting one of his own playbills into the victim's pocket for the sake of publicity. It is bad taste, but nothing more sinister.'

'Do you think him capable of solving this case before us, George?'

'Sir – I am no longer certain of what any man is capable.'

NINETEEN

———◆◆———

Fog lay thick upon the river districts earlier the following day, masking all within its shifting shroud. Buildings became shadows; hulls loomed as leviathans; phantasmal bridges spanned mere air. Out on the black water, there was little sense of being cradled by the broad metropolis – rather, one peered at amorphous shores and felt adrift off some savage continent.

The oars clunked in the police galley and Inspector Newsome opened his senses to the *aqua incognita* about them. Cranes and chains sounded from wharfs. The shouts of coal-whippers echoed flatly from unseen colliers. The disembodied flames of a purlboat's brazier cast an orange halo and it signalled its presence with a regular bell. Presently, the sky darkened above them: London-bridge.

In that shadow, Mr Newsome brooded on the previous evening's meeting with Sir Richard. As expected, the master of the *Aurora* had made a fuss about that pencil illustration of the dead mate and Sir Richard had delivered the predictable lecture on virtue. Still, nobody yet knew about the tooth, and the other clues in the case were vague enough that he felt he maintained the advantage. Today was the day he would capitalize on it.

The galley bottom scraped on gravel beneath the massive inner walls of an arch and the mud thereabouts made itself known through a dank, vaporous breath.

'Here we go, sir,' said the first constable. 'I am told that this is where some of the toshers enter the sewers. Low tide is approaching and they congregate at this time.'

The inspector looked dubiously up the mud bank and into the fog. Something moved there: some limby shape that might have been human or spectral.

'Ho! You there by the sewer outlet!' he called to the form. 'Come down to the water here.'

A person materialized through veils of moisture: a tosher in his eccentric working attire of greasy leather coat, thick canvas trousers and long gutta-percha boots. A policeman's bullseye lamp was strapped to his chest and gave out a flickering beam as he picked his way across the detritus with the aid of a tall hoe. Too late, he saw that the caller was a Thames policeman.

'Fear not, man,' said Mr Newsome, perceiving the man's hesitation. 'It matters not to me that you enter the sewers. Indeed, I would like to ask you about your experiences there.'

'Sir – it's true I'm about to go in,' said the tosher. 'There're but five or six hours when I can do my work before the tide seals the holes . . . Might you ask me your questions when I return?'

'No. This is a matter of urgency. How long have you worked in the sewers? Do you know them well?'

'As well as any man. I've laboured there for upwards of seven years and I've seen most of what there is to see.'

'Very good. You are the fellow to suit my needs. I have reason to believe—'

'Sir – time's wasting. This is my work, my livelihood . . .'

'And this is a police matter! I could take you down to Wapping if I chose.'

'I don't refuse your questions, sir . . . it's just that . . . Why don't you accompany me if you're so eager? I'll show you what you seek more readily than I can tell you about it . . .'

Inspector Newsome weighed the proposition. He looked to his constables in the galley, neither of whom seemed especially perturbed at the idea of their superior venturing into the sewers without them. His deliberations were rapid.

'Constables – I will go with this gentleman. If I do not return to this place before the tide covers the bank, you are to see that Sir Richard Mayne himself is notified directly without delay. Here is my notebook, which you will give to him. It contains information of great value to a case he is engaged upon and is therefore too valuable for me to risk soaking in filth. See that *nobody* looks at it – and I include both of you – unless I am irretrievably lost to the river. Am I sufficiently clear upon that point?'

'Yes, sir,' came the dual response.

His instructions thus given to the increasingly bemused constables, he reached under his seat and took out a bundle wrapped in oilcloth. This he stuffed securely in his coat pocket before stepping out of the galley onto the bank.

'Five hours, gentlemen, or when the tide begins to rise,' was his parting shot. Then he was gone into the fog with the tosher, the pair of them swirling gradually into invisibility.

The constables waited just two heartbeats before jostling to open the notebook.

'You're not dressed for the sewers, sir,' said the tosher as the two walked towards the outlet. 'If you can wait until tomorrow, I could—'

'No. I have had quite enough of this infernal river. I will tolerate wet feet today if it means one less day in a boat.'

'As you wish – though I fear wet feet'll be the least of it, sir. I've a spare lamp you may use . . . Here, let me help you into the harness.'

Mr Newsome allowed himself to be fitted with the leather shoulder straps that positioned the metal box at the centre of his chest. Meanwhile, the smell of the sewer insinuated itself into the fog: a warm exhalation from the city's innards. It was excremental to be sure, but also bore scents of something else entirely – some ageless accumulation of rotting matter that seemed to seep from the very strata of London's history.

'It's a good day today,' said the tosher. 'The rain's been light and the flow is meagre, see? It's all likely to change shortly, of course, on account of these incessant north-easterlies. Raise the tide something awful they will.'

They stood before the aperture itself, twice as tall as a man but letting forth a modest enough output of grey-brown water over the bank and into the river. It steamed slightly as it emerged and carried with it items of a more substantial form, which Mr Newsome declined to examine in greater detail.

'The grey is mostly ash,' said the tosher, affixing a hat with a long rearward-facing flap and pulling on some long leathern gloves. 'The brown is—'

'Thank you – I believe I may know what the brown is.' Mr Newsome observed the preparations of his guide and attempted to follow suit, folding up the collar of his coat and rolling cuffs over his gloves. 'Is it safe inside? Will there be rats?'

'O yes, there're plenty of rats, but we've an understanding, they and I. We seek different prizes and have no need for conflict. Only remember these few points: step only where I step, never touch the roof, shout out if you smell gas . . . and never be out of my sight. Are you ready?'

'I suppose so. Let us proceed.'

Mr Newsome cast a last look towards the river, which was now lost in impenetrable whorls of moisture. Even the bridge itself had been mostly consumed, presenting but a few yards of brickwork like a ruin from a lost age.

'Keep to the edge,' said the tosher as he splashed through a few inches of murky effluvia. 'There's a deeper channel down the centre that takes most of the flow. You don't want to be up to your thighs in *that*.'

'Quite. Tell me – what is the extent of these passages?'

'The extent? Why, I don't believe any man knows, sir. I myself have gone as far as Holborn and Clerkenwell and glimpsed the city thereabouts through the street's gulley holes. There're passages and chambers from the time of Queen Bess and before.'

'I mean to ask if there are large spaces under the city where a man might keep animals or . . . or perhaps store materials.'

'Ha! What curious notions you have, sir! The air and the damp make the sewers a poor place to keep anything except the —— of the populace, pardon my language.'

'Have you ever encountered any animal larger than a rat down here?'

'Ah – you've been listening to the tales of the mudlarks, have you? I've seen no beasts myself but there is one among our number – a fellow called Bates – who claims to have heard noises in the tunnels about Wapping.'

'Noises? What noises?'

'O, he's old and touched with lunacy is old Bates. Too

much gas, I suspect. The sewers have their own noises, see? They channel sound in curious ways, like the tubes and cavities of our very own ears. Say a manufactory pours a quantity of hot water down the drain in Westminster – in Stepney you might hear thunder as a result. Or say a passage collapses at Cheapside – here, near the bridge, you would think it above your very head. These are your strange noises. It's just the sewers.'

'What of animal prints seen in the mud at low tide? Or rats chewed by a larger predator? Have you never witnessed such things?'

'Sir – I once saw an eel as thick as a man's thigh, but it was dead. I've seen rats that could pass for cats, but nothing stranger. As for your prints . . . well, let's say a normal cat walks upon the mud . . . then the mud shifts and expands according to its nature and the print suddenly appears larger than it was. *These* are the so-called "mysteries" of the mudlarks. You'll be disappointed if that is what you have come to find.'

The two men had now passed some few hundred yards into the tunnel, which had narrowed gradually to the comfortable height of a man. What had been a faintly foetid smell by the river, however, was now increasing in intensity to something that pinched the inspector's nostrils with its eggy reek. Daylight had faded with every step further into the gloom and the lamps upon their chests had now become the sole illumination, casting a dim orange light upon the slime-glistening brickwork.

'Breathe through your mouth if you can,' said the tosher, taking the right tunnel as they approached a fork. This passage in turn branched off right at a number of intervals and the sewer-hunter decisively took the third one as they continued deeper under the metropolis. 'Can you hear it, sir? Can you hear the city?'

They paused their splashing footsteps momentarily and Mr Newsome struggled to disallow the smell from entering his nose. Amid the trickle and drip of the tunnel, a faint rumbling came to them: a throbbing *basso* note that seemed to emanate from both above and below. Was that the sound of a million souls and their industry: the countless carts and wagons, hooves and feet, manufactories and railways and markets?

'When there is silence down here, *that's* when I will worry,' said the tosher, continuing again towards his goal.

'Where are we going?' said Mr Newsome, wiping something viscous from his cheek with a look of disgust.

'Alas, sir, there are many of us harvesting the sewers. One must explore deeper and deeper to enjoy the spoils. Today, I enter a new branch.'

'Spoils? What spoils? I have seen nothing more than some scraps of wood amid a bilious soup of filth.'

'You'll see, sir. You'll see.'

'I certainly hope to. Tell me – I imagine a man accustomed to searching the sewers must eventually become inured to the smell. Is that so?'

'That's quite the case, sir. I have made smells at home that have disgusted me more.'

'I . . . I mean to say that a man may spend time down here and emerge into the city not perhaps realizing how he stinks. He then goes among the crowds quite oblivious to the abhorrence he evokes.'

'I'm careful to wash my hands and feet every day, sir, but I dare say there're some of my kin that are less particular.'

'I believe I have met one. Do you know a fellow who is

rather short and who has the look of a boy about his face? He is . . . well, let us say he is not a talkative fellow.'

'I can't recall the man from your description, though there are some boys who do this work. Wait a moment – I must now consult my map . . . shine your lamp at me for a moment, won't you?'

Mr Newsome obliged, and the tosher reached into his coat behind the lamp and withdrew a piece of wood about the size and shape of a dinner plate that was strung around his neck on a piece of leather twine. Etched into its surface with a fine chisel was a bewildering network of lines and branches annotated with letters. He turned the circular board according to their current location and then counted off some of the apertures visible to them before returning the 'map' reverently to its place and proceeding still further into the dark passages.

'Is that your own guide to the sewers?' asked Mr Newsome. 'I would be very interested to make an imprint of it.'

'You wouldn't read it, sir, for it is coded. Only I know how to read it, and I would not part with it if you threw me in gaol. Indeed, I would burn it before I would allow another man to gain possession of it. It has taken me many years to create and is the envy of all shoremen.'

'I see. Then perhaps you can tell me how extensive it is. Might it extend to Wapping and its environs?'

'There are indeed sewers thereabouts – old ones, too. But they are often the most treacherous and likely to collapse. Righty-ho, I think we have just about reached our destination . . .'

Mr Newsome looked around in the perpetual night and realized that he was utterly lost. Only the masonry had changed during their meandering about the *cloacae* of this putrid underworld: from the ordered, well-cut stone of the larger tunnels to the rotting ancient bricks of their current location. Here, the effluent around their ankles did not appear to flow, but sat stagnating with an opaque film upon its surface.

'How is *this* a destination? What do you expect to find here?' asked Mr Newsome, watching with considerable distaste as the tosher removed a glove and plunged his hand beyond the wrist into the mire. Thus submerged, he seemed to grope about the submerged crevices with the greatest of attention.

'O, you'd be surprised what lurks here among the dung of generations, sir. Whatever gets flushed or dropped or washed away at every house and street up there arrives down here sooner or later. It's all here between the bricks where they lack mortar – the older, the better. I dare say there's a king's fortune beneath the city if one had the time to search every inch.'

'I see nothing but slime and the soil of generations.'

'Ah, but it is not about what you can see, sir; it's about what you know. I would expect a man of your profession to be familiar with the notion.'

'You are indeed a philosopher of the sewers.'

'Mock me all you like, sir – but you might be surprised what I make in a year by wading in the city's waste. I might even venture to say it's more than you earn.'

'I have yet to see any evidence of it.'

The tosher ceased his probings of the pestilential brickwork for a moment and looked at his guest, whose uniform trousers were now saturated to the knee, and whose shoulders glistened with multiple drips of permeating ooze.

'Imagine this if you can, sir. Metal attracts metal, see, and as the centuries pass, the bits of metal washed here gather in the natural dips and crannies. Thereafter, it corrodes and fuses – precious matter and base metal altogether. Well, sir, it lies and it accumulates and it swells and it waits for a man like me to come along and pick it up. I have heard of these conglomerate masses as large and as heavy as a boulder – all amalgamated pins and nails and silver . . . but also gold, which does not corrode, sir. Find one of those tangled rusty masses and you find the treasure of centuries within it. You just need a hammer to break it open.'

The tosher then went back to his obscene harvest with an emphatic vigour. For his part, Mr Newsome showed that he was unimpressed with the lesson and cast a nervous eye at his pocket watch. Almost two hours had elapsed since they had left the river.

'I really do think we should be return—'

'Aha!'

The tosher's hand emerged shining wetly in the lamplight and brandished a small object, which he polished on a sleeve.

'Do you see that?' he said with evident delight. '*Here's* your treasure, sir! I cannot make out the detail and it is some-what blackened, but I'll warrant from its weight that this is a King James silver sixpence. I have found them before.'

Mr Newsome was incredulous despite himself. 'King James?'

'Indeed! And I'll warrant there's more besides. Metal attracts metal, didn't I say? We still have time before the tide . . . and it makes little difference if we miss it. I have known men stay the night down here – it's quite safe if you have light and provided it does not rain. Why not get your hands down and see what you can find . . . ?'

His look of disgust said that Mr Newsome did not favour the opportunity. Instead, he again attempted to discern their location relative to the surface. The preponderance of right turns suggested that they had proceeded broadly east. Could it be that the Tower was above them? Or perhaps the rotting alleys of East Smithfield passed overhead, threatening at any moment to wash a river of steaming cess down around their knees. In this place, he mused, in the very living bowel of the city, men became mere parasites, picking at the constipated detritus of history.

It was while engaged in such thoughts that something caught his eye: a flickering light glimpsed in another tunnel leading away from where they stood. He tilted his head and thought he heard the faintest *plash* of sodden footsteps.

'Did you see that?' he whispered to the still searching tosher. 'There was another light in the tunnel there.'

'Another of my kind, I expect. There are enough of us.'

'But you said this was undiscovered territory.'

'Then I advise you to keep quiet and turn your light away from that passage. There's no need to worry – we'll be leaving shortly.'

'I should speak with the other fellow also. Wait for me here.'

'It is better that you stay with me. You don't want to be going off . . . sir? Sir!'

But Mr Newsome had set off splashing into the other tunnel, where the light he had seen was becoming dimmer.

'Ho! You there! Wait a moment if you please!' he shouted into the vanishing blackness.

His shouts echoed dankly along the sewer and seemed to return to him from both directions. The tunnel was clearly a very old one and became smaller as he strode, forcing him to bend further and further until he reached a parting of the ways, where four other mouths let forth their gurgling stream into a larger pipe. He stopped, looking back to be sure of his return path. Then the light he was chasing showed itself again and appeared to be vanishing into a branch from the sewer straight ahead.

He determined to venture only that far before returning to his friend with the wooden map. But as he hurried towards that branch and peered into it, he caught the briefest flash of the person he was pursuing: the *silhouette* of a hatless head, hair apparently stiff with dirt and a figure of seemingly boyish dimensions . . . the selfsame man who had leaped in handcuffs from the police galley? He who had loitered at Pickle Herring?

'Stop! Thames Police!'

Mr Newsome rushed to where he had seen the figure, heedless now of the stinking matter that soaked him to the thighs and splashed across his uniform jacket. Here was *his* treasure, just out of reach within the subterranean viscera of the city.

'I said halt!'

Mr Newsome arrived at another nodal point, his own voice still reverberating wetly through the brickwork, and searched once more for the fugitive light. Which tunnel now? There seemed to be no sign of illumination but his own.

He tried to control his breathing that he might better hear the footsteps of his quarry, but there was none. The man had no doubt extinguished his lamp and paused silently in his flight. Now it was only a case of who would move first . . . but the tide was ineluctably rising and only one of them likely had the knowledge to escape without aid.

He waited a few more heavy heartbeats, hearing nothing but the constant telluric rumble and the conjoined flow of a thousand foetid streams. Seconds passed into minutes, and still nothing. Time to make a decision – he had to return.

He kicked the wall in frustration and set back the way he had come. Back along that same tunnel to the place he had glimpsed the figure; back further to where the tunnels divided and then straight on . . . but which one was 'straight on'? It had seemed at the time that he had proceeded in a direct line from one passage to the next, but now he faced two that might qualify. Both looked identical from his vantage point.

'Hello there!' he called out to his guide. 'It is I: the Thames Police inspector. Can you hear me?'

No reply.

'I say – I am close to you but cannot see you. Could you move in front of the tunnel I previously ventured down? I cannot remember which one it is . . .'

No sight or sound of any human presence.

Grinding his jaw, Mr Newsome selected the sewer on the left and walked down it to the end. But once there, he did not recognize the place in which his tosher had found the silver coin. So, returning whence he had come, he took the right-hand option and discovered soon enough that the brickwork therein was in a state of partial collapse – quite dangerous, and clearly not the right tunnel.

He returned to the meeting place of all and determined to take the third tunnel, which, though it seemed not at all to be the one he had originally emerged from, must indeed be the correct one.

It was not. At least, it brought him to no place that seemed remotely familiar. Indeed, nothing seemed familiar. It all looked the same: the maddening uniformity of the bricks, the perpetually trickling liquid, the flickering shadows thrown by his chest-mounted lamp . . .

'Where are you, man?'

His own voice replied: a sound oddly magnified and

distorted through the endless masonry roots of the metropolis, a repeating note of creeping panic – a sound to unnerve any man.

He held his breath and strained to hear any indication of his tosher guide: the faintest splash of foot or distant cough. But there was only the constant trickle of liquid and that great elemental moan of the city throbbing through the brickwork all about him . . .

And then something else.

It came to him from a distance, channelled through the network of ancient and modern cavities: a low, guttural note that seemed half growl, half roar – a sound that could have been an irregularity of the sewer's flow . . . or one made by an animal. A large animal.

At this sound, there followed another no less perturbing: that of a thousand unseen rats stirring from their vile crevices into the water, where they squeaked and splashed and scratched in evident agitation. The sub-city tunnels were alive with it.

Mr Newsome checked his watch with a hand that refused to shake. The river had now risen. The sewer mouth was closed. He was trapped, abandoned: lost beneath the vast, teeming mass of London's urban fabric.

He wondered whether the oil in the lamp would last.

TWENTY

The glow of the fire was the only illumination in that modest parlour in Lambeth. It shone in Mr Williamson's eyes as he sat alone, staring sightlessly into the flames. His notebook lay open on his knees, and numerous other sheets of paper were scattered on the floor about him. Katherine's chair – his dead wife's chair – had been moved from its accompanying location by the hearth to sit instead beside the wall. It was dark outside, yet the curtains remained unclosed, providing a dim reflection of the man in the window's black panes.

Held loosely in his right hand was a tract recently pressed upon him by an earnest young man in the habit of hectoring the crowds outside the theatres of Haymarket:

BEWARE THE LURE OF THE MAGDALENE!

Be not blinded by her beauty, for she has no higher morality. Sin and deprivation is all she knows. Cast down your eyes upon seeing her, for she is Eve proffering the cankered apple.

Take not that fruit! Look not into her eyes – she is serpent beneath her smile, and her forked tongue leads Man into temptation as surely as Christ was tempted by the Devil himself . . .

He crumpled the paper into a ball and threw it towards the fire, where it at once began to uncurl languorously among the flames – a bright heart of combustion even amid the burning coals. In a moment, it was naught but frail ash.

A sudden knock at the street door startled him from his reveries.

He remained sitting.

Again the sharp rapping at the door and the voice he had hoped not to hear:

'George – it is I: Noah. I know you are awake; I have seen the firelight through the window. George?'

Mr Williamson closed the notebook with a sigh and made a perfunctory effort to clear some of the papers around him. Still, he did not stand.

'George?' came the voice from outside. 'Are you safe? In ten seconds, I will assume you are being held against your will and must force open the door . . .'

Finally, he stood and ventured into the hall, where he opened the street door to peer out through the crack. He had been prepared to rebuff his visiter, but circumstances persuaded otherwise.

'My G—, Noah! What has happened to you?'

Noah Dyson was bleeding freely from a long cut to the forehead above his left eye. His unkempt clothes (an incongruous oilskin *ensemble*) were likewise spotted and smeared with blood – whether his own or another's was unclear.

'May I enter, George? I have important intelligence on the *Aurora* case.'

'Were you attacked?'

'It is more complicated than that . . . and I fear that my

attacker will soon know your address if he is observing and sees me dawdling on the step talking to a gap in the door.'

'Yes, yes – I suppose you must come in.'

Noah cast a final look at the street behind him and entered.

'I will get something for your wounds,' said Mr Williamson. 'Pull a seat in front of the fire.'

'Have you any brandy?' called Noah, taking Katherine's chair and settling it before the hearth.

'I do not keep spiritous liquor in the house,' said Mr Williamson, returning with a small brown glass bottle and a strip of cotton cloth. 'This is chymist's alcohol to clean your cuts.'

Noah sniffed the bottle's neck and set about cleaning the lacerations above his eye and across his knuckles. If the preparation stung, he showed no sign of it. Then, with that task completed, he sighed and swigged heavily from the bottle, coughing as the concentrated spirit burned his throat and brought tears to his eyes.

'I believe it is not to be taken internally,' said Mr Williamson, taking his seat.

'The bitterest medicine is sometimes the most efficacious, is it not?'

'Hmm. Are we to speak in riddles, or will you tell me what has happened?'

'I am a great advocate of honesty and clarity, at least where trusted fellows are concerned. Are we trusted fellows, George? You were keen enough to escape my presence at the London Dock when Sir Richard was about. Did he see me whisper to you and reprimand you for it?'

'He is no longer my superior. I do not work for him.'

'Indeed, but you evade my question all the same. I will not press you to tell me what you would rather keep confidential . . . but only tell me this: are we still working together on this mystery of the *Aurora*? Would you prefer me no longer to call at your house?'

'Hmm. Hmm. Noah – there are things . . .'

'Are you ashamed to be associated with one such as myself? Do Ben and I sully your good name in the eyes of Sir Richard and those other guardians of justice? Has he, I wonder, hinted that your return to the Detective Force is dependent on your not associating with the likes of me? I sit here bloodied in the name of a cause I undertook in partnership with you. At least afford me the respect of a frank answer.'

Mr Williamson sighed. 'It is something of that sort, Noah.'

'Then let us speak candidly. Is that what you truly want: a return to the Force?'

'Noah, I . . . I no longer know. Since I left – or rather, since I was shouldered aside by Inspector Newsome – I have led a purposeless existence. I have engaged in employment beneath my ability. I have fallen into habits unbecoming—'

'What habits? You walk the streets. You work. You do not even keep brandy in your house!'

'I have become degenerate in my thoughts.'

'O, not this nonsense again. You are referring to the girl Charlotte, of course. Have you been visiting her rooms at Golden-square? Have you been paying for her favours?'

'Certainly not!'

'Then what sin have you committed other than that of being a man? You think of her often – it is natural enough if she is attractive. It is what she lives for: to captivate men such as you.'

'I . . . I dream of her. Indecent dreams . . .'

'Of course you do. There is no need to blush so. Our

animal urges are always stronger than our higher sensibilities. But, George – if I may venture some advice: you cannot love a whore. She does not seek it and will not be persuaded of it. Her body is her commodity and you cannot afford it for a lifetime. These street girls do not marry. They will not be saved except through the benediction of wealth.'

'Hmm. You are right, of course.'

'But despite knowing this higher truth, you cannot control your feelings. Such is the paradox, and flaw, of all religion, George.'

'I will not tolerate any of your blasphemy, Noah . . .'

'It is religion – not desire – that tortures you, George. It is religion that is your inner dictator. Your feelings for Charlotte are natural and pure . . . but only as long as they are lustful. Do not confuse this with love.'

'Hmm. Hmm. I . . . it is a personal matter. I must examine my soul for guidance. In the meantime . . . I hope you will respect my disinclination to discuss it further.'

'I will, but you know you can speak to me on the subject without shame whenever you wish. I have seen the world, George. I have seen horizons and civilizations that you – a man only of the city – cannot conceive. There is more to this human flesh than nave and steeple, than right and wrong . . .'

'I know you have had a different life than I, but . . .'

'Men change, George. Some become better; some become worse. It is within our power to choose.'

'Hmm – now you sound like Sir Richard . . .'

'Ha! That is a comparison I would never have expected.'

Mr Williamson did not share the laughter, but turned his gaze once more upon the flames.

'Very well,' said Noah, perceiving the dark curtain of melancholy descending upon his friend. 'I need hardly tell you

that Mr Newsome will be pursuing whatever means necessary to solve the case, whether or not they meet Sir Richard's
notions of morality. Will you discuss the *Aurora* with me, or
should I leave you to your fire?'

'Noah . . . I . . . Tell me about how you received your
injuries.'

'Good. These cuts were dealt me not two hours ago by
that mysterious Italian fellow of our recent acquaintance. As
you might expect, it was not all one way – I gave a good account of myself.'

'What happened? How did you locate him?'

'That is the most curious thing. I was seeking Eldritch
Batchem among the shipping districts and I quite accidentally
saw the Italian surreptitiously observing none other than our
russet-capped "investigator".'

'Wait – the Italian was *secretly* observing Eldritch
Batchem? Why would he do such a thing? And on whose
behalf? I cannot imagine Mr Batchem asking his own associate to watch him.'

'Precisely. If not Batchem, who *is* watching all of the players in this drama, and why?'

'Is it possible that Mr Batchem engineered this in order to
confuse us and cast our gaze elsewhere?'

'I have considered it, of course – but no man could have
predicted I would be at Ratcliff-highway at that time or
place. In truth, this development now seems more logical. For
all his sophistry, Batchem is not particularly sophisticated in
his methods, whereas I think we can both agree that the Italian is an admirable exemplar of thievery, observation and
stealth. Would such a man work for our be-capped buffoon?'

'Hmm. It is a persuasive argument. As I said the other
day, I first encountered this Italian *before* Mr Batchem's the-

atrical address and Mr Timbs's challenge. Was he, I wonder, observing me on a matter unconnected with any investigation into the *Aurora*'s disappearance? Or, rather, in *anticipation* of such an investigation – in order to gauge what kind of detective I might be? I cannot fathom what other reason he, or his masters, could have for engineering that strange incident.'

'I, too, sense that my life has been under scrutiny – and not only scrutiny, but also manipulation. Let us not forget the article in *the London Monitor*. Did it not strike you as strange how much privileged information was revealed there? At the time, I wondered at Batchem having the wherewithal to discern those facts. But now I think about the Italian . . . *he* strikes me as the kind of man who might be able to learn such detail – or who might work with another who has that ability.'

'Hmm. Then if not Eldritch Batchem, for whom *does* the Italian work? Does it not seem possible that whoever is behind these recent deaths and the disappearance of the vessel is also behind our Italian?'

'Quite. And if that is the case, I venture to suggest that we are not dealing with mere smugglers. There is a greater intelligence at work here. If, as now seems likely, Batchem was *not* responsible for the article in *the Monitor*, it would appear someone has been seeking to cast suspicion, quite successfully, on him at the same time as disparagement is heaped on us. Someone, in short, is not only trying to throw the investigation off the scent but also to damage or denigrate its investigators in the process. Have you heard what has happened to my business concerns as a result of that article?'

'Hmm. Hmm. I have heard rumours.'

'My entire stock confiscated and the manufactory closed until the extent of duties owed can be determined. It is also said that the East India Company is asking about irregularities in the exports. I am fortunate that my real name appears on no documentation and that my workforce knows nothing of my address.'

'Hmm. I fear you are quite correct: we face a greater threat than we first imagined. Did you learn nothing more in your altercation with the Italian? There must be something more – some further hint or clue.' Mr Williamson reached for his notebook. 'Tell me *precisely* what happened.'

Noah could not help but smile at the detective's unchanging method. 'Very well. It was like this, George: after ascertaining that Batchem was the subject of observation, I turned my attention instead to the pursuer. And, frankly, I have never seen such ability. Within minutes, he seemed to sense that he was being watched and began to look around him. Only with the greatest efforts did I manage to remain unseen, but it was inevitable he would finally discern my design and my identity.'

'He attacked you?'

'Not immediately. His primary interest was Batchem so he persisted in his pursuit with the frustrating knowledge that I, his shadow, would also benefit. Clearly, he could not allow me that advantage. He would have to ensure my silence. In such a way did we follow Batchem about the environs of Ratcliff-highway for almost an hour, watching him enquire at public houses and among the seafaring classes thereabouts.'

'What was the nature of his investigation?'

'I will come to that in a moment. However, when it became clear that Batchem was returning west to his hotel, the Italian appeared promptly to vanish. One moment he was in my vision and the next he was gone, perhaps as a wagon passed through my line of sight. Evidently, he expected me to pursue him in the vicinity of my last sighting: down an alley between two shops. It was clearly a trap, but I was in an intemperate humour and rather relished the challenge. Moreover, I was armed, as I knew he must also be.'

'Noah . . . tell me that you did not kill the man.'

'Your mortal soul need not bear that burden. I entered the alley with my dagger drawn and saw no sign of him – not even a scent. But I felt he was there, lurking. No doubt he was expecting a cautious approach, so I took the opposite action and proceeded noisily, whistling and kicking at debris for all the world like a passing sailor planning to use the space as a toilet. Such a strategy would perhaps give him pause and a moment of doubt as to whether I was indeed the one who had been observing him. It was a successful ruse: I saw him peep out from behind a buttress and our eyes met.'

'And what of the man? Did he speak? Did he show any fear?'

'Quite the contrary. He smiled and nodded as if to ac-knowledge an equal in his deceptive art. But there could be no conversation. He leaped at me with a thin stiletto blade and we fought. I will admit he was an accomplished man with a knife, but we were evenly matched and I left him with a gash to his neck. As soon as he realized he could not easily kill me, he took the sensible decision and fled.'

'You did not think to follow him? He might have led you to the one who controls him.'

'I believe that *two* bloodied men running through Ratcliff-highway may have excited the wrong kind of attention, George. And in any event, we need only look behind us if we want to locate the fellow again. Think also of this: whoever controls the man now knows what we know.'

'Hmm. What *do* we know? That some invisible hand

controls a murderous Italian? That Eldritch Batchem is not perhaps the person we had assumed him to be? I see little improvement in our current position.'

'As I say, whoever is watching this investigation is also visible through their observation of it. They will follow where we lead.'

'Or they will kill us, Noah.'

'They have resisted that course of action thus far – though I cannot explain why. Perhaps it is a case of seeing how close we come to the solution before they strike. The only course of action is to proceed with what we know. Either we will reach the end of this mystery, or we will again encounter its perpetrators during our attempts.'

'Hmm. You said that Mr Batchem was pursuing his own avenues of investigation about Ratcliff-highway. What of those?'

'Quite. Taking advantage of my bloodied state, I returned to the sites of his earlier questioning and lied that a man in a red cap had just assaulted me. Had they seen such a man? Some replied that they had and that he had been asking about the first mate of the *Aurora*, a fellow named Hampton. I trust he was not among those found in barrels?'

'That is correct. He is the one mariner not accounted for, although I fear Mr Batchem's searches are quite in vain – it seems Inspector Newsome showed a likeness of this fellow Hampton to the ship-owner some days ago. Sir Richard believes the body was pulled out of the river by the Thames Police shortly after the vessel went missing.'

'It matters not. One of the men to whom I spoke had suggested to Batchem that he might visit the rat fights at the Forecastle public house off Ratcliff-highway this evening. It is apparently a well-attended spectacle and somebody there may know of first mate Hampton. Therefore, if I sought redress from my "attacker" I might follow suit and visit the place.'

'I know the Forecastle by reputation,' said Mr Williamson. "Drinking, dogs and death" – that's what the local constables say about the place.'

'Well, we might consider a trip to "the rats" if that is where Batchem is to be. If we attend, it is highly possible our Italian, or one of his fellows, might also make an appearance.'

'Hmm. It seems a hazardous course – or a possible trap. Did you learn nothing further from your visits among the receivers? Perhaps that is a safer route.'

'I have Ben watching the large silk emporium on Ludgatehill. It seems they are about to receive a large order from a dubious source. I am afraid, however, that Inspector Newsome has had the same idea – I met him there just before the discovery at the London Dock. What of our Mr Cullen? Have you had any reports from his labour at the wharfs?'

'Nothing useful as yet. He remains there still as far as I know.'

'Do you doubt his ability? '

'He was a dutiful and honest constable. Time will tell if he has a detective's capacity for broader thought. Inspector Newsome clearly did not think so.'

'A detective might be many things, might he not? Your "broader thought" is Mr Newsome's cunning and ruthlessness. I might say that my own advantage is knowledge and experience of the city. Perhaps Mr Cullen's dogged persistence will be the particular trait that improves him.'

'We will see. He is a good man and I wish him well. I fear, however, that his goodness and devotion will lead him one day to harm. He has a young man's thirst for justice.'

'Harm comes to us all, George. Surviving it is what makes us men.'

'Hmm. Hmm.'

'Well, we will see what Ben and Mr Cullen bring to the investigation. More information is the thing. What did you discover at Waterloo-bridge? I assume it was murder?'

'Undoubtedly. I believe the killer ascended the bridge by rope from a vessel floating upon the river itself – an endeavour requiring significant skill.'

'That should surprise me, but our dealings with the Italian lead me to believe that we are at odds with a group of uncommonly impressive talents. We may assume, then, that the murder upon the bridge was therefore another example of a conspicuous warning of the kind we saw at the London Dock – a signal for anyone with knowledge of the missing brig to hold their peace or forever be no more.'

'It would certainly seem so. There is one more minor point, however: the toll-collector said that, apart from a missing hat and the wound to his throat, William Barton was otherwise in a composed state of dress when he staggered out of the fog.'

'And this leads you to believe that he perhaps knew his killer . . . that perhaps they exchanged some words but did not struggle.'

'Either that or the attack was so swift and invisible that Mr Barton saw nothing.'

'I rather suspect the former. If we could only learn more of the Detective Force's investigation into the events at the London Dock, we might be able . . . Wait a moment. George? That averted glance tells me that perhaps we *do* know more. Or rather *you* do.'

'I . . . it is true that I have been fortunate enough to

discern a number of details through . . . through an old acquaintance in the Force.'

'Were you planning to tell me?'

'Am *I* under investigation now, Noah? Must I account for my every movement? Do I ask you how or where you find *your* information? I am sure it is best that I do not know.'

'Very well. I will not question your sources. Tell me what you know only if you wish. I trust you did not bleed in order to acquire it.'

'Hmm. There are few clues to follow. The fatal barrels were evidently swapped with those in the original consignment. Nobody saw anything, of course.'

'That in itself is a clue.'

'Quite. As far as I can tell, the only useful piece of information to come out of the investigation thus far is that the alien barrels had traces of both muscovado sugar and tobacco about their hoops and staves.'

'Which means they were rolled through other warehouses to reach their destination. That tells us little.'

'It tells us that the barrels most likely originated elsewhere than London Dock, for there is no practical reason why they would have picked up those residues at the London Dock, where the respective storehouses are quite separately located. The suggestion is rather that the barrels came from a single warehouse or landing that contains many forms of cargo – the kind of businesses, for example, found along the river wharfs rather than in the docks.'

'You are right, George. And such privately owned places would also offer more privacy in the act of embarrelling those unfortunate sailors.'

'But there are hundreds of such quays and wharfs and platforms. Where could we begin?'

'I admit I have no idea, but I know a place where we might begin to ask, and where we might perhaps find more answers to our multiplying questions.'

'The Forecastle.'

'"Drinking, dogs and death", George? Shall we make an evening of it?'

'Hmm. It would seem so.'

TWENTY-ONE

As the tides of the river ebb and flow according to the timeless balance of the waters, so there is a natural equilibrium in the shared existence of men. Thus, as Inspector Newsome found himself cruelly imprisoned in the visceral vaults of the city, I found myself free.

Once again, my labour and fortitude in the face of the inimical blank page had seen me emerge from penury, the printer's press (as ever) my *deus ex machina*. They may take my bed, my clothes, my copy and my freedom, but they may never take the writer's soul, which – like the golden goose – is abundantly fecund.

Naturally, in those first days, I compensated for my months of deprivation by gorging myself on chops and pies and porter until I thought my cheeks would tear and my belly pop. I sought out the busiest, noisiest streets and the smokiest, most raucous congregations to feel once more like a citizen of this great and glorious chaos that is London. Along Waterloo-road, meanwhile, I sated more carnal needs unto the very threshold of stumbling anaemia.

Alas, with enjoyment of liberty comes further bills, and I was soon again but a whisker away from the magistrate's bench if I could not quickly turn my hand to further column inches on the *Aurora* case and to my continuing researches into the murky past of one Eldritch Batchem. And so I went in search of the latest knowledge among the taverns of Fleet-street, where those news-grubbers of my bastard kin – the penny-a-liners, scribblers, fire-watchers and pseudo-literary liars – gathered to steal each other's stories and make the nation's print.

Needless to say, the detective mania continued apace. For all its soiled reputation, *the London Monitor* had started a fire that the London Dock murders had fanned into a conflagration. At every coffee-house fireplace along Fleet-street, the questions were the same: what is the Detective Force doing to solve these latest crimes? Why does no murderer yet stand before a judge? Is the Custom House complicit? Where is the *Aurora*? Will Eldritch Batchem be the man to solve the crimes? Is Sir Richard Mayne to resign his position as Police Commissioner at the will of Her Majesty?

The following, from a *Times* correspondent, might stand as a representative example of the mood gripping the city:

Dear Sirs

Must not the world wonder that here, at the heart of its richest and most illustrious port, seven documented murders and the theft of an entire vessel have recently been perpetrated? Is it not a matter for national shame that those warehouses into which the wealth of nations are entrusted may apparently be entered at will, and invisibly, by the common criminal? Indeed, it is an outrage to both our moral and our commercial standing in the eyes of multiplicitous nations that such crimes remain unpunished.

I am modest in my claims that I possess some investigative acumen of my own, and the course of action seems a clear one. Whence came those barrels containing the unfortunate mariners? Who made them, and where? How did they find their way into the spirit vault and on whose authority? Answer these questions and you answer how the bodies became thus entombed.

As for the tragic Mr Timbs, there is a rumour that he was warned by his killers some days prior to his death. Why did not the Metropolitan Police offer him protection even as he courageously led them simultaneously to the truth and to his end?

I put these questions to the investigators of London – Eldritch Batchem among them – in the name of clarity, justice and in the true spirit of detection.

Yours
Aloysius Dent
Oxenden-street

Thus does the populace at large (and its correspondents in particular) demonstrate their anodyne mediocrity. It was all to me a stale debate, and proof enough of what I had already sensed: that the greater headline lay hidden beneath rather than atop this story. Who was the man calling himself Eldritch Batchem?

Absent he may have been from the London Dock three days before, but he was not one to shy from attention where it might aggrandize his investigative efforts. Accordingly, his *riposte* could be found in the very next day's edition of *the Times*:

Dear Sirs

I read with interest Mr Aloysius Dent's communication of yesterday on the case of the *Aurora*, and concur wholeheartedly with his assertion that it is an outrage. Where I must disagree, however, is with his claim to 'investigative acumen'.

An amateur would naturally look first to the provenance of the barrels and their route into the spirit vault, but he would do so in error. It was clear to me (if not to the Metropolitan Police) that the bodies left at the dock were *intended* to be found as a form of grisly display. Therefore, the perpetrators will have taken all measures to avoid leaving clues. Readers may be assured that I am not at liberty to reveal here the *true* path of the investigation as I pursue it.

As to the recent letter in these pages from Sir Richard Mayne, in which he refutes my verdict on the Waterloo-bridge suicide, I can only pity the investigative methods employed. His 'solution' of murder is both fanciful and relies upon a misreading of unrelated evidence that is now so 'conveniently' erased by the passage of time and traffic.

I remain, in the service of justice and truth,

Yours,
Eldritch Batchem
Investigator by Royal Appointment

A trip to Whitecross-street gaol to learn more about the man was clearly imperative. There would be inmates still resident who might recall the curious Mr Crawford (or Crowley), who, with his perpetually gloved hands, his maniacal neatness and his disturbed dreams, was no doubt a memorable figure to those who had been immured with him. And did not I myself fully appreciate that even the most private man will sometimes open the lockbox of his soul to those who have shared the same melancholy fate?

Of course, there was no use simply visiting the gaol and enquiring after the inmate in question. Previous journalistic endeavours had shown that the deputy governor guarded the keeper's office like an administrative Beefeater and would reveal nothing whatsoever without a letter of introduction or an official edict. A more circuitous approach had to be taken – one more native to my inquisitive bent.

Accordingly, three days after the London Dock murders, I could be found standing before the lofty frontage of that house of correction on Whitecross-street during the morning visiting period. If I appeared to be a simple vendor of beer with my barrow of brown glass before me, and if I squinted histrionically through spectacles seemingly no less opaque than my bottles, one may be sure it was with a grander design.

'Two porters, please,' said a pretty young woman, opening her purse. Her two small be-suited sons (infant undertakers both) stood alongside her, staring morosely at their polished shoes.

'Certainly, ma'am,' I replied. Then, with a myopic peer: 'I know Mr Dixon likes his morning porter, eh?'

'Excuse me, sir? I know no Mr Dixon.'

Another theatrical *moue* of ocular impairment: 'O, forgive me, ma'am! I mistook you for Mrs Dixon. I see now that you are Mrs Talbot. These peepers of mine!'

'I . . . I am afraid you are again mistaken, sir. I am Mrs Dickinson.'

'O, curse these useless eyes of mine! I do apologize. How could I have not recognized Roger's pretty wife? Your sons are the very image of him!'

'Roger?'

'Your husband was the finest glove-maker of Oxford-street, ma'am, if you don't mind me saying so. It is a travesty what his creditors have reduced him to.'

One of the boys giggled and mimicked my wrinkled squint to the other.

'Sir . . . my husband is called Herbert and is a banking clerk. I am afraid we must be going now. Good day to you.'

I maintained my optic confusion only until the innocent Mrs Dickinson had entered the gaol. Then I swiftly cast aside the spectacles and rolled the barrow away, ever grateful for the limitless capacity of our race to be embarrassed by awkwardness.

And a mere four hours later, I was back for the afternoon visitation period without the beer and spectacles, though with a basket containing bread and eggs. This time, I was an erstwhile colleague of that unfortunate banker's clerk Herbert Dickinson, he with the lovely wife and the two melancholy sons forced to grow with the shame of debt upon their bloodline. The poor man had complained of his prison diet and it was only fitting that I do whatever I could to supplement his gruel.

Once inside, however, I made no futile attempt to locate any Mr Dickinson. Rather, I made for the Middlesex ward of the gaol, crossing the spacious flagged yard and through the dolorous family scenes of the receiving ward to where I knew the day room of the debtors lay. My quarry was not the ashen fathers, the wasted husbands or the dissipated sons – rather, I sought the debtor without visiters: the long-term resident who has passed through the grief and shame of insolvency to find a home of sorts behind those walls. It is these men who are the unofficial ledgers and historians of inmates past, and of whom there are always one or two in every debtors' gaol. Indeed, here was one now sitting at the common table . . .

As his roomates received tearful kisses and sustaining victuals, he reclined insouciantly in a chair and smoked his long clay pipe with a smirk playing about his eyes. Dressed in a fading and oft-repaired suit, he was greying about the temples and must have been fifty years old. At my entry, he cast a comprehensive gaze of enquiry about my person and allowed himself a broad smile around the mouthpiece of the pipe.

'Ah, you'll be here about Eldritch Batchem,' he said.

I admit I was too startled to respond.

'Assuredly, you have the look of the penny-a-liner about you,' he said. 'The worn shoe leather, the suit of clothes that *was* fine when you bought it some years past, the inky fingertips and, yes, the furtive air of conspiracy as you venture here with not the slightest intention of visiting one of us poor debtors. But becalm yourself – I will not call the turnkeys! I myself am one of your accursed fraternity . . . or, at least, I once was.'

I took a seat at the table. A smell of stale food and un-flushed latrines predominated. 'Yes – I am a writer. I . . . I have brought you eggs and bread.'

'Ha! Of course you have, you duplicitous ———! I remember using such ruses myself to sniff out a story. I will not ask what machinations you employed to gain entry to this place, but I salute them. I trust you are not a stranger to the debtors' prison?'

'Horsemonger-lane. I wrote myself free just a few days past.'

'Yes, your appearance is more emaciated even than our

characteristically malnourished ilk. You have the look of grey incarceration about you still.'

'Well – I seek to add colour. I am on the scent of a story.'

'And you have heard somewhere that he was once here, "by royal appointment", one might almost say. Ha!'

'To my knowledge, Eldritch Batchem was never an inmate of this gaol.'

'No – but Thomas Crawford was,' said the fellow with a wink. 'He did not wear a tweed suit or a russet cap, but he was wont to wear his gloves continually.'

'What makes you think the two are the same man?'

'More pertinently – what makes *you* think so?'

'Call it supposition or intuition. One who knew this Crawford has remarked that there are similarities of character and voice with him who now calls himself Eldritch Batchem. Evidently you have had the same idea.'

'I have not seen the figure of Batchem, though I have read of his exploits in the papers. *Your* writing, perhaps? No matter – certain visiters here have remarked upon the same.'

'Did you know him?'

'Nobody knew him. He would not be known.'

'But you lived in his company and observed him: his excessively methodical nature, his irritable temperament, his nightmares . . .'

'Your research is thorough. Yes, he was a resident here perhaps six or eight months past and I had occasion to study him.'

'For how long did he stay?'

'It was curiously brief, that is true. It may have been as few as six weeks and then he was gone, his debts evidently cleared at a stroke.'

'Then he worked while he was here? How did he buy his freedom?'

'I never saw him do a thing but read newspapers. I supposed at the time that a benefactor must have bought his freedom, though he received not a single visiter as far as I can recall.'

'He spoke to no one? Not even when first admitted and the walls closed all around him?'

'The man was a veritable Sphinx, as parsimonious with his words as he was presumably profligate with his spending. O, but he was observant in his way: always with a secret eye or ear upon his fellow debtors. Yes – a suspicious one, to be sure. I barely saw him once they moved him to a private room.'

'Was that not highly unorthodox in itself?'

'Well, quite – but the dreams . . . he was keeping the whole ward awake with his gibberings. It was for the benefit of all that he was removed.'

'You are telling me nothing I do not already know, but I feel certain – if you were a writer of any quality – that you have made your own conjectures upon the man. Will you tell me, or must I leave and take my researches elsewhere?'

The debtor smiled and applied himself to his pipe for a moment. This unexpected interlude in his otherwise daily tedium was clearly affording him some amusement and he would not be hurried to its conclusion. At the same time, he seemed to be debating whether to reveal what he knew. Then, with a smile:

'I believe the key to the man is in his hands rather than yours.'

'So – a riddle. You refer perhaps to his insistence on wearing his gloves at all times.'

'That . . . and a particular disinclination to shake hands.'

'Evidently he has something to hide: some identifying characteristic that might otherwise prevent any protean inclinations. A tattoo? Some infirmity or deformity? A false hand? I see from your smile that you know very well what it is . . .'

'And why should I tell you? Ha! What writer gives away his secrets so that another may profit?'

'You have had your chance and you have not taken it. Or, at least, you have a part of the bigger story but not the whole. With respect, you are old and tired; you no longer have the requisite spark to weather the ceaseless challenges of the writer's life. It is why you smoke your pipe in peace here and live off the charity of others: content in your final defeat. I assume it is book publishing that has brought you to your sorry state?'

'Ah, books. Do not speak to me of books. Ha! If I had a penny for every book printed at my own risk, or for every copyright I have given up to pay a debt – well, I would be a debtor nevertheless. But you are quite right: it is a game for young men. My hands have lost their strength. My eyes . . .'

'Then tell me what you know. Let a younger man enjoy the freedom you can never again taste.'

'Perhaps for a credit in your eventual work . . . ?' He smiled, but his eyes were yearning.

'Let us be frank. Even if I did promise you such a credit, we both know I would be lying. Tell me, or do not tell me – but do not make me sit here longer amid this smell.'

'Ha! You truly have a heart of iron. You are a writer born, not made. Very well, very well – I will tell you. But I fear you may not believe me. I hardly believe it myself. Eldritch Batchem is a polydactyl.'

His face betrayed no mocking smirk or lie-revealing eva-
sion of gaze – only the pure satisfaction of revelation.

'How many?' I said.

'He has six fingers on each hand. I saw them myself – each
perfectly formed – as he washed at a basin. Look carefully
at those perpetual gloves of his and you will see only five
fingers, but the middle one is broader than the rest. Almost
twice as broad, in fact, to accommodate the extraneous digit.
I understand the condition is exceptionally rare.'

The obfuscating veil of personal history shifted and the
likely origins of Crawford/Batchem flashed before me. His
behaviour, his dreams, his hands – all suggested one irresistible conclusion about his past that I must prove.

'Ah, I believe you have it now: the next step in your investigation of the investigator! Ha!'

'Perhaps. Tell me – was there ever one called "Liveridge"
imprisoned here?'

'Not to my knowledge. But there is one so called in the
tortured soul of Eldritch Batchem, is there not?'

'I have heard that he spoke the name in his dreams.'

'In his nightmares only, and always incoherently. Whatever the true import of that name, it is one that for Mr
Batchem (or Mr Crawford if you prefer) is bound up in
anguish, fear or guilt. Whatever the secrets and shadows of
the man, they will find illumination in the decryption of that
single hieroglyphic.'

'I have no doubt of it. He now styles himself a "detective"
and pontificates on all matters pertaining to that art, but did
he ever show such interest while here at Whitecross-street?
What might have moved him since to grow that strange
beard and adopt his curious costume?'

'The man I observed was haughty and self-important.

Such traits require, or rather demand, an audience to achieve their fullest fruition. Indeed, for someone so determined in his pursuit of privacy, I believe he relished his notoriety. His every act of wilful seclusion brought him increasingly before our gaze.'

'Quite the paradox. Well, I thank you for your time, but I now have a story to pursue.'

'Wait . . . I do not even know your name.'

'What is a name? I am what you were, and will likely become what you are. Good day.'

And as I pursued my scant but telling discoveries at White-cross-street to their natural conclusions, the figure of Eldritch Batchem himself was blindly investigating his way to a violent encounter that would take him, unwittingly, to the black heart of the mystery he pursued.

Perseverance is undoubtedly one trait of the effective investigator, and he had been tireless in his interrogations among the shipping districts. Somewhere – in some smoky den or hectic wharf or greasy-cobbled court – he had heard a name mentioned. In time, that name had no doubt occurred again, and recurred until the chaos of beery and boorish answers revealed a thread.

The name was that of a particular wharf at Wapping.

It was, according to rumour, a place where ships moored (unofficially) if their allotted berth was temporarily taken. It was, they said, a place where one might find occasional work outside the normal dock hours. It was also, seemingly, a landing point at which almost every manner of cargo was received. More importantly, those who mentioned it at all did so with an accompanying glance over the shoulder, a wink or a confidential hand over the mouth.

Dusk was settling over the city as Eldritch Batchem strolled along Cinnamon-street, his russet cap and tweed suit drawing the comments and catcalls of sailors thereabouts. Public houses cast their gaslight across darkening lanes and the dank breath of the river rose among the muddy thoroughfares to claim them for the night.

Down onto Wapping-street he walked and ever eastwards past the Thames Tunnel to where the gas flares of the wharf in question silvered the warehouses and masts about it. As was its custom, the landing stage was busy with the offloading of a vessel and a steady procession of bales was being disgorged from the hold towards the gaping doors of the storehouse. The intoxicating sweetness of the cool evening air bespoke Virginia tobacco.

Or rather, that was the predominating scent. There was also another, less aromatic, which twitched at Eldritch Batchem's nostrils and caused him to look about for its source. He had smelled that nauseating compost of drains, mud and excrement previously on walking about Wapping-street, and had simultaneously felt that he was being watched. The sensation now was similar.

And there, leaning against a piling at the water's edge, was a short fellow who unblinkingly returned the gaze directed at him. A particularly grubby-looking specimen of indeterminate age (he might almost have been a boy), his face was oddly expressionless and his eyes were jet buttons.

'Do you work here at the wharf, young fellow?' said Eldritch Batchem, approaching his observer.

No reply.

'I am a detective seeking the missing brig *Aurora* and I was hoping to ask some questions hereabouts. I wonder if you would be so kind as to . . .'

An inadvertent flicker of the little man's eyes caused the investigator to turn quickly and look behind him, whereupon he was rendered quite speechless by what he saw.

Standing but a yard from him was the very double of the reeking fellow at the piling: the same height, the same clothes and the same pallid death-mask face – even the same black button eyes. There was not a detail to separate them.

'Well I . . . brothers!' said Eldritch Batchem, turning rapidly back and forth between the two for comparison.

But as he turned and re-turned, they moved silently closer towards him. Before he could react to the threat, he saw the sweep of an arm and the flash of a razor at his throat.

The blade sliced skin and blood ran forth.

'O! O! I am slain!' he cried as he dropped to the heavy planks of the wharf, gloved hands fluttering wetly about his neck as the russet cap fell free.

Of the two dozen men loading there, not a single one noticed anything. Or, at least, that is what they would have said if asked.

TWENTY-TWO

The bulldog's bulbous eyes stared sightlessly back at Mr Williamson from the wall-mounted glass case. Once a vigorous specimen of the rat-killing art, the animal was now reduced to a poorly upholstered parody of itself: legs exaggeratedly bowed, mangy jaw askew, and overstuffed to the point of seeming inflated. The plaque below its memorial proclaimed *Dancer: four-hundred rats in five minutes.*

'I saw um when ee wus alive,' said a virulently red-faced gentleman, nudging Mr Williamson in the ribs. 'Killed rats quicker than a feller wi' an 'ammer, did old Dancer.'

'Indeed?'

'O, aye. 'Tis a crime what they done to 'is memory. 'E looks more like a carp these days.'

'Quite.'

'Not seen yer 'ere before. 'Ere for the rats, are yer?'

'Yes. For the rats.'

Mr Williamson peered through the smoke of the Forecastle's seething parlour but could not see Noah. It was barely eight o'clock and the place was already raucously full of Ratcliff-highway's sailors, coachmen, rope-makers, biscuit-bakers, watermen and assorted ladies, both professional and domestic. Amid the general hubbub, there was the occasional yelp of terriers, bulldogs and optimistic mongrels tethered to table legs or sitting upon the laps of their owners.

Perceiving his interlocutor was otherwise preoccupied, the dog-fancier turned from Mr Williamson to another fellow and began a discussion on the merits of the ditch rat versus the sewer rat. Mr Williamson then gratefully returned his attention to the crowds, hopeful of glimpsing the Italian, or – less likely, it seemed – Eldritch Batchem himself. The dense and hazy fug made visibility limited, but would perhaps also offer him the same advantage against those who might observe *him*.

What was it that Eldritch Batchem had hoped to learn here? Was it, as Noah had suggested, merely an extension of his interrogations around the district? Or was he following a more specific trail? More to the point, was anyone who knew of the *Aurora*'s fate likely to reveal anything to a detective in the aftermath of those gruesome murders at the London Dock? The message had been clear enough: speak and you will die.

It was indeed a frustrating case, even in Mr Williamson's broad experience. There was no breathing witness to question, no accessible crime scene but the river itself, and no identifiable villain save the thousands of shoreline labourers and the elusive Italian. Its murders took place in nocturnal fog or unseen in supposedly locked fortresses of cargo, while the only trace of the vessel itself was a tabulated wake left through Custom House ledgers. Would this be the case that finally proved too diffuse for him to solve?

'Eldritch Batchem will find the vessel and the murderer, you mark my words.'

Mr Williamson looked up. The speaker was an omnibus

conductor standing immediately to his left and conversing with another fellow in the same line of work.

'Now then – I am not so sure,' replied the other. 'Did you not read that he was wrong about the Waterloo-bridge crime? The police are saying it was a clear case of murder – not suicide as Batchem said.'

'They would say that, wouldn't they? He has run rings around them.'

'There is evidence to the contrary.'

'What evidence?'

'They cannot reveal it all on account of putting the murderers on their guard.'

'That is rather convenient for them. Mark my words: it will be Mr Batchem who is triumphant. I will put money on it.'

'How much?'

'Well, I . . .'

Mr Williamson stopped listening and made to stand. He had seen Noah beckoning from the other side of the heaving parlour, where he was sitting with a trio of rough-looking river workers.

'This is my colleague Mr Williamson,' said Noah to his table mates as the detective approached. 'George – these gentlemen have had an interesting recent encounter with a certain "investigator" of our acquaintance. The ballast-raker here has quite a tale.'

'Is that right?' said Mr Williamson, taking a seat and examining the ballastmen with Noah. 'What manner of encounter?'

'As I was tellin' Mr Dyson 'ere,' said their leader, 'the —— in the red 'at came into a vessel I was rakin' at St Katharine's and assaulted me.'

'Eldritch Batchem *assaulted* you? Why would he do such a thing?' said Mr Williamson.

'I admit I was short with 'im and told 'im he couldn't enter, but 'e got quite upset and pushed me against the 'ull. Look at my 'ead!'

The ballast-raker pulled off his cap and exhibited the still-seeping gash.

'Hmm – that is indeed a nasty wound. What was he asking about?'

'Some ——— nonsense about workin' with a shovel and our work with the ballast. I told 'im nothin' and neither did my boys.'

Noah nudged the ballast-raker. 'Show Mr Williamson the glove.'

'Aye, we 'ad a bit of a scuffle and I pulled off 'is glove. I 'ave it 'ere.'

Mr Williamson took the proffered glove and examined it. 'Hmm. Fine-quality leather and stitching to be sure – no doubt made especially for the wearer. Average size and . . . what is this?'

Noah smiled but said nothing. Seeing that the ballast-raker was about to speak, he held the man's arm.

'One of the fingers is broader than the others,' continued Mr Williamson. He put his own hand into the glove and palpated the larger middle finger with an expression of enquiry. And, in a moment, his face showed the incredulity of understanding.

Noah laughed and nodded.

'Six ——— fingers!' blurted the ballast-raker. 'I saw 'em, but I didn't believe it at first. The man is a *devil* – I saw it in 'is eyes when 'e struck me. 'E threatened 'e would kill me if I told a soul.'

'Hmm. Hmm. This is most odd and unexpected, Noah,' said Mr Williamson, 'but it casts no further light on our case. So Mr Batchem has been asking about ballast; I have also had the same thought. That is no revelation.'

'Do not dismiss this information, George. I feel sure we will be able to learn more about Batchem knowing what we know. There is clearly more (quite literally) to the man than I had anticipated, and it is always beneficial to know another man's secrets, is it not?'

'Hmm. I believe it would be more useful to ask our fellows here about wharfs along the river. Have you not already done so?'

'I was about to. Gentlemen – I have no doubt that you have worked on vessels up and down the river. If I were to ask you to name wharfs where both tobacco *and* muscovado sugar are loaded – or in neighbouring warehouses, say – would that be a large number?'

The three ballastmen assumed expressions of cogitation, sorting through the catalogues of riverine locations in their heads. As they did so, Noah cast a surreptitious glance of concern at Mr Williamson, who was now disinterestedly fixated on the beery throng of the Forecastle. A man of characteristically grey moods, the ex-detective sergeant had seemed darker of late. Even the oddity of this latest discovery appeared not to rouse him.

'Well, there's Pickle Herring,' said the ballast-raker. 'They 'ave a bit of most things there.'

'Indeed,' said Noah, 'but there is also a quantity of coal landed there and we are not looking for coal dust.'

'What about Nine Elms wharf?' said one of the heavers. 'Moggach's warehouse 'as sugar and tobacco, don't it?'

'No, it 'as tobacco and *rum*,' said the ballast-raker. 'There are the West India Docks, of course, but their tobacco and sugar stores are at a distance from each other if I remember.'

'Fryin' Pan wharf at Wappin',' offered the heaver who had not yet spoken. 'I seen 'em unloadin' everythin' there: tobacca, wool, sugar, silks, furs . . . not coal. Never seen coa—'

There was a sudden pause. The ballast-raker had cast a severe look at the speaker. Noah caught it, and Mr Williamson evidently sensed it, turning his attention back from the parlour to the table.

'Who has a warehouse at Frying Pan wharf?' said Noah as nonchalantly as he could.

'O, it's not so much a ware'ouse,' said the ballast-raker with a careless gesture of the hand. 'Vessels sometimes stop there if their proper berth is taken, you know. At least, that's what I've 'eard.'

'And do Custom House officials receive ships there officially?' said Mr Williamson with renewed attention.

'If the ship 'as a landin' warrant, why not?' said the ballast-raker. 'I deal in ballast, sir – I don't pay attention to things that don't concern me. Fryin' Pan wharf doesn't concern me. It's none of our business, is it, mates?'

The two heavers shook their heads mutely and stared at the tabletop.

'Hmm,' said Mr Williamson.

'Well . . . can I buy you another drink, gentlemen?' said Noah with a clap of his hands.

'No. I think it's time for the rats,' said the ballast-raker, fumbling earnestly for his watch.

At that very moment, the barman rang a large brass ship's bell and a thrill of excitement passed through the parlour. Dogs recognized the sound and began barking. A door was thrown open and a slow rolling thunder of boots began to sound across the wooden floor towards the stairs led, it seemed, by three eager ballastmen.

'Shall we adjourn above?' said Noah to Mr Williamson.

'I suppose we might,' replied the latter.

'What is the matter, George? You are quite unlike yourself. Did you not just observe that awkwardness when the heaver mentioned Frying Pan wharf? I would not be surprised if every river worker here knows more than the police about the disappearance of that brig . . . and you are the man to extract it from them. Have you seen any sign of Batchem or the Italian?'

'Nothing.'

'Well, that is perhaps to our advantage. Let us follow the throng upstairs and see what else we can learn. Tomorrow, we will meet with Ben and Mr Cullen to gather all we know.'

'You have not yet spoken with Benjamin?'

'No, but that is not unusual. If he is not still at Ludgate-hill, he will be at a theatre somewhere. I will speak to him later. Now – let us make haste . . .'

The two joined the remaining enthusiasts in venturing up the narrow wooden staircase to the room above, which presented a scene even more populously cacophonous than the parlour had been. In the centre was a pit of about six feet in diameter with a waist-high rim encircling it and a large gas chandelier suspended centrally above. All around the pit, men sat on banked benches or stood leaning over the rim to loudly debate the merits of the sturdy bulldog that sniffed about the white-painted floor within.

Noah indicated that they should take different viewing positions and Mr Williamson ascended one of the benches to take a seat between a bulky fellow with coal dust glistening in his beard and an American sailor in a red worsted shirt who introduced himself with a wink and a gobbet of chewing tobacco that narrowly missed the detective's shoes. Pipe smoke twisted beneath the startling illumination of the gas chandelier and there was a powerful smell of gin in the air.

'Welcome, welcome all!' came a shout from the doorway: the portly landlord himself.

A colossal cheer and stamping of feet went up and the assembled dogs again began their chorus of anticipation.

'Tonight, we will see some fine examples of the rat-killing art,' said the landlord, 'including my own precious terrier Claymore, who will attempt fifty rats in five minutes! But first, perhaps some of you will try your animals. Who is this in the pit? A fine bulldog, it seems. Is he a brave one?'

'He is called Prince,' shouted a fellow at the rim, evidently the owner. 'I will try him on ten rats.'

'Very well – let us test his mettle. The rats, the rats – bring the rats!'

The volume in the room rose higher as the audience scrutinized the animal before them and placed bets on whether Prince would kill all of his rats. Meanwhile, a singular personage came through the door hoisting a writhing canvas sack over his shoulder. The fellow, who seemed to walk lightly upon his toes, could have been no taller than five feet and wore a long, thick beard that extended south to his sternum and north almost to his eyes. Long wiry hair stood out alarmingly from his scalp and reached down to touch his shoulders. As he passed through the crowd, dogs growled and worried at his heels.

'Mr Baudrons – have you got some good ones for us?' shouted the landlord with a theatrical gesture.

The hairy little man nodded and continued to the pit, where he climbed over the rim with the aid of some wooden steps. Once inside, he indicated that Prince's owner should restrain him until the ten rats could be extracted. He then unbound the neck of the twitching sack and reached in with a bare hand to extract the first of the damp and filth-matted vermin by its thick brown tail. With each successive rat, the room became more and more suffused with the putrid stench of the sewer until ten of the abominations huddled in a roiling mass of fur and tails by the pit's rim.

By now, dogs all over the room were whimpering or barking at the unholy aroma and speculation among the crowd had reached a hiatus. Meanwhile Noah and Mr Williamson used the general focus upon the arena to cast their eyes over the crowds for any sign of their Italian in disguise. Of him, however, there was no sign among the motley gathering – though there was another present whose atrocious bodily odour was to some degree now masked by the smell of the rats.

He named Baudrons climbed back out of the ring and signalled to the landlord with a nod.

'Release the dog! Let Prince seek his coronation!' shouted the landlord.

A cheer erupted and the bulldog approached the seething pile with dainty caution. Unsure, he put an exploratory nose to it . . . but withdrew a mere second later, yelping and dancing madly about with a rat attached firmly to his snout.

A great laugh of derision erupted from the crowd and continued as Prince sought urgently to prise the creature from his nose with a flailing paw. The humiliated owner reached urgently into the pit and jabbed his pocket knife at the rat, whereupon it let go and scuttled back to the group seemingly none the worse for wear. Prince, however, had had quite enough and sat licking at his nose with no more interest in the proceedings.

'That was rather a poor show,' said Noah to the man standing next to him at the pit's edge: the fellow called Baudrons.

'I have no resspect for dogz, ssir,' replied the diminutive fellow. 'Foolissh animalz, they are. A good cat would not cower sso before an animal but a quarter of itz ssize. I ssupply the ratz, certainly, but I have no regard for the dogz.'

'They are sewer rats, are they?'

'Indeed, ssir. They are the mosst obsstreperouss ssince they musst fight for their food. Your ditch and river rat iss fat and sspoilt in hiss fare.'

'I expect you are quite an authority on the matter.'

'Not esspecially, ssir. Catz are my province. I am cat masster at the London Dock.'

'Is that right? A terrible business two days past, was it not? In fact, you must have been about your duties at around the time the crimes in the furnace were perpetrated. I wonder if you saw or heard anything?'

'I have already sspoken to the Thamez Police on the matter.'

'The *Thames* Police? Perhaps you mean the Detective Police . . .'

'Not at all. A red-haired fellow in uniform, he waz. Quite impertinent, and no friend to catz. He ssmelled of boatz.'

'Inspector Newsome,' said Noah.

Another enormous cheer interrupted their conversation as a feisty terrier (a substitute for the tremulous Prince) tossed a dead rat over the rim into a fellow's lap. Noah took the opportunity to wave across at Mr Williamson and indicate that he should come to join them.

'I don't recall hiss giving a name,' said Mr Baudrons.

'On what did he question you?'

'Az you ssay: about the night of the deathss. I ssaw nothing.'

'And that was the extent of your conversation with him?'

'That, and a tooth he wanted to know about.'

'A tooth? A human tooth?'

'No, ssir – an animal'z tooth he found. Very likely a lion or tiger, I would ssay.'

Noah looked dubiously at the pinched and hirsute face of his interlocutor. It seemed to show no signs of guile or deception.

Mr Williamson arrived meanwhile and stood alongside, shaking his head at Noah's raised eyebrow of enquiry: no, there was still no sign of the Italian or of Eldritch Batchem.

'This is a fellow of mine,' said Noah to Mr Baudrons. 'He is a genuine detective – not a uniformed policeman. George – this gentleman is the cat master of London Dock and has been interviewed by Inspector Newsome about a large animal tooth. What do you make of that?'

At the name of his former superior, Mr Williamson blinked and seemed to return from his hitherto abstracted realm. 'Hmm. Inspector Newsome is indeed a curious man. Did he reveal where he found the tooth or to what it might pertain?'

'He did not, ssir, though he assked me if ssuch a large animal might live in the ssewerz, and about the sstoriez of the mudlarkz. They claim to ssee footprintz in the mud, you know.'

Noah and Mr Williamson exchanged a glance of mutual bafflement. Had Mr Newsome's descent into uniform rendered the man insane?

'And did he seem to suggest that this tooth was in any way connected to his investigation into the deaths in the spirit vault or Queen's Pipe?' said Noah.

'No, ssir. No indication of that at all.'

A reverberating collective yell filled the room. The land-lord's champion terrier Claymore was about to enter the pit and Mr Baudrons excused himself to fetch a fresh consignment of rats from downstairs.

'What do you make of that?' said Noah, looking swiftly around the banked benches to see if anyone had been watching their conversation with Mr Baudrons.

'I admit I have no idea,' said Mr Williamson, 'but whatever else he may be, the inspector is not stupid. There must be something in his enquiries. The sewers, the mud banks . . . could there be some connection with that body he apparently pulled from the river?'

'It is the only connection I can think of. But how to proceed . . . ?'

Mr Baudrons entered the room once more, this time aided by another man in carrying a large rusting wire cage that teemed with claws, wet fur and thick cable tails. Together they traversed the wooden stairs into the pit and poured the heaving brown mass onto the ground, where it swarmed briefly in exploratory arcs before instinctively forming a protective mound. The crowd cheered appreciatively at the general size and robustness of the specimens, and Mr Baudrons took a small bow.

But as he raised his head from that bow, he seemed to pause as if remembering or sensing something. His eyes seemed to flicker across one quadrant of the benches, and then he retired from the pit so that Claymore might try his luck at fifty rats. Noah, however, had caught the moment and touched Mr Williamson's arm.

'Another good selection of vermin,' said Noah as Mr Baudrons rejoined them.

'Yess, all quite filthy and dizeazed . . .' came the some-what distracted reply.

'Did you notice somebody you know in the crowd just then, Mr Baudrons? I saw you look up into the crowd.'

'No . . . no, it waz a ssmell.'

'The smell of the rats? They are quite pungent, are they not?'

'Not the ratz. They have their own disstinct aroma. No – I have ssmelled that other ssmell before: ssomething of the ssewerz, but with a human sscent alsso. Mosst unpleasant. It waz in the tobacco warehousse of the dock that night – that night they found the fellow in the kiln. My ssoldierz ssmelled it alsso . . .'

'Who? Who is it in the audience that smells so,' said Noah. 'Did you detect him from the pit?'

'I think I might know who,' said Mr Williamson, his eyes fixed on a short man towards the back of the benches.

Noah's eyes followed the line of the gaze and saw the man. Despite the press of humanity, there was a distinct space either side of the fellow in question, who appeared even from that distance to be a grubby specimen. His hair was thick with grime and his clothing dark with accumulated dirt. More significantly, he seemed to be showing no interest in the blood-and-fur phrenzy of the pit, but rather stared with blank manikin eyes at the three now studying him. If he was surprised or afraid to be identified, he showed not a sign of it.

'George – I wonder if you would like to situate yourself by the doorway while I approach that little man,' said Noah, beginning to make his way around the inner rim of the benches without taking his eyes from his target.

Mr Williamson did immediately as bidden, picking a way through the flailing arms and jostling figures all about him.

The doughty Claymore had by this point dispatched almost forty of the sewer rats, whose bodies lay twitching or inert about the blood-spattered circle. It was the height of the evening's entertainment and there was much money to be made or lost upon the next thirty seconds.

Only now did the stinking man on the benches appear to perceive he was to be trapped, and, like a rat himself, looked rapidly about for a means of escape. The door to the stairway was distant, and Mr Williamson was struggling through bodies to reach it. Meanwhile, Noah came ever closer with an unwavering stare of intent.

Neither of his pursuers could have anticipated what next occurred.

With an agility betrayed by his stature, the stinking fellow vaulted over the rear of the benches and dropped some eight feet into the perimeter space by the wall. An uncurtained window there had been whitewashed over and this he shattered with a determined kick that was barely heard above the clamour of Claymore's final seconds in the pit.

Pausing only to clear any remaining shards from the frame's lower edge with his boot, the man then crawled out backwards to hang with both hands from the sill above the alley beside the public house. By the time Noah arrived at the window, his quarry had already dropped from the first floor to land with a jolting grunt in the mud below.

Noah risked his head over the parapet and saw the little fellow exchanging words with a colossal man whose face seemed to swirl with strange blue-black shadows: the distinctive curlicued tattooing of those odd Antipodean warriors occasionally encountered about the world's shipping districts. At the sight of Noah, this giant raised a pistol and let off a shot that smashed the remaining pane even as his target jerked back inside.

'Are you wounded?' asked a rapidly approaching Mr Williamson.

Noah removed glass shards from his shoulders. 'I am unharmed. He went through the window here and his accomplice fired at me.'

'Who? The Italian?'

'No – a South Sea islander. An enormous fellow.'

'A harpooner, perhaps?'

'Very likely. I saw his face and would know him again.'

'We must go and apprehend them. Quickly!'

'George – wait! It is futile; they will be already gone by the time we descend to the street. Even if they are not, the islander is armed and physically more than a match for both of us. Let us instead be content to act on the knowledge we have.'

'What knowledge? The man has escaped.'

'If nothing else, we know we are looking for a small malodorous man and a huge one with a tattooed face. Let us also add the Italian and we have three quite distinctive characters to seek – all the better if they are associates. When we meet with Ben and Mr Cullen, I rather suspect we will be in possession of the requisite materials to finally solve this mystery.'

'Hmm.'

'I am glad you agree. Now – did Claymore kill his fifty rats? I had five pounds on him to succeed . . .'

TWENTY-THREE

Mr Cullen's first sensation on regaining consciousness was the pain in the back of his head. An exploratory hand proved what he already knew: he had been clubbed senseless, the assault leaving a raw gash upon the back of his scull. He was now lying face down on a cold stone floor.

Though the very act of thinking seemed to hurt, he tried to reconstruct how he might have been attacked and by whom. He clearly recalled a man coming to him at the gates of the London Dock and telling him that Mr Rigby needed an extra hand to unload some cargo. Then he and the messenger had re-entered the dock and boarded a ship, the *Concordia*, which had travelled a matter of twenty minutes or so east to Frying Pan wharf.

The mood on board had been somewhat tense. A number of men evidently chosen for their strength had looked at Mr Cullen with frank distrust and at each other with questioning glances. They had coldly rejected his few attempts to engage in the jocular riverine idiom he had sought so hard to master. Meanwhile, Mr Rigby observed all with an unfathomable gaze and exchanged some private comment with the reeking little fellow who had also been waiting outside the dock gates.

On arrival at the wharf, Mr Cullen had sought to redeem himself by wholeheartedly putting his back into the work, hoisting barrels out of the hold and then descending to the shore to further transport the cargo into the open warehouse. It had been dark by this point, but gas flares illuminated the wharf with their pale brilliance and rendered the toiling lumpers figures in a startling riverside lithograph.

The work had proceeded thus, in eerie silence but for the song of the tackle and the rumble of barrels, for over an hour. Then, finding himself momentarily alone in the part of the warehouse where the barrels were being stored, Mr Cullen had taken the opportunity to take a circuitous route back to the doors.

Nothing seemed particularly amiss. It was a warehouse like any other, albeit rather eclectically stocked with a variety of material ranging from spirits to tobacco and from tea to bales of cloth. Such storehouses tended to be owned by proprietors who dealt only in a limited trade, but an exception was hardly to be questioned.

However, when a draught of cold musty air had caught Mr Cullen on his return to the wharf, he had paused, curious, to investigate from whence it came. There was a faint smell of drains about it, and his first thought was that there was perhaps an old well in the rear of the building. He was engaged in peering between fat bales of cotton at what appeared to be a broad rusty iron hatch in the floor when Mr Rigby appeared silently behind him.

'What're yer doin' there, lumper?' the tattooed foreman had said.

'O, I . . . I thought I smelled a well, Mr Rigby, sir.'

'A *well*? Yer not 'ere to be smellin' wells, are yer?'

'No, sir. Sorry, sir. I'll get back to the ship.'

'Or perhaps yer were lookin' for somethin' other . . . ?'

'What? No . . . I . . .'

'Get back to the *Concordia*. I knew I was wrong to give yer a chance.'

'Yes, sir . . .'

And he had started to return to the wharf, never to reach it.

Had it been Mr Rigby who had struck him? Or was it some other unseen assailant? There had been the blow, a flash of white light, and then only blackness. He did not even recall striking the floor.

Now he appeared to be in some manner of dim, candle-lit cell – though it was not like any police gaol he had ever seen. The dark stonework smelled damp and its huge rough blocks looked old. A rusting iron door showed no eye slot, no knob and no shutter at the bottom for the ingress of food. There was no bed or any other furniture. Indeed, it was difficult to make out any finer detail in the light from the single candle burning in a simple wooden holder on the ground at the centre of the room.

He struggled into a sitting position and felt nausea rush upon him. The knees of his trousers had been ripped in his fall, though any grazing of the skin thereabouts was insignificant when compared to the pain in his head. He checked about his person and found that nothing seemed to have been taken from his pockets.

Gathering his senses, he became gradually aware of something odd: the absolute silence. There was no sound of traffic, or of people, or of the building itself: a bang of door or creaking floor. One would expect to hear *something* of the city, even the vibration of a passing goods wagon, but there was not the merest hint of sound. Rather, he had the impression of being locked within walls of such immense thickness that no sign of life could penetrate from outside.

Most men would have felt the chill hand of fear in such a place. Some would have wept at their predicament. Mr Cullen felt only shame at having caused inevitable disappointment to his fellows, who would surely discover his absence and waste valuable time trying to locate him rather than pursuing the case at hand. Mr Williamson would not say anything, of course, but the loss of confidence would be palpable in his every expression thereafter . . . Unless Mr Cullen could effect an escape and report his discoveries with all haste.

He sought to order his thoughts. What exactly was there to report? He had seen nothing untoward. Indeed, he had nothing to reveal but a feeling of vague dubiety and a blow to the head at Frying Pan wharf. River men were a rough sort and he had likely exceeded his role of mere lumper with his curiosity.

But the cell? Why imprison him when they might have more easily bundled him into the river wrapped in heavy chain? Whatever the reasoning, there was something highly illegitimate about the proceedings and Mr Williamson would expect to hear the particulars.

He stood uneasily and approached the door, which appeared even rustier on closer inspection. The atmosphere was clearly extremely damp. He rested an ear against the cold iron and tried to discern any voices beyond, but there was nothing. A keyhole revealed only darkness (or perhaps an escutcheon plate) on the other side. He paused in frustration. What would Noah or Mr Williamson do? What further methods might they employ to transform ignorance into knowledge?

He put his nose to the space at the bottom of the door and sniffed. The smell of wet stone and drains was similar to what he had experienced at Frying Pan wharf, and there was a faint but unmistakable whiff of new tobacco. Good – that was a connection of sorts. It was possible that he had not been moved far from the warehouse in his unconscious state.

Now for a closer examination of the room itself. He forced himself to look with fresh eyes at the bare space: thick stone flags upon the floor, with some remnants of hay here and there; an uncommonly tall ceiling that seemed to narrow as it rose into impenetrable shadow; large rough-hewn blocks of dark stone. It was, in truth, more a dungeon than a cell.

Only the candle struck a discordant note. Amid such grimness, it was an incongruous kindness to the prisoner, who might sooner be broken by the darkness and silence. He approached it cautiously, half expecting some fatal mech-anism to spring into life at his step, but all suspicion faded when he came within arm's reach. It was nothing more than a simple candle in a rudimentary holder.

Rather, it was perhaps *too* simple. Why give the prisoner the means to explore his dungeon when there could be no means of escape? Unless, of course, that was the entire point: to taunt him. There was a certain malice in providing a means of illumination that consumed itself even as it prom-ised the impending inevitability of absolute blackness.

Despite his circumstances, Mr Cullen could not help but smile. He had made a deduction: the detail of the candle said something about whoever had imprisoned him. It was some-thing he could tell Mr Williamson.

Not to be cowed, he took up the candle and went to the wall by the door that he might examine it more closely. In so doing, he understood just why the light had been provided. Under the dim orange glow of the flame, he saw that there was an obvious tidemark around the room where water had evidently filled the space at intervals. It was almost as high as he was tall, and it suggested something else: the door must itself be at the bottom of a descending corridor so that any water could seep under it without flooding another chamber. There was most likely a set of stairs heading upwards from the doorway, which in turn explained the silence of the room. He was probably below the level of the ground.

Another deduction: was this to be the means by which he would die – trapped here as the room filled with water? He recalled the tales he had heard at the docks about the river breaking its banks and flooding the surrounding districts. Was he now in one of those districts?

He was pondering this when a sound within the room startled him: a low moaning that could only come from a man. He looked about him but saw nothing. He looked up and saw no aperture in the disappearing ceiling from which the noise may have come. Then, holding the candle before him, he stepped tentatively over the flagstones to examine the far side of the room.

And there, lying flat along the bottom of a wall, was apparently a long bundle of rags. So dark, still and shapeless was it that he had previously taken it for a shadow in the brickwork. But it was no shadow. It was a man of considerable height, his dark clothes evidently made darker still by water stains and grime. Clearly, he was emerging from the same oblivion of unconsciousness his observer had so recently experienced.

A dark face appeared dimly from beneath an arm.

'Ben?' said Mr Cullen.

The hand that reached to touch the bloody spot at the base of the scull was undoubtedly black. The face that turned squinting to the light exhibited a milky eye.

'My G—, Ben! It *is* you! How did . . . what . . . let me help you up.'

Benjamin took the extended hand and pulled himself into a sitting position. His face in the candlelight showed that he had sustained other minor injuries, perhaps in his fall. Dried blood was crusted beneath his nose and there was a cut under his healthy eye. He waved a hand about the room and shrugged interrogatively.

'Where are we?' interpreted Mr Cullen. 'I admit I have no idea, Ben. I believe it is a cell under the ground in the vicinity of Frying Pan wharf, but how or why I came to be here is something I cannot explain. There was some unloading and I was doing extra work for a certain Mr Rigby . . . but how did you come to be here?'

Benjamin began his rapid exposition of signs but stopped after only a few moments when Mr Cullen's utter incomprehension became clear. Instead, he sighed and resorted to the simple dumb-show mimicking of a frying pan, accompanying it with a tongueless approximation of a sizzling sausage.

'You too were brought to Frying Pan wharf? So the place *does* mean something in the *Aurora* case!'

Benjamin nodded wearily. Whatever they had learned was useless inside a subterranean cell.

Mr Cullen could not know, of course, how Benjamin had found his way to that cell, how he had kept the noisome fellow from Ludgate-hill under his observation until they alighted at Execution Dock and thence through the twisting streets of that riverside district towards the environs of Frying Pan wharf. There, the little man had entered the large warehouse without hesitation and still without any apparent suspicion that he was being followed. Benjamin had loitered briefly, acutely aware that his attire did not suit the environment and that every minute he tarried was an invitation for further attention. Thus, within a few minutes, he had determined to absent himself from the place and report back to Noah about the likely source of the illicit silk.

But as he had turned to walk back to the ferry platform, he was faced with the very same diminutive fellow he had been pursuing. It did not seem remotely possible that the man had emerged from a different part of the warehouse and circled the streets unseen to arrive behind Benjamin in such a short time – yet there he was, staring blankly up at his Negro shadow with a painted face that was quite devoid of emotion.

The two had paused in that silent *tableau* of recognition: one of them incapable of speech and the other showing no inclination towards it. Pursuer wordlessly acknowledged the pursued. Mutual accusation was implicit.

Benjamin shrugged good-naturedly: such was the nature of the game. Who was to make the next move? The stinking boy-man simply gazed unblinking.

And something had crashed heavily against the base of Benjamin's scull. As he dropped into blackness, confusion was the overwhelming sensation. Who had managed to come so close to him without revealing the slightest noise or indication of their presence? It was quite unnatural . . .

'Ben? Ben? Are you all right?' Mr Cullen brought the candle closer. 'You seem quite distant. Perhaps the knock on your head? He must have been a sturdy fellow to get the better of you!'

Benjamin nodded absently and looked about the cell.

'I have made a thorough examination of the place, Ben. There is but one door. The ceiling, as you see, tapers off into shadow. I suspect that it is sometimes flooded. A curious place, to be sure. What do you think? What is our best course of action? Will Noah be coming for us?'

Benjamin shook his head. Nobody knew about their location but the people who had imprisoned them. Or, rather, lured them – it was too large a coincidence that they would find themselves in the same cell . . . which in turn suggested that whoever was behind the disappearance of the *Aurora* had been observing their observers for some time.

'Why so glum, Ben? Have hope! I am certain that Noah and Mr Williamson are doing their utmost to find us. Once they discern that we have gone . . .'

But Benjamin was toying with the iron ring about his ankle, his single eye turned inward upon some other place and time – a place, similarly, of incarceration, darkness and fear.

'What we need is a plan, Ben. Something similar to the time we took Mr Williamson from Giltspur-street. Perhaps . . . perhaps if we leave a bundle of clothes where you were lying and then, when somebody enters, they will mistake the pile for your figure. We will have the advantage of surprise . . . Ben – what *is* that metal band about your ankle? Is it some ornament particular to the Negro?'

Benjamin laughed – not his usual hearty *basso* note, but rather a short expiration quite bereft of mirth. Yes, it was indeed an 'ornament particular to the Negro' – at least, the Negro as he continued to live in the United States, the Negro that Benjamin had once been. Free in England he might be, but his predicament at that moment was a clear enough indication that freedom could still be forcibly taken at any point.

Could a simple, honest soul such as Mr Cullen ever truly understand the infernal abyss from which his cellmate had fought to escape? Could he, who had known liberty from birth, conceive the asphyxiating sensation of returning to the incarcerated state?

Benjamin indicated that Mr Cullen should sit opposite him and place the candle once more upon the cold stone flags between them. He pointed to his own eyes with forked fingers and then at Mr Cullen's with a single definitive finger: watch my hands and my face. Hear my story. Understand me.

Mr Cullen, for his part, observed the terrible solemnity in that single functioning eye and nodded. He would try his best to read the hieratical language of fingers and palms, which, though often arcane, was also broadly imitative.

And so, illuminated by the meagre light of a single flame, Benjamin began his narration, hands moving slowly to acclimatize his listener to the wordless tongue. A palm held low showed the stature of the enslaved boy. Raised to waist height, it bespoke the crops all about him. Curved and hooked, it became a scythe. The work was reaping or picking, while fingers flickering from above called forth a relentless Mississippi sun.

Only the hands spoke, but the body and the face were mirrors to the story. His one eye, unfocused, on the past, Benjamin became a different man: no longer the lofty well-built Negro of common acquaintance, but one cowed and nervous beneath the hateful gaze of the field overseers – a boy reduced to human livestock, a boy reduced to the function of sweeper, cutter, carrier, washer, digger.

Here was a boy that slept uncovered on cold stone and who worked hungry, knowing neither his parents nor how old he was. He was inquisitive. He had questions that might kill him if asked. And his two sharp eyes saw the things that awaited him: the naked bodies suspended on hooks and flayed until their backs hung wetly in tatters; the sickening stench of branded flesh; the whippings that demanded screams and then demanded silence; the casual bludgeon; the hateful seduction; the immolation of the falsely accused.

He grew to be naturally big and strong: a finer man, he knew, than those who worked him under the gun. At such a size, and with such strength, he inspired admiration and fear in equal measure – the former for his ox-like endurance and the latter for what he might one day do with it. So if they drunkenly tied him to a post and beat him blind on an occasional Saturday evening, it was merely to curb his sinful pride and show him he was a lesser man.

He and his kin sang as they worked – tunes and rhythms born not of any learned musical knowledge but from the life in each that had not been caged. They used words beyond their understanding, words sung to them by unknown mothers who had received them from *their* mothers a continent away. The words mattered not – only their utterance: a prayer for some, a lament for others, a sole unfettered expression for all.

And how Benjamin had loved to sing! Always the first to start and the last to finish, he sang at work and he sang at rest. In song, there was a means to tell himself the story of each day, mimicking everything from the to-and-fro of the saw to the cries of the beasts, from the creak of the gate to the beat of the hammer. In song, his imagination was free.

In song, he gave an impression of carefree happiness that could not be tolerated. In song, he mocked those who would reduce him to an ignorant beast. First, they warned him. Then they flogged him. But he could no more stop singing than thinking. He infuriated them beyond tolerance. So they pulled out his tongue with pincers heated in the smithy forge.

After that there was only silence – silence and a hatred

that would not be placated until Benjamin could flee and see his tormentors repaid. From that moment, his single eye sought every distant copse, cloud and horizon. What he had lost in voice he would invest in careful study of his captors: their comings and goings, their means of transport and the timetables of their trips. Northwards lay freedom, and he would be free.

In the meantime, he dissimulated servility and exaggerated his subjugation. Tongueless now, he had become the beast they had wanted – a dumb, passive implement. But his labour earned him food and his food earned him the endurance he would shortly need. Strength and imagination were the parts of him they could not tear away with cauterizing iron.

Then, escape, when it came, was an ordeal – all the more so since his self-willed emancipation was paid for with the unrestrained murder of those who had dared silence his song. He was pursued for days through the fields, through the brush, through the rivers and forests and hills. His feet bled with hard distance and his skin was torn by thorny flight. At every crossroads, bridge and river port, there were sentinels, patrols, guards and guns. Dogs chased his scent relentlessly.

But he ran, away from slavery and away from death. He ran to freedom in the ports of the north, where the oceans beckoned and where he might turn his strength to a lifetime of liberty. It would be the limitless horizons of the sea that gave him new birth.

Beneath the sails of his new life, he made a vow. Never again would he permit another man to put chains on him or imprison him. He had been silenced, but he would live for pleasure and savour every day. He would dress as finely as his pocket would allow; he would eat to satisfy his stature; he would walk tall with pride and be subservient to no man.

And he would retain that band of iron about his ankle to remind him of these promises to himself . . .

Benjamin lowered his hands, breathing more heavily now with the force of his narration. Sweat glistened on his face in the candlelight and the seeing eye burned with its flame.

Mr Cullen felt his mouth dry and his palms damp. He searched for something to say in response, and, finding nothing commensurate, merely nodded. He understood.

The candle guttered and died.

The cell was thrown into utter blackness.

TWENTY-FOUR

By no measure could Inspector Newsome be termed religious. He had seen enough evil to know that Man's sin was eternal and never to be cleansed – not even if an ocean of salvation were to wash through the metropolis. Nevertheless, a childhood of forcible scripture remained with him, flickering unbidden across his thoughts when stirred by some circumstance or other. One such line now seemed particularly insistent: *And Jonah was in the belly of the fish three days and three nights.*

In those first moments of realization that he was abandoned, he had fought to remain composed. There was no immediate danger. He had light from the chest-strapped bullseye lamp. He was not exposed to extremes of temperature. He had not yet experienced thirst or hunger. In his coat pocket, he had a roll of oilcloth containing a sheathed dagger and a pistol loaded with shot lest his life fall into danger. No, the greatest threat in such a situation was the fragility of one's own soul. Men went mad in gaol or on vessels adrift at sea; might not the same occur within the very bowels of the city?

The thing was to remain calm: to ignore the endlessly ramifying darkness all about and to think about one's options. Perhaps the tosher would return at the next tide to see what had become of the policeman he had abandoned. In that eventuality, Mr Newsome's best course of action was to remain as near to his point of abandonment as possible and to simply pass the hours with patience and fortitude.

On the other hand, would the tosher willingly return to face the inevitable wrath caused by his unannounced departure? Admittedly, another of his soiled brotherhood may happen along the same tunnel in a few hours' time . . . or he may not.

Such uncertainty was not to be tolerated. Action was required. Should the inspector assume that all water flowed towards the river and take that direction in the certainty of arriving at a broad sewer mouth? Or would such an avenue lead to drowning as the tidal flood washed about the tunnels? Though most outflows were, he knew, sealed with iron baffles that opened and closed with the pressure of the river, the older sewers were still open to the flood. He looked at his watch – there were perhaps five more hours before the tide changed in his favour.

Had not the tosher said that it was sometimes possible to glimpse the city through the gulley holes in the streets themselves? If so, it might therefore be possible to seek out one of the broader tunnels that ran beneath the broad thoroughfares and call to a passer-by that he was trapped. In such a way, his exact location could be discerned and a tosher sent to rescue him. It seemed a fair solution . . . with the single caveat that he would thereafter (and in perpetuity) be known as that unfortunate detective who was trapped down a drain. The idea was therefore rapidly dismissed from his mind.

One clearly desirable action remained: he would endeavour to continue the investigation unhindered by the inconvenience of his imprisonment deep beneath the earth.

Neither night nor inclement weather could hinder him here within the endless caverns of filth. It had, after all, been the search for clues that had led him here, and there was no reason why he might not utilize the next few hours precisely towards that end.

Thus determined, he unwrapped the pistol from its oil-cloth and slipped it snugly behind one of the lamp straps across his chest. The sheathed dagger, he tucked behind his belt where he might grasp it at a moment's notice. Then he stilled his breathing, the better to listen and calmly attune his previously fevered thoughts to his environment and the task at hand.

The tunnels dripped and gurgled with distorted echoes. Distant splashes be-spoke rats and splats of matter slopping down drains. A plutonic wind brought variously the heat of vegetal decay or the cold aroma of the grave. But there seemed no sign of human life – no rhythmic step or cough or scrape of shoe. The answers were all here, below; he was sure of it. Where to begin?

Somewhere among the multiplying channels of that putrid Hades was the reeking little man of Pickle Herring and Nightingale-lane. When last glimpsed, the fellow had been carrying a Davy lamp rather than the cumbersome specimen upon Mr Newsome's chest. Such lamps were arguably brighter than the bullseye, but they also contained less oil. Therefore, unless the enemy had an extra supply with him, his lamp would not last until the tides changed . . . which rather suggested he was heading to a place where he might access more oil – a place, perhaps, where he might bide his time while the waters sealed all within. Certainly, the stench and general appearance of the chap suggested that he spent much time in the sewers.

And what of the mysterious animal tooth? Was it not the only tangible clue as to the death of first mate Hampton, as well as a suggestion of something lurking in the sewers? Was it really a leap of the imagination that the beast was some manner of protector or deterrent? Here, beneath the city, where no customs man or detective would think to investigate, the cargo of that missing vessel could be hidden beyond all eyes.

So he walked, no longer noticing his saturated feet and legs, and searched the brickwork about him for any clues to the regular passage of men. Had the water been splashed above its natural level by a passing foot? Had successive hands left a greasy mark on a ledge? Was there some natural, intuitive route to be discerned through the larger tunnels as one sometimes navigates unknown city streets with an accumulated urban sensibility? His senses were alive for the merest clue.

And then he saw it.

It was easy to miss in the dimness of the lamp's illumination, but clarity was achieved by directing the beam immediately upon the curious marking: a pale chalk sign made at shoulder level by some human hand. The hieroglyph (a circle bisected horizontally by a line that extended each side beyond the diameter) resembled no letter or symbol he recognized. He had not previously noticed such things as he accompanied the tosher, and the man had apparently shown no inclination to look for them. Even so, the chalk circle surely had to be some marker or directional aid used by the sewer hunters – or by others using those dank passages.

Mr Newsome considered the device for any inherent meaning. Did the circle represent the tunnel itself and the bisecting line an arrow of sorts? Appearing as it did on a corner where a large sewer formed a junction with two more, perhaps the sign related to that specific arrangement of tunnels and directed its reader in a particular manner. But what manner?

He knew enough of the criminal codes of burglars and pickpockets to appreciate that no single, isolated symbol was intelligible. Only by drawing conclusions from a number of them could some pattern be deduced. And excitement gripped him – here, it seemed, was the key to his deliverance from the underworld, if only he could interpret the code.

He splashed across the sewer to check the other corner for similar marks and was satisfied to see a chalk circle there also. This one, however, featured an inconclusive vertical bisecting line. What now?

Neither direction seemed more obviously propitious than its alternative, so he took the right-hand (more inviting?) option indicated by the vertical line and trudged ankle-deep along the tunnel in search of another mark. As he went, he reflected the truth of what the tosher had told him: that the smell became, after some time, no worse than certain streets above. There were rats, true, but they showed little inclination to trouble him and seemed content to swim from his approach. Indeed, in the dull beam of the lamp, he might almost imagine himself on a midnight beat among the rotten pre-pyrean alleys of Wapping or Rotherhithe.

Another division of the labyrinth presented itself and other symbols emerged from the darkness: on one corner a circle with three vertical lines bisecting it, and on the other a repetition of the first sign he had seen. A deduction – the vertical lines denoted how many apertures stood between the walker and his next direction, while the horizontal line marked a closed avenue? There was only one way to confirm it: to venture in the direction suggested by the tri-linear mark and note what markings occurred between that point and the third furcation. If he was right, the horizontal line would appear at the first two apertures and some other vertical device at the third.

It proved to be the case, and the third tunnel he encountered presented two vertical lines through a circle. Nevertheless, Mr Newsome restrained his pleasure. He was so hopelessly lost that he knew not in which direction he was proceeding. Was this a route to freedom, or one deeper into the innards of the city? Some time-withered and primitive faculty of his brain told him that the latter was most likely, and that he was moving – or being drawn – inexorably towards some essential core. Whatever the case, it was surely better to be at the end or the beginning than in the futile and featureless centre.

Thus did he navigate, peering at walls, counting channels and travelling ever deeper into those unmapped and unknown regions. By now, it was becoming clearer that he had long since left the masonry of his own century and was venturing within the forgotten constructions of a more distant history. Hereabouts, the tunnels were narrower and fashioned from an eclectic combination of material. Water stood stagnant and unmoving in pools dammed by refuse. The beam of the lamp picked out foundations of long-ruined structures. It seemed barely credible that any tosher had come this far, but the chalk markings continued to lead him.

Remembering the instructions of his guide, Mr Newsome was careful to avoid touching the roof of the tunnels as it became lower. In fact, it was while crouching to pass a particularly precipitous piece of hanging stonework that his dagger slipped from his belt into the murky water. Without hesitating, he plunged his hand into the coldness and brushed fingers among slimy crevices before he was able to grasp the handle and retrieve the weapon, dripping strands of unspeakable matter back into the water.

But there had also been something else down there: some small object wedged betwixt the bricks. He weighed disgust against curiosity. It might be a clue: something dropped by the man he pursued. His hand, after all, was already thoroughly begrimed . . .

Once again, and with a grimace of distaste, he dipped into the murky liquid and groped where he had previously felt the object. And there, standing on its end, was what felt like a coin. He pinched it firmly between thumb and forefinger and tugged it free of the mortar's grip.

It was a sovereign: grimy, but untarnished by its centuries-long submersion in filth. He rubbed the face with a dirty thumb and read the Latin formulae with an unfamiliarity that soon became wonder: *Fra et Hib Regina Elizabeth D.G.* A crowned, enthroned figure pressed into the gold made its provenance clearer still.

'My G—!' muttered Mr Newsome, putting the coin reverently into a trouser pocket. How far into the city's roots had he roamed – and how much further would he go?

His pondering was interrupted by another horripilating instance of *that* sound: the bestial roar and the subsequent agitation of countless rats. Now, however, it seemed much, much closer.

He felt his blood pounding in his temples. A sudden sickening thought occurred: what if the markings he had been following were warnings rather than invitations? Not 'come this way' but rather 'avoid these passages at all costs!' Was he now within the territory of the beast? Might it smell him and come prowling silently for his bones?

He gripped the dagger and tried to control his breathing. There was no further sound but the endless echoing of the original cry through the sewer system.

The moment of fear slowly ebbed and rationality reined control. If the markings pertained to the beast, they would surely present the same symbol each time: one of prevention and dissuasion as opposed to their clear numerical indications of progress. There was nothing else but to continue as bidden in the hope that whoever had made the markings was familiar with the maze and had safeguarded their own well-being.

So he walked ever further into the city's deepest ancient seepings, determinedly resisting the urge to look at his watch, or at the level of remaining oil in the lamp, or to consider the immense weight of the world far above him. Instead, he busied his mind with the case at hand, which, like the tangled masonry veins immuring him, was a realm of disconnected junctures in need of a map.

In the light of the London Dock deaths, it now seemed clear enough that the tidewaiter William Barton had been murdered on Waterloo-bridge. Evidently he had known too much of the *Aurora*'s disappearance. Perhaps he had been greedy, or merely indiscreet. Whatever the reason, it had proved necessary to silence him as it had been necessary to extinguish the lives of ship-owner Josiah Timbs and the crew who had chosen to remain on board.

Such deductions, however, simply generated more confusion. The audacious spectacle of the murders was counter to all good sense and seemed positively to invite investigation. And yet every clue – the tooth, the lack of any possible suspect on Waterloo-bridge, the impossibility of those embarrelled mariners – mocked all detectives with absurdity. The perpetrator behind the missing brig was clearly either an imbecile or a genius. Mr Newsome hoped earnestly for the former.

Strangest of all: nobody knew anything. Of course, criminals were always reluctant to help the police with any useful witness testimony, but his impression on this case was that the ignorance was largely genuine. Why else had the remaining crew of the ill-fated vessel been allowed to live? They had obviously seen and heard nothing. Or perhaps the river workers knew enough to know that an averted eye was the most advisable policy. Those who did see died.

The same conclusion kept occurring: what better place for the root of this criminal endeavour than beneath the city itself? Here, all was hidden from view and sealed tomb-like against sound . . .

He paused and listened.

Had that been the distinctive modulation of a human voice?

There it was again: muffled by stone and carried via the auricular convolutions of the sewers – most definitely a man (or men) speaking.

But which direction? Should the inspector continue to trust the chalk symbols, or rush instead towards the apparent *locus* of the voice? Caution suggested the former, but at an accelerated pace lest he lose his chance.

He checked his pistol, took the dagger in his hand and followed the hieroglyphs with a rapid but assiduously quiet step, shuffling through the water rather than splashing. As he did so, the chalk circles led him into a space quite unlike anything he had seen thus far.

The tunnel hereabouts was fashioned from uniformly thin, reddish bricks and well finished with fine mortar.

Indeed, were it not for the heavy accretion of grime and mould, the work might have been done the week before. Moreover, the passage did not appear to be a sewer at all, but rose gradually out of the water to reveal baked clay paving more suited to pedestrians than to the passage of effluvia. He stepped out of the mire.

The voices became more distinct as he proceeded. They reverberated oddly in a manner that suggested a vast cavern ahead rather than the confining sewer. And as he trod damply over the mercifully dry ground, he perceived the true antiquity of the place he had entered. For there, on the floor ahead, lay a large tessellated image in blue and white: a handsome mosaic of some aquatic god holding a trident and with weeds entangled in his lengthy beard. Fish of many kinds were illustrated about him, and a legend at the image's base proclaimed 'Thamesis'.

Too agitated by this point to wonder at what he saw, Mr Newsome was becoming gradually aware that the dim light of his lamp was being replaced by illumination emanating from the end of the passage in which he walked – illumination that had the pale look of fixed gaslight rather than a swaying oil lamp. Incredible though it seemed, there was no denying the vision.

Multiple voices were now clearly audible, while various other sounds suggested that some form of activity was taking place: a rhythmical rattle, a crash of something hitting the ground, a trundling of wooden wheels . . . and now, as he came nearer to the tunnel's end, a combination of smells. Tobacco was first to strike his nostrils . . . then the mustiness of wine barrels . . . then pungent hides . . .

An ornate arch built into that curious brickwork marked the apparent conclusion of the passage. Mr Newsome extinguished his lamp and approached it in a state of nervous excitement, walking on the balls of his feet and bent almost double as if to avoid being seen. On arrival, he saw that the corridor extended further left and right of the arch. He crouched close to the wall beneath the aperture and removed his hat that he might raise his head above and peer into the brilliantly lighted space beyond.

He could barely believe what he saw.

There, below, was a colossal vault made of the same brickwork and clay as the corridor: evidently some lofty Roman temple or cistern that had lain hidden for millennia. Only now it was a warehouse stocked with every imaginable cargo: barrels stacked high in timber frames . . . pyramids of bales reaching almost to the roof . . . a mass of copper-banded chests nestling close by copious drums of tangled ivory tusks . . . great piles of precariously leaning hides . . . chests used as blocks in a tremendous edifice of produce from every port across the globe. Above it all, three tremendous gas chandeliers served to bathe the entire startling spectacle in bright objective light.

Yet, despite the magnitude of the space and its multifarious contents, very few men were present. Mr Newsome watched (with restricted breath) as a burly fellow with heavily tattooed forearms loaded cases onto a trolley and pushed them out of view, whistling as he went. Another pair of figures then appeared from behind the barrel stacks: the reeking little man and another who appeared to be of Mediterranean extract – perhaps an Italian. Speaking in a language unfamiliar to the inspector, the two made their way towards a sturdy iron-banded door, where the Italian used the heel of a long pointed knife to rap their presence.

The door opened inwards. There was a glimpse of flickering firelight within. They entered, and the door banged closed with a resounding echo.

Up at his arched vantage point, Mr Newsome felt his heart hammering beneath the lamp still strapped to his chest. A rush of conflicting thoughts and urges assailed him. Here – in this bountiful, scandalous treasury of undoubtedly smuggled goods – was the solution to the case. Here was his guaranteed return to the Detective Force and his redemption in the eyes of Sir Richard. Here, also, was a deadly snare into which he had irreversibly stepped. He was one man with one bullet in his pistol and not enough lamp oil to venture back through the sewers. Success (and acclaim) lay down in the warehouse among the criminals . . . as did the likelihood of death, for, assuredly, no man would be permitted to see this and live.

As he stared unblinkingly at the door, it opened once again. The same two men exited, the Italian now pushing an inert figure strapped to a cargo trolley.

Mr Newsome eyes opened still wider. The bound man wore a tweed suit and had a pointed beard. A length of blood-mottled fabric circled his neck. A russet cap had been stuffed roughly into his jacket's breast pocket and he was missing a glove.

Eldritch Batchem.

Mr Newsome's fingers throbbed with a rush of blood. Heat flushed his face. Was the investigator dead? Had he been interrogated in that room? How on earth had *he* found his way to this infernal place?

But there was little time to ponder further on that conundrum, for the door was opening again from within. A shape emerged from the flame-marred darkness and, for a second, its face was caught in the scientific light of the gas. At least, it had once been a face.

Mr Newsome's heart staggered. A nauseating faintness coursed momentarily through him. He had seen that face before. It was a face he had once looked upon with fear and hatred – a face he thought he had last seen charred and dead and hanging from the basket of a flaming balloon. It had been further scarred by that incident, but there could be no mistaking the eyes and the unnerving rubious jaw. The murderous incendiary Lucius Boyle was still alive, and evidently the orchestrator of this entire outrage surrounding the *Aurora*.

TWENTY-FIVE

Benjamin was missing and in danger. Noah was now sure of it.

He had not returned home the night Noah had visited the Forecastle. There had been no note, no message at all, no sign that Benjamin had returned to their riverside address at any time since leaving for the coffee house on Ludgate-hill.

True, it was not unknown for the lofty fellow to visit a theatre and return in the early hours. He had even, on occasion, returned at noon the next day from his unknown debauches – but this situation was quite different. For one thing, if he *was* to spend a night at the shows, he only ever went out in his very finest clothes (which remained in his room). For another, he knew that Noah was eager to hear any news concerning the silk emporium and he would not willingly have made his friend wait.

More significantly still, Noah simply felt it. The two had a fellowship that was quite literally beyond words. One understood the other as a physical presence – or as an absence. Their orbits exerted a reciprocal gravity.

And so, as Noah strode down Fleet-street that morning, his aspect was of such ferocious determination (not to mention the late injuries sustained in his fight with the Italian) that the crowds seemed to quail and part before his momentum lest violence occur to their persons. He entered the coffee house on Ludgate-hill with a resounding clatter of the door that caused all present to look up from their business.

'May I help you, sir?' asked the proprietor from his counter, perceiving that the precipitous entrant was not in search of coffee.

'There was a tall Negro gentleman here yesterday,' said Noah.

'Indeed there was, sir. He sat there at the window for hours and hours, he did, gazing across the street.'

Noah went to the place indicated and glanced rapidly about the table and floor, much to the consternation of the two young clerks occupying the seats.

'Did he leave anything behind when he went? A note, perhaps?' called Noah over his shoulder to the proprietor.

'Only the money he owed, sir. He was certainly a curiously silent chap. A friend of yours?'

'Did he read a newspaper while here?'

'Why, yes. He quite devoured yesterday's edition of *the Times*. But see here, sir, you are rather disturbing my—'

'Do you have it still?'

'Ah . . . I believe so. By the fire there – we use the old editions for kindling . . .'

Noah stepped rapidly between intrigued customers and pulled out three copies of the previous day's *Times*, hastily rustling through each page for some sign known only to him: some note or message his friend may have left. With the second copy, he found what he was looking for on the first page: Benjamin's distinctive black pencil mark around a personal advertisement:

ποταμιάνοι: παπαγάλος στο τηγάνι

The words made him pause. Where had he recently read something similar?

With the customers now muttering to each other about his behaviour, and the proprietor equivocating over some manner of intervention, Noah cast previous editions of *the Times* to the floor until he came to the one he had read in his own parlour some eight days previously. There, on the front page, was the advertisement he was thinking of:

ποταμιάνοι: αυγή στο τηγάνι

'Sir, your behaviour is rather irregular . . .' ventured the proprietor, approaching from his counter.

'Then bring me a cup of coffee in the Arab style and see to your other customers without disturbing me further,' said Noah, distractedly taking a seat by the fire and spreading the newspapers on the table before him.

The circled lines were in a rough form of modern Greek – that much was clear. But it was a grammatically suspect strain that made him doubt whether they had been placed by a native Hellene. For example, the nouns 'αυγή' and 'παπα-γάλος' were missing their articles: 'την' and 'O' respectively. And what on earth was 'ποταμιάνοι'? He knew that 'ποταμι' was the Greek word for river and that the 'οι' suffix represented a plural . . . so could the term refer to those who worked on or occupied the river?

As for 'τηγάνι', he knew it only as an informal place name

in the southern extremity of the Greek mainland – a rough Peloponnesian coast of pirates and fighting men. But was not that particular place so named for its barren landscape of flat rocks which became so hot in summer that one might actually cook on them – 'τηγάνι' meant 'frying pan' in Greek.

The proprietor brought the coffee to the table and Noah smelled the sweetness of cardamom. He reached obliquely for the cup without taking his eyes from the words, burning the tip of his tongue in the process.

Frying Pan wharf – the reference was irresistible. But what of the rest?

The first advertisement seemed to refer to 'αυγή' – 'eggs'? Such a translation made no sense whatsoever: 'Rivermen – the eggs to the frying pan'. Noah searched his memory for scraps of language, remembered phrases, curious proverbs and arcane grammars. He had often mixed his ancient and demotic Greek when a mariner in those balmy seas . . .

And then he smiled at his mistake. He had confused his vocabulary. The word was not 'eggs' at all. *That* word was 'αυγά'. Rather, the sentence in *the Times* alluded to the word for 'dawn': 'The dawn to the frying pan'.

He shook his head in consternation and sipped again at the coffee, which was quite excellent. The phrase still made no sense at all. Unless . . .

'Αυγή' might be the modern Greek for dawn, but the Latin was 'Aurora'. The *Aurora* to Frying Pan wharf: a code and an instruction. He checked the date: the advertisement had been printed two days before the eponymous brig had vanished.

Noah's mind buzzed with the audacity of placing such a thing in a newspaper before the eyes of the whole city. It was truly an outrageous gesture of derision at the supposed authority of the police and Customs – just as the subsequent murders had been. The same hand must surely have been at work in both.

The ripples from Benjamin's pencil circle seemed to repeat ever outwards into supposition and conjecture. Why Greek? Was the Italian in fact a Greek? Or were these men much better educated than the average river worker? Such a code certainly suggested a sophistication of method beyond anything so far imagined by the investigators.

Noah looked again at what his friend had marked in the coffee-house edition. The line was identical but for the word 'παπαγάλος'. Was this the next vessel to be taken? If the code was indeed an instruction, another ship would disappear the very next day.

In Greek, 'παπαγάλος' meant 'parrot': admittedly, an untypical name for an ocean-going ship. Clearly – as with the *Aurora* – it alluded to something else . . . but he could think of no mythological, historical or linguistic analogue that might also be a vessel name. Was there perhaps a code book possessed by the 'rivermen' which directed them how to interpret the words used in *the Times*?

Noah finished his coffee and banged the cup on the table. Such ruminations were doing nothing to find Benjamin. He looked up to see the proprietor still observing him with unease.

'You there!' called Noah. 'Did you recall what time the Negro fellow left this house?'

'It was shortly before dusk, I believe,' said the proprietor.

'And in which direction?'

'I cannot be sure, sir. I do not observe all of my customers so closely.'

'Very well. I thank you for your assistance. You are also

to be congratulated on the quality of your coffee.' Noah folded the marked pages into a pocket, dropped some coins on his saucer and walked out with a determined pace.

He arrived moments later at the selfsame silk emporium at which he had recently passed himself off as a buyer for the Swiss National Opera. The lady at the counter recognized him immediately, but did not seem at all happy to see him. Had Mr Newsome shattered the opera ruse?

'O, good day to you, sir.'

'Is it? I assume that my order is ready to collect.'

'It is a rather unusual case, sir. Shall we step into the stockroom?'

'If we must.'

Noah was allowed behind the counter and through the door into the room at the rear. All appeared exactly as it had before.

'I must apologize, sir,' said the lady. 'It is most unusual, but . . . your order has not arrived.'

'What! Did your agent not visit to collect my list?'

'O yes, yes, he did, sir.' As before, she seemed to wrinkle her nose at the memory. 'But the goods have not been delivered. Such a thing has never previously occurred. This . . . supplier is usually most trustworthy.'

'What time did the agent come here?'

'I cannot recall precisely . . . some time before dusk yesterday, perhaps.'

'This agent – is he a short fellow with a blank face and a stench of the sewers about him?'

'I . . . I am not at liberty to discuss our suppliers.'

'Does he perhaps have a foreign accent?'

'Sir, your questions are inappropriate. You are not a policema—'

Noah withdrew his dagger, all pretence now abandoned. 'A man's life is in danger – and now so is yours. Tell me!'

'O! O! A small man, yes! He smells terribly. I have never heard his voice – he just holds out a hand for the orders.'

'For how long have you dealt with him?'

'I . . . I . . . O, will you kill me, sir?'

'How long?'

'For . . . for six months or so. Please – take anything you like but do not murder me!'

'Cease your whimpering. I am neither a thief nor a murderer. Do you know if this fellow went directly to his warehouse after visiting you?'

'He does not speak, I . . . I cannot answer your question.'

'Does he enter as I did, through the shop, or via a rear door?'

'The . . . the tradesman's entrance – there at the back of the storeroom.'

'Thank you. I bid you good day.'

'But . . . your silk. Your deposit . . .'

'Keep both – and your silence. You will never see me again.'

Noah exited through the tradesman's doorway indicated (leaving the unfortunate lady shaking in distress) and found himself in a rank alley alongside the emporium. Had Benjamin been here? There was no indication of his unusually large boots in the mud, though one tiny sole print did suggest a child or a man of diminutive stature.

Noah stood and pondered for a moment as the noise of Ludgate-hill echoed between the buildings towards him. How might the pursuit have been effected? Along the streets, where a man might lose his pursuer among the crowds and carts? Or along the river where no shadow might easily lurk?

In light of the little man's odour and riverine inclinations, the latter seemed more likely.

The nearest ferry platform to where he stood was at Blackfriars-bridge, and the quickest way to arrive there – he realized with foreboding – was to walk past his very own house. It seemed, indeed, that with each successive step towards the *Aurora*, the various investigators of the case were being drawn more irresistibly into a trap that had long been prepared for them.

But there was no choice – his friend was most likely to be found at Frying Pan wharf. Noah tested the edge of his dagger against a thumb and strode southwards to the river.

TWENTY-SIX

'Inspector Newsome is missing.'

The speaker was Sir Richard Mayne: agitated, clutching a notebook, and standing at the street door of Mr Williamson's house. A cab rather than a police carriage stood waiting on the cobbles outside.

'Sir Richard – I . . . it is a pleasure . . . but . . .'

'May I enter, George? I would rather not be seen here.'

'Of course . . . of course.'

Mr Williamson directed the Commissioner of the Metropolitan Police to his modest parlour and nervously stoked the fire as Sir Richard took a seat. The distinguished gentleman was clearly very ill at ease.

'Could I make you a cup of tea, sir?' said Mr Williamson, fastening his top shirt button.

'Thank you, but no. As I said, the inspector is missing. It is a most difficult situation and one requiring urgent action.'

'Indeed, sir . . . but may I ask why you have come to me?'

'George – I need hardly explain the humiliation I would suffer if the newspapers discovered that one of my inspectors had vanished – particularly *this* inspector. Can you imagine the headlines? It is something I will not tolerate. Much as I am tempted to leave the man to his fate, I am obliged to find him.'

'Yes, sir . . . but . . .'

'I cannot use the Metropolitan Police for this. You know how constables gossip. The two who work with him in the galley have been sent down to Brighton until this sorry mess is cleaned up. In the meantime, I must turn to a sober, reliable man who can discreetly aid me. George – you are that man.'

'Hmm. Hmm. When you say that he has vanished, what precisely do you mean?'

'Yesterday, at low tide, he left his constables and ventured into the sewers at London-bridge with a tosher as his guide. Some few hours later, the tosher returned alone and told the waiting constables that the inspector had wilfully chased off after some shadow.'

'That does rather sound like a thing Mr Newsome might do.'

'Quite. The fact of the matter is that the tide then rose and sealed him under the city. He is certainly lost and possibly even drowned.'

'Hmm. I see – but I have no knowledge of the sewers. Is it not the best policy simply to send the tosher back to find him?'

'Under other circumstances, you would be correct, but I have been given this.' Sir Richard held up the notebook handed to the inspector's constables for safekeeping. 'In it, Mr Newsome has kept notes of his independent investigation into the disappearance of the *Aurora* and the intelligence that led him into the sewers. I think it is time for you and I to have a frank conversation about what we know. A man's life and the solution to a crime may depend on such cooperation.'

'Hmm. Hmm. I fear that your words are truer than you know. Mr Cullen has also seemingly vanished.'

'Who is Mr Cullen?'

'He was a constable until quite recently. He worked with the inspector on the Holywell-street—'

'Yes. I recall the fellow: tall, burly, rather slow. Is he working with you now?'

'I would not say he was "slow" . . .'

'No matter. You say he has vanished?'

'It would seem so. He was working at the docks to collect information from the various river workers and has been re-porting to me every evening. Last night, I heard nothing and I am afraid some harm may have befallen him. He is normally most reliable.'

'What was the tenor of his investigations at the docks?'

'Our . . . rather, *my* assumption was that any smuggling operation of a comparable magnitude to the *Aurora*'s disap-pearance must require significant manpower to unload the vessel. Mr Cullen was attempting to discover if any such casual labourers knew of the missing brig.'

'It seems he found something,' said Sir Richard.

'Evidently, but I have no idea what. He had heard ru-mours, allusions, expressions of indiscretion or deceit, but nothing probative. I suppose you could send constables into the dock to investigate his disappearance, but that would only put the criminals on their guard.'

'Yes, "the criminals". Who *are* these criminals of whom we speak, George? The evidence of their crime is everywhere, but it is as tobacco smoke in a room that contains no cigar or pipe. We must solve this crime.'

'Hmm. Hmm. Perhaps we can start with that notebook you have. May I see it?'

'Of course – though I am afraid his hand is somewhat illegible in places. I have folded the corner of the page on which he began this investigation.'

Mr Williamson took the notebook and opened it at the marked page. The account began with the recovery of first mate Hampton from the river near London-bridge and continued with the subsequent autopsy at Wapping station.

Sir Richard, meanwhile, looked around at the modest, even austere, home of the man who had once been the Detective Force's most lauded investigator: one who had embodied the spirit of the modern police and the new London. The walls were uniformly bare but for a piece of fading embroidery under glass.

'An animal tooth?' said Mr Williamson, looking up.

'Yes. One might hardly believe it if the inspector had not gone to such lengths to pursue it. When the constables questioned the tosher, he said that the inspector had been quite persistent in his enquiries about "monsters".'

'Hmm.'

'What do you make of the incident at Nightingale-lane? Have you reached that part?'

'A moment please . . . hmm . . . ah: the stinking little man.'

'Have you come across that fellow in your own investigations?'

'Yes . . . but subsequently, and it seems from the inspector's account here that the fellow surely died. I cannot imagine any man leaping into the river with his wrists in irons and surviving the experience.'

'Well . . . continue reading and we will discuss it further when you have finished.'

Mr Williamson did so, his eyes following the lines with the greatest attention. If nothing else, it was an insight into the mind of a man who for so long had been his superior in the Detective Force. Finally, he was forced to pause.

'Hmm. It seems there is a page torn out here; was this how you received the notebook?'

'I admit that I removed a page to spare Mr Newsome any embarrassment,' said Sir Richard. 'It has no bearing on the case, I assure you.'

'Perhaps you will let me be the judge of that, sir. You have come here today to call upon any skills I may have as a detective. It is possible you have missed some minor word or hint in the torn-out page that would mean more to me.'

'I do not believe so, George, but I will respect your experience. I suppose the circumstances are pressing enough to exculpate me from any accusation of impropriety. He should perhaps have excised the sheet himself . . .'

Sir Richard extracted the carefully folded page from his breast pocket and passed it to Mr Williamson, who opened it and leaned back in his chair to digest the (apparently hastily scrawled) contents:

Williamson – the man is working in collusion with that d—— transportee Dyson and his dusky servant again, I know it. I will be d—— if I let the —— beat me on this case. He, and that buffoonish —— Batchem, will reflect with humiliation on the time they challenged me. Whatever happens, the old mare Mayne will take me back, by G—!

'Hmm. Hmm. I apologize, Sir Richard. You are quite right: there is nothing of use here.'

'Inspector Newsome is . . . an able detective,' said Sir Richard. 'Able, but significantly flawed.'

'Yes, sir. I imagine now might be a pertinent time to raise the matter of that contract I signed in your office.'

'Circumstances have changed, George. Let us be frank. Mr Newsome is no longer at liberty to pursue the case and you . . . well, it appears you may not have adhered to its every condition.'

'Then may I assume that neither I nor Mr Newsome will be permitted to return to the Detective Force?'

'I believe that now is not the time for such discussions. Of more urgent importance is—'

'Sir Richard – with the greatest respect – the fate of Mr Newsome is not important to me. That contract I signed has more significance.'

'Very well. Then perhaps we might first discuss your associations with this fellow Noah Dyson . . .'

Mr Williamson was about to speak when a tremendous banging came at the street door. He did not move from his seat.

'Are you going to answer the door, George?' said Sir Richard. 'It may be your Mr Cullen returned from his recent discoveries. Please – grant him entry. I would be interested to hear his testimony.'

Mr Williamson stood and approached the door with a combination of hope and dread. Whoever stood on the other side of the door, the subsequent conversation was likely to be problematic. With a large intake of breath, he unlatched the lock and twisted the door knob.

It was Noah, his right hand quite covered in blood and more blood spattered on his bare neck. His dark woollen overcoat hid any further gore.

'George – I believe I have just killed a man.'

Mr Williamson's legs weakened and he felt the colour drain from his face.

'Let me in, for G—'s sake – did you not hear what I said?'

Noah pushed his way past into the short corridor and closed the door behind him. 'It was that stinking little fellow from the dog fights . . . and there was another one: an identical twin. They attacked me and I defended myself. I have virtually run here from Frying Pan wharf. Will you make me some very sweet tea? Then we must return in force. Is Mr Cullen here? They have Ben – I am sure of it. And that is not all . . .'

'Restrain yourself, Noah!' hissed Mr Williamson. Sir Richard Mayne is here – in the parlour – at this very moment.'

'*What!*'

'He must not see you bespattered with blood like this. It would be better if he did not see you at all.'

'But why is he . . . ? No matter, it is time for you to make a decision, George.'

'For G—'s sake, Noah . . . this is no time to . . . Will you just go into the kitchen and at least wash your hands!'

'Perhaps I must make the decision for you.'

'No . . . !'

Noah brushed aside the feeble attempt at obstruction and strode into the parlour, where Sir Richard Mayne was sitting by the fire. The two men appraised each other with magnanimous animosity.

'I believe you are sitting in my seat, Commissioner,' said Noah.

'And you, Mr Dyson, appear to bear the clear evidence of a murder about your person – which crime, I believe, carries the sterner penalty.'

'Sir, I can explain this situation,' said Mr Williamson, entering the parlour in a state of pale anxiety.

'I would be glad for you to do so,' said Sir Richard, entwining his long fingers on his lap.

'Noah . . . that is to say, Mr Dyson . . . whom I first became acquainted with when I was compelled to work with him (much against my will) on the Lucius Boyle case, has, of late, become an . . . an occasional informer, who, infrequently, I . . .'

Noah held up a hand for Mr Williamson to stop the *charade*. 'Sir Richard – let me speak frankly. There is no time for dithering. The blood you see on my hands belonged to a man who tried to kill me not one hour past because I have discovered – through the guidance and expertise of Mr Williamson – the secret behind the *Aurora*'s disappearance. As we sit here, my one true friend is, I believe, a prisoner of the men who stole the vessel. I cannot act alone: they are too many. The strength of the Metropolitan Police is needed.'

Sir Richard looked from Noah to Mr Williamson, evidently weighing what he had heard against the illegality he strongly suspected.

'Perhaps you are thinking,' continued Noah, 'that the life of a Negro man is inconsequential. Others have believed so. But know this: another is also at great risk – one whose life it may be particularly beneficial for you to save . . .'

Noah took a soiled tan-coloured glove out of his trouser pocket and threw it to Mr Williamson. 'George – perhaps you could identify the wearer of this. I found it near the place where I was ambushed. The stains on the palm and fingers are blood – the wearer's own, I would wager.'

Mr Williamson at once saw the larger middle finger and nodded. 'Sir Richard – this glove belongs to Eldritch Batchem. We have established that the man has an extra finger on each hand and wears specially made gloves such as this one. It seems Noah is correct.'

Sir Richard wordlessly indicated that he would like to examine the glove, and did so with a look of concern.

'I might add,' said Noah, 'that we have seen nothing of the man for some time. Yes, there was that letter in *the Times*, but neither I nor Mr Williamson have recently seen him or heard of his activity.'

'May I tell Noah what you have told me, Sir Richard?' said Mr Williamson. 'It seems that, together, we three may possess all elements of the solution.'

Sir Richard hesitated, the limp glove still in his hand, then merely nodded, fearing perhaps that anything he said might be used against him later.

'Noah – they have Mr Newsome also,' said Mr Williamson. 'At least, he is lost among the sewers in pursuit of the missing brig. Mr Cullen, too, has vanished from the docks.'

Noah digested the information. A muscle twitched in his jaw. 'Very well – the time to act is now. Sir Richard – will you strike at the enemy with me, or act against me?'

'If I may offer my own opinion,' interjected Mr Williamson, 'public opinion will favour a rapid and dramatic gesture that brings the criminals to justice. They need never know how, or from where, the police obtained their intelligence – only that a great crime was solved.'

'You speak like a man who has spent too much time amidst the sophistry of thieves, George,' said Sir Richard, indicating Noah as the contaminating influence.

'Or with Inspector Newsome,' said Mr Williamson.

Sir Richard acknowledged the point with a regretful downward glance. He re-examined the bloodied figure of Noah, and a Manichean struggle raged beneath the police commissioner's placid exterior. A decision was imperative. His was typical of the barrister.

'Very well. I must hear everything that you know, Mr Dyson. If I find it persuasive, I will act in the interests of justice and throw my full authority behind the correct course of action.'

'And in turn,' said Noah, 'I would ask that you share all that *you* know, Sir Richard, so that we can establish a mutual trust.'

'Need I remind you, sir, that I am the commissioner of—'

'Actions, not titles, earn trust, Sir Richard. Have we an agreement?'

'Very well. Perhaps you will earn *my* trust, Mr Dyson, by being the first to speak.'

Noah allowed himself a half-concealed smile of respect for this man who, whatever his religion, politics or ethics, was one who deserved it. Still standing, he now took the seat vacated by Mr Williamson and began:

'Mr Williamson knows most of what I can recount – and I suspect he has already told you much of that. Our investigation was furthered just last evening at the Forecastle public house, where we expected to encounter Eldritch Batchem. Instead, we observed a short, malodorous man escape with remarkable agility through a window when approached. Another rat-fancier – an employee from the London Dock – had identified the man's particular odour as being one he had smelled in the tobacco warehouse the night of Mr Timbs's murder . . .'

'You refer to the so-called cat master, perhaps,' said Sir Richard. 'I have read of him in Inspector Newsome's notebook.'

'I know of no such notebook,' said Noah. 'But yes, the fellow was Baudrons. Arriving immediately at the broken window, I heard the stinking little man exchange some words in a foreign tongue with a tattooed harpooner in the alley below. I now believe it may have been Greek.'

'You did not mention any such foreign tongue to me at the time,' said Mr Williamson with a reproving look.

'I admit that, in the urgency of the moment, I thought I had simply heard a strong accent or garbled diction. Subsequent discoveries, however, suggest otherwise. Sir Richard – take a look at these circled advertisements from *the Times*.'

Noah unfolded the scraps and handed them to the commissioner.

'Ah, Greek, is it?' said Sir Richard, scrutinizing the lines. 'I am afraid I am not well acquainted with the modern form . . . something about a river is it?'

'It is in fact a code: an announcement to certain men of the river to steal a particular vessel. The first instance refers to 'αυγή': the Greek word for 'dawn'. The Latin is, of course—'

'*Aurora*,' said Sir Richard gravely. 'But where was the vessel to be taken? I do not recognize the word . . .'

'"Frying pan". It is Frying Pan wharf – the same place, I believe, to which my friend followed the stinking man after he visited a known silk receiver on Ludgate-hill . . . the same place alluded to in highly dubious terms by an indiscreet ballast-heaver at the Forecastle . . . the same place I was attacked this morning when I ventured there.'

The police commissioner was nodding vigorously now as the pieces of his own puzzle shifted into comprehension. 'Gentlemen – this confirms what I have recently heard from Mr Jackson, the Inspector General of Customs. It seems his investigation has turned up a further quantity of blank landing warrants hidden at the Custom House itself. As before, they bear the name of Principle Officer Gregory, but at least two of them have been partially completed, listing Frying Pan wharf as the unloading point. It seemed suggestive enough, but now I see there is a stronger connection.'

'Do you know anything of the wharf, sir?' asked Mr Williamson, leaning now against the back of Noah's seat.

'I asked my clerks about the place and the only recollection any of them had was that early excavations for the Thames tunnel were to begin there. It seems, however, that some Roman ruins were found below the surface thereabouts and so the work was moved some few hundred feet west where the ground was easier to work. The warehouses that now stand on the original site have been built subsequently.'

Noah turned to look at Mr Williamson, who had evidently had the same thought and voiced it: 'Might those Roman building works exist still beneath the modern warehouses? And might they extend to subterranean chambers that might store cargoes unseen and unregistered by the Customs men who patrol those shores?'

'Mr Dyson,' said Sir Richard, 'if that Greek is indeed a code, what is the name of the second vessel mentioned . . . and are we to assume that it will be taken within the next twenty-four hours, if not already?'

'The word is "parrot", but the actual ship name is likely to be something tangential or metaphorically related. Perhaps your clerks will be able to get to Gravesend, to the Custom House and to Trinity House to see what vessels have arrived into the Port of London most recently? As for the likelihood of this other vessel being taken as the *Aurora* was, that all depends on how confident these people feel. They evidently know that a large police investigation is underway. Indeed, they have taken a number of the investigators involved. Does that make them bolder, I wonder, or more cautious? If the former, we might reasonably expect the ship (whatever its real name) to be taken tomorrow.'

'Yes, I follow your reasoning,' said Sir Richard. 'The advert has been placed, which would seem to suggest intent. Perhaps the perpetrators of these crimes simply have no fear.'

'Or perhaps it is a test to see how much we really know,' said Mr Williamson. 'As we pursue this new vessel, they may watch us to gauge our strength. Alternatively, it may all be a ruse to direct our attention elsewhere.'

'That is quite possible,' said Sir Richard. 'Nevertheless, I believe the time has come to act. We will investigate the identity and movements of this other ship, the "Parrot", and we will strike at Frying Pan wharf.'

'So – to action!' said Noah, making to stand.

'Wait,' said Sir Richard with a firm voice. 'I understand your haste; I also have a man in danger – but let us understand the nature of our challenge. This wharf is evidently a dangerous place. It is peopled by numerous men of the roughest sort who care nothing for the law and who have already killed to keep their secret. If we go there, it will be in daylight with a contingent of brave policemen, with the foreknowledge of the vessel to be taken and with the benefit of a flood tide that gives our galleys room to manoeuvre. We must also be accompanied by men of the Custom House, who will verify what is illicit and confiscate it. I trust that a man of your sense cannot argue with these criteria, Mr Dyson.'

'I suppose not.'

'I understand that you wish to rush madly and alone at that warehouse with dagger in hand, but you would almost certainly be killed or taken prisoner. If your friend is still alive, his best hope is for an orchestrated assault from the Metropolitan Police, which will take some time to organize. Can we agree upon that?'

'Noah?' said Mr Williamson. 'Sir Richard speaks perfect sense. I know it is difficult for you to wait – and that Ben is more your concern than the missing brig – but they are many and you are one. Deaths may result.'

'All right,' said Noah, finally. 'It will be tomorrow. But I have my own ideas on how to proceed. Listen . . .'

TWENTY-SEVEN

Thus did the three remaining investigators sit in conference beside the fire at Mr Williamson's home. Afternoon dimmed into dusk; gaslamps were lit; night absorbed smoke into a still darker sky. Any curious passer-by might have stood gazing through those uncurtained windows at the *tableau* of earnest discussion within and wondered at the characters present.

Who, for example, was the sober-looking gentleman with the pock-marked face? A bookkeeper or a clerk, perhaps? He spoke little, but listened to the others with clear intent. The one with the grey eyes and broken nose was quite a different sort, expressing himself volubly by means of gestures and extemporized diagrams. *He* – an engineer or some manner of radical? – might have been the leader of the three were it not for the gravity of the third figure: the oldest and most patrician, whose eyes possessed a great intelligence. It was a vaguely familiar face . . . but unlikely to be anyone of great authority in this part of London.

Certainly, one seldom knows what or who to believe in the great metropolis. Three fellows glimpsed through a window could be businessmen, plotters or thieves. A man wearing a russet cap might call himself Crawford or Batchem and be taken as either if there is no contradictory evidence. A detective might adopt a uniform and seem a common policeman, while a constable might equally divest himself of epaulettes and become a detective.

In such ways do metamorphoses occur and perspectives change in the city of tides. Men likewise rise and fall according to the vagaries of the moon, or fate, or will. Where were they all on that night before the raid on Frying Pan wharf?

Inspector Newsome's heart had barely calmed since witnessing the villains in the warehouse. The longer he remained crouching there in the corridor by the arch, the more frozen with fearful inertia became his filth-soaked legs. Discovery by one of the criminals or their band was surely imminent. Action was imperative – but to what end?

Should he venture back the way he had come and lurk about the sewers until his lamp faded and blackness became his tomb? Might he attempt to find another source of oil to light his journey back to the river? Or should he descend into the warehouse and test his own life against those men who could kill him without their crime ever being discovered? He had one bullet and a dagger; at least one of the others also possessed a blade and was likely to be more adept in its use.

As he cogitated thus, he saw with a jolt of horror that he had left damp footprints all along the corridor to where he now rested. No doubt these could be traced directly from the sewer, raising a general alarm and stirring every murderous hand against the intruder. He had to move – and keep moving – in the hope that his trail would dry before being discovered. But move where?

With determination he stood once more and peered

through the arch. Nobody seemed to be present below. The only course of action was to follow the corridor either left or right and see where it took him. Left or right – life or death? He reached into his trouser pocket and took out the Elizabethan sovereign he had found. Heads or tails?

He went right, following an apparent gallery punctuated with more arches looking over the warehouse space. He walked cautiously and without destination – merely to move – and in the hope that an idea would occur to him. The pistol remained gripped firmly in his palm.

Inevitably, there could be no rescue from the Metropolitan Police. This place had remained secret for a long time, either because no tosher knew of its existence, or because those who did had been silenced. It was not at all rare for a decomposing sewer-hunter to be found by excavators of some new street, or for a body to be washed out into the river. Perhaps, indeed, the animal he had been seeking was one of Cerberus's race: a fearsome beast let loose among the vile passages to dissuade and devour.

Where was the creature? Was it that very moment sniffing at his path of damp footsteps and growing ever closer? Would one pistol shot be enough to fell it? And would that loud report bring the criminals running to effect what the animal had not?

A stone stairway fell away to his left: a long, steep descent of around thirty feet ending dimly in a rusting iron door. Moss and slime flourished around the lower stairs suggesting a regular influx of water, and there was an unmistakable smell of the river. Excitement animated his spirit – was this a possible means of escape?

Cogitating no further, Mr Newsome descended towards the iron door, upon whose rusty knob was a length of cord holding a large antique key. He put an exploratory ear to the metal and heard nothing beyond. He slid aside the escutcheon plate noiselessly and peered into blackness. Was it better to be on the *other* side of that door? Might it lead him to freedom? If required, he had just a little oil left in his lamp and a box of lucifers in a dry coat pocket . . .

Still holding the pistol, he inserted the key into the hole and turned it with a scraping of corroded parts. He pushed with his shoulder and the heavy door groaned inwards . . .

After the candle had died, Benjamin and Mr Cullen had sat listening to each other's breath and occasional shuffling in search of warmth on the cold stone flags. No other sound or needle of light intruded into that Hadean cell.

'Will we die here, Ben?' said Mr Cullen.

Silence answered as an unseen gesture.

'I am not afraid to die . . . only, I had hoped one day to marry a nice girl. I am still quite a young man . . . O, this is unbearable! I would rather they had provided no light at all than to give it and let it die. There must be *something* we can do to escape this place!'

Benjamin breathed steadily, part of the darkness.

'Wait . . . Ben – do you hear that . . . ?'

Footsteps were indeed approaching – perhaps two or three pairs of boots echoing from afar. Within the cell, they strained to hear more detail.

The people were now apparently descending a flight of stairs towards the door, and . . . was one of the footfalls impaired in some way, as if the fellow was being half-dragged or carried?

'Ben!' whispered Mr Cullen, 'I will wait by the side of the door. When it opens, I will force whoever enters into the cell.

We can dispatch them together and make our escape. Are you ready?'

A scraping boot indicated Benjamin's preparations.

The key rattled in the lock. The door opened a crack. A shaft of dim light cut across the flagstones inside. Mr Cullen stepped vigorously forward in anticipation of grasping a shirt front . . .

Instead, a virtually inert body was thrown into the cell and into the open arms of Mr Cullen, who toppled over backwards under the dead weight. As he fell, he caught the merest glimpse of two forms (one short, one tall) silhouetted against the stairs . . . then the door closed with a reverberating clang. Blackness returned.

'A dead man, Ben!' said Mr Cullen, his hands going over the body for some kind of identification. 'Can you smell the blood, Ben?'

Benjamin made his way towards the voice and aided in the examination of the body.

'O . . . wait a minute . . . I think he is breathing!'

And, indeed, the increasingly vivid body began to groan and writhe as if regaining consciousness.

'Who are you, sir?' said Mr Cullen. 'Were you also taken at Frying Pan wharf? Are you a police detective?'

'A det . . . a detec-tive,' croaked the figure weakly.

'Do the police know we are here? Is there to be a rescue?'

'My . . . neck . . . razor . . .'

Mr Cullen felt along the prone body and realized that what he had previously imagined to be a scarf about the neck was more likely a makeshift bandage. Close to, the smell of blood was unmistakable.

'They have cut your throat, sir? If you can speak, I suspect the wound is not deep. Have heart – you may live.'

'I have solved . . . *Aur-ora* . . . I have solved . . .' gasped the invisible fellow.

Benjamin, meanwhile, had extracted something wadded in the gentleman's breast pocket and was manipulating it now, employing black fingers in that black space. It was some manner of garment: a circle of material, a label, stitching – a cap? He reached with blind urgency for Mr Cullen's hand and pressed the item into it.

'O . . . what is this?'

Benjamin allowed his friend a moment to palpate the cap then drew Mr Cullen's hand in his own towards the injured man's beard, where entangled fingers tugged at a point of coarse hair. There was a sudden intake of breath from Mr Cullen.

'Eldritch Batchem!'

'*I* have solved . . . the case,' rasped the investigator thus identified. 'I . . . have found . . . murderers. Frying Pan . . .'

'My G—, Ben! Do these people have us *all* in custody?' said Mr Cullen.

The question hung unanswered in the damp air.

'I have . . . solved,' croaked the prone form, fading now. 'The villain is found . . . Liveridge . . . forgive me . . .'

'Calm yourself, Mr Batchem,' said Mr Cullen. 'Who attacked you? Can you describe him? Who is the murderer?'

'I . . . I . . . a mask of evil. O, Liveridge!'

'His name is Liveridge? I do not understand you . . .'

But the wounded man had clearly exhausted himself, or been exhausted by what he had endured. A black hand settled softly on Mr Cullen's arm: leave the poor fellow alone.

For some minutes, none spoke, each occupied with the flurry of his own thoughts. Eldritch Batchem wheezed softly and made no attempt to sit.

Then, once again, there was a dry scraping of the key in the lock. The door groaned open and a shadowy figure appeared in the frame, looking cautiously inside . . .

. . . Mr Newsome almost exclaimed as his eyes became accustomed to the gloom and he saw the three gentlemen squinting back at him. Benjamin, the traitorous Mr Cullen, and the infernal stage-detective Eldritch Batchem – all together on the damp stone flags. A rush of impressions and conclusions assailed him . . .

'Mr Newsome!' cried Mr Cullen with unrestrained amazement. 'You have come to free us!'

Benjamin's single eye also could not repress its wonder. He began to stand, but his amazement turned instantaneously to fury . . .

Without a word or gesture, Mr Newsome rapidly closed and locked the door, dropping the key into his trouser pocket where it clinked against the gold coin.

Fulminations and execrations rained then upon the door from within and the inspector thought it better to distance himself from that place with all haste . . .

It was fully night when Noah finally left Mr Williamson's house. The wind tugged at his coat tails and he inhaled deeply at the distinctive perfume of Lambeth air: the lead smelters' poison, the breweries' yeasty steam, Beaufoy's acrid vinegar works and, of course, the eternal river mud and streets that had yet to see the modern age of progress.

Of a mind to walk, he instinctively headed north past the dark emptiness of Vauxhall Gardens to where Fore-street ran its sordid and dilapidated course parallel to the Thames. Here, glowing cigar tips twitched within shadowy passages at approaching footfalls, and gaslamps mocked the centuries-old structures as they bowed under the pressure of time. But Noah felt no trepidation. In this jungle, he had always been a predator.

As he walked, he could not help but reflect upon the vagaries of London. One might be rich or poor, sinful or righteous, and the city would strew one's path with trials all the same. A house or livelihood lost, an unexpected betrayal, an unjust incarceration, the omniscient eye and illimitable reach of authority, the abduction of a friend. The strong rose above the filth; the weak were pulled into the torrent and drowned. Every child of the city knew as much.

Benjamin would be found and freed – that was the only concern. The *Aurora* and its cargo could be d——. Sir Richard Mayne and his perfidious Inspector Newsome could be d——. Even the benevolent and well-meaning gentleman detective Mr Williamson could be d—— if he wished to place justice higher than one man's life. In London, one stepped first, hit hardest and took one's chances at the expense of others. Trust was temporary, and friendship all too often fleeting. Every child of the city knew as much.

The damp earth of the archbishop's gardens now sweetened the air as he traversed Church-street and passed closer to the river. Venerable Westminster-bridge showed itself a many-humped beast lumbering across the choppy waters, and Noah paused to look at the river. Behind him was that great seat of Christianity, Lambeth Palace. Before him was a deity that pre-dated the Cross. Had not articles of pagan faith been found upon the shore: those clay and stone supplications marked with forgotten ancient tongues?

A Christian prayer or a pagan propitiation? Noah had long ago found the former to be futile. He took out his dagger and weighed it in his palm, turning it so that the moon played along the blade. Was it an offering worthy of the river god? Would it please the ageless power enough to grant a wish? Noah muttered something to the waves: half promise, half hope. And he tossed the dagger with all strength into the black depths of ageless Thamesis.

Mr Williamson watched the fire die but did not stand to revive it. Sir Richard and Noah had left some hours previously and the house seemed emptier now than before their arrival. It was late, but he could not think of sleep.

The following day would be a tempestuous one – quite literally so if the wind whining about his walls was anything to go by. He should, perhaps, have been in higher spirits, having been approached for help by Sir Richard, but his thoughts were otherwise occupied. He thought of earnest Mr Cullen, possibly dead at the bottom of the river. He thought of Benjamin, who had once saved him from certain death. He thought also of Noah, whose life seemed uncommonly tainted of late by involuntary association with the Metropolitan Police.

And, much against his will, he thought of Charlotte. Rather, the girl contaminated his mind, entering unbidden into his every private moment. Even there, where he had lived in virtuous contentment with his wife Katherine, the street girl tormented him with memories and visions and sensations that would not let him sleep.

Noah could see it, of course. For him, the solution was as simple as imbibing the spirit until a surfeit of it caused all charm to fade . . . either that or until the spirit rendered one a slave to its intoxication. What was stronger – the man or his temptation?

'Go to her, George,' Noah had said on leaving. 'Tomorrow there may be pistols and knives. Tomorrow we may die. Will you go to your grave knowing that a mere girl had tortured you so? Go to her as a detective, as the policeman you once were, and see her for what she is. Rid her from your thoughts.'

Mr Williamson put on his coat and hat. He would go for a walk to clear his head and consider the day to come. He would cross Vauxhall-bridge and take note of the river in this uncommon wind. He would walk north beside the penitentiary to Whitehall and perhaps have a cup of coffee thereabouts to revive his mind.

Or he would walk past those coffee houses towards Haymarket and head up towards Windmill-street, intently noting female faces all along those sinful thoroughfares. He might even go as far as Golden-square, where the habitually uncurtained illumination of one specific residence caused one to pause and glance idly inside as if to see what sort of person lived there.

If she saw him standing watch, she might wave with a smile and come to the street door. She might beckon him up the stairs and remark that his face was somehow familiar. Would the gentleman like a cup of tea, perhaps? The fire inside was warm and it was terribly windy out.

Her perfume would be as he remembered it. Her large, dark eyes would mock the sobriety of his own. He would take off his hat and enter with an expression not of ardour or lust or longing, but of crucifixion.

Later still, and long past midnight, a single office at Scotland Yard showed its illuminated window to the night. Within, Sir Richard Mayne was marshalling the forces of justice in preparation for daylight.

Clerks and messengers had been roused from their beds and sent off about the city to wake others, who in turn would write orders and dispatch their own men in an ever-outwards ripple of readiness. The Thames Police station at Wapping called in extra men and sought additional galleys for their use. The police fire boat and steam launch were put on stand-by for first light. The Horse Guards were told to be aware of imminent police activity that might require armed support. The Lord Mayor issued a general alarm to all police stations within the vicinity of Frying Pan wharf, advising them to have men ready if needed. Even the Home Office was notified of a possible disturbance by the river.

Similarly, Trinity House was apprised of the situation and requested to keep its lumbering ballast machines clear of the wharf at high tide. In response, it graciously offered a lighter and a number of strong honest men should they be required to purge this corruption finally from river trade.

Almanacks were consulted. Low tide would be half past eight that morning. High tide would be half past two in the afternoon, after which there would be dead water and the best opportunity for action.

Sir Richard showed no apprehension or indecision as he signed orders, drafted instructions and received runners. But as dawn approached, so did a creeping doubt.

And so, as the players in this drama lived out their various stories on that night – frustrated, imprisoned, wounded or in moral peril – the metropolis was in the early stages of its own imminent convulsion. The north-east wind, which had been building for days, now reached a new intensity, whipping up clouds of ash from the streets and channelling them through alleys in blinding vortices. Chimney pots came loose and crashed to the cobbles; rigging whistled and whipped against masts in the docks; galleys and wherries rocked against their tethers at stairs all along the river.

At Deptford, one particular vessel, the *Prince Peacock* out of Calais, was moored for the night. Its mariners rocked in their hammocks, oblivious to the creaks and rattles of their vessel or the hull-slapping waves. At flood tide, their progress to St Katharine's would be all the easier with the favourable wind . . . if indeed they ever reached their final mooring.

Down near Pickle Herring-street, the 'Thames sage' John Tarr stirred uneasily from his shore-side abode and ventured out onto the mud to observe the waters. He cast a weather eye at the moon-silvered clouds. He watched the racing scalloped crests upon a mercury surface. He noted the thicket of swaying masts along the far shore – a consequence of that persistent north-easterly that drove more vessels than usual into the heart of the city.

Not only vessels, he must have mused, but also great volumes of water driven from the sea into the gaping coastal mouth of the river. Certainly, it was that time of the year when inundations might occur. He appeared to nod and mumble something to himself, or to the sky. Then he returned briskly to his den, leaving up Tripe-alley just a few minutes later with a full seaman's bag over his shoulder.

TWENTY-EIGHT

Daylight and the ebb tide brought wonder among the many thousands working by the river. By half past eight, the waters seemed to have receded to a greater extent than many could recall, revealing the broad channel almost to its bed at certain points.

Between St Saviour's and the London Dock, a mere ribbon of flat, brown water remained amid a great expanse of shining mud that was itself littered with the unveiled detritus of centuries. Sodden barrels, still-corked bottles, pipe fragments, saturated coal, slithery lengths of discarded rope, and pottery of every hue could be seen there, along with the bones of some long-forgotten wreck emerging blackly from the mire's grasp.

Naturally, the mudlarks were out in force, swarming like insects over the river's unexpected nakedness. Not only they, but any number of street boys, apprentices and costermongers, for whom the novelty was akin to the old frost fairs of memory. And above the whole filthy carnival, an unimaginable composted miasma arose that suggested the very fundament of the city had been momentarily laid bare.

Yet despite the early low tide, the Port of London was as

busy as it had been for months. Almost a third more vessels than usual had been blown upriver by that persistent wind of recent days and the shores seemed as crowded with men and wagons as London-bridge. At every dock, wharf, quay and bank, cranes rattled, wheels trundled, boots rapped out lumber tattoos, and the thunder of landing cargo echoed around warehouse fronts.

It was indeed a populous and detailed canvas from the gallery of London – a mere fragment of time soon to be erased by the incoming flood. But if one were to take a magnifying glass to its epic scope and peer into the shadows, one would notice certain other characters waiting expectantly among the throng . . .

Shortly before noon, for example, the grand *façade* of the Custom House was concealing a congregation of some considerable significance. Mr Williamson sat towards the rear of a large smoky room crowded with chattering uniformed policemen and Custom House officials, all of whom were engaged in the most energetic speculation as to the reason for their presence there. When the large panelled door opened, an immediate hush came over the room, followed by urgent muttering as Sir Richard Mayne entered with the Inspector General of Customs, Mr Jackson.

'Gentlemen,' began the latter in a stentorian tone, 'I thank you all for volunteering for this extra duty, which, as you have no doubt already gathered, concerns a matter of the greatest importance to the commerce and reputation of this building, and to the city as a whole. One might say it began with the murder of Mr William Barton on Waterloo-bridge nine days ago, but I regret to say that the crimes facing us are greater, and stretch further back even than that. I am sure most of you know the commissioner of police; I will let him continue.'

Sir Richard Mayne nodded sombrely in acknowledgement. 'Thank you Mr Jackson, and I thank you gathered gentlemen for your time. I will be brief: a large and well-established smuggling operation has recently been identified by the Detective Force. It is behind the disappearance of the brig *Aurora* and behind a number of rather grisly murders. Not only that, but a Thames policeman has also apparently been abducted by this band of brigands.'

A wave of comment rippled through the audience, the occasional *sotto-voce* mention of 'Newsome' showing that the secret had not been kept as well as the commissioner might have hoped.

'Gentlemen!' continued Sir Richard with a grimace, 'the focus of our action today will be Frying Pan wharf at Wapping. The police steam launch is waiting before this building and will transport many of us to that place as the high tide becomes still water. I will be frank – there may be danger and you constables may have to use your truncheons. A battle, however, is not our aim. Mr Jackson – perhaps you will explain . . .'

'Indeed,' continued the inspector general. 'The purpose of our raid is to enter the warehouse and confiscate all cargo for which there is no documentation – particularly anything we can connect to the original manifest of the *Aurora*. It also seems very likely that there is a concealed storeroom at the site. If our colleagues in the police can find that space, we Customs men will impound everything within it and discern its origins as comprehensively as possible. All miscreants we encounter will be arrested and closely questioned on the matter of the missing brig. Does anybody have a question?'

No hand was raised.

'Very well,' said Sir Richard. 'Allow me to describe our

raid in greater detail. It is not our intention simply to descend in force upon the wharf, which may give senior members of this group a chance to escape. Rather, an advance force will first dock there on a vessel named the *Prince Peacock* . . .'

And as Sir Richard laid out the events to come, Mr Williamson sat silently impassive amid so much eager anticipation. Though dressed in his civilian clothes, he had been issued with a truncheon and a reinforced constable's top hat. One might perhaps have said that the expression on his face was one of calm readiness for the task ahead – but a dark unease permeated his every thought. He remained unshaven since the day before, and his eyes were hollows of shadow.

Long after he and the many other fellows had vacated the room to board the launch, his truncheon and hat remained intentionally upon the seat.

Noah Dyson scratched irritably for the dozenth time at the false beard he was wearing. Ludicrous as it looked, it made a remarkable difference to his appearance, creating an authentic impression of the brawny sailor who had been at sea for months. More importantly, it might briefly fool the Italian, the surviving stinking little man or anyone else who had been observing him over the past few days.

Had he really killed the twin of that malodorous midget? The two of them had leaped upon him like dogs the day before, clinging too close for him to effectively bring the dagger into play. Only when one of them had been literally thrown to the ground did he have the chance to slash at a throat. Certainly, the man had bled profusely and lain quite inert as Noah made his escape.

The incident had caused him to reflect anew what kind of men would so readily wreak murder upon those who came close to discovering their secret. First some of the crew of the *Aurora*, then the braggart William Barton, then Eldritch Batchem. Had Mr Cullen, Benjamin and Mr Newsome all gone the same way? The enemy was utterly ruthless. But retribution was imminent.

Noah looked up at the *Prince Peacock*'s filigree of rigging, masts, spars, booms and braces *silhouetted* against heavy grey cloud. Most sails were now furled for docking, and the crew were largely occupied below decks to hide their true number. It was a sight to transport him temporarily to any one of the world's oceans and to evoke memories of his previous life. The smell of oakum, the crunch of salt on timber, the billow of canvas and *thrum* of wind-plucked rope . . .

'Mr Dyson, sir? The tide is quite risen. We are ready to dock.'

Noah came out of his reverie to see the *Prince Peacock*'s (genuine) first mate standing at his side. 'Very well,' he replied. 'You may retire to the master's quarters as I oversee our landing. Stay there, whatever may occur, and you will be safe.'

He strolled forward to the port bow and saw Frying Pan wharf ahead. The large warehouse doors were open and a newly loaded lighter was just heaving to from its moorings. Noah smiled and felt his blood hot in his veins. Nobody on shore could have the slightest inclination about what was to happen next.

He turned back to the decks, inserted two fingers into his mouth and gave a shrill whistle. 'All right, boys! Bring us in to the wharf. Coils at the ready there . . . man the capstans . . . haul that jib . . . easy to starboard, mates . . . easy I say!'

It should here be noted that while those scurrying mariners were all experienced with rope and sail, none but the first mate was of the original *Prince Peacock* crew (themselves removed earlier that morning at Greenwich). Rather, they were a composite band of volunteer Thames Police and Custom House officers in plain clothes who might unload the vessel and, should the need arise, be on hand to offer a ready fist and truncheon.

'That's right, lads!' continued Noah with gusto. 'Toss the cables there! We are coming to. Are you ready to break out the cargo, boys?'

The ship settled into its berth as gently as an infant into its cradle. The ropes were pulled tight and the gangplank clattered down onto the stone edge of Frying Pan wharf.

Immediately, a stalwart and suspicious-looking man with luxuriantly tattooed forearms approached the foot of the plank as if to block Noah's descent. 'Hoi! What's this?' he shouted. 'We're expectin' no vessel here! I was told yer would dock at . . .'

'Whom do I have the pleasure of addressing?' said Noah from behind his beard.

'Rigby, of course – I'm foreman of this wharf and I say we're expectin' no *Prince Peacock* 'ere.'

'The landing warrant says different, sir.' Noah stepped assuredly down the plank and handed Mr Rigby the Custom House document, watching him scrutinize it with ever greater confusion . . . as well he might.

'Where's yer tidewaiter?' said Mr Rigby with a truculent glare.

'Why, he is right here . . .' Noah indicated a genuine uniformed Custom House tidewaiter procured for just this eventuality.

The man saw his cue and came forward. 'Is there a problem, foreman?'

'Where'd yer get this warrant, tidewaiter?'

'From the landing-waiter, of course, after he reported our arrival at the Long Room. It is all quite clear: a hold full of Brussels lace and French silk bolts to Frying Pan wharf . . .'

Mr Rigby scratched his head and cast a look back to the warehouse, muttering to himself: 'This wasn't supposed to . . .'

'If you will ready your lumpers and alert the warehouse-man, we will begin unloading immediately,' said Noah, whistling once again for his men to unload the holds.

'*Wait, d—— you!*' exclaimed Mr Rigby. 'You'll wait 'ere while I check on this with . . . with my master. Unload *nothin'*, understand?'

And with this, Mr Rigby strode with great vigour into the darkness of the warehouse. A number of lumpers around the wharf had already stopped work and were observing the scene with a mixture of amusement and dubiety.

Noah cast a quick look along the river and saw the police launch's prow nestled among colliers over at Elephant stairs on the Rotherhithe shore. He winked at the tidewaiter by his side and called out to his crew: 'Down planks, men! Break out the trolleys. Unload, unload . . . ! All cargo into the warehouse there!'

Thus, when Mr Rigby emerged rapidly and red-faced from the shadows a few minutes later, it was to see pulleys already in play on the vessel's decks and a number of men approaching him with crates on trolleys. Apoplexy seized him at once.

'I thought I told yer: no ——— unloadin'! Take it back or I'll crush yer 'eads, I swear!'

'Sorry, sir,' said Noah, himself carrying a large crate, 'the warrant says Frying Pan wharf and that's exactly where we must unload.'

'Why, you . . . !'

Mr Rigby aimed a tremendous kick at the crate in Noah's arms, almost knocking him over and causing the crate to drop to the ground where it cracked along one edge. Its contents could now be glimpsed through the splintered wood.

'Hold up!' said Mr Rigby on peering within. 'That's no lace or silk . . . it looks like . . . old newspapers! What's goin' on 'ere . . . ?'

Those sundry lumpers on shore who had not already stopped work to watch the show paused in their work. There was certainly nothing like a good fight to liven up the tedium of their daily toil.

Mr Rigby turned hateful eyes immediately upon Noah, but was quite unprepared for the reaction of this artificially bearded false mate.

Noah stepped rapidly around the fallen crate and grasped the material at the foreman's throat with a powerful hand. At the same time, he swiftly produced a boatman's knife and made sure his victim could feel the cold metal edge just below his jaw. He spoke with a chilling malevolence:

'The Negro with the milky eye – tell me where he is imprisoned or I will cut you from ear to ear.'

Just inches from Noah's face, Mr Rigby's eyes at first showed surprise rather than fear. Then understanding seemed to flicker across them and he grinned with vulpine self-assurance.

'Cut me, then, why don't yer! No copper or Customs man can do it in plain sight . . .'

Noah's knee flashed forcefully into the softness of Mr Rigby's abdomen and the latter dropped like a sack of grain to the wharf.

'Unfortunately for you, I am neither,' said Noah to the groaning form at his feet. He extracted a whistle on a cord from beneath his shirt and turned to blow it sharply three times towards his vessel. 'All inside, men! The signal! The signal!'

The crew remaining on the *Prince Peacock* reached for a number of green hand flags and waved them furiously in the direction of Elephant stairs, where a great plume of rising smoke showed the police launch about to dart across the river.

The raid had begun in earnest.

Noah strode towards the open doors of the warehouse, but, even as he did so, shouts echoed inside the structure and the great wooden panels began to roll shut on their metal rails.

'Quick, lads! The door . . . we must block the door!' shouted Noah to the crew at his back, who were now pouring from the vessel towards the warehouse.

But the native lumpers of Frying Pan wharf would not remain passive. They exchanged glances. They instinctively reached for their hammers and pry bars and knives. Had they not just witnessed that bearded first mate brutally assault their foreman Mr Rigby? Had they not seen with their own eyes that crate split open and common newsprint spill forth? Something highly dubious was afoot, and the Thames lumper recognizes only one tool of debate . . .

A colossal masculine roar went up as the wharf lumpers descended *en masse* upon the men of the *Prince Peacock*. And chaos took hold on the shore: a tremendous scuffle of boots on stone, punctuating cries of pain, whistles blowing and the grunts of men reduced to beasts as they rolled violently entangled upon the ground.

Noah drove an elbow into the throat of a fellow trying to grab him from behind and raced for the still-closing doors of the warehouse. All support was now engaged in grappling and punching, while the police launch was still fifty yards from the wharf. There was no time to lose – he must enter alone and take his chances.

With a final leap, he passed sideways through the shrinking gap in the doors even as they brushed him front and back. He rolled on stone flags and righted himself quickly to see a fellow each side of the huge panels – evidently rather frightened clerks rather than lumpers. Both were now urgently hammering wedges betwixt door and rail while simultaneously watching the intruder with great apprehension. There seemed to be nobody else inside.

Noah reached for his knife and addressed the two in a tone that did not invite dissension: 'Tell me where the Negro is kept and I will not harm you.'

'There is no Negro here,' said one tremulously.

'He is above six feet. He has a milky eye and a scar about his neck. Tell me – where have you seen him?'

The two looked at each other in apparently genuine bafflement, then back at Noah with shrugs. They were mere clerks – their sole province was the ledger and the scales. Battle meanwhile raged beyond the doors, bodies or implements occasionally striking against it with a resounding crash.

Noah glared. 'Open the warehouse immediately. Remove the wedges or I swear I will kill you both as you stand.'

Again, the two men exchanged urgent glances. Noah was equidistant between them. He could not catch them both. Evidently realizing this, they seemed to reach the same decision simultaneously and both ran from Noah into the cavernous hall of the warehouse.

He furiously kicked away the wedges with a muttered curse and hefted a door ajar to aid the imminent influx of police. Then he turned from the *mêlée* outside and examined the interior of the place, casting his eyes around at the barrels, bales, stacks and stores that rose almost to the grubby skylights. Ben was here somewhere.

Noah set off down determinedly down the passage immediately facing him: a long avenue of tobacco bales exuding their sweetly intoxicating scent. There had to be a concealed stairway or a locked vault . . . some manner of anteroom or passage, most likely towards the rear of the place.

As he reached the end of that aisle, a draught of cold musty air washed over his perspiring face and he stopped. There was a distinctive smell of damp stone and drains to it . . . and it appeared to be emanating from behind a stack of cotton bales. He gripped the seaman's knife in readiness and moved closer to peer between shadowy cracks.

There, behind the cargo, appeared to be a large rusty iron hatch in the stone flags. It was undoubtedly the origin of the draught, which even now set frigid fingers at his neck.

Noah hauled aside the cotton bales, which though huge in dimension were naturally light enough. Moments later, he was able to prise open the hatch's lock with his knife and lift the cold metal plate to reveal a sunken platform containing a double-handled crank mechanism – evidently some manner of device for descending to a lower level of the warehouse. It was big enough to take perhaps four large barrels at a time.

Without a further thought, he clasped the knife between his teeth, jumped down on to the platform and unhooked the ratchet lock. He then set to work with the iron crank handles and the platform descended almost soundlessly on greasy teeth into a brickwork shaft that was clearly of greater antiquity than the warehouse itself.

In a matter of seconds, brilliant gaslight began to flood in over his boots and rise slowly up his legs. A bewildering array of scents rose to meet his nose: exotic spices of India, ambergris, brandy barrels, hides and horn . . .

Noah worked the mechanism with greater speed. He felt the platform settle with a clang against its base and turned to see a colossal chamber at which he could merely gape in wonder. The gas chandeliers, the ranks of barrels, the stacks of casks . . . here was a sultan's treasure, a city of gold – a subterranean smugglers' storehouse to defy the eyes and stir the imagination.

Something moved at the periphery of his vision. Noah took the knife from his mouth. A figure emerged cat-like from among the cargo.

The Italian.

And he was pointing a pistol unwaveringly at Noah's heart.

When the police steam launch arrived at Frying Pan wharf upon a great black wave of haste, it was to witness a vast riot in hectic progress. Perhaps fifty men were now engaged in a chaos of noisy battle that had left sticks, broken bottles and unconscious bleeding men littering the shore.

Up at the prow, Sir Richard gazed down upon the scene with combined horror and anger. Those men on the *Prince Peacock* had been told explicitly that they were to simply guard the warehouse and hold it until the uniformed police arrived on the launch. No doubt the volatile Mr Dyson had wrought his customary effect upon the wharf's lumpers.

Sir Richard nodded slightly to his Thames Police superintendent and whistles began to blow. The vessel was secured and planks were dropped. The superintendent let forth a blistering military yell:

'Truncheons at the ready, men! Take all miscreants into custody! Surround and secure the warehouse! Go! Go!'

Uniformed police poured from the launch with a collective cry and added their truncheons to the violence already
vividly extant.

Following them at a more studied pace, Mr Williamson
latterly descended the plank bereft of hat or weapon, moving
somnambulistically to where bars and fists flew with bloodied abandon.

'George – what are you doing!' cried Sir Richard from the
prow, too far away now to be heard amid the cacophony.
'Wait for the uniformed men! George, you might be killed!'

But there was another matter even more pressing – one
that none of the combatants had yet had occasion to notice.
A Custom House officer arrived panting by Sir Richard's side.

'Commissioner, sir!'

'Yes, what is it?' said Sir Richard, still watching Mr
Williamson's stately progress into oblivion.

'Sir – the river . . . it is still rising . . .'

'Of course it is. Why are you bothering me with this
news?'

'I . . . I think you do not understand me, sir. High
water was fifteen minutes ago according to the almanacks,
but – see – it continues to rise and rise. The north-easterlies,
sir . . . it is going above the wharf edge. It may flood the
whole of Wapping as it did a couple of years past. Millions of
pounds' worth of cargo may be lost to the flood!'

Sir Richard looked where bidden and saw that the river
level was indeed at the very limit of the wharf and beginning to lap over it. He recalled with cold dread what had
happened at the last such tide: Bankside submerged from
St Saviours to Holland-street . . . Blackwall entirely under
water . . . warehouses and cellars breached as far as Vauxhall . . . corn, flour and tobacco stocks ruined by the turbid
waters . . .

The men of the Thames Police would again be urgently required to help rescue cargo and citizens all along the river, and yet here they were engaged *en masse* in a furious battle at Frying Pan wharf. The newspaper reports would be scathing . . .

'My G—,' muttered Sir Richard, realizing where the greater responsibility lay. 'We must call back the uniformed men. We must sound the retreat.'

'But Mr Dyson is already inside the warehouse, sir . . .'

'I know that, but the Thames Police does not serve him alone. I have no doubt he can protect himself. Now – sound the retreat and see about securing as many pumps as you can . . .'

And as the constables of the Thames Police were recalled with great difficulty from their violent endeavours, the river went on rising. It rushed up stairs, inundated quays and encroached ever further into the thoroughfares themselves. At Bermondsey and Shadwell, rats poured in their hundreds from the sewers to be attacked by men armed with shovels. Cellars filled with filthy streams; fires were doused in the very hearths of riverside public houses; wherries drifted beneath gaslamps in streets rendered abruptly Venetian. Even Tower and Custom House wharfs were covered, and Scotland Yard itself became a muddy lagoon.

By three o'clock, much within the immediate river basin was below water and the river had risen higher than at any time in the previous five years. Barrels and sodden bales drifted amid vessels. Horses pulling wagons of fugitive stock were splashed to their bellies. Everywhere, the men of the Thames Police were labouring to minimize the damage.

No lives had yet been lost to the flood – but at least three were in immediate peril within a secret subterranean cell . . .

TWENTY-NINE

'Ben? Can you hear that?' said Mr Cullen.

There was a grunted affirmative.

'It sounds like water . . . flowing water. It seems to be behind the walls.'

They listened in the blackness to what seemed a distant stream. The rasping breath of Eldritch Batchem came thickly from the space between them. *He* had not stirred or spoken for some time.

'O! My legs! Ben – my legs are wet! The water is coming in somehow!'

Both men stood splashing to their feet.

'It smells like the river. If it rises as high as the mark I saw on the wall, we will be in trouble for sure, Ben.'

Silence from Benjamin, then a bubbling from the figure at their feet.

'O, he is drowning!' said Mr Cullen.

A sodden body was dragged blindly from the centre of the floor to where it could be propped sitting against a wall. The water was now ankle-high.

'Where is it coming from, Ben? Up through the floor? Beneath the door? I cannot tell. Can we plug it? We must do *something*…'

362

Doubly silenced, Benjamin waded to the iron door and began to feel around it for any hint of weakness. There was no discernible flow beneath, indicating that the exterior was flooding at the same pace. He hammered on it with a meaty fist and found it utterly unyielding.

'Ben? What are we to do? The water is now almost to my knees. How are we to escape? I see no . . . I see no possibility of survival.'

Benjamin sighed, and spoke. Tongueless as it was, the utterance seemed clear enough:

'No-ah.'

'That is a nasty cut you have on your neck,' said Noah, standing before the Italian.

The latter gave a half smile. His pistol remained steady. He used his free hand to indicate where he had similarly marked Noah in their altercation at Ratcliff-highway.

'Yes, you are a skilful enough fellow,' said Noah. 'Perhaps you are a thief; perhaps you are a murderer. I do not care – I have no argument with you. I care nothing for the cargo in this Aladdin's warehouse, or for its origins. I am not a policeman. I seek only my friend the Negro. Where is he?'

The Italian gave no sign that he had heard or understood.

'Now is your chance to flee,' said Noah. 'A hundred policemen and Customs officials will descend upon this place in moments – you must know that. Is there no other way out of this chamber? Take it now. I will not stop you.'

The Italian's eyes seemed to flicker momentarily towards a thick, iron-banded door to his right.

Noah caught the glance and smiled. 'The exit is there? But if it were, I suspect you would already have used it. Ah . . . perhaps your master is still here, in that room there, and you are afraid to flee until he has made his own escape. That is a commendable act of duty. But, as I say, the raid has already begun and . . .'

Noah's pause was occasioned by a startling change in the Italian's expression. Rather than staring intently at the intruder's face, he was now seemingly transfixed by the pool of water trickling from the platform and spreading outwards across the dry floor of the warehouse.

Noah looked up and saw that the brick shaft through which he had descended was now quite streaming with water. He remembered the abnormally low morning tide and made the automatic connection.

'My friend – the Thames is clearly in flood. In a matter of minutes, all this will be chest-deep in water. Time is short. What are you going to do?'

As if to reinforce his words, a crash and urgent voices echoed down the shaft from the warehouse above.

The Italian raised the gun and sighted along its barrel at Noah's heart.

'*Halt!* Thames Police! Drop your weapon!'

Both Noah and the Italian started at the cry.

A figure holding a pistol emerged from behind a stack of crates – a thoroughly begrimed fellow reeking obscenely of the sewers and with a thatch of curly red hair seemingly aflame atop his head. A constable's bullseye lamp was strapped to his chest and his eyes burned with a lunatic intensity.

'Inspector Newsome – I never believed I would be pleased to see you,' said Noah.

'I care nothing if he shoots you, Mr Dyson. It is his testimony I seek to secure . . . put that gun down, I say!'

The Italian now grinned and slowly turned his weapon on Mr Newsome.

'This is my final warning . . .' said the latter.

There was a sharp report and the pistol jumped in the Italian's hand. Inspector Newsome dropped to the ground with a grunt and lay immobile.

Noah was already in motion and reached the Italian before he could turn in response. The base of the seaman's knife connected solidly with a temple and the Italian collapsed to his knees half-sensible.

'The Negro – where is he? He has a scar about his thr—'

But the blow had been too powerful. The Italian's eyes rolled upwards into his scull and he toppled on his side.

'———!' screamed Noah, kicking at the unconscious form.

His cry resounded within the lofty chamber. The cloud of smoke from the discharged weapon hung still in the air. He withdrew a pair of handcuffs and tethered the Italian wrist-to-ankle before going to examine Mr Newsome's body.

It was unmoving. Noah slapped the face for a reaction and saw none. A dark stain was spreading from beneath the bullseye lamp on the chest. He searched roughly through the pockets for anything of use to the investigation, finding only a large rusty key on a cord, a dagger, a box of lucifers, a gold coin and the large animal tooth wrapped in a piece of cloth. He put all into his own pockets and looked about him. Soon, policemen would find the shaft and begin to descend. Where was Benjamin?

The iron-banded door. Noah ran at it and aimed a tremendous kick just above the knob. The lock ripped through the jamb. The door flew open in a shower of splinters.

Empty. The room looked like a clerk's office: a broad wooden desk with neatly sorted piles of paper, a bookshelf with ledgers, a large-scale map of the river with all stairs, wharfs and docks marked upon it. A fire smouldered in the grate. There was no other exit to be seen.

He sniffed the warm air within. There was a scent of cigar smoke and of a match having been struck. There was the smell of a man. Whoever had fled had done so recently.

Water seeped black and silent over the threshold and into the room. The voices of policemen continued to echo distantly from the warehouse above, though there was no movement of the platform. Noah returned to the vault and looked wildly for another door or passage. There seemed to be a gallery running around the upper portion of the walls.

'Ben! Ben – can you hear me? Make a sound if you can hear me!'

The space swallowed his voice.

There was a thud of boots as one of the *Prince Peacock*'s 'crew' landed at the bottom of the shaft. The fellow observed the two bodies and Noah standing between them. He nodded an understanding and set to work with the hand crank to raise the platform and bring more men.

Then a noise: a distant clanging of metal that came to Noah indistinctly through the labyrinth. There was a pattern to it – a regular beat of desperation, a hand where no tongue could cry. Benjamin . . .

Mr Williamson passed like a spirit through the fury of the wharf. Weapons struck, arms flailed and curses were hurled, yet he walked unarmed and unscathed amid the madness. Even as the tide of men turned at the sound of the retreat, he continued towards the warehouse doors as if borne there by the rising waters.

Inside, he moved automatically towards where a few of Noah's plain-clothes crew were peering down a brickwork shaft and calling to one of their number who had evidently dropped there. One of the group noticed his approach and stood to attention:

'Sir – we heard a gunshot below! Robinson is raising the platform now.'

A top hat emerged gradually from the hole, followed by a face and a torso working an iron mechanism with great excitement.

'All aboard, lads!' called he who had raised the platform. 'There's a giant warehouse below. Two bodies lie dead already.'

Four of them jumped the remaining two feet and beckoned for Mr Williamson to join them. He may have worn no uniform but, to a man, they knew exactly who he was.

'What bodies? Who did you see?' said Mr Williamson as they descended.

'It was very quick, sir. One fellow lying in cuffs . . . he had long dark hair. The other was more distant, also on the ground. Mr Noah Dyson was standing between them and acknowledged me. Sir . . . I wonder if we may ask you: who is this fellow Dyson? The superintendent suggested he is some manner of agent . . .'

'Then an agent he is.'

The platform descended into water and the men gazed in muttered wonder at the reflected spectacle before them. Two inert bodies lay as islands. There was no sign of Noah.

'To work, gentlemen,' said Mr Williamson. 'Detain and arrest whoever you find.'

The men splashed away like hounds after a scent and Mr Williamson approached the first body: the Italian. Lying awkwardly on his side, he was not dead but breathing shallowly in his oblivion. A pair of police handcuffs bound his left wrist to his right ankle. Noah's work, perhaps.

The other form lay supine, its submerged red hair a straggling coral growth about the head and the face frozen in the grimace of its end. Inspector Newsome – even in death did he frown at the world. Mr Williamson searched himself for grief or sorrow and found neither.

A half-open door drew him, the floating wood splinters about it suggesting an earlier scene of action. He entered cautiously and beheld the same space witnessed by Noah just minutes previously. But Mr Williamson was calmer. He observed the room coolly and saw more: a wooden chair with blood smeared on its back and with a length of twine still tied to one rear leg – evidence of an interrogation? Had Mr Cullen or Benjamin been tethered here? If so, had notes been made?

He examined the documents on the desk: predominantly vessel manifests, wharf records, shipping lists from *the Times* and completed landing warrants. These he rolled and tucked into an inside pocket as evidence.

He next tried the drawers and found them locked – an impediment soon overcome with a heavy fireside poker that quite destroyed the lacquered wood and brass trimmings of the drawer fronts. His hand thus admitted, he groped among more papers and took hold of a book bound in calf skin: a diary.

He turned to the last page and saw with horror his own name written in the regular copperplate script:

Williamson visits the whore at Golden-square and stays
two hours. Leaves after midnight looking troubled and
furtive. Noah walks back through Lambeth and across

Waterloo to his home. Mayne returns to Scotland Yard, where his light burns until three o'clock . . .

He flicked to the previous page and back further, his eyes darting over the lines. It was all there: every meeting, every enquiry, every step he had taken right back to that curious incident before the steps of the Queen's Theatre. And not just concerning *his* activity, but also Noah, Benjamin, Eldritch Batchem and Sir Richard – all reduced to *dramatis personae* in another man's story.

Questions buzzed about his mind. Who was the owner of the diary? What was his interest in these men? What else did he know and how might he use it? Had, indeed, the document been left here on purpose as a provocation? Only a thorough examination of it would reveal such deeper truths, and there was no time now. The room was clearly full of incriminating evidence.

He paused. Had that been the faintest swish of water? Not the intemperate splashing of the still questing crew, but a stealthy and much closer step.

He took hold of the poker and remained utterly still lest his own movements send out traitorous ripples. A sound of heavy breathing seemed to approach the office. A shadow fell across the threshold. He raised the weapon in readiness.

And the hairs upon his scalp prickled in chill terror.

There, in the doorway, was the beast sought for so long by Mr Newsome, its great leonine head matted with dirty water and its yellow eyes fixed with lethal intent upon the frail flesh of Mr Williamson . . .

'Ben! I can hear you, Ben!' called Noah as he rushed along the upper gallery towards the apparent source of the clanging noise.

Yet the signal was fading and becoming less frequent even as he closed the distance. Was Ben tiring in his efforts? Or was it that the rising waters were slowly isolating his place of incarceration? Soon, there was no sound at all.

'Ben! I am close! Do not stop!'

He halted abruptly. A stone stairway to his left descended into a well of dark water whose surface writhed as if fed from below. The stairs clearly led somewhere: a deeper vault or to the sewers themselves. And as he watched the murky level rise, he thought he felt a presence there: some living spark, some silent-shrill entreaty that called him closer . . .

Ben?

He plunged into the water – knee-deep, thigh-deep, chest-deep – until his very eyes passed into the cold black realm and his hands groped still lower along a slime-slathered wall. Blind, deaf and mute, he finally felt his boot strike an impediment. His fingers then found the same flat, corroded surface. A door? He reached unseeing into a pocket and withdrew the knife, using its heel to rap his presence on the metal sheet.

Silence. Just the pressure in his chest and the water in his ears.

Then a vibrating hammer blow of response: life beyond.

Noah ran frustrated hands over the door and found a knob. He pulled. He pushed. He kicked furiously at the un-yielding mass and let forth a bubbling execration. His breath was almost gone. The blows still sounded from within.

The key?

He jerked it out of his trouser pocket and fumbled cold-fingered to move the escutcheon aside and find the hole. He turned the key. He pulled the door open against the pressure of water. He reached into the void.

A large black hand grasped at Noah's from the blackness.

Noah seized it and hauled the body out towards the ascending stairs.

Another limb flailed and Noah took hold of a thick wrist, tugging it forcefully from death to life.

And with the final dregs of breath almost gone, he himself staggered heavily up the stairs until his head broke the surface. Merciful air rushed into starving lungs and light once again filled his eyes.

Benjamin and Mr Cullen were slumped panting and saturated on the upper stairs. Noah waded clear of the water and nodded to them with an easy smile that belied the depth of his relief.

'Inside . . .' gasped a dripping Mr Cullen, 'Eldritch Batchem . . . is still inside.'

Benjamin spoke briefly with his hands.

Noah nodded. 'If his throat has been cut and he was immobile, then I agree: he is already dead. He is older and less hearty than you two, and all air inside is now certainly gone. We must think of ourselves and flee while we have the chance. The river is in flood and the secret warehouse is under siege.'

'A secret warehouse?' said Mr Cullen.

'I wonder – do you even know that you are at Frying Pan wharf? No matter – the river continues to invade. We must go to safety above.'

Now knee-deep in water, Mr Williamson had barely moved. The poker remained aloft. His arm was beginning to tire with the effort of immobility. He dare not blink. He dare hardly breathe.

For its part, the great, shaggy-headed lion observed him with similar stillness. It sniffed the air, flicked its tail, and set forth a lazy pink tongue about its massive chops.

Time telescoped. Waterfalls of filth and the plashing footsteps of the questing crew sounded distantly from the warehouse beyond. Lion and man appraised each other in an expectant *tableau*.

And Mr Williamson's fear turned gradually to empathy. For all its size and threat, the beast was, in truth, a rather pitiful specimen of its kind: soiled with grime, emaciated about the ribs, conspicuously missing a large incisor, and utterly bedraggled by its cloacal abode. It clearly no more wanted to be there than he did. If it sometimes roared, it was through imprisoned despair rather than aggression. If it had indeed torn at the flesh of first mate Hampton's corpse, it had no doubt been in abject hunger rather than violence.

He slowly lowered the poker to the desk.

As if in acknowledgement of the gesture, the lion blinked, shook its vast head, cast a final proprietorial look about the room and exited almost silently in the same direction it had come.

Mr Williamson slumped with both hands flat on the desk and exhaled deeply, his head downwards in prayer or relief or some darker mortal thoughts. He was in the same posture when a panting crew-member arrived excitedly at the door.

'No criminals to be found! Not a single . . . O, are you all right, sir?'

'Did you not see the lion?'

'A *lion*, sir? Like in the zoo? I have seen nothing of the kind and I have looked everywhere.'

'In this very room just moments ago . . . Never mind. Have you explored every possible entrance and exit?'

'Indeed. There is a gallery above and a couple of passages leading from it down into water – the sewers perhaps. We

also found Mr Dyson with two other gents he says are colleagues of his. One was a terrifying Negr—'

'I know them. Was there another: a bearded fellow?'

'No, sir. I have seen no such—'

'Now listen – you and your fellows are to gather as many
ledgers and documents as you can carry from this room and
take them aloft with all haste. Do you understand? Where is
Mr Dyson now?'

'He has already ascended with the others.'

'Hmm. Well, gather your fellows and get immediately to
work in this room.'

'Yes, sir!'

The fellow ran off to fetch his colleagues and Mr Williamson went out into the warehouse to see sundry cargo bobbing
upon the flood. The water was now mid-thigh and rising
continually – more than high enough to drown the insensible
and handcuffed Italian . . . their only living witness!

He waded urgently to where the man had lain bound, but
could feel nothing with his feet. Had he misremembered the
exact position? He submerged his arm to the shoulder in icy
black water and swirled a hand madly about in search of the
body.

Nothing. Not a limb nor a garment nor a clutch of
hair . . .

Then his fingers touched metal. He withdrew a pistol
and tossed it irritably towards the clerk's office. Plunging in
again, he grazed another object and knew immediately from
long experience what he held – a pair of police handcuffs.
These he withdrew, staring incredulously at their unlocked
mechanism. Was it truly possible that the Italian had been
revived by the cold water at his face and somehow freed himself to escape beneath the surface of the murky pool?

He looked over to where Mr Newsome had lain and saw only water. The corpse had been subsumed. A shiver passed through him: a grim foreboding combined with the river's chill that seemed to harrow him quite to the bone.

'Men – it is time to leave. Take all you can carry from that room. Let us abandon this infernal place to the river . . .'

THIRTY

By nightfall, it was a different city that presented itself to the investigative glare of the gaslights – a city released, a city quite transformed by the inundation of its ancient flow. At Westminster and Bermondsey, at Tower and Rotherhithe, at Wapping and Shadwell and Limehouse, the shoreline streets were clotted ankle-deep with reeking mud. Cellars were bailed by bucket; stairs seeped and trickled; ferry piers sagged as prehistoric swamps. Rat corpses and assorted flotsam collected where the ebb tide had eddied.

The entire Port of London had suffered that day: dry goods tainted, buoyant goods lost, loaded barges subsumed where they lay on the banks, and almost every wharf a greater or lesser victim of the invading flood. Only the diligent work of the Thames Police had prevented a greater catastrophe. It was thanks alone to their readiness and manpower that a great quantity of cargo had been decisively removed from danger.

That uniformed presence had been particularly concentrated around the many warehouses of Wapping, and notably at Frying Pan wharf. Indeed, a cordon of men seemed to guard the place long after the waters had departed, standing sentinel with flaming torches as if expecting another assault.

It was perhaps midnight when certain senior officers of the Custom House and the police arrived by steam launch and ventured inside the sealed building. That they later emerged mud-caked and saturated carrying dozens of dripping bundles seemed to suggest that they had found what they sought.

In fact, daylight would raise more questions than answers, and the meeting that occurred some thirty hours after those momentous events would follow a pattern to which its participants had become rather accustomed . . .

'Mr Dyson – I thank you for attending,' said Sir Richard Mayne, standing to receive his final guest with a firm handshake. 'I accept that you do so out of good grace rather than by compulsion.'

Noah nodded a greeting to the other gentlemen in that Scotland Yard office: a sombre-looking George Williamson, and Mr Jackson, Inspector General of Customs, who raised a quizzical eyebrow at the newly arrived fellow. Was this the 'agent' his men had spoken of with combined admiration and mistrust?

'So, gentlemen – to business,' said Sir Richard, taking his seat at the large oaken desk that was today covered with water-crinkled ledgers, stained sheets and blotted books. A smell of the river rose palpably from the material, though it was all now quite dry.

'As you may know, men of the Metropolitan Police and the Custom House re-entered that remarkable chamber below Frying Pan wharf the night before last to fully document the scale of its depredations and to settle the issue with legal finality. Before I proceed in that direction, however, I first have a number of questions for Misters Williamson and Dyson.'

The aforementioned two looked briefly and without guile at each other, then back at the speaker. They had already revealed all they knew in the hours following the raid. There was nothing more to hide.

'Very well,' continued Sir Richard, 'both of you gentlemen reported seeing the body of Inspector Newsome. I have your statements here and they tally in their detail. My question is simple enough: are you absolutely certain he was dead?'

'Wait,' said Noah, sitting forward, 'am I to assume from your question that no body was recovered?'

'That is correct. George – it seems you were last to see him . . .'

'Indeed. I stood over him and saw no evidence of life,' said Mr Williamson. 'When I left the chamber, the water was already above the level of his body.'

'So you cannot say with all certitude that he was still there?' said Sir Richard.

'Hmm. I suppose not. But I saw no breath when I examined him . . . and Noah saw him shot.'

'That is right,' said Noah. 'I believe I even heard the bullet strike him. I saw him fall and lie unmoving. Perhaps the receding current moved him.'

'Every inch of that warehouse has been examined, Mr Dyson,' said Sir Richard. 'It may indeed be true that the inspector is dead – and a great tragedy it is – but the fact remains that no body has been recovered.'

'No body at all?' said Noah. 'What of Eldritch Batchem? He was incarcerated in the same cell as Mr Cullen and my fellow. His throat had been cut and he was immobile. His corpse must be there. I gave full particulars of this to your men.'

'So your testimony says,' said Sir Richard, locating the document on his desk, 'but, again, there is no body to be found. Not he or the "Italian" to whom you both refer. How do you explain this singular lack of evidence?'

'I can only think that the waters have flushed them all out through the sewers,' said Noah with a shrug. 'The fact that Mr Newsome was there at all is clear evidence of a network leading to the river. Perhaps we will find them in a week or two, swollen and floating by a ferry pier at Rotherhithe.'

'Perhaps, perhaps,' said Sir Richard in a less than credulous tone. 'It is unfortunate enough that the dead bodies will receive no civilized burial. What is much worse is the evident escape of this "Italian". And what of this smelly little fellow or the South Sea Islander mentioned in your testimonies? There is not a single trace of them also.'

Noah and Mr Williamson exchanged glances and the former opted to reply:

'It seems clear enough that all are close associates of the orchestrating criminal behind these crimes. The smelly man alone may be connected to the deaths at the dock by his curious odour, and we have evidence that he was instrumental in the taking of both Benjamin and Mr Cullen. I can only assume that they escaped together, or at least to the same place. Find one and you will find them all – although I would be surprised if any is now to be found in this country. They are too distinctive to remain.'

'I see,' muttered Sir Richard dourly. 'This is most unsatisfactory. On the matter of mysteries, I wonder if we might also touch briefly upon Mr Williamson's "Minotaur" encounter.'

'If you are referring to the lion, I have said all there is to say on the matter,' said Mr Williamson.

'Quite. But nobody else saw the beast – not Mr Dyson, not those fellows who entered with you – not any of the men who ventured back into the place that night. Why, there were not even any footprints in the abundant mud.'

'Am I being called a liar?' said Mr Williamson. 'Inspector Newsome thought there was a beast in the sewers and I saw that beast. The waters ebb . . . the footprints are erased . . . the beast re-enters the sewers and is lost once again leaving no trace. Must I *further* explain what I saw? Am I a drunken costermonger to be disbelieved in such a manner?'

'Becalm yourself, George,' said Sir Richard. 'I am merely attempting to understand every detail. So much of what happened in that chamber cannot now be explained by the physical evidence.'

'Hmm.' Mr Williamson turned his head to stare blackly into the fire.

Sir Richard's expression was one of concern, but he retained his sense of decorum. '*Ahem*, well, let us turn to something more empirical. Mr Jackson – perhaps you could summarize what you have learned from the reclaimed ledgers.'

The nautically attired Mr Jackson nodded his assent. 'A large proportion of the stock listed on the manifest of the missing brig *Aurora* was indeed found in the hidden chamber – notably the French silk. As for the other cargoes stored there, a consignment of port and fifty bales of Virginia tobacco are reliably documented as stolen. We are combing through the remaining material at present and I have no doubt all cargo therein will prove to be illicit.'

'How is it possible such an outrage could occur barely a mile from the Custom House itself?' said Noah to Mr Jackson.

'Excuse me, sir, but who are you to address me so?' said

Mr Jackson. 'What is your rank? Did I hear your name as "Dyson"?'

'Mr Dyson is *not* a member of the Metropolitan Police,' said Sir Richard. 'He has aided investigations in a purely *un*official capacity. Nevertheless, perhaps I can rephrase his question more civilly on my own behalf. Can we be sure this will never occur again?'

'In truth, Sir Richard, I can be sure of nothing. As long as there are dishonest men motivated by money or threatened with violence, there will be crime. I need hardly explain this to you. However, you may be assured I will be conducting a thorough review of my men and procedures.'

'I suppose that is all I can ask. Is it at least possible to reconstruct and take lessons from the fate of the *Aurora*?'

'For that, Sir Richard, I must turn to your men here, who have evidently spent more time investigating the evidence.'

Sir Richard acknowledged this and looked to Mr Williamson. 'George? Will you speak? What can we say of this case that is conclusive?'

'Hmm. Hmm. All evidence would seem to suggest that on arrival in London, the vessel was logged by a landing-waiter and reported to the Custom House as per the standard procedure. Thereafter, a landing warrant was issued to moor and unload – presumably for the correct berth at St Katharine's?'

Mr Jackson nodded.

'I suppose we will never know if that was the warrant received by the first mate of the *Aurora*,' continued Mr Williamson. 'Most likely it was a fraudulent note prepared by the tidewaiter William Barton (himself conspicuously murdered for some indiscretion some few hours later). Barton then aboard, around half of the crew were allowed ashore by lighter and the rest were necessarily killed and embarrelled – apart from first mate Hampton, who must have discerned the plan earlier and been slain for his discovery.'

'A gruesome and sorry tale,' said Mr Jackson.

'And still worse,' said Mr Williamson, 'with the death of the persistent ship-owner Mr Timbs. Nothing could have been a greater threat to the secrecy of this criminal band than his public announcement at the Queen's Theatre – where each of us was conspicuous in our way. Thereafter, when one of us came too close, he was taken: the fate of Noah's friend, our Mr Cullen, and the investigator Eldritch Batchem.'

'But they were not immediately killed as the others were,' said Sir Richard. 'Why do you imagine that to be?'

'Hmm. I could not say. Perhaps to lure their colleagues so that all could be eliminated at a stroke? The cell at Frying Pan wharf may well have been a death sentence regardless of the adverse tide, so perhaps they were intended to die after all.'

'I see your point,' said Sir Richard. 'Please, do not let me interrupt your narration . . .'

'Well, the rest we know. The *Aurora* docks at Frying Pan wharf, is divested of her cargo by sundry lumpers led by this Mr Rigby, and then the vessel itself either spirited away under a new name, or destroyed.'

'Do you have any proof at all of this?' said Mr Jackson. 'The *Aurora* may still be in port.'

'Hmm. I have not previously mentioned to any of you that I discovered a vessel's name plaque below Waterloo-bridge. It was charred almost beyond recognition, but it appeared to be that of the *Aurora*.'

'What? Why . . . why did you withhold such important information?' said Sir Richard, bristling at the revelation.

Noah, also, could clearly not disguise his feelings at the omission, but said nothing.

'In truth, I concluded that the discovery was of little con-sequence,' said Mr Williamson. 'Even if it was the genuine name plaque of the vessel, how might that have helped me? I already knew it was missing, perhaps destroyed. At the same time, anyone may fashion a plaque and set fire to it. Perhaps I was *meant* to find it. I imagine the real ship is now somewhere out on the oceans: owned by whoever killed Mr Timbs. In fact, the real clue in this case was that code in *the Times*, without which we may never have known about the *Prince Peacock*.'

'And even then, I am not sure we had the right ship,' said Noah. 'The foreman Mr Rigby was utterly confused at its arrival.'

'It was the closest name to "parrot" that we could find in the Long Room lists,' said Mr Jackson. 'Is it possible that these criminals simply knew of the raid in advance?'

'I fear you may be right,' said Sir Richard. 'According to Mr Dyson's testimony, the wharf foreman seemed to suggest that no vessel was supposed to arrive. Perhaps the code had been nullified by subsequent intelligence. Certainly, there are many men on the river who must have known of it.'

'Nevertheless,' said Noah, 'the quantity of lumpers wait-ing at the wharf would seem to suggest that trouble was expected even if the vessel was not.'

'Perhaps,' said Sir Richard. 'But it matters not. The raid was successful.'

'I wonder if I may enquire,' said Mr Jackson. 'Where are your criminals? I have heard mention of a small, malodorous man, a long-haired Italian, even a South Sea harpooner . . . Who is behind this organization? Who killed all of those men? I see many crimes, but few men in custody but your foreman and some sundry lumpers.'

The question hung in the air. Silence crackled with the fire in the grate.

'You are quite correct, of course, Mr Jackson,' said Sir Richard with a sigh. 'We may have solved the crime, but we have few criminals. Whoever they are, they operate through fear and threat. The nature of the murders says as much: every man along the river must know that failure to cooperate will end in a gruesome death. There may indeed be one leader, but that odd Greek code suggests there are many of them working unseen. I regret to admit it, but we have seen only the tentacle tips of this monster.'

'Hmm. Hmm . . . I admit there is another piece of evidence I have not yet submitted . . .' said Mr Williamson, almost at a whisper.

All turned surprised to see his face a mask of blushing guilt.

'George, this is a serious matter. If you—' began Sir Richard.

Mr Williamson extracted the leather-bound diary from an inside breast pocket and leaned over to lay it gently on the desk. 'In that volume, you will find all of our activities – even you, Mr Jackson – documented daily since shortly *before* the *Aurora*'s disappearance and its announcement by Mr Timbs. I found it in the clerk's room in the hidden chamber.'

'What!' said Sir Richard.

Mr Jackson paled and looked quite nauseous.

Noah stared incredulously at the book and then at his friend.

'So it was you who smashed the drawers of that desk?' said Sir Richard. 'My men assumed it was the fleeing criminal.' He snatched up the book and turned to the last page. 'A leaf has been torn out at the end here . . .'

'That is how I found it,' said Mr Williamson, knowing well enough that other pages were also missing – pages he would have no one else read.

'Which rather implies the owner of this book wanted us to find and read it to know what he knows,' said Sir Richard. 'Well, this is . . . this changes the whole complexion of . . . To what purpose would somebody observe us *before* our investigation?'

'I am no policeman,' said Mr Jackson, 'but it seems to me that this fellow – whoever he is – has quite turned the principles of investigation on their head. Rather than you following his clues, *he* follows *yours* and leaves a trail of false or contradictory evidence to be found. It almost seems a game with him. Why, I might even offer that this whole business with the *Aurora* has been a challenge or entertainment to test the mettle of his adversaries. His very murders have been utterly outrageous in their conspicuousness, as if taunting you to solve them.'

'As you say, Mr Jackson – you are no policeman,' said Sir Richard. 'The idea is quite . . . quite ludicrous.'

Mr Jackson merely frowned and roughly adjusted a cuff.

'He knows where we live,' said Noah with a leaden note. 'He has been observing us through his agents and learning more about us. In allowing the diary to be found, he shows us he is more powerful in his watchful invisibility. He shows us what he knows.'

'Let us not be dramatic, Mr Dyson . . .' said Sir Richard.

'Think of it,' said Noah: 'Has not the whole *charade* been engineered by him from the start? The flyer in William Barton's pocket, and the warning note to Josiah Timbs – both were advertisements for Batchem's show. What if the intention was always to lure us – his *dramatis personae* – into the theatre that evening to set the challenge. He was perhaps there watching us. We should make a close comparison of the writing in this diary and on the note to Timbs . . .'

'I really think that you are exagg—' said Sir Richard.

'And what of that article in *the London Monitor*?' continued Noah. 'It became clear some time ago that it was not the work of Eldritch Batchem but intended, rather, to *appear* as such. Two evenings ago, after I left Mr Williamson's house, I took the liberty of doing what none of us had previously thought to do: I called in at the offices of *the Monitor* and enquired, in terms that would admit no equivocation, who actually did place that article. And do you know what I learned?'

The other three gentlemen merely stared in anticipation.

'I learned that the article was delivered anonymously by hand along with one hundred pounds in cash and a request that the piece run the following day. Naturally, the editor of that gutter publication could not refuse. So I ask the question again – who would wish our ruination so earnestly? Who would lure us into a case and seek to frustrate our investigation of it? Who would perpetrate murders of such wilful complexity merely to draw attention to them?'

Mr Jackson seemed even more ill at ease.

Mr Williamson had become quite pale.

'Enough of this mood!' said Sir Richard. 'You speak, Mr Dyson, as if we were utterly vanquished, but we have quite smashed the criminal enterprise of this fellow and driven him to flee. He has nowhere to hide and we will seize him. In the meantime, the Metropolitan Police has many of the lumpers from Frying Pan wharf in custody and the secret warehouse itself to pick clean of evidence. We will make all exertions to locate this Italian and these smelly little men – both of whom seem rather conspicuous. The arrest of this fellow is but a matter of time.'

'He knows where we live. He is a ruthless murderer. Do you think he will wait?' said Noah.

'I will not abandon you or Mr Williamson,' said Sir Richard. 'I have involved you in this and I will ensure your safety whatever measures are required. I and the thousands of men at my command will not rest until this person is gaoled. There are many remaining avenues of investigation to pursue . . .'

But neither Noah nor Mr Williamson was now listening. Instead, each was engaged in his own thoughts upon the implications of the case – each understanding that the writer of that diary would not be found by any common investigation. Here was a man who had sought not to kill them, but to ruin them by attacking livelihood and reputation. Here was a man who had targeted their friends. His actions were no mere crimes. He acted from some more inexplicably personal imperative. As long as he and his minions were at liberty, the investigators could not feel safe, could not walk down any street with anonymity. Decisive and collaborative action would be necessary – action that would not wear a uniform or bear the stamp of Sir Richard's legitimacy.

They exchanged glances. Together, they were stronger – time and experience had proved as much. They had Benjamin and Mr Cullen in support. The prize this time would not be justice, but freedom itself.

Both nodded slightly. The deal was made.

As one might expect, the disappearance of Eldritch Batchem was a matter of the greatest public interest in those following days. He who had been such a conspicuous voice of detection had now seemingly vanished as completely as the vessel he had sought.

Some maintained that he could not possibly be dead and that he continued to pursue the case in secret, this being the only way to track the criminals. Others solemnly accepted the police reports of his death, praising his heroic sacrifice in the battle against smugglers. In certain quarters, it was remarked darkly that his disappearance just as the police raided the warehouse was no coincidence at all – that, in fact, the russet-capped enigma knew more about those murders than any man (except the murderer himself) should.

One thing was certain: the most talked-about revelation of all concerning the life and alleged death of Eldritch Batchem was published just two days after the high tide in that ill-famed rag *the London Monitor*. Purporting to be a singular and authentic history of the man, it was a publishing sensation that saw editions changing hands for two and three times the cover price once all had sold out. As for the author of the piece, he also made a significant sum – enough, assuredly, to stay beyond the magistrate's reach for another six months, and to earn himself the considerable envy of the city's penny-a-liners.

It was I.

I had learned much about the man during those hectic days of the *Aurora* case, albeit barely enough for an *exposé*. Nevertheless, the skilled writer is able – through the galvanic alchemy of the fictive art – to fuse fact and conjecture into genuine truth. Eldritch Batchem was an unfinished story: a conglomeration of disassociated episodes whom I would write whole.

My beginning, at least, was certain: Eldritch Batchem

had been born a supernumerary horror, six perfect fingers on each imperfect hand. People had smarted in disgust, their coos souring on tongues as they perceived the taint of disfigurement. His own mother recoiled at what she had made and could not bear to look upon it. Her love curdled in shame.

What end for an innocent child too abominable to suckle? Why, the same end as greets so many others of the city's lost: he was abandoned nameless as a foundling at the hospital gates, there to be raised by proxy, named by a committee and dropped into a ward with the loveless progeny of magdalenes and beggars.

From such places do those like Eldritch Batchem emerge. The child competes for attention among half a hundred other tiny souls, or retires inwards to the safety of solitude. Possessions are collective or none. Cared for by nobody, the unfortunates make their own stories for a life of sustaining artifice.

Only by means of many footsore researches among London's orphanages and hospitals did I learn more, blessed by the fact that a twelve-fingered boy is most definitely remembered, whether he is called Crawford or Batchem . . . or Liveridge.

And at the illustrious Foundling Hospital on Guildford-street, I found my man. Thomas Liveridge had been admitted, aged just two days, some forty-three years previously. Born illegitimately to a prostitute, the infant had kept his birth name and had survived the perilous early years to become a delightful (albeit diminutive) boy beloved of all at the hospital. Inquisitive, attractive, and of a naturally loving nature, he was quite the most popular little chap of his age group. His fingers, however, numbered only ten.

Young Thomas's closest confidant during that first decade was rather more abundantly endowed with digits. *He* was called John Shakespeare (according to the Guildford-street mania for bestowing illustrious names) and was quite a different story. Left in a basket at the door aged one, he was silent, secretive and possessive from his earliest infancy. He was, nevertheless, a child of developed intellect: a teller of stories with which to entertain his fellow Thomas long after the candles had been extinguished.

Thus they lived out their collective childhood, cheating mortality and growing robust. In time, as is occasionally the case, little Thomas soon took the fancy of an esteemed benefactor whose barren wife could not bear to see the sweet boy apprenticed to a rough boot-maker or weaver. Might not they take him as their own and educate him in a manner more befitting his charm? Arrangements were duly made, and young Thomas quite danced with glee at the thought of presents and carriage rides and of a life immeasurably more blessed than his fellows.

More blessed, certainly, than his closest friend: the six-fingered lad facing a lifetime of exclusion and grim curiosity. As might be expected, Shakespeare/Crawford/Batchem took the good news without good grace. Indeed, his rage on learning that his closest, his only, fellow was to abandon him was so intemperate that he had to be restrained and given laudanum. He did not speak for days, choosing instead to remain, against all official strictures and solicitations, beneath his bed sheets muttering incessantly to himself.

That might have been the end of it, but the true conclusion was more tragic still. It is not uncommon for children to die at these institutions, but such fatalities are usually among the youngest, and attributable to such ailments as convulsions or inflammation of the bowels. Falling to one's death from an upper-storey window at midnight on the eve of one's salvation, however, might be considered decidedly *un*common.

The investigation had been discreet enough. Nobody could say for sure what had motivated fortunate Thomas Liveridge to imbibe his friend's phial of laudanum and leap from the dormitory window. Nobody could explain how the other sleeping children had seen or heard nothing untoward. Nobody wanted to speculate too closely about the distinct six-fingered hand print on the pane in question. In fact, when John Shakespeare was apprenticed one year before the customary age of release – sent forth with twenty rather than the usual ten pounds to ease his way in the world – nobody at Guildford-street sought to ask any further questions on the matter.

Had he, indeed, murdered his closest friend rather than lose him to another? Had *this* been the childhood crime that would torture him thence, drive him ultimately towards a phantasy of investigation and make him a public speaker upon the very nature of his own blackest deed? Perhaps. Like teardrops, man's deepest sins seep forth unbidden.

Where the boy went then, I cannot discern. He did not stay long with the weaver to whom he was sent, and was no doubt absorbed soon after into the great ravening nowhere of London. Here, a mere walking shadow down dark streets and within the insensate crush of crowds, a man may lose himself so comprehensively that he may find himself anew.

Such was the essence of my article in *the London Monitor*: a construction (I admit) of equal parts fact and fancy – a tale signifying nothing but the vagaries of fate. Regarding the mysterious investigation of the Green Drawing Room, I had been able to learn nothing more. Indeed, of Eldritch Batchem's life between apprenticeship and insolvency, there was only a void of speculation and wonder. Of his death also, there was only rumour, for no body was ever found. He had come from nowhere and returned there just as inexplicably with the erasing wash of the river's tides.

No matter; I leave truth to the philosopher and revelation to the chaplain. *My* province is the inner theatre of the mind, for whose performance I always prefer payment over applause.

But before the curtain falls, let us cast a departing glance across the city stage to watch over them all: Noah stalking nervously alone among the faceless streets, Benjamin and Mr Cullen at the musical theatres of Haymarket, Mr Williamson drawn irresistibly by a siren of passion along midnight avenues to Golden-square, and Sir Richard at his unending committee meetings and court hearings.

Had any of them known the true identity of the criminal behind the *Aurora*'s theft, however, they would have felt a profounder unease. In fact, only one man knew the terrible entirety of the truth – and knew it with the singular advantage of the villain not knowing it was known.

It was two days after that disastrous tide, and the banks of the river were more crowded than ever with mudlarks picking through the filth for newly revealed treasures. Since a boy had unearthed a slimy leather bag full of Spanish gold between Southwark-bridge and Blackfriars-bridge, even shop girls and apprentices could be found wrist-deep in the mire, combing excrement for hidden wealth.

By London-bridge on that bright, still day, the silent herd of scavengers were given reason to pause shortly before noon. At first, the sounds from the sewer were assumed to be that of a fat eel or drowning dog thrashing in the shallow outflow. But as it persisted, they heard the unmistakable sloshing rhythm of footsteps approach.

"'Tis the beast . . .' mumbled an Irish hag, describing the shape of the Holy Cross upon her breast.

But it was no myth that emerged from the hellish mouth. Nor, at first sight, did it seem completely human. Rather, it was a vision of reeking degradation: clothes soaked with vile matter, hair quite tortured with grime, face besmirched with two days and nights of smoking oil, hands made blackened claws by ancient brick, and pained eyes squinting at the light of freedom.

Inspector Albert Newsome.

By what means had he navigated his way through the poisonous labyrinth and sustained himself without food or water during that purgatory? How had he escaped from the flooded chamber and found oil enough to light his way through passages quite blocked with the river's flow? These are answers for another time. More pressing, perhaps, is the matter of his unholy resurrection.

In truth, he had never died. The Italian's shot had been perfectly aimed at his adversary's heart, but that heart had been covered with the policeman's bullseye lamp. Metal was pierced, glass was broken and oil was spilled, but no skin or bone was damaged. If he fell, it was merely the colossal jolt of the impact over his precious organ that knocked him shocked and insensible, manifesting in him all the visible signs of death. A physician might even tell us that his body ceased to live momentarily, as sometimes happens with those wrongfully interred.

It was in this unanimated state that his form, shifted and buoyed by the swirling currents, was carried among the cargo with the other flotsam until a wave of frigid water lapped up his nose to wake him with a splutter and a cry. By then, he was alone in the murk of Thamesis's ancient realm – alone but in possession of the singular dreadful knowledge that must surely restore him to his former stature. Only he knew the secret identity of the criminal who had so invisibly observed them all.

And as the mudlarks backed away in fear from the filthy apparition before them, Inspector Newsome cast his eyes over the blackened chimneys and warehouses of Southwark, over the massed packets and colliers of the rancid river, over the smoke-choked sky and the hovering chymical miasma. Truly, London was the greatest city in the world.

A smile almost touched his lips and, with a viscous, sucking step, he made his way wearily towards Scotland Yard.

Acknowledgements

Moniczka – muse and amused
Rodzinie Radeckich – *za wszystko*
Monika Wolny – fault-finder extraordinaire
Jennifer White – once again, for the card
Sarah Armstrong and family – fine people all
Professor Laura Marcus – catalyst for Williamson's world